Earth Lost Without Power

Earth Lost Without Power

The Neutron Bomb

By

L. S. Wood

ARPress

ILLUMINATING IDEAS.
EMPOWERING VOICES

ARPress
45 Dan Road Suite 36
Canton MA 02021

Hotline: 1(888) 821-0229
Fax: 1(508) 545-7580

Ordering Information:
Quantity Sales. Special discounts are available on quantity purchases by corporations, associations, and others. For details, contact the publisher at the address above.

Printed in the United States of America.

ISBN-13   Paperback   979-8-89356-877-6
               eBook   979-8-89356-878-3

Library of Congress Control Number: 2024909128

Table of Contents

CHAPTER ONE
Hitler's Germany..1

CHAPTER TWO
Red Alert..8

CHAPTER THREE
The Detonator..16

CHAPTER FOUR
The Word..18

CHAPTER FIVE
The Convoy..21

CHAPTER SIX
Facts Unknown 26

CHAPTER SEVEN
The Arrival of Brass..29

CHAPTER EIGHT
Curiosity Killed the Cat 36

CHAPTER NINE
Bye Bye Biplane 42

CHAPTER TEN
The Downfall of the Neutron Bomb..44

CHAPTER ELEVEN
The Great Launch 49

CHAPTER TWELVE
The Flaw 52

CHAPTER THIRTEEN
A Horrific Sighting..61

CHAPTER FOURTEEN
The Unexpected Furry of Futility 63

CHAPTER FIFTEEN
The Final Decision 71

CHAPTER SIXTEEN
The Eye in the Sky..76

CHAPTER SEVENTEEN
The Big Flash 80

CHAPTER EIGHTEEN
Devastation in the Air 85

CHAPTER NINETEEN
The Lucky Ones...90

CHAPTER TWENTY
Empty Skies over Earth 93

CHAPTER TWENTY-ONE
The Clearing Sheen 96

CHAPTER TWENTY-TWO
The Gruesome Sight...103

CHAPTER TWENTY-THREE
Eyes toward the Heavens 106

CHAPTER TWENTY-FOUR
A Prayer for a Daughter, a Mother, a Wife............................107

CHAPTER TWENTY-FIVE
Decaying Death March 109

CHAPTER TWENTY-SIX
The Light of Night...111

CHAPTER TWENTY-SEVEN
A Long Hard Year 114

CHAPTER TWENTY-EIGHT
Preparing the Twitchel for Flight 118

CHAPTER TWENTY-NINE
Returning Home 122

CHAPTER THIRTY
Did They or Didn't They...132

CHAPTER THIRTY-ONE
The Loss of Thunder in the Skies..............................139

CHAPTER THIRTY-TWO
Tried to Reach Out 141

CHAPTER THIRTY-THREE
The Big Question 145

CHAPTER THIRTY-FOUR
The Long Wait 160

CHAPTER THIRTY-FIVE
The Reunion 166

CHAPTER THIRTY-SIX
The White House 181

CHAPTER THIRTY-SEVEN
Substitute Duty 187

CHAPTER THIRTY-EIGHT
The Arrival Home 202

CHAPTER THIRTY-NINE
Daring Pilots 217

CHAPTER FORTY
Sunday Morning Mass 219

CHAPTER FORTY-ONE
The Visitor 223

CHAPTER FORTY-TWO
Orders to Fly Again 226

CHAPTER FORTY-THREE
Early Morning Exercise 241

CHAPTER FORTY-FOUR
The Night Before Takeoff 250

CHAPTER FORTY-FIVE
The Time To Fly 253

CHAPTER FORTY-SIX
The Final Countdown 257

CHAPTER FORTY-SEVEN
The Lottery for Life or Death 273

CHAPTER FORTY-EIGHT
Excitement of a Sighting 281

CHAPTER FORTY-NINE
The Beautiful Launch 283

CHAPTER FIFTY
The Departure 298

CHAPTER FIFTY-ONE
The Suffering 324

CHAPTER FIFTY-TWO
Back on the Farm 326

CHAPTER FIFTY-THREE
Hope 328

CHAPTER FIFTY-FOUR
Back Aboard the Space Station 329

CHAPTER FIFTY-FIVE
Survival in Space 332

CHAPTER FIFTY-SIX
The Stay of Time 335

CHAPTER FIFTY-SEVEN
Let the Lottery Begin 340

CHAPTER FIFTY-EIGHT
Going Home 357

CHAPTER FIFTY-NINE
The Eye of the Storm 364

CHAPTER SIXTY
The Great Escape 369

CHAPTER SIXTY-ONE
The Capsule 374

CHAPTER SIXTY-TWO
The Gargantua 1st Wave 386

CHAPTER SIXTY-THREE
A New Day for Life 394

CHAPTER SIXTY-FOUR
The Long Wait 397

CHAPTER SIXTY-FIVE
A Tiny Sailboat 399

CHAPTER SIXTY-SIX
The Watchful Eye in the Sky 404

CHAPTER SIXTY-SEVEN
Stone Deaf Ears 409

CHAPTER SIXTY-EIGHT
The Seventh Day 411

CHAPTER SIXTY-NINE
The Friendly Port of Call 413

CHAPTER SEVENTY
The Last Shuttle of the Fleet 416

CHAPTER SEVENTY-ONE
Going Home 421

CHAPTER SEVENTY-TWO
The Last Flight to Space 427

CHAPTER SEVENTY-THREE
The Choice of no Return 442

CHAPTER SEVENTY-FOUR
The Decision 448

CHAPTER SEVENTY-FIVE
The Last Mercy Mission 459

CHAPTER SEVENTY-SIX
Safely in Orbit 463

CHAPTER SEVENTY-SEVEN
The Happy Eye in the Sky 466

CHAPTER SEVENTY-EIGHT
A Friendly Voice in Space 469

CHAPTER SEVENTY-NINE
The Docking 471

CHAPTER EIGHTY
The Last Stage 476

CHAPTER EIGHTY-ONE
The Return 479

CHAPTER EIGHTY-TWO
The Sonic Boom 485

CHAPTER EIGHTY-THREE
A Lonely Cloud 493

CHAPTER EIGHTY-FOUR
The Loss of a Mission 496

CHAPTER EIGHTY-FIVE
Manny Eyes Focused on the Heavens 501

CHAPTER EIGHTY-SIX
Home at Last 505

CHAPTER EIGHTY-SEVEN
The Celebration 507

CHAPTER ONE

Hitler's Germany

During the 1940's with World War II playing out in full-scale battle abroad, Hitler's new Germany was in its final stages in its attempt to develop and detonate the first atomic nuclear device ever known to mankind. This new weaponry would facilitate his warring Germany to triumphant control over the entire world.

The Norwegian ferry, the SF Hydro, leaving Norway for a German port, was blown up and sunk by Norwegian resistance forces in its attempt to deliver the special liquid cargo it carried. The cargo onboard was an enriched heavy water required by Hitler's scientists in making the new atomic weaponry. The ship had to be sunk in order to slow Hitler's scientists down long enough for the united allies from the western world to bring the nuclear age into fruition. The special heavy water was in railroad tanker cars on the ferry sailing towards Germany, and would afford Hitler's physicists in their efforts to produce the deadly weaponry they would use against the world.

The acidic heavy water was laden with suspended neutrons floating wildly in the water. The enriched liquid was made possible by passing massive amounts of highly charged electrical values in strong voltage through ordinary water treated with potash. The proses raised the waters acidic level to a high acidic level above the 14ph+ percentage. The heavy water when mixed properly would turn raw uranium into usable plutonium uranium for the new weaponry they were trying so desperately to make.

In the United States during this time, volunteers by the hundreds worked diligently on a similar project. They all worked to perform new applications in mathematical equations, in order to defeat the power seeking Germans in bringing to fruition the first atomic bomb and weaponry ever made.

Volunteers worked tirelessly in order to keep Hitler's militaristic Germany from ruling the planet. A strong effort by everyone, the Manhattan project came to fruition in record time. Many sleepless nights encountered by the dedicated people around the United States working on different mathematical problems developing and completing the weaponry of destruction for war and peaceful purposes as well.

Involved in the Manhattan project, were two very highly trained doctors in physics. Both were busy calculating, anxiously toiling away at their jobs in a bombproof shelter. The secret laboratory was made up of modular formed steel cubicles with pre-stressed concrete construction applied to their outer sidewalls. The U.S. Government purposely hid the Trinity testing facility buried beneath the hot remote desert sands of Los Alamos, New Mexico.

Dr. Charles A. Swatter and his associate Dr. Roger K. Sterling, with their trustworthy staff, were vigorously at work testing all mathematical equations calculated and sent in from around the country in the stability of raw materials needed to complete the complicated project. The doctors tested and retested mathematical equations over and over again within their busy minds.

They had to design a molecular fusion formula to calculate the outcome of this new weaponry using the first unnatural division in high quality properties of altered plutonic uranium. In detonation, the fusion would split atoms in nanosecond timing, turning the new substance into as fast an acting division upon millions in concentrated uranium atoms simultaneously exploding into trillions if not bazillions of tiny little atomic fragments.

The massive heat generated by these gases would first push out from its epicenter and then be sucked instantaneously back to its point of origin. If their calculations were right, the explosion would cause a reverse action thrusting masses of debris and smoke rapidly skyward up into the earth's atmosphere as a massive mushroom flume high above the earth's crust. The two doctors assigned to this special project were highly recognized American physicists. Both committed against time for world peace in accomplishing the first ever massive atomic nuclear device.

The hefty bombs would have to be loaded into the fuselage of a large Army Air Force bomber, and then quickly flown abroad to the enemy's homeland in order to help end the world war.

Heads of states from around the world and the United States anticipated the making of this new weaponry would bring world peace to the globe and an end to wars caused by evil forces around the earth forever.

The new bomb required a special highly enriched plutonic uranium ore. The purest most stable uranium ore they could find. The ore used in making this particular bomb had been obtain from a once thriving gold mine found deep in the Alaskan wilderness. An old gold miner found the highly enriched organic substance strictly by accident. He discovered the uranium ore after becoming severely sick from the ore's high radioactive strength as he dug further down into his gold claim, deep within the rugged wilderness of Alaska's last frontier.

The radioactive strength in this plutonic ore read very high very powerful on the first manmade neophyte radiation-detecting device ever made by man. A new sensing device made for detecting radioactive potency in any radioactive material.

The doctors worked feverishly hard with these two materials to bring them together to react with one another with great force. One substance made by man, the other material made natural by origin. Using mathematical formulas in safely developing these new devices before some other hostile nation of mass destruction might first invent them.

One day, these atomic devices might supply electrical power to the world around, and put an end to all the millions of tons in coal burned daily by the electrical power-generating plants around the world. Their many smokestacks shooting out tons of massive deadly toxic emissions daily, destroying the earth's atmosphere and air we breathe with dense smog, killing the ozone layer surrounding the planet that protects it from the sun.

The main goal in the nuclear project was to put an end to the raging World War II fully engrossed across the seas, both east and west of the American coastlines. The doctors not knowing at the time that the new weaponry would be sent to the islands of Japan, instead of going over to warring Germany where the new bombs were intended to go in the first place.

Days filled with exhausting hours away from their loved ones consumed by the urgent project. The doctors confined themselves similar to prisoners of war, of their own making, within the confines of the hidden laboratory below the hot desert sands in total solitude. The physicists, whether asleep at home or awake at work, continually worked mind-bogglingly hard trying to find a link to the solution to the demise in the worthy project.

They labored from the early morning hours of day until the late of the night and sometimes into the break of daylight without sleep, trying hard to bring prompt closure to this very needy project that they were in command of. With the world depending on them, they had the weight of the planet resting upon their shoulders. Their loving, understanding wives did not bother their husbands, knowing they were dedicated patriots to their country and the safety of their loved ones abroad and at home. Their children did not understand their father's absence at the time, but would understand later on in the outcome.

They painstakingly laid out what lay ahead in creating the deadly device to bring it to fruition for world peace. The government did not want a single word leaked out about the experiments going on at the facilities especially to the doctors' wives, children or relatives. They were afraid that if they knew anything about the special project that they might become primary targets of an enemy undercover agent. The doctors were extremely lonely from being gone from their families for so long.

Minutes away by vehicle from the main entrance to the laboratory inside the same compound was an Army Air Force airfield. It included a fully staffed Army ground force assigned to the field for additional protection. The airfield was built for added security in protecting the experimental laboratory by air with a strong defense airbase equipped with the most modern fighter aircraft warring machines newly owned by the United States military.

These pilots assigned to this special airfield were of the highest top-gun quality flying aviators on constant standby alert, ready to respond in a spilt second notice should a red alert sound out at the air station. These pilots were on the ready should any aircraft, especially an enemy aircraft, approach the facilities from the air, or should a small foreign ground force breach the U.S. borders or shorelines, and attempt a go of it against the special security defense mechanisms put in place surrounding the fortress and laboratory facility.

The laboratory's main entrance into the special underground facility was located several minutes away by car from its center point to its outer bordering circumference and security points. They built the compound in the shape of a large wagon wheel, protected by a modern day electrified monitor -sensing fence surrounding its most outer perimeter.

The new electronic fence ran on a no amp, low current, high sensitive sonar sensing wave link, first of its kind silicone wiring device, equipped with high frequency sensitivity receiving and sending sensors.

This enabled the laboratory's security monitors to pick up the smallest of tiny non-threatening rodents or smaller animals that might amble up close to the fence while eating grassy mounds in sod and plant life growing in or around the sandy dunes located around the facility.

The radar screen at the command center was similar a sonar screen used in a submarine, but ten times larger. Three trained soldier airmen stood or sat at their duty stations at all times in front of the security screen, monitoring it's every detection transmitted upon its surface.

All three simultaneously watched for intruders. They could tell by the numbers generated in binary code from the fence, as those patterns generate into figures on the screen. The screen monitored twenty-four hours a day, three hundred and sixty five days a year.

They would watch this screen until fruition of the experimental bomb or its sudden end decided by a high military ranking officer, or a higher-ranking government official due to the extreme cost, too great for the country to manage or if not needed for the end of the war had come, whichever came first. A second security fence around the compound was a fortified fortress fence placed just a few feet inside the main security sensing wire.

The coiled up lethal wires installed for additional security in case an assembly of unfriendly aliens from a foreign land tried to scale it. Guard shacks were located every few thousand feet apart dotting the outer perimeter of the facility to increase its measure in securing the post. These guard shacks were securely connected with an assortment of telephone lines surrounding the facilities buried at different intervals in depths underground, should a small force or enemy try to break into the compound.

The guards stationed in these shacks were supposed to report any low flying aircraft flying below the radar-detecting devices surrounding the compound trying to fly over the facilities to the main dispatch. To enter, one would first have to enter through a stringent security measurement point put into place at the secluded Army airfield. There they would first have to pass through a tight securities screening station, and then proceed through another gated area to gain access to the lengthy dirt roadway leading out the desert to the laboratory's entrance.

Every pilot and soldier stationed at the Army Air-Force airfield were all top security personnel, having been background checked one by one, and hand selected to serve the country at this special facility. With top security in place, men without top security badges at the base were not allowed beyond the inner boundaries from within their restricted duty area.

None of the men stationed there were allowed to venture too near the main entrance to the hidden laboratory's entrance inside the compounds epicenter, except for a few selected individuals, having many eyes watching over their entrance by higher-ranking individuals than they were.

All personnel at the facilities singularly picked out by military securities personnel located at the newly formed military leaders facilities in Washington D.C., and recommended by military leaders from around the nation. These pilots had proven themselves worthy as topnotch pilots in the new aircraft they flew at their designated fighter training flight schools they all attended. These pilots were dedicated airmen, brothers to one another, loyal to all, to their country, and ready to fly into combat at a moment's notice. Ready to give up their lives against all odds to protect the new security compound they were assigned to protect against all foreign troops or enemy aircraft, whichever might try to breach the compound's high security system.

On many occasions, the base pilots scrambled in order to escort a lost or very curious civilian pilot away from the restricted airspace above the experimental desert compound. Maybe a pilot was out for a fun-filled day or afternoon of flying, or others who may have lost their way while flying cross-country from one state to another who did not know about the newly enforced restricted air space over the small piece of desert floor below in New Mexico.

The young hotshot military pilots loved there assigned flying missions. They took great pleasure in every opportunity they had in escorting a pilot away from the compound when they had the chance to do so.

It seemed like a joyful way to practice one's military flight training out on some poor soul and having a whole hell of a lot of fun in doing it at the same time. Most pilots hoped it would all be in fun and not a real combat mission, whilst some of the young members on the team hoped for some real action in the sky over the desert, even if it was in their own back yard and country.

CHAPTER TWO

Red Alert

Mr. Stew Jones, a well liked but gruff old chap flyer was lucky to be alive as he was a self-trained pilot when he was a young lad. He purchased his first two-winged airplane along with a friend who bought one also. The two did not know a thing about flying these aircrafts until they both jumped up into the cockpits of their beasts, and became a couple of young flying aces who loved to barnstorm people for the sheer fun of scaring the hell out of everyone on the ground below them.

One bright sunny day, he was out flying along all alone in his old open cockpit biplane. For some unforeseen reason, he knew nothing about the newly restricted air space of a no fly zone over the desert. He was out flying along minding his own business, he thought, when he became half scared to death. Suddenly from out of nowhere, a squadron of military wartime fighter airplanes surrounded his little old biplane midair out over the desolate desert in the bright of midday. He not knowingly had crossed over the invisible forbidden fly-zone airspace line drawn in the desert sands below flying not far from a newly built restricted research complex.

The squadron leader hand motioned Mr. Jones to leave the restricted airspace at once by signaling him off by hand-waving at him as one very young determined hotshot fighter pilot, fired a blast from his wing-mounted machine guns.

White smoke from tracer bullets he was firing went flashing out from his wing guns, as he went zooming out in front and across old Stew's flight path. He had flown his warring plane right in front of old Stew's double winged aircraft, coming just inches away from him. He thought this stupid young bastard pilot had almost run right into him on purpose it was such a close encounter.

He got the message real fast when a second warring aircraft came zooming in at him from the opposite side of his old aircraft at a similar high speed. The second young fool pilot zoomed up across from his right in front of him as the other one had done with both his winged machine guns ablaze, just barely in front of his old biplane.

Stew could see quite clearly the smoky trails left behind from the tracer bullets fired in front of him from the second plane as he had seen from the first dip shit pilot's spray of bullets fired. He knew these damn fool warring fliers were not fooling around with him. The nose cone on the second aircraft looked more like a flying shark right up out the ocean ready to eat him alive.

After adjusting his old tired eyes and affixing them on the aircraft zooming in front of him, he almost wet his pants in fright seeing the sharp looking teeth painted on the cowling cover over the plane's engine. Especially for the way the fool pilots were acting toward him, as if he was an enemy pilot from a foreign land attacking their country.

He figured it would not be long before he and his old Betsy biplane would be full of lead, if he did not do something real fast. Old Stew quickly yanked real hard right on his flight control stick sticking up between his two legs, and pushed it hard forward with a quick hard thrust. This placed his old two-winged biplane into a straight downward hard right roll out of the way of this crazy bunch of squadron flying maniacs.

He left in the direction the head pilot leading this bunch, the squadron commander, had intended for him to go. He did it in quite the military tactic fashion in his departing performance in evading this bunch of crazy flying bastards he thought, hoping they would not follow him and drive him deep into the desert floor below. The old coot really impressed the squadron commander with his quick instinctive military avoidance tactic.

The evasive maneuver was impressive for any pilot seeing Stew was an aging old fart of a pilot flying alone in an old frail looking relic of an aircraft not looking too flight worthy having no machine guns attached to it in any form, and ordered his squadron not to follow behind him, or to tantalize him any further.

Seeing he was fleeing the area as ordered, they returned to the airbase to await upon another stray pilot to enter the no-fly zone, and scare the hell right out of them if they could or take on a real enemy aircraft.

The squadron pilots both young and old got their jollies off by scaring the crap out of anyone they could find out in the desert flying too near the restricted airspace fly zone. They laughed like hell half the night away after returning to base telling their stories to anyone who would listen about the encounters they had with these unfortunate pilots of chance, until it was late and time to call it a night and retire to their bunks for an evening's rest.

Old Stew Jones had to make an unexpected detour around the restricted fly area circling way up around to the north of the compound. He managed to land at a small farm and airfield not far from where he had run into the first demise of his last long flight he would ever make. He luckily landed at an airfield to refuel his aircraft low on fuel. He was running on gas fumes as his fuel tank was so empty in order to allow him to accomplish his preplanned cross-country flight to his destination. Filling his old airplane fuel tank with gasoline enabled him to fly to his destination.

He flew off again into the bright blue sky above the desert, flying cross-country far out and around the restricted airspace over the new compound getting some very worthy advice from the farmer gent managing the small farms airfield he had landed at to refuel.

After an extended hour-long unplanned flight around the new compound, he finally managed to land his old biplane Betsy. He landing her safely at his old school chum's farm and home. His final destination and last flight ever to Silver Stone Creak just south of the new military laboratory facility and testing site.

Stew looked at the wind directional windsock attached above Brad's old barn. Just his sucky lucky luck, same as the rest of this damn day had been going for him so far. He would have to land his bird down the airstrip into the wind away from Brad's house and barn instead of up the field towards the barn and house his usual way when he flew there.

He gave it quick thought about landing his old bird with the wind up the field, but knew by doing so it would jeopardize his safe control over the plane near the ground, and did not want to become another dead statistic of a pilot for not using common sense when it came to making a safe landing. He knew landing into the wind was best control of his aircraft, and the right thing to do.

He knew his reaction time in flying old Betsy was not as it once was, so he set his bird down on the homemade airstrip with his biplane going into the wind as it should. He slowed old Betsy down finally at the far end of the airfield by the barbed wire cattle fence. He gave the engine a quick burst of fuel using the throttle, spinning his old bird around, and then slowly taxied his old biplane up the airfield strip to Brad's house and barn at the far end of the bumpy landing strip.

He slowly reached down, and turned the knob beside his left leg shutting off the priming valve and fuel lines to the plane's multi cylinder engine. He was preparing to put his old faithful Betsy to rest for the night, or two or three nights for an anticipated long stay with his friend Brad. When he finally regrouped himself from the long flight with enough energy and strength, he disembarked up and out the rear cockpit from his old biplane, getting himself down off his aircraft.

His face was still painted pale white from fright, almost white as a ghost. His skin color looked drained, as white as a preacher's insipid white collar, from being so damn heart attack frightened just over an hour or so before from that stressful experience he had with all those stupid flying military pilots he had encountered earlier that afternoon. He felt half way between life and death it seemed, with his heart still racing like a racehorse that had just finished running the Kentucky Derby.

Brad Shaw and Old Stew were the ones who bought the two very similar airplanes together. He was also his old high school chum from way back in the 1870's many long school years in the past. Stew enjoyed visiting him on special occasions at least once or twice a year. He loved to muse over their old times in their youthful younger years as wild young lads during the good old hay days of horse and buggy days of old like when they would dare one another to jump off the rear roof of the barn or grab a rattlesnake by its tail and snap it in the air as if it was a bull's whip, breaking the snakes neck, skinning it, and cooking it up over a campfire to eat. They were two hellions.

The stories from yesteryear told on these special visits were repeated a thousand times over, but it rejuvenated their aging minds as they laughed wholeheartedly about them, as it brought them back to a time in youthfulness they once so loved.

Brad watched as his friend Stew slowly stepped out Old Betsy's rear cockpit all stooped over as if in pain. He watched him slowly crawl out the fuselage down to the walking pad on the lower wing, and as he slowly shuffled his aging feet along down the frail wing to its end, jumping down to the ground below him in a painful bound. He landed tepidly on both of his sore feet, almost falling over to the ground on his face. Brad thought it very funny not seeing Old Stew jump down off his bird with his quick old fancy foot stepping way, thinking there might be something drastically wrong with his old friend.

Stew began badass mad rambling on about his encounter earlier that afternoon with the warring squadron of fighter planes. He profusely started swearing out loud to his old bud Brad about the near mishap he had just experienced northeast of Silver Stone Creek. He was steaming mad beside himself and sizzling over the damn situation to Brad.

He sounded volcanically eruptive releasing built up pressure in pure anger, for he had been thinking about the disruptive incident all the way there since refueling his old biplane Betsy.He was truly pissed off about the whole encounter having taken place.

It was supposed to be a relaxing flight over to Brad's farm as it usually was. He was expecting to enjoy the solitude in the quiet clear blue sky above on the flight, and was looking forward to a couple of well-deserved needy relaxing days with his old friend. Maybe he would stay a week or more with nothing to do but talk about happy days of old. He was just plain bullshit about the incident, and could not wait to get out whatever had bottled up inside him off his chest. He erupted like an exploding volcano before even saying hello to his old friend Brad.

"Ran into a whole damn bunch of those stupid damn asshole military highfalutin military fool hearty flying dip shits bastards up there in the air, Brad. Northeast of here this afternoon, Brad. Phew, a whole bunch of them stupid damn fools anyway. Really do not know for sure how many there were, but it was a bunch. They were all flying them there damn new high fancy fast flying machines with teeth sticking out all over the damn cowlings out-over their engine covers, the bastards! They surrounded the plane, Brad, just like a bunch of hungry locusts or a bunch of angry swarming honeybees. The bastards thinking me some sort a damned criminal or something out there going to harm the world, the way those bastards came flying up at me from all different directions. You might have thought I was one of those damn German enemies trying to take over the whole countries airspace all by myself around here in the desert, or something like that, I don't' know? One of the damn sons-of-bitches shot his machine guns off at us or almost at us. He shot it off right in front old Betsy here, and me. He scared the hell right out of us, Brad, and I almost pissed my pants. Thought for sure those sons-of-bitches were going to kill us both just to have a couple of freaking falling targets to get some damn killing practice in flying and shooting on us, with all those new fancy warplanes they were flying.

Maybe the bastards just wanted to fly around and watch us bury ourselves in to the damn desert floor below. Wanted to give the whole bunch them bastards the freaking fickle finger of fate I did, if you know what I mean. I decided it not a good idea to fickle finger them off at the time.

What in hell is going on up there, Brad? Did the damn Nazis, or them war seeking Japanese bastards land over here or something?"

"No Stew, the damned Nazis have not landed over here yet, nor have the warring Japanese landed here either. We sure as hell hope neither of them ever does land over here. You had better calm down a bit Stew, or you are going to have a heart attack.

There is talk going around about some new fang-dangled military fortress base being built up north of here somewhere. They do not let anyone from around these parts here, nowhere near the damn place. Guess its top secret or something, Stew. No one really knows.

I hear tell by some the folk round here, there is going to be some sort of a testing on some new kind of special weaponry of war up there, or some brand new fancy flying airplanes they don't want anyone to see. Something real secret going on up there no one knows about. As if they were making special kites to carry tiny bombs over enemy lines being made for all anyone around here knows. Don't really know much about it, Stew, and do not really gives a cat's ass or cares either. Guess I am just too old to care about things like that anymore. It is just a whole bunch of hearsay and speculation in gossip being spread about the countryside by some of the towns folk that is all I know.

Folk around these parts hear, been telling people they got some poor Doctor folk over Niceville way working up there at the new airfield, or something like that. Poor kinfolk of his do not have any privacy to themselves at all.

Listen to this, Stew. This doctors kids has got to goes off to school with a military escort every day, everywhere they go, as does his lovely wife. They even go when she goes out to the damn store just to do some simple grocery shopping or goes to get her damn hair done. No way to live I tell you, is it? Having some strangers around your family all the time just does not seem quite right, does it Stu?

"Cannot say I would want to live my life that way, Brad! They probably have to have a damn escort just to go off to the damn bathroom, too.

It is not anyway we would want to live our lives. You got any that good old homemade brew of your, that special scotch you make so good for a very needy pal? That experience I had today with all those damn assholes flying up there, makes a man kind a thirsty for some of the good stuff, if you know what I mean?"

"You know I do, Stew. Have a brand new fresh bottle along with several others in stash. Several new capped up bottles never been opened up yet. Have them well hidden away as usual. Put the bottles out in the grain stores bin in the barn. Saved the bottles out there for special days just like this one and other special days that might arise at different times.

Then some days just to forget about another tomorrow coming. Saved out a bottle or two of my scotch just for you to take along back home with you when you go. I'll fetch your bags Stew from the front cockpit of old Betsy here so we can go off up to the house for you to have a good shot or two of my special brew and to relax a wee bit while we chat.

Just cannot believe why those stupid assholes did that to you up there today, Stew. There should be some sort of federal law against those damn fool highflying cowboys up there doing such a thing to innocent ordinary people like us, or too anybody.

If old Jessie and I had been up there with you Stew, we would have shot the bunch of those asshole fools the middle finger. Got myself a real short fuse when it comes to fools like them stupid bastards even if they did try to shoot us down.

We would have given them bastards a good run for their money if we were up there with you, Stew. We do talk pretty damn big for old farts right. Let us get you and your bags up to the house, then I shall fix the two of us up with a good strong drink to get your stay started. Maybe I should get out my old twin winged bird myself, and go half way back home with you, just to see what those bastards would do if there were the two of us up there flying around? We could give them damn cowboys a real good run for their money they would never forget, couldn't we?

CHAPTER THREE

The Detonator

"Look at this Charles, I cannot believe it. We have the answer right here in front of us! You would not think the solution was this simple. All we have to do is install a small sensitivity, activating chamber on the impact-detonating device. There the activating detonation switch could be used anywhere in the world just by using the changing pressure in altitude to activate it. We can place it alongside the atmospheric pressure regulating switch in the altimeter's sensory pressure activity device, having the falling pressure in altitude at the delivery site activate the switch in its decent. I mean the rising pressure in the switch causing the detonator to activate right before the egg hits the damn ground wherever we were to deliver it. We can hatch this egg anywhere we want to. We can set this jewel off at any height in the atmosphere anywhere around the globe that we possibly want too. We can preset the altitude sensor to correspond with the height of altitude wherever we want to position the bomb to detonate. The bombardier can even set the activating pressure switch after takeoff or just before releasing it.

Now, we don't have to work any longer on that stupid timely anti-plunging detonator-activating device we have been racking our puny little brains out on for this past long month. Why did you not see the simplicity in this problem before, Charles? I mean why had we not seen how foolishly simple the whole- damn solution was before? It is so damn simple that one of my two little kids could have worked this problem out all by themselves."

It has just been so damn plain crazy around here! The solution to this whole damn problem has been staring us in the face right along for months. With a newly designed activating altimeter pressure regulating sensory switch in hand, we should be ready to test the atomic nuclear device in just about a week, more or even less is my guess. I will have the boys in instrumentation get going on this right away, and start work on the pressure switch now. In the meantime, I will call Washington and get permission from General Carey and the Security Council to detonate the Egg as soon as we have their permission.

While Nate and his crew readied the pressure switch, we can simulate the barometric pressure change in altitude by using an oxygen 02 cylinder canister with an airline along with a pressure switch connected to an air line with an operative pressure-regulating valve.

I will call Washington straight away and get going on getting the Egg's nest assembled."

CHAPTER FOUR

The Word

"Good afternoon, General Carey's office, Lieutenant Moody speaking. How may I be of assistance?" "Lieutenant Moody, this is Red Duck calling! Is General Carey available in his office today, please?" "One moment please, Red Duck, I will connect you straight to General Carey, sir. He was just talking about you to the staff this morning, sir. Is everything all right, sir?" "Everything is better than all right, thank you!" "He will be pleased to hear that, Red Duck!"

"This is General Carey, how may I help you?" "Hello General, this is Red Duck Charlie calling, sir. I need your permission to lay up for the construction of building the nest for the hatching of the Egg, sir." "Yes, sir, Red Duck, you definitely have our permission for the nest construction to begin in order to hatch the Egg. I want to meet personally with you and your staff prior to the Egg's detonation. The egg's securities staff should be at the testing facilities by the week's end. You have our permission, Red Duck, to call on base civil engineering on our behalf. You can have Major Wood issue the necessary instructions to his men for the nest to be constructed straight away, Charles. Major Wood can have his office call securities here in Washington if there are any questions or concerns in constructing the nest. I will see you soon, Red Duck." "Good day, General."

"Hello! Hello! Damn fool phone lines anyway! Hello, operations, operations, is anybody working in there today?" "Good morning

18

operations, this is Staff Sgt. Morris speaking, how may I direct your telephone call this morning." "Sergeant Morris! This is Red Duck calling from laboratory Expo, Delta, and Charlie would you please patch this call through to Major Wood at once, Sergeant Morris, if you wouldn't mind please!"

Charles's voice sounded dreadfully irritated to Sergeant Morris's ears on the phone line. "One moment please, Red Duck, I will connect you straight away, sir." "Operations, Major Wood speaking". "Major Wood, this is Red Duck Charlie, from Expo, Delta, Charlie calling, sir. We are ready for construction to begin on the nest for the Egg at Expo, Delta, Charlie, key word Bravo, Major Wood. We will be ready to hatch the Egg as soon as you can have the egg's nest constructed for its hatching, sir. Securities in Washington want you to furnish the men, the materials, and the security forces straight away, sir. They are counting on your timely preparation in the nest's completion for its hatching, Major, at your earliest convenience, sir. I have followed the strict chain of command as directed, Major Wood. Orders in proper chain command by General Carey, Sir. I have called to alert General Carey on our progress and our needs. I have secured through him the proper channel of permission and the projects code name for the Mannequin Towered Nest, sir, to be built straight away with your help, Major."

"What is the word and code given to this project, Red Duck?" Captain-Colonel-Major-Duck-Delta-Major-Wood-Duck-Charlie-Wood-Major, Major Wood."

"The code name is correct Red Duck. The preparations for the nest shall get underway immediately. I will have the nest prepared for hatching shortly, Red Duck." "Thank you, Major Wood, and have a good day."

"Everything is ready to go, Roger. The nest preparations are underway as we speak. We had better get a move on fine tuning this new baby before we forget what I said we have to do with that pressure sensory altitude activating device. What a mouth full. We will be able to activate the new device safely from the new concrete steel bunkered facility once the Egg finds the cradle at the nesting sight. I still cannot

believe we did not think of that simple little idea of using a pressure switch a long time ago. I bet my little boy, Billy, could have figured that switch idea out all by his lonesome just by playing with that new erector set that Sally and I gave him for Christmas last year. It is a real shame sometimes that we cannot see the damn forest for the trees it seems. Especially when the entire world is counting on us for a solution to everyone's dire need in peace and tranquility. If only people from around the world could get along, there wouldn't be a need for all this fighting crap and stuff, and the world would be one heck of a lot better off place to live for everyone."

It is truly amazing, how it takes a few crazed-up individuals who greedily want what another individual or whole country have that they don't have. They go after them in war or any other means they have to secure themselves that which does not belong to them. Greed in individuals, kills any spirit of love or tranquility for others, and for what?

Why do people not let others around the world live happily? Let them enjoy what they have and not want to be tyrants in the world who want power over all others. Oh well, enough said! Let us get back to work on this warhead that will put an end to all that greedy stuff, right Roger?" "Yes, Charlie!"

CHAPTER FIVE

The Convoy

Several crews of electricians, plumbers, carpenters, and many heavy equipment operators from base's civil engineering who had been waiting around for months, finally had the go ahead to assemble for their mission. The crews quickly assembled in the civil engineering yard and prepared for an immediate departure on their expected but unsure assignment. The excited workers instantly mobilized the second Major Wood gave them orders for the preparation of the coded duty venture they were all assigned to perform at this special Army airbase.

Many large stacked up heavy wood, sheathing, and other equipment of supplies for the nest construction had been previously loaded onto many military vehicles that were parked inside the motor pool gated area. The trucks had been sitting there locked away in the desert all covered up with large protective tarps over them for months. It behooved the many military men to what their real assignment was going to be.

The majority of men who were stationed out in the country's vast hot desert were basically doing nothing but sitting around being bored out of their minds. Most of the time they waited to move out with whatever was beneath the many tarp-covered trucks, and bring it somewhere out in the desert or wherever their orders would lead them. This type of wishy washy assignment with a war going on abroad confused the hell out of all the men.

With orders given to engineering to assemble, the men in civil engineering ran to their different loaded motor vehicles, similar military fighter pilots running from their preparation rooms to their military fighter aircraft, ready to take off and fight the enemy in a moment's notice.

By 1200 hours Eastern Time, the convoy of military trucks had reached its first checkpoint between guard shacks numbered 48 and 49 respectively. The guards assigned the two out-posts were taken-a-back with the sudden surprise of the large convoy approaching them as it rolled up between their two positions from within the compound.

The soldiers on duty demanded to know why hadn't they been notified about what was going to take place. Due to the top security of the special orders given by General Carey, and the special matter at hand, they were not notified. All phone lines except the invasion phone lines had previously been shut down at base communications prior the convoy leaving the base. All other personal phone lines would remain down until further notice after the nest was complete. All regular non-high security communication phone lines were strictly off limits to all personnel until further notice.

A messenger on a motorcycle went around to all Charlie check-point positions informing the personnel on duty there, not to use any phone lines. They were to use the designated red line in case a dire emergency arose. If an enemy was approaching their post or attempting to breach their station, they could use the phone line, and only then! Any personnel using phones other than for military reasons of any kind from their secured position's would be dealt with severely by a full military court martial, and would spend many years behind bars in a military detention center.

General Carey did not want anyone outside the base knowing anything about what was taking place out in the desert at that time. He didn't want any of the lines between the guard shacks to get tampered with or tapped into. He didn't want any alien force to prevent the hatching of this very formable device at a most crucial time in the life of the war and the forthcoming of human freedom around the globe. Tough security was imminent with this special assignment.

Security in the Egg's development was the main reason for all the safeguards put into place. None of the guards on duty at their assigned guard shacks knew anything about what was taking place in the desert until completion of the experiment was to take place. Even then, the guards stationed in their shacks were in the dark to what was taking place around them.

A crew with many phone linemen went to work immediately digging up new trenches in the desert floor, and laying out mile after mile of new phone line cables and connectors buried deep beneath the sands in the desert. The rest of the large convoy of trucks proceeded out across the desert sands to a new opening breached in the fence for access to the hatching sight. Another linemen crew came quickly along behind the first burying the newly dropped wire beneath the sands in the hot desert floor protecting them from passing vehicles traveling to and from the new gated area. The lines were being buried deep in the sand to protect them from damage, and prevent immediate access to them for ease of tampering or tapping into them for espionage reasons.

The air around the compound became an even more top security issue, as the airmen stationed at the base flew continual missions around the perimeter of the facilities and out over the nesting site around the clock to keep any and all enemies and other stray pilots away from the facilities prior to the detonation of the egg.

Not knowing it, Old Stew Jones just happened to be the unfortunate pilot flying too close to the compound that day when they surprised him. The squadron was returning back to the airstrip after spending several long tiring hours flying around and around in circles about the outer perimeter surrounding the compound protecting its airspace, a couple days prior to the egg being detonated. The guards on duty at guard shacks number 48 and 49 Charlie stations, upon arrival of the convoy, received strict orders to stay put inside their posts, and to wait quietly there. They were not to use any phone lines under any circumstances until new orders arrived for them to do so. Their new orders would come down to them by way of special messenger in a specially sealed envelope under the private seal of the base commander.

An additional six heavily-armed men were stationed instantly with them as additional protection at their volatile post.

They were to help guard the new opening made in the base perimeters fence of the top security outpost along with an armored vehicle equipped with two machine guns and a grenade launcher. These new men would take over all communications with base control using decoding radio messengering while the breach in the fence was unprotected.

Prior to the convoy leaving the main base, messengers went out to all the perimeter guard shack posts around the compound to inform them of maneuvers taking place in the desert that day, and to ignore any dusty flumes being made inside the compound made by all the trucks rolling over the dusty sands. All guards shacks except for numbers 48 and 49.

A second guard shack, quickly erected just twenty feet away from the original number 49 guard shack, was called number 49½. This was to protect both sides of the newly installed swinging gates against unlawful access to the compound.

Delta Charlie Bravo Two post number 491/2 guard shack would become the new focal point of the new nesting facilities communication post. No one without the direct permission of either Major Wood from civil engineering or that of General Carey from military defense headquarters in Washington D.C. could enter or leave through the newly gated area. No one could exit out of the compound through this gated area without one of a newly developed electronically engraved insignia pass, which recorded the movement of all personnel each way through the gate of the compound.

Almost immediately upon arrival, the top security sensing tracking wire was dug up, cut, spliced, and then reburied in the new roadway made in the fence. The twelve-foot high protection fence had been breached and re-gated. The military convoy of trucks with a full platoon of military police and armored guard carriers escorted the vehicles out of the newly installed gate and proceeded northward toward the site where the nest and its control buildings were to be erected.

Another couple of miles further north in the desert from the main facilities was another gated compound which required top security clearance for entry. A small guard force was assigned to this much smaller circular compound way out in the desert.

A change of guards took place a couple of times per shift, depending on the heat of the day and the cold of the night out in the desert. Some of the men were becoming slaphappy while protecting the small fenced-in area.

They wondered why anyone in their right mind would want to protect such a small postage-stamp size parcel of land, the size of a single city block barren of any life other than a single blade of witch grass. It was the home of a passing rattlesnake or two and a flowering cactus growing by the post shack, way the hell out in no-man's land. They all figured the land beneath the desert floor had to have some value to it. It had to be rich in oil, a gold mine, or some other great value for their government to assign an entire platoon of military police to protect the wasteland 24/7.

CHAPTER SIX

Facts Unknown

None of the scientists making the nuclear bomb knew what the extent of damage this new atomic fusion in raw materials would have on the earth as it was the first of its kind ever detonated on the planet. It left many scientists with doubts in their mind as to what might occur to the earth's core the minute the fusion in atoms took place. What other catastrophic events other than a humongous blast would be produced or occur when the splitting of this manmade matter, was not clearly known to the scientists of specific matter in material science.

These scientists could only muse through deduction of equation in mathematical science as what to expect from the catastrophic reaction in splitting these atoms all at once might have or could cause near the epicenter of the explosion and the immediate earth surrounding the explosion.

By some unforeseen circumstance, the raw materials below the earth's surface sizzling with flowing magma beneath the desert floor near the blast site if laced with hot liquid uranium, anything was possible to happen to the planet when the blast occurred.

If the first splitting of an atom caused an acute adverse unstoppable worldwide atomic splitting reaction, the world once known to mankind as planet earth, might just possibly disintegrate into billions, trillions, and possibly zillions of tiny fragmented pieces of molten rock and turn itself instantly into space dust. The reaction could occur in a matter of

mille-seconds, and none of the earths' population would be any the wiser for it.

The scientists who were working diligently on the project had taken every precaution they could think of into heightened scientific formulas. They gave it their best in scientific judgment and painstaking reflection on the physical subject matter they had at hand before coming to their conclusion of the worst scenario that could happen to the planet. They were sure it should not or would not come down to that, or at least they hoped not.

The scientists figured that if it did occur, no one on the face of the earth would feel the pain from the instant blast, as all would turn instantly into space dust, including them. They all laughed about it. "What the hell" the scientists thought, "ashes to ashes, and dust to dust. Everyone on planet earth was born to die, and the sooner would not be as bad as the later if Hitler's Germany did manage to take control over the entire world."

Everyone knew there would be no peace on earth or the possibility of living freely ever again, quietly or securely around the globe for any of its inhabitants. Not until Hitler's' sick total genocide prevailed all over the earth with his enforced annihilation of imperfect human beings, except for his sick desire of a total population with all blond haired and a blue-eyed race of human beings. He had no use for any human beings that did not fit his credibility of being born perfect except for his soldiers fighting for him. If they should die fighting for his cause, he did not care. Hitler would stop at nothing. He would destroy the children of any blond haired blue-eyed followers if they produced children with different colored hair or eyes that were not of his liking. He would even take the lives of his own children and his children's children if they were not born perfect in his mind's eye. Everyone knew he was a sick-minded lunatic and needed to be stopped immediately. Even if this new weaponry destroyed the earth, it would not be as bad as living under a dictator like Hitler.

General Carey heard just prior to leaving Washington, D.C. to go to the nesting site for the new bomb that the Japanese Emperor was preparing his military ready to join forces with Germany to take whatever spoils of war they could muster up from the war for themselves. The humbug around Washington, D.C. was that the Japanese could become a problematical country to deal with if they did enter the war at that time, and this new weaponry might have to be used against them as well as on German soil.

Time was running out for the allies abroad, and the need for the special bomb to bring lasting peace to the earth was in desperate need.

CHAPTER SEVEN

The Arrival of Brass

General Carey flew in from Washington, D.C. to the hot sands of New Mexico's northern desert on the second day after informing the president and his confidant staff that the Manhattan Project leaders were ready and now prepared to test the first nuclear prototype of the atomic bomb. He was extremely anxious to take part in this new historic event for humanity arriving at the experimental facilities at 1600 hours their time in the desert that afternoon.

"Good afternoon, General Carey", "And the same to you, Charles. Good to see you, too, Roger. Is the Egg ready to have its shell cracked open yet?" "No, sir, General Carey, the Egg is not quite ready to hatch. We are mostly ready, but want to explore the demeanor of the first chain reaction possibilities of this first split atom just a little further. Nothing to worry about though General Carey just a little more material and mathematical figuring to go over on my part, that's all."

"I was in communication with Major Wood on my way over here to see you Roger. He said the nest should be ready in just about another four days or less, is that a problem with you gentlemen?"

"No, sir. General Carey, not a problem at all."

"I guess the workmen are quite curious to know why we are building a 100 foot tower that looks similar to a giant wind-powered water well without a blade attached way out here in the middle of no-man's land in the desert so important. I guess everyone will know by the end of next week, right?" "You bet they will, General, and undoubtedly so will the rest of the nation and the world. The news media, if we let them, will take this huge blast and make it bigger and well known around the country and around the world. The Manhattan project will not be top secret any longer after this baby hatches itself, even out here in no-man's land!"

"Hey, Sergeant Wise, why the hell are we way out here in no-man's land erecting this stupid looking water tower without a well attached to its under-belly anyway?" "We do not really know boys. You know the old military saying don't you, and how it goes? It is not up to us to ask that silly question why boys, it is only up to us to do or die! Now boys, a lot more sawing on those planks and a lot less flapping those jaws of yours, and we might get this damn project off the ground a whole hell of a lot sooner than later! With a wee bit of luck and my sweet Irish temper boys, we just might have this stupid waterless tower completed and ready to fly before General Carey arrives from Washington D. C. to inspect our work! Now let's stop all this yakking and get attacking this project pronto!"

"What do you mean, General Carey, Sergeant? Do you mean the real chief, the head chief, the big cheese of the military armed services from the capital, that General Carey?" "That is the one boys, the one and only General Carey!"

With everyone realizing who was coming to inspect their work at the tower site, the work on the nesting tower took on a vigorous double time in their efforts. Just the thought of General Carey inspecting their work scared the hell out of most of them.

The men's hands flew at the heads of nails with hammers as if a machinegun was set on rapid fire. Handsaws sang out in musical tune, singing away cutting quickly back and forth across the surface of the boards beneath them. Their speedy rhythm caused tiny wood shavings to flow down toward the ground in a constant stream of sawdust.

If General Carey, head of the entire military armed services, was coming all the way out here to the desert to this hellhole to inspect their work, then the tower they were building must be something of great significance.

On the fourth very long hard day of hot work on the special erection in building the Egg's nest, a motorcade of several vehicles approached the nesting site from the direction of the main laboratory complex.

The motorcade speeding across the deserts-sands sent up a huge cloud flume of dry desert dust about twenty five and more feet up into the clear day air. Each Jeep had one of the scientific doctors in it along with a couple of special military men to protect the doctors from any harm should any come near them. In another specially equipped vehicle sat General Carey along with two his military aids for assisting and serving him.

The caravan first stopped at a huge crater made in the desert floor created by several bulldozers and heavy equipment. The area was halfway between the breached fence of the main compound and the small fenced in compound at the nesting site. The crew of select craftsmen from civil engineering had put together a cylindrical shaped cement operations headquarters building, buried half beneath the surface of the desert's sands and had lined the several outer concrete walls in the making of the building with a thick lead lined shielding. A small dozer with an angled blade was busy at work backfilling a trench laced with many cables running northward toward the nesting location several miles to its north.

The two doctors with General Carey were extremely pleased with the progress the civil engineering group was having finishing the special project of building the controlling facilities, and were anxious to see how the nest way out in the middle of the desert was coming along.

Construction at the nesting site had to be in its final phase in the top-secret project to keep away any crafty spies from foreign lands. The government wanted the rest of the world to be in total darkness and unaware in its development. The idea of making the atomic bomb came from a Germany scientist whose plans were stolen by the united allies. The Germans were busy working on the bomb, but at a much slower scientifically overrated and complicated mathematical rate of speed.

They were using improper quantities of heavy water concentrate in all their computations with incorrect formulas in purifying contaminated raw uranium into plutonium for their nuclear bomb's creation.

The design and prototype of the experimental American atomic weaponry in their arsenal was sought out by other countries in their quest to fulfill their own deadly needs.

The design for the first jet engine built by the Germans was also attached to these plans; a new weapon of destruction used against innocent lives the Germans attacking innocent victims over the English Channel, with buzz bombings attacking England. The buzz bomb was one of the greatest determining factors behind why this new atomic bomb the world was so desperately needed, abroad. In the beginning, bits and pieces of the Manhattan project were scattered around our country in its first stages to deter any foreign spy from getting immediate access to the entire project.

General Carey's motorcade proceeded along the new pathway on the desert floor to the north towards the nesting site where the tower for the nest was in its final phase. The busy soldiers in the field all called to attention as soon as General Carey exited his vehicle in the small motorcade convoy. "Carry on men," General Carey yelled out at the top of his voice, "You are all doing an exquisite job out here. Carry on men."

"Good afternoon General Carey and a good afternoon to you Major Wood." "I certainly hope this nesting project meets or exceeds your highest standards of quality control with detailed specifications in structure and buildings in this project, sir."

"A fine job well done, Major Wood, well done. We surely hope this work is what you and Roger was expecting, Charlie. If there are any changes that need to be done that you or Roger deem necessary for the nest, this is certainly the time to make them all known to us so we can make the changes before we complete the job. To modify the tower after completion would be real time consuming if not impractical at that stage of the game." "Everything looks first-rate, General Carey." "Day after tomorrow, Major Wood, the doctors and I would like the

Egg brought out here and positioned in the nest for proper fitness and inspection". "Everything is just about ready for it, General, and will be in order I am sure for the arrival of the Egg on site, sir."

General Carey, Major Wood, Charlie, and Roger followed the trained engineering staff slowly around the nesting site, as they took out the drafted blueprints showing the tower's size and measurements. The engineers began measuring the prints with their slide rules. They measured longitudes and latitudes in precise measurements for the nest's proper height, width, depth, and weight.

Taking into account and overlooking the final progress taking shape around them with the greatest in admiration for the fine work accomplished so far on the structure in such a short notice of time, it was truly amazing all this work had taken shape in such a short time.

The military men in the field were like little preprogrammed robots, as every move made by them was not wasted, as the nesting site was coming together in slow rapid motion right in front of the ones from the convoy. Fruition of the long project was now inevitable, and the first real test of the new atomic bomb was just a day or two away.

The dignitaries returned to the nesting site early the second morning after the first inspection as planned. Placing the Egg into the tall nest was like Cinderella sliding on the glass slipper the handsome prince had placed on her. The nest cradle fit the Egg with perfection. Soldiers in the field did not quite know what to expect when the Egg was placed down into its final nesting place. They were confused as to why they had built this tall tower way out in the desert to hold a ball made from steel that looked more like a wrecking ball way out in the middle of these hot sands. They had no idea what was going on and never would until a few days later.

Their mission in the hot desert was now complete even though it seemed a bit ridiculous to them. They had brought fruition to their temporary assignment that lasted a long time out in the middle of nowhere. Their new orders now were to pick up their tools of trade immediately, and to load them back onto the vehicles they used and returns back to the Army Air Force headquarters. As soon as most returned to the airbase, they were to again pack up all the necessary equipment from civil engineering to leave the facilities empty of materials and vacate the premises immediately for their new assignments awaiting in sealed envelopes back at headquarters. Most all of their new orders would send the men halfway round the world to join their counterparts in the fight for world peace.

They were to take time off and spend quality time at home with their loved ones for a couple of days before moving out to their new assignments. They were ordered to not mention their last assignment to anyone they ran into while on leave. This didn't make any sense to the soldiers.

There was a horrific war going on across the sea. They were one by one hand selected out of their fighting units, then stationed way the hell out here in the middle of no-man's land, in the New Mexico desert where scorpions, tarantulas, and rattlesnakes lived. Living there and having nothing to do for the past several months except sit around and wait for their assignment. They were told nothing about this special mission up front. Foolish orders sent them rushing out into the hot desert sands in northern New Mexico to accomplish their silly mission in record time. They were to build a foolish looking tower with scaffolding, several other smaller wooden structures representing empty houses, along with a few cinderblock cement out buildings. Some made of wood, some steel structured buildings alike and all with different roof designs for no apparent reason. All were built not far from the tower. Now to pack up and leave did not make any sense to any of them. Nothing about this ridiculous assignment made any sense to them. The project left an awful lot of unspoken questions of confusion unanswered to most all who wondered what the importance of this top-secret military mission was that they had just accomplished. They packed up their equipment and left without further wondering what they had really just accomplished for their country.

The soldiers, who had been working around the clock all week long on the construction of the safety bunker, felt similar to everyone else at the sight. Why would their government or any other government build a six layered cylindrical silo shaped bunker from cinder blocks lined with several layers in thick lead blanketed sheathing? Each lead shield was fitted between each cinderblock layer, and then filling in the empty cavities of the cinder blocks with full strength high intensity concrete that would stop a mortar attack. Why would they do all this, and then place a one-inch thick sheet of preformed armored steel plating around the whole outside of the entire structure?

It just did not make much sense to any of the soldiers who feverishly labored in the sweltering heat of day and the cold raw of night in extreme adverse conditions to make this stupid structure that did not do anything useful without any information as to why they were there in the first place. Nothing made any sense to most as they were only doing as told to do as soldiers, and happy to be of service to their country no matter what this whole thing was about.

They all assumed that the bunkered silo structure they were building was to be a bomb-proofed structure of some sort. It was definitely a bomb shelter built to withstand the strongest of all modern man-made bombs. All they could do at that point of time was to complete their task and leave the area immediately.

Most would leave their assignments in the desert feeling bewildered to what it was all about, but would soon in the months to follow find out that their stay in the hot desert sands was worth their while with the end of the war that followed the dropping of the newly invented atomic bomb.

CHAPTER EIGHT

Curiosity Killed the Cat

Mr. Stewart Jones had just taken off down the grassy runway from his old friend Brad's bumpy backyard landing strip. Brad stood by the landing strip, and waved his friend a friendly goodbye as he roared off down the airstrip and into the air. He flew off into the bright blue of the early morning sky without a cloud anywhere, a perfect day for flying. He was flying back home to his daughter's home where he lived and kept his old Waco biplane undercover out in one of her empty barns near their airfield. He was feeling quite chipper this day about going back home to see his daughter and his grandchildren, and their children.

He felt quite satisfied with himself and life for the time being, leaving his old friend Brad's farm behind, especially after spending a few very relaxing well enjoyed days of reminiscing about the fun they had in times of old when they were both much younger and more mischievous.

Just as old Stuart's wheels on his vintage biplane left the grassy runway, a very important message began broadcasting out over the local public radio channels in the immediate area of Brad's farm and the surrounding area that also encompassed the new laboratory and military compound to the far north and northeast of his farm.

The special broadcast reported there was going to be the detonation of a very large-scale bomb in the testing area above the new airbase forty miles to the north northeast of town. It was only going to be a test. No one in the immediate area should become distressed if they saw a very sizeable looking white funnel cloud appear in the sky above the desert floor after hearing a large blast or feeling the earth shake beneath ones feet or rattled their homes like a mild earthquake. It would not be a tornado, an earthquake, or even that of the enemy of Hitler's army invading the country. It was only our government testing a very strong new weapon for our protection.

All fighter aircraft squadrons from the testing facilities airfield were now out flying in a circular pattern one hundred or better miles outside the compound in circles around the area of the testing sight. They were there to keep out all stray aircraft that had not heard the warning about this specific test which was going to take place early that day, who might fly their aircraft too close to the testing area, and get themselves along with their passengers hurt or killed by the super blast.

Neither these pilots, nor any of the men in charge of the test that day had any idea there might be one unique pilot flying alone in and around within the restricted fly zone. Mr. Jones had missed the very important message of the day, the broadcast about no one to fly within fifty or less miles of the restricted blast location to the north.

Had Stew landed his small aircraft at the local airfield twenty miles south of Brad's farm, a warning not to fly that day was hanging on the doors to all the hangers. He and his plane would have been forbidden and not allowed to take off from the airfield that day. Then again it was Stew Jones, and old Stew never did like listening or taking orders or advice from any strangers.

Stew sure as hell, would not want to put his old friend Brad out by having to have him drive those extra twenty or less miles to pick him up at the airfield. Especially being quite capable of landing his plane right there at the farm where Brad kept his old twin winged biplane out in the barn. The one he and Stew had bought together when they both purchased their two twin winged biplanes as a package deal, but Brad had not flown his in a couple of years now. Old Brad had had a couple of near mishaps in his last few attempts in landing at his farm as his eyesight and depth perception was failing him, and he knew better than chance another flight, for the next might be his last.

Stew flew his biplane Betsy north northeasterly as he had always done in the past on his return trips back home to his daughter's house where he always kept his plane. He hoped this beautiful day wouldn't be spoiled like his last flight by him meeting up again with those damn fool highflying knuckleheaded dip shits he had encountered on his way down to Brad's.

He almost wished he would meet up with the bunch of smart asses again on his way home. He was ready for them this time having topped off his fuel tank at Brad's farm. Even though he had a tank full of fuel, he would probably do what they demanded.

This time though, he would give them bastards the fickle finger of fate. A sign they so well deserved. He might even show those sons-a-bitches just what his old Betsy twin winged biplane could do that theirs could not do, knowing damn well he could outmaneuver them by doing flips, barrel rolls, and dives they couldn't possibly do with their fancy flying machines. Nah, the day was just too damn nice, and he didn't really need the aggravation or grief of running into them again.

Old Stew could not help but notice flying home not far from Brad's home there was a new perimeter fence he had never seen before down on the desert floor below. He was now flying within the surrounding restricted air space and looking down to see its many deserted outhouse-looking guard shacks dotting along the fence below. Seeing he had not had any military visitors come flying up at him like maniacs as before, he decided to follow this new fence for a while northwesterly instead of his usual path to the northeast.

He noticed a large breached gated opening in the huge fence gates wide open with a new scratched out road leading directly north. He banked his twin-winged aircraft to the right, changing his flight path again, and followed the road leading towards the north. He had plenty of fuel on board for another hundred extra miles or more of flying, and the weather was just perfect for a little countryside joyriding and sightseeing to extend his pleasant ride this fine day while flying home.

Turning the old biplane, he banked it softly right and followed the roadway. Old Stew spotted a short rounded flat-topped building

sticking straight up out of the desert floor a couple of miles up the road. It looked half buried beneath the sand in the desert floor. Behind the round structure, lay another separate bunker looking like a half round open style garage closed in on one side of the circle with a couple of military Jeeps, two duce and a half military trucks, and a couple of other vehicles tucked away inside it.

He veered his flight path away from the new structures thinking they may have had something to do with his encounter a few days earlier with the warring squadron of fighter planes. Not wanting to run into them again, nor get himself noticed by anyone below who might look up and detect him even though he did not see anyone roaming around the grounds outside or any movement of any vehicles below, he decided it was best to avoid them.

He proceeded more northeasterly on a course back towards home and turned old Betsy towards the east. He discovered out of the corner of his left eye, a newly erected wind powered bladeless water well tower built further up the road from the buildings that he had just veered away from. It stood tall without a fan on its top in order to run the water pump below it. It looked as if someone had placed a big round black baseball or a big balloon on top the tower. This really got the best of his very inquisitive curiosity to boiling.

A water well towered wind mill without a wind powered fan atop to run it, stood tall like a pyramid all alone among several smaller looking outer buildings in the desert he had never witnessed before on his numerous flights to his friend Brad's house. They looked all newly built with tire tracks and bulldozer tracks still fresh in the sand up north in the bright early morning sun, out in the open desert like the fencing he had just noticed, and flown over.

What the hell was going on down there, he wondered. His curiosity got the best of him for a second time in just a short period of only a few minutes or less. He veered his old bi-plane off course again towards the north northwest one more time to see what the 100-foot tall towered structure jetting up out the desert floor was all about a few miles up the road. He needed to get a grasp on what was going on down there, to take a good look, and see if he could figure out what it really was.

Maybe it was the beginning of a new settlement way out in the desert of some kind.

There was no sign of any cattle, bison, or even that of a stray horse roaming the immediate area of the desert below him that might be in need of such a fine looking watering well. These newly built structures got the best of his revolving imagination and subconscious. He had to see what someone was up to way out there in the middle of the uninhabited desert as he flew closer and closer to the structures and the tall tower up ahead of him, still wondering what it was all about.

Four, Three, Two, One, DETONATION! An arc of light more brilliant than the sun of daylight flashed blindingly bright with the first splitting and fusion of atoms. The reaction in the bomb exploding made a large mushroom shaped funnel cloud roar instantly skyward from the nesting site. For many miles around, anyone watching could see the cloud rise high above the desert floor. The explosion sent a huge volume in red hot air rushing instantly outward from its epicenter. Immediately after exploding, it imploded. It pulled the air back into a vast vacuum, causing larger amounts of air to be sucked back to the point of fusion, and instantly sent it skyward. It sucked vast amounts of sand, gravel, and fragments of the structures the soldiers had previously assembled near the Egg's nesting structure back with it. The several observers of the first nuclear bomb explosion were safely hidden down in the protective bombproof observatory. They watched the action from a safe distance away as the massive blast in fusion separation of atomic particles sent out a huge shock wave across the desert floor. The hot shockwave flattened the buildings of wood, concrete, and steel.

General Carey, Roger, Charles, and their staff watched the detonation from the protected bunker several miles away. They carefully watched the reversed action in the blasts shockwave go out and then immediately reverse backwards towards its point of origin. The blast sucked the hot air back from across the area it had traveled too, and up into the atmosphere above the desert floor. It instantly contaminated the blast zone's atmosphere high above the Earth with radioactive micro-molecular fragmented dust particles that would travel across the United States to New England in the next several days. The cloud of radioactive particles dropped radioactive dust all over the country and its inhabitants.

This first blast caused the beginning of many cases of cancer to the skin, bones, and the blood supply of the people living in the United States. U. S. Officials from the government had no idea what the residual fallout from this atomic bomb blasts in pink particles would do to the many unsuspecting citizens across their country. The first explosion would cause years of sickness, grief, and birth defects. No one knew the full effect this bomb test and bombings abroad would cause to the vast population around the globe or to their own people. The ill effects caused by the blast would follow the experiment in atomic fusion into the next century and possibly into centuries to come after that, until it might someday annihilate the populous around the world. Newborn babies around the world would be born without limbs, while many would develop leukemia. A life of worldwide wretchedness would follow the population of the planet for a lifetime, and spread into their offspring as their children's children had their children, and their children had theirs.

CHAPTER NINE

Bye Bye Biplane

Old Stewart Jones never knew what hit him, the fusion in atoms hit him so fast. He and his biplane were instantly gone within a nanosecond of time, instantaneously vaporized when the Egg split its shell and hatched. Surely, old Stew felt no pain in going from dust to dust and ashes to ashes as it happened so fast.

One to two seconds prior to the clock ticking down to zero, Dr. Charles and several others in the observatory thought they noticed a small twin-winged aircraft flying a hundred or more feet above the nesting tower that looked like a large dragonfly, or airplane. It was a mere second too close and too late for him or any of the others in the observatory to do anything about stopping the countdown even if it had been a plane. None of them at their monitoring stations had the necessary controls in front of them to deactivated and stop the procedure. They were watching the blast through a newly developed televised camera lens imagining system using sound waves to transport imagery though the air by radio wave frequency to a set of conversion tubes and onto a picture screen. Maybe it had been an ordinary housefly or other bug on the lens of the camera that made them all think it was an aircraft, or was it?

Brad never heard from his old friend Stew ever again, but did feel the blast and shockwave that took his good friend's life from him. It seemed Stew had just vanished from the face of the earth into the thin air of the planet. Dr. Charles had heard of the missing man and his old biplane, as did the others watching that day through the monitors. They as well as the others surmised that it must have been the missing man's biplane they had all witnessed for a slit second's time flying over the nest at the precise time of detonation.

Dr. Charles felt guilty and confused with life after that. He and his friend Roger had helped develop such a destructive device that was so lethal to the planet's inhabitants. He and the others who had been involved in the bomb's fruition would fret daily in the back of their subconscious minds. Most everyone bottled up the deep emotion changing circumstances caused by the device until the day would come when they all would die of natural causes, they hoped.

Some fretted continually every day about how many innocent Japanese lives the bomb would take to end the war. The sudden death of old Stew haunted the ones who had noticed him for a split second and then he was gone. Many who thought they were individually responsible for the great loss of lives, took their own lives by not being able to live with the thought that they were the ones responsible for the great loss in life. They all knew they were going straight to hell after death, and why prolong the howling agony of their continual revolving minds about it while still alive just waiting for their last agonizing day to come.

The testing of the first atomic bomb in its nesting site went very well, beyond everybody's wildest dreams or expectations. It was supposed to be the bomb that ended all wars, but it only stopped the Japanese and the Germans, ending the Second World War. The cold war between great powers of the world prevailed for many more years to come after that deadly time in history.

CHAPTER TEN

The Downfall of the Neutron Bomb

In a new experimental laboratory located in Russia, not far from the city of Moscow, several scientific doctors were working hard on developing the newest in deadly wartime bombs ever made in peacetime, the neutron bomb.

Dr. Ivan Scavonivich and his associate doctors were busy trying to work calmly while being rushed by their superiors for the speedy completion in the prototype of new living creatures, human beings, and animal annihilating warhead. It would be new to science, an electrical agent dispersing nuclear device. The neutron bomb would be the deadliest bomb the world would never forget for years to come.

This new bomb was to be the most brilliant of all manmade bombs ever invented by modern day technology. The new bomb would kill all animal life within miles of its detonation, but would not destroy the integrity of any buildings or plant life surrounding its point of detonation. It would leave the surrounding area safe and usable, unlike the atomic bomb did by leaving the surrounding area demolished and unusable for many years due to radiation contamination. This very deadly bomb in its infancy stages was produced and made ready for some very greedy leaders who wanted to conquer vast areas of land for their own selfish reasons of power in wealth, as did Hitler, and other power seeking reasons.

Work in the Russian laboratory on this new deadly device was proceeding quite well for the doctors in charge of its testing and their vast team of scientific associates. The work had gone so well in its development stage that it was time for this new weapons testing. Massive data files in all its phases in calculated theory resulted in mental debilitating testing and killing anguish. The Russian leaders had their scientist perform inhumane testing on many of the country's prisoners and animals in cages that showed great results in its annihilation of living creatures.

The new bomb held a significant imbalance with multiple effects for the large amounts in wild neutrons that they each could hold. Especially the bomb's massive concentrated properties of neutron masses when used in large uncontrolled amounts. This new device proved very dangerous to even those handling these very insensitive imbalanced properties of nature.

The scientists used extreme caution while handling the wild concentrated properties of nature's unforgivable strength, considered more dangerous than the most toxic poison known to human. Extreme caution was never used properly in manufacturing this destructive animal tissue and life menacing neutralizing properties of life that they were making. The greedy men did not care about its consequences to their own scientists, for they just wanted these weapons available for their own use in their arsenal of mass life destruction. This would enable them in controlling the populous around the world, and they could get away with mass producing this new weapon in secrecy and having its use at their immediate disposal.

This newly developed neutron-killing device consisted mostly of neutrons in immeasurable amounts of condensed concentration. Heavy water was reduced to its smallest size ever, then harnessed in capsules no bigger than a woman's sewing thimble, capable of releasing their deadly force out into the earth's atmosphere with the firing of a simple device no bigger than that of a pyrotechnic firecracker. The result of the small blast would cause devastation to life felt for miles around its detonation. These larger neutron elements the Russian scientists reduced down and condensed to impartial neutron particles. All these concentrated particles carried a reverse non-electrical charge, and were regarded by scientific minds around the world as the most dangerous of all unstable elements of materials known to humanity and to the animal kingdom.

Similar to all other bombs of mass destruction, the reduced neutron devices needed handling with the greatest of care, for they could result in instant death to those handling them and to all other animal life forms in and around the area for several miles, if not more for they didn't really know. The properties of them so highly unstable, no one truly knew for sure just what would happen when they are released into the atmosphere.

Not one of the fearless greedy leaders in the Kremlin at the time wanted to be anywhere near the testing sites when they performed their testing. The destructive properties these new bombs were capable of causing if handled wrong, made the new Russian leaders extremely nervous.

They wanted the new weaponry for their own military arsenal, but none wanted to be anywhere near or around the devices when being tested for many various reasons. They all knew the bizarre dangers the sudden release of these neutralizing neutrons were capable of causing, and did not understand the lasting effects these new devices would have on future living creatures. Not one of the cowards wanted to gamble an incident making them perish into the unconsciousness or death because of their own fears of its danger, or lack in knowledge about the new deadly device they all wanted mass-produced right away for their greedy use. With world control over the deadly device in hand, they figured Russia would become the world's number one super power, able to control everyone around the globe like puppets on a string.

In the United States, a similar device in its arsenal protection plan was under way. In an experimental laboratory located in Lexington, Massachusetts, they worked on developing a similar prototype of the deadly Neutron bomb with safety in mind.

Dr. Norman Andrews, Prof. Jeffrey Jefferson, and their colleagues in science were busy in the final stages of putting together their quality control and final touches on their very own neutron bomb. This weapon was very similar to the one their Russian counterparts were hurriedly building, but with a great deal more caution placed into their new device of weaponry. They were using more modern measure of reliable safety devices affixed to them than were their counterpart Russians.

The Americans had been carefully studying the long term effects these deadly neutron bombs could have on innocent victims outside the ramification of its destructive point of impact, along with what long term effects might have on Mother Nature herself. These scientists wanted to know more about the reproduction of wildlife animals and other creatures living in the area of a blast. They meticulously preplanned and re-planned what to put into place prior to a detonation of such a deadly device.

No one wanted to affect the precious balance of Mother Nature's earth surrounding the testing sight. This category of bomb could pose a more deadly outcome on the entire planet than the atomic bomb. This particular deadly bomb needed a more suitable assembly in the number of neutrons correlated in it, and the explosive properties in its payload properly measured out so not to increase its magnitude of life taking destruction worldwide.

With the wrong and incorrect mixture of deadly elements in its protonic payload wrongly subtracted and an incorrect amount of electrons improperly balanced in the original formulated in its making, the bomb could be extremely dangerous to everyone. Great adverse effects could result with instant grief and devastation of an entire population around the globe with drastic outcomes.

Massive power losses might occur worldwide around the globe resulting from the improper influx and imbalance of the earth's magnetic fields with severe consequences resulting in a true imbalance of gravity with great measures of imbalance for all living creatures. It could cause great black outs similar to large solar flare ups in space caused when there are solar storms on the face of the sun, but possibly more devastating to the earth, if the blast was uncontrollable by some simple means.

Spies did their best in keeping their comrades informed of any counterpart scientists' progress in the development of this new weapon. A new self-installed leadership over Russia took place after a deadly cue against the Russian leader that the good people of Russia had elected to govern their country. This small group of men decided they wanted to be in the lead of promoting the first Star Wars syndrome scare tactic throughout the entire world like no other nation had ever encountered or seen before.

The United Nations Assembly in New York warned these newly self-installed Russian leaders of the new eastern world, several times to not mass-produce these kinds of new highly insensitive neutron weapons of mass destruction.

This group of greedy new leaders of Russia continually bragged to the world about having this new power of control over the entire planet. They broadcasted it to all the leaders around the world, and didn't care about the proven safety mechanisms necessary for any kind of human safety. Scientists from around the globe knew this and feared for their control over the populous around the world. These new leaders discarded all warnings from world leaders and their own concerned scientist. These greedy men ordered several hundreds of these multi-headed molt chambered sensitivity activated bombing devices mass-produced under the cover of night in several of their large secured factories. They would not inform the leaders of the world what was taking place so they might add these weapons to their arsenal of mass destruction. Under the secrecy of darkness, they accomplished the task without the world knowing it somehow before any spies found out about their secret creations.

All this, for wanting to show the world a supremacy in their becoming the new leading super power around the world in their race to the Star Wars era of controlling the world in short time by using outer space as their weapon dispersing plan of control of the earth.

CHAPTER ELEVEN

The Great Launch

Countries around the globe were in total shock when the great missile launch from within the Russian empire took place. The United States and Canada scrambled every fighter aircraft they had available, as did all the other countries around the world. The United States put their SAC missile defense systems instantly on red alert. Eastern ally countries aimed their missiles toward Russia, as well as friends of Russia re-aimed theirs if need be.

Allied atomic submarines cruising the vast seas and waterways around the world, positioned themselves to launch an enormous offensive attack toward the Russian empire. It looked to the world that the Russian people were launching a third world war attack around the globe, as everyone on the ground of planet earth prepared to fight back at all costs.

The Russian leaders broadcasted a special message to the world powers just seconds prior to the great launch. They informed everyone around the globe that they were going to be sending a large-scaled fleet, a quantity of their own protective missiles into outer space as a weapons package for security in defending their own people. The multitude of missiles were going to be orbiting the earth, and were not a threat to anyone on earth as long as everyone around the globe left the Russian empire alone to do whatever they wanted to do in their own provinces and elsewhere if they so choose to do so. They did not volunteer or give any better explanation than elsewhere, or somewhere or anywhere as they broadcast their boastful informational message to the world.

The Russians had secretly built rocket launching pads within the structures of many old abandoned factories concealing their plans from everyone by using the darkness of night. This included some of their very own top-notch military officials in their own defense systems. The elite spy system around the world did not function in finding out about the Great Russian missile launch until it was too late, and the launch was under way. Hundreds of radar screens from around the world established contact with the several hundred Russian rockets taking flight. Friendly ally countries went into an instant frenzied panic attack in disbelief and concern what the Russian empire was up to. The entire atmosphere surrounding the earth became chaotically busy with every kind of military warplane known to humankind that could fly that day.

Immediately, all military National Guard fighter pilots around the United States reported to active duty. Emergency phone numbers rang out all across the country from east to west and north to south at their places of employment and at their homes. The voice on the other end of the phone was telling the reservists to leave their places of employment and homes immediately, and to report at once to their military units or squadrons as soon as humanly possible. The world was in a frenzied red alert and needed everyone at his or her post in order to protect his or her country.

The launch of Russian missiles never swayed or altered from their direct courses in flight straight up putting them all into their own orbit around the globe. Not a one failed to launch.

World leaders from around earth expected some of the missiles to do just the opposite at any given moment in time, but all flew precisely as the Russian leaders had said they would. Every missile shot strait toward the heavens above and into their own precise orbits.

The missiles raced around the globe like race cars on a circular race track until they were in their predetermined orbiting positions the Russians had preprogrammed into their onboard computers. The missiles positioned themselves in strategic locations around the earth in order to defend their homeland against all aggressive countries around the world. The Russian leaders said it was for their protection only, but it looked more like a preplanned positioning of their new missiles for the future purpose of an invasion on earth instead for the sole purpose of protecting their homeland.

Countries around the world voiced loud despair in Russia's overzealous act and show of unnecessary force surrounding the globe with their missiles of mass destruction. NATO, with great concern for its assembly, demanded to know the true reason from these new Russian leaders. The tyranny of the new Russia with its newly self-installed military leaders boasted strongly about the new Russian superiority they now had over the rest of the vast world as the world's newest, greatest, and now most superior super power of all times in the history of the world. They were now not afraid of any country around the planet, especially the flawed weakness of the once super power, the United States of America.

The Russian's boasted how the world was at their mercy now, and no one not even other powers of the world were ever to interfere with what they chose to do globally, or they would pick a location in Great Britain for retaliation of interference. They would prove it to everyone on the face of Planet Earth just what this new power of accomplishment would mean to the ones who just might try to oppose their supremacy.

CHAPTER TWELVE

The Flaw

Within days of the bizarre Russian missile launch, the United States intelligence network received some very troubling information from a very troubled Russian scientist through its strategic spy system. He claimed he had been one of several scientists working on the severely faulty guiding systems installed in all the missiles now orbiting the globe. They were using old relic equipment in their guiding protection systems. These old units of guidance control were hurriedly modified to get these many missiles aloft to show supremacy to the world. By using the below-grade insulating materials and installing it into the orbiting missiles could prove fatal to many inhabitants around the world, and most importantly to the citizens of Russia as well.

An American double agent spy who had gathered all this information had an entire layout of the newly modified Russian missiles guiding systems, schematics, and plans with him as he entered the Pentagon with this very disturbing news. He had paid dearly for the plans or at least his own brother and partner had. His only living brother was with him at the time of contact when the subject scientist gave up the sets of plans and lost his life in helping him secure the plans for the U.S. Government.

Steven barely escaped his pursuers himself as he ducked quickly into an open doorway down through a maze of buildings through alley ways in and out of doorways and escaping his pursuers. He miraculously managed to search and find another informant for his sanctuary, and in time with his help over the last few weeks, made his flight to freedom. The mission turned out to be a true success for the department except for the loss of his brother, whom he dearly loved and admired, who had recruited him into a life of being a double agent for his country.

The biggest problem with the new schematics the Russians had designed and interfaced into their missiles guiding system was in decoding them and breaking down their new and very difficult sophisticated code that they had installed in all of their missiles.

An overzealous Russian computer whiz somehow electronically had interfaced an emergency coding device with codes in instant swapping within the new computerized blueprint plans. The security in the guiding systems on these missiles, along with other bizarre schemes with internal triggering micro switches, were installed to protect the missiles while in orbit from interception by an enemy cargo space craft trying to destroy the missiles one by one, and eliminating Russia from being the new world power.

Computer scalpers both young and old from around the country were brought into the pentagon's most highly secured computer laboratory facility in Washington D.C. in order to help break this very new to electronics, ridiculously encoded micro coded whiz bang young Russian scientist had almost un-flawlessly developed.

Too bad, they had not used such care in using quality-controlled materials in their speedy production of them as well as in the designing the new defense mechanism for the security of these destructive missiles orbiting the earth.

It took several long weeks of rounding up computer scalpers from around the country and computer whizzes working for the government to help in this awesome tedious project, to come up with a plan to break this protection code and plan.

These ludicrously new computer codes would instantly make new avenues in recourse penetration for the protection of entry into its protected flight program. This way no enemy force from below by chance could find the radio frequency on the craft and destroy the missiles before they could return to earth to seek out their intended targets and distribute the multiple small deadly missiles stored within their nose cones. Each of these smaller missiles inside their mother missiles had their own condensed collection of neutron explosives and guiding systems to seek out many targeted areas for instant killing of it pray.

One sixteen year old computer wizard that had been brought into the program for hacking into many government computers around the country, was apprehended by federal agents in a small community college in Montana. He had lastly accessed a highly sophisticatedly protected government project, by using his high IQ. He put a small self-made, simple macro buffeting softening code into the Russian guiding system to block the ever-changing code, and it worked. After coming up with the coded solution in code recovery, the many charges against him brought by the U. S. Government were dropped. The officials he was working under secured him a job working with his government even though he was under age. His new job, instead of him hacking into their sophisticated programs, would now have him develop new specialty coded programs for other computer intelligent people like himself, so others would not be able to hack into any other concealment programs of high security for his government.

With the Russians highly sophisticated decoding program broken, they discovered the many guiding system flaws in the missiles floating around the earth in space. It showed the guiding protection systems for recovery that the Russians had developed and installed in their many missiles would be extremely dangerous. The system was not only dangerous to all the countries around the world, but it was as dangerous to their own country of Russia as it was to the entire planet earth below.

No one incorporated any serious scientific thought of common sense into the seriousness of the required sophistication needed in this new guiding and protection system.

A child using a toy erector set would have put more thought into his project than these egotistical new leaders who wanted immediate recognition of their new supremacy. The foolish action taken by the so-called highly intelligent Russia leaders, in need of control of their country, proved their arrogance. Especially after finding out the truth about these flawed guiding systems they over eagerly installed in their so-called brilliant Star Wars Defense System. One of the Russian scientists who had been working on the Russian defense systems and neutron bomb guiding systems defected from Russia to the U.S. Lucky for him, the United States government gave him asylum in their country under an alias protective name and a job to help to try to stop a worldwide catastrophe from taking shape. He would do anything possible to help the United States succeed in its lone fight against a weapon no one had any control over, except for the Russian leaders who could put an end to the standoff of the missiles by blowing them all up with the simple push of a single button.

They were too damn obstinate to act out for the good of humanity, or even their own people. These few newly self-installed military Russian leaders had previously killed for their new position as leaders. The new leaders vowed to the world that the many deadly rockets they had placed into space orbit were fail safe, explaining to the world their superiority in these newly sophisticated fail-safe systems they had personally overseen in all the installations in each of their rockets.

They bragged about how each missile cone had been filled with many smaller war-headed missiles each, and they would only be used if the leaders around the world did not stop messing around with their every whim. The new Russian leaders continually boasted about a new modern day scientific accomplishment that they had performed over and over again to the world.

They were trying to explain to everyone just how great their missiles really were, but were losing world confidence in the way they continually boasted about their safety for everyone. The world was a much safer place to live now as they continued on to reinforce everyone around the globe. Safer except if a strong foreign force or nation try to invade their country, or try to stop them from doing whatever they damn well pleased around the globe. Only then would they put their defense Star Wars mechanisms into full-scale force against their enemy. They now had doubts about the many missiles in space themselves, but refused to acknowledge it to the world that something could go wrong with them at any moment.

The new leaders of Russia were still afraid of Great Britain, the United States, and a couple of other weaker powers around the globe, because they knew if they started something, these powers would be on top of them like flies on a cow manure pile. Several of the Russian scientists who had worked on the secret project, tried to warn their newly self-installed leaders of Russia openly on the streets of Moscow. They tried hard to explain to them about the great dangers that were now lurking high above the earth, so others would hear their warning plea for their people. Several of the scientists who dared to voice their opinions openly and try to warn their leaders in front of the media were immediately sent off to prison in Siberia to be forgotten about, as well as their families just for being their relatives.

The only lucky doctors were the ones who had defected to the U.S. One by taking a vacation to Austria with his family right after the launch and was able to leave Russia for their security. He did not voice his opinion openly as he knew the outcome would be devastating just like the missiles, and wanted to escape the country before the countries around the world attacked Russia for their blunder.

A second doctor was able to defect from Russia by escaping to the United States by securing permission to travel to a science convention in Italy. He never showed up for the convention and never returned back home to Russia. The Kremlin was now seeking both doctors for defecting, and ordered them both killed upon sight by the soviets KGB force who had spies in the United States.

The very few remaining scientist not imprisoned worked frantically on the faulty guiding protection systems and did not dare voice their opinions in their opposition openly. They tried to repair the defects installed in the systems from down on earth without any success. The one who knew the most about the coded system was in prison in Siberia along with his coworkers and families. Along with several hundred friendly communication and weather satellites was the International Space Station mostly manned by Soviet cosmonauts at the present, taking their turn using the laboratory in the sky for their own personal experiments, supposedly to help humankind around the world and not just for their country alone. They had left for the International Space

Station just prior to the new leaders of Russia taking control over their country. One of the new military leaders had put orders into the hand of one of the cosmonauts to give to the officer in charge of the space station to stay concealed until the end of his stay in space.

There was nothing any scientists on earth could do to rectify the faulty switches, relays, guiding gyros or the extensively and extremely sensitivity sensing mechanisms that had already been installed into the faulty war headed missiles circling the earth. The entire fleet of Soviet missiles were ready to bring catastrophic results to the world below if activated.

It was possible that any one, two, three, ten, or even possibly every rocket above could all converge on a single target that could possibly be the best that could happen except for being over Russian Moscow, the scientists explained to their bold thoughtless leaders that this was possible, and could happen at any time.

After many long tiring hours of debating back and forth with the friendly countries trying to negotiate with the stubborn Russian leaders about the dangers they initiated into space, they confessed to their guilt of unnecessary speed of putting all these rockets into orbit without further precautionary measures put into place.

The Soviet leaders would not have confessed to their own guilt or stupidity if it had not been for one of their own multi-headed neutron rockets descended back to earth over Russia and exploded the week before. The returning missile killed many farmers in the producing region around Russia. The small independent missiles in its nose cone did not leave their mother ship, and all exploded on reentry over Russia causing a gigantic catastrophe. The farm hands, their families, along with all the livestock, foul of the air, and wildlife in fields for miles around perished due to the mishap of a single missile carrying its multiple war-headed armed missiles in its nose cone.

The so-called perfect Russian security system installed in all the missiles did not work well in space, and had caused a catastrophic event to take place in their country, and now waiting to happen to some other unsuspecting nation down on earth somewhere.

The new Soviet leaders understood they were at extreme risk as were many other inhabitants around the earth to the perils they had caused lurking in the once peaceful and now very menacing heavens above caused by them.

Through joint efforts by many nations, top electronically-minded scientists from around the world met in Washington, D.C. trying to ward off any potential danger which might result in the near future. They willfully put their scientific minds together and devised a system in which to retrieve the menacing missiles one by one, if necessary, and to deactivate them all.

Should these sensitive missiles allow for the luxury of all being reclaimed before returning back to earth and destroying another village, town, or city! They had to be stopped, and the sooner the better for everyone's safety including the new Russian empire that placed them in orbit.

The nosecones affixed to each missile had their own safety devices attached to them that would sense the size of an approaching spacecraft trying to capture it, and remove it from its orbit. The sensing device installed in its tracking system would activate to keep any nation such as the United States from being able to intercept them with their space shuttle fleet.

The sensory device would activate the rockets propulsion engine, and send the unit hurling back towards the earth to accomplish its dreaded works of destroying heavily populated nations.

These missiles would also kill the livestock for miles around, and the many insects, and other living creatures in the vicinity with its many deadly exploding neutron bomb missiles.

The one stray lone fox missile which had come back to earth all by itself exploding over Russia, caused havoc and great unrest in its nation. The missile never went to its intended programmed target and never meant to explode in or over Russia. The new leaders of the Kremlin explained that it must have had its sensitivity capture mechanism activated somehow by accident and allowing it to return to earth. A satellite passing too close to it or a quick passing space stone speeding quickly nearby on its way to or by earth and had accidently activated the capture recovery sensory device. The new Russian leaders didn't want to give any better explanation than the simplest one as they were afraid if they told the rest of the world the truth about the faulty missiles, even the good people of Russia would turn on them by massive assemblies in force and take back their country by a revolution that they didn't want.

All the sensitivity devices manufactured and installed in these missiles, had no quality control in place for speed of quick development and their quick delivery. They made them using a mixture of silicon and rubber together for the cable sheathing on which a constant bombardment of ultraviolet light from the sun instantly started to decompose the instant they all reached orbit. Quick unnatural aging on its rubberized skin made the rockets extremely vulnerable to something as small as a speck of space dust, if it passed too closely by its sensitivity sensing firing mechanism to wake the guiding system alive and fire up the main rocket to life. In turn, it would activate the target seeking mechanism on the tight grouped miniature missiles held in their nose cones with the many war headed neutron missiles located therein.

The missile that returned to earth by its lonesome over Russia didn't respond to any of its preprogrammed settings installed to where it was supposed to go, and attacked its maker's land. This worried the new Russian leaders. They all knew what they did was wrong, and knew they would pay for their blunder in the near future somehow.

Meetings of smart-minded scientists were being held daily by hundreds of scientists worldwide to help fend off the fate of the poor situation lurking in the heavens above. While these meetings were taking place, a crew of highly trained United States military astronauts from NASA, were blasting off from Cape Canaveral's Space Center in Florida.

All information attached to this mission was for the shuttle to intercept one of the many potentially menacing rockets lurking above, and bring it back to earth. When safely back on earth, a team of trained men would disarm the payload of neutron bomb mini missiles held in its nose cone. The approach to the rocket had to be precise from a forty-five degree angle from its starboard side facing the earth in which the sensing device was not set to detect any movement at that angle, an engineer figured out in the missiles electronic electrical schematics. This was the only flaw anyone could come up with that might help the people on earth overcome a most destructive situation.

Should the shuttle approach the missile from behind, straight on, or on any angle other than a forty five degree angle from deep space, it would sense the spacecraft and activate the sensing mechanism by firing its rocket, immediately sending the missile back towards the earth and its intended preprogrammed targets, if its guiding mechanisms were working properly.

It would take a period of several long years to accomplish the retrieval of all these menacing missiles if this mission was to be successful. It would try to make one successful mission per week or until all the menacing missiles were retrieved and defused.

As the crew aboard the Twitchel was passing out through the Ionosphere and into outer space, a small shower of meteorite fragments of stone and dry ice from Haley's Comet came passing by the earth as it began to rain down from its long tail behind it toward earth. The meteor shower began bouncing millions of tiny pebbles of Comet fragmented particles of dry ice, dust, and stone from the Twitchel's fuselage, wings, and windshield like hail in a severe thundershower before a tornado might strike the earth. Radio communications from the Twitchel back to earth through the storm of static dust was horrendous as the crew of the Twitchel leveled out into their desired orbital path in order to retrieve their first missile of the many they were hoping to retrieve in their first recovery mission.

Suddenly the entire crew's eyes bloomed with disapproving horror written all over their stunned faces hidden behind their face shields. None onboard could believe what their eyes were watching take place before them as hundreds of small thruster rockets came instantly to life before their very eyes. They didn't understand what the horrendous outcome of what they were witnessing would be. They presumed it was not to be a pristine outcome for them later on in the mission as they were now having to deal with whatever the results would be.

CHAPTER THIRTEEN

A Horrific Sighting

Out the Twitchel's main glass windshield, the crew witnessed the entire fleet of Soviet neutron missiles in their immediate area and around the globe come simultaneously to life. One missile after another took flight back toward the earth without delay. The crew aboard the shuttle knew the shower of ice and stone must have breached the sensitive sensing mechanisms on all the rockets at precisely the same exact time. The supposedly secured failsafe missile system the Russian leaders so boldly bragged about to all nations around the globe, had failed in record time. In less than a ten-second time lap, they all had failed. One missile's rocket booster after another brought their solid fueled propulsion systems to life. The circumference around planet earth looked like a multitude of fighter jet squadrons that had all thrown their ignition switches to their rocketed aircraft on, all at the same precise time.

The blackness of the shuttle's orbit became aglow with a significant number of burning solid-fueled rockets littering the darkness of space above the globe alight. The quiet heavens became alive with hundreds of deadly Soviet multi-headed neutron warheads, every one of them heading back to the earth under full power.

Every missile activated by their own faulty propulsion safeguard guiding systems. They were all alive and were following their preprogrammed missions back toward earth to seek out and destroy their prioritized predetermined destiny of destruction to start killing all living creatures within their pre-plotted return sequence. Every location on earth that these deadly inoculating missiles of death were going to alight was sure to be heavily populated. Each missile with its own unique design made ready to cause drastic chaotic grief to thousands in lost human life along with an undetermined number of domestic and wild animals alike.

This new weaponry of destruction would snuff out all life almost instantly where it detonated and for miles around as well. The populous around the world were not ready for such a disaster as this one was going to cause. The leaders from around the globe would stop at nothing to stop it from happening to the citizens of their countries.

The Soviet leaders did not have a plan to stop such a massive invasion as the one taking place other than to destroy all of the rockets with the push of a single button. Prior to this disastrous mishap, they had had full control over every rocket in orbit in space, so they thought. They thought they could send them back to earth one at a time to show everyone around the globe they were the true rulers of the planet above everyone else. Now it was different, and they did not know what to do next.

CHAPTER FOURTEEN

The Unexpected Furry of Futility

"Houston control, this is the U. S. Space Shuttle Twitchel, over!" "Go ahead Twitchel!" "Command Center Houston, we have a severe code red alert taking place up here." "What type of code red problem do you have, Twitchel? What is your dilemma, be more specific?"

"Believe me, Houston, this is a true special red coded alert. The entire fleet of neutron war headed missiles up here is everyone's problem, Houston. The entire fleet of the war headed missiles have all been activated. They have all fired themselves up, Houston. All rocket powered motors have been ignited, command center. All the missiles we can see from our position are all heading back toward earth under full power as we speak, Houston!"

"Repeat your transmission Twitchel. Static down here is terrible on our receptor network, Twitchel, please repeat". "All neutron war headed missiles have all activated themselves, Houston, and are all heading back toward earth under full power!"

"Roger, Twitchel. We have all neutron missiles heading back toward earth under full power, Twitchel?" "Correct Houston. Transmission is correct, Houston! All soviet rockets have ignited themselves and are heading back to earth as we speak."

"General Hamilton, we have a very severe problem. The soviet rockets have all activated themselves somehow and are all heading back toward earth as we speak."

General Hamilton ran to the main control room at command center central. He quickly picked up the red colored phone and began almost screaming into its mouthpiece. "This is General Hamilton from NASA Control Center, gentleman. We have a red alert on our hands. Repeat. We have an all-out red alert on our hands.

Men, the scatter run has begun, I repeat, the scatter run has begun! We have a massive scatter run underway as all Soviet rockets are heading back toward earth under full power".

The scatter run was the pre-designated code name given if anything thing went array with the recovery mission on any one or more of the rockets in orbit if one was to return to the earth under its own power without being snagged by the recovering unit, the shuttle Twitchel. Every nation around the globe with fighter planes scrambled their aircrafts into immediate action, hoping to intercept any stray missiles returning from above their nations.

The perpetrators coming to earth needed to be taken out of the sky immediately before they were able to disperse any of their heavily armed and very deadly payloads from their nosecones. Everyone knew the rocket's nosecones had a dozen or more highly sensitive neutron activated war-headed mini missiles in them. Each rocket was capable of shooting these assorted Minnie-Rockets off in an assortment of different directions to seek out their own preprogrammed targets of ill repute.

Every military aircraft around the world were capable of flying were to blow up every missile they could before they would be able to reach their preprogrammed destinations or have the chance to activate any of the many altimeter detonator sensory devices installed in them.

The United States and the Soviet Union scrambled every available fighter aircraft they had on land and sea in unison with all the other nations around the globe. The sky became a scattered air arena full of aircraft searching out the unsuspecting enemy no one ever expected to return to earth this way. The pilots aboard these aircrafts in the air thought they were in pursuit of a single stray missile in their area coming back toward the earth, searching frantically for the one menacing unit.

They did not realize they were in for one hell of a fight, a fight of a lifetime, and for their very lives as well.

An accumulation in hundreds upon thousands of jet fighter pilots from around the globe flew their warring aircraft into the air to seek out and destroy their foe across the heavens approaching the earth. After becoming airborne, all were informed of their missions by their commanding unit officers as to what they would be up against by facing this deadly enemy. This enemy was more dangerous than just flying up and engaging in an air-to-air combat dogfight with another flying ace of their own caliber in another aircraft similar to theirs in the once friendly skies they all had guarded over their countries. They would be up against an enemy with more strength and magnitude than they had. An enemy with a computerized mind with the fastest decision making computers for their computerized brains ever built into an aircraft, or vehicle of mass destruction. These flying fortresses of destruction would become a challenge to the best of the best of flying aces, and it would be a miracle if any of the warring planes in the sky would prevail in their missions to seeking out and destroy the enemy.

The quick response computerized guiding systems installed in them could fend off any capable fighter aircraft that might come into destructive range of them or try to pursue them in their rapid descents back toward the earth in order to accomplish their deadly missions.

The primary goal in each rocket was to seek out a predetermined location in the sky over the earth's crust. They were to find a high densely populated region over the planet in a specific country, and then activate the many nosecone missiles to eject their deadly payloads in many smaller more deadly missiles out over their intended targeted area, killing the enemy. All missiles were preprogrammed to accomplish their deadly tasks with a full squadron of highly trained fighter pilots in warplanes in hot pursuit of them on their deadly mission runs.

The time of day along with their location in orbit above the earth would greatly signify what targets they would seek out and destroy as they descended back toward earth from the heavens. The time preprogrammed into each rocket had a revolving clock program of the day's rotation in the rockets computers which activated and governed each missile by the power of the magnetic fields generated by the earth's magnetic polar caps energy transmitting fields of magnetism, governing their location by the earth's constant rotation.

These deadly rockets were continually signaling their positioning aloft status in orbit by radio signaling their positions to the other missiles in orbit avoiding satellites in their orbit. This was the only good part in their preprogramming the many rockets, giving them a better chance to avoid recovery by an adversary or even their own makers.

The faulty missiles had no conscious or guilt built into them. Surely, not a one cared who they killed, if it was their own maker if he or she was in its path when it came back to earth. Something drastically wrong had gone array in their preprogramming of destinations.

The Soviets knew it when they tried to reprogram them in orbit not to returns back to earth. To seek out another orbit above until a future time when they would be needed to show supremacy to the world below. The faulty programs installed had failed, as none would responded to commands broadcast to them by their command center to abort the mission and stay put in orbit until a later date in time when needed.

In the United States, all emergency broadcasting network systems around the country went into immediate action broadcasting the warning of the approaching menace. Every radio and television station around the country, dropped what they were broadcasting, and turned to warning their viewers of the peril which was about to take place around the globe. Every communication satellite circling the earth was pouring out important warning messages sent to them and they back to the earth below.

People around the world having any kind of electronic messaging equipment were informed that the faulty Soviet missiles had erupted into a full-scale case of scientific disarray, as a deadly reality was about to affect everyone on planet earth with their imbalanced deadly payloads.

This was not just another case of another Orson Wells broadcasting his fable with his made up story about the invasion on the world by aliens from another planet. This was a true war crime brought on by the greedy Russian leaders. The situation was an unconscionable not well thought out incident cast down onto the many inhabitants of the earth including all its wildlife and domestic animal life there on, including birds and insects that fly.

A very unfortunate invasion brought on by the few new Soviet Union leaders' stupidity. An unprovoked invasion brought down from space on everyone no matter where they lived on planet earth including their own people of Russia.

The emergency broadcasting system warned that everyone should in some way take immediate shelter and cover well below the earth's crust and surface if possible and hurry in doing so before it becomes too late. The ones not able to seek cover will all perish, it broadcasted. "This is not a test, the broadcasters repeated over and over again over the airways of their networking stations. Take cover immediately. Seek out shelter of any kind in the lowest parts of your homes or at your places of employment. Take cover wherever you can possibly be safe from the approaching menace from hell. Take cover in water wells, in basements of skyscrapers, in cellars of homes like you would if a tornado was to be coming. Whatever you do, take immediate cover in a well-secured area away from windows, doors, and outside walls. Take all of your children, your family pets, and any other animals you can with you if possible. This is not a test. Please take cover immediately."

Every town, city, and community around the whole wide world engaged their warning sirens into full action along with every available whistle shrilling, and all horns blowing out a call of distress, warning everyone within ear shot from them to heed some sort of warning.

Many concerned people around the world put themselves in harm's way. They jeopardized themselves trying hard in vain to send out messages of warning to people from bells in steeples, horns of all sorts, along with loudspeakers installed out on commons and in parks. The citizens of the world, along with their many animals and the other poor creatures around the planet, were in a state of peril from the descending manmade menace approaching the earth quickly and quietly from the heavens above. Soon it would be too late to do anything to save themselves from the disaster ready to happen at any moment.

People around the planet were scrambling around trying to take cover in complete shock as they ran. People around the world wondered how anything this atrocious could possibly take place in one's lifetime. The leaders of the world should have known better than let anything this ludicrous take place in these new most modern times of technology. Maybe this was God's way of putting an end to man's existence on planet earth as they once knew it.

The populous of the world became frantic hearing about the horrific dangers broadcast to them by the emergency broadcasting equipment sending out its many warnings. People in deep sound sleeps were rudely awakened from their rest by loud horns. Sirens blasting from police cruisers driving around neighborhoods trying to warn people, while others out and about shopping were being warned in supermarkets and other types of stores to leave their shopping carts behind where they were and go immediately home to be with their loved ones.

Worldly inhabitants sought shelter in storage food coolers, their basements, or wherever else they could go in finding immediate shelter from this new type of deadly bomb that would kill all humankind and animal life alike in its path. They did not understand how a bomb of this magnitude could kill everyone including their pets and other animals, and yet would leave their buildings, trees, vegetation, and all the likes unscathed in its path of eminent destruction.

Peoples' actions around the planet looked more like a scene right out an Alfred Hitchcock fable. A horror movie scene coming to life, as all were getting ready to die by an approaching invisible ghost. Everyone had a very sick feeling about the world they were living in, as they once knew it to be, was about to come to an abrupt end. The world was going to burn up in flames, as predicted in the Bible, and all were going to burn in hell except for the meek.

People became instantly panic-stricken hearing the warnings. Groups of people began leaving their places of employment by the hundreds of thousands stampeding over each other trying to flee. To where ever they were supposed to go, they did not know. City streets along with subways became almost instantly jammed. Transportation systems became instantly over crowded with masses of people trying to flee the big cities and towns, trying to flee and return back home to be with their loved ones so they might die together.

Hundreds instantly began running out of patience with the massive overcrowding in the streets. So many of them became instantly hostile, extremely irritated with one another, as impatient drivers trying to flee the city began running over people in the streets and on city sidewalks to get around enormous traffic jams on the roadways to escape the crowds. Some drivers sped out of control to get back to their homes, causing enormous accidents along roadways. No one would stop to see if anyone was dead or alive or in desperate need of immediate medical attention. It seemed no one cared about life and humanity any more.

The news media had been warning the world this would happen one day. Sending out warning after daily warning, and now it had all come to fruition and everyone knew the end of the world was near. Thousands and upon thousands of the city dwellers and workers became trapped while trying to escape the cities. They could not escape the wrath of overcrowding in the streets. Many sought their hurried ways into the many churches within the city limits, crushing innocent people young and old on their way into the overcrowded doorways, killing many older people and children by plainly knocking them down and crushing them beneath their stampeding feet. Every person on the streets was acting like people trying to flee a burning building. In this case, the people were trying to get inside a holy structure as soon as they could instead of staying outside of its holy walls and face the devil himself.

These hostile people all wanted to be in the house of the Lord when the final seconds of the world came to its providence. Most people thought it would not be more than a billionth of a second when the world came to its end. Many people having sinned wanted to rebuke to the Lord in confession before they died and had to face him at the pearly gates of heaven when they arrived. People did not know what to expect or how to protect themselves from the evil forces about to descend down on them from out of the blue.

Rival gangs of city juveniles hearing the extreme news dispersed, going their own separate ways to be with family or someone they thought might care about them. Everyone who heard the deadly warnings about death approaching them felt the same as others did. What was going to happen to he or she, feeling the end of the world would soon be upon them before the end of the day was to come, or even sooner. It was all up to the good Lord above now, or was it up to the Russian leaders to stop this intrusive fate of the world?

CHAPTER FIFTEEN

The Final Decision

Precious seconds, hell no, precious minutes had already wasted away in failed communication talks between the space agency, the President of the United States, his leaders of the armed forces, and the greedy leaders occupying the Kremlin now. The world was in a state of panic, and no one on the face of planet Earth knew the next proper step to take in this serous dilemma.

The President of United States requested and then demanded, slamming his fist down on his desk yelling at the stubborn Soviet leaders that they push the damn activating panic detonation button. Whatever the button's name was that would allow all these deadly missiles still in orbit to explode simultaneously, before any might possibly regain entry back into the earth's atmosphere and rain down death upon everyone below them. Leaders from around the world hoped by pushing the panic button it would leave the Earth safe from this potency of death that the missiles carried with them.

This created a big dilemma the Kremlin did not want to deal with if they detonated the missiles in space. Afraid these exploding missiles would kill the astronauts onboard the U. S. Twitchel as well as all the cosmonauts aboard the international space station.

They did not care about the lives of those on the space station, but the Soviet leaders were afraid the ramifications it would cause leaders from around the world, angry for killing the few innocent people in outer space.

The President of the United States demanded they push the panic button at once, and was willing to sacrifice the several lives of his people in orbit in order to save the millions if not billions of lives it might cost the world below if they didn't do it right away.

It was not a matter of seconds in who would be right or who would be wrong at this critical time. He demanded they do the right thing by pushing the damn button that would cost the least amount of lives, and to make it happen now! Everyone onboard the Twitchel knew the president was right about his hard decision and scared as hell for themselves, but more afraid for their loved ones back home on earth, than they were for themselves.

The cowardly soviet leaders were intimidated. They had no idea what would happen if they were to blow all the neutron missiles up all at the very same time. They had not given it any forethought or afterthought when they had initially installed the safety device for this type of protection. They thought they would never have to use it. More thought out scientific data should have gone into their hurried production of all these many killers.

Along with a separate activating device installed in each missile with its own special frequency in order to be watched over from earth and destroyed one by one if necessary. The Soviet leaders had not given it any thought about separate safety devices they were all in such a damn hast to become the super power of supremacy over the planet. Caution and any safety features were not number one on their priority list at the hasty time of missile production, and now it was too late even for them to come up with a good lie about how safe their new rocketry systems were.

Leaders from countries around Earth both large and small were heavily yelling and screaming at the Soviet leaders over their special connected communication lines to blow up the damn missiles before they might regain entry back into the earth's atmosphere, or it might be too late for everyone, including them. The Soviet leaders were all hoping for a damn miracle to happen, which did not. It was now all upon their greedy little shoulders to either act now or face a continental tribunal court system later on for their actions and they knew it.

Military pilots in the air knew their treacherous missions. They were to seek out and destroy as many enemy missiles they could before they had time to activate and deploy their deadly payloads in neutron warheads mini-missiles of great strength to the earth. If these missiles nose-cone canopy covers were to open in flight, they would deploy their twelve, twenty, or more activated warheads they were carrying. It all depended upon the size of the carrying rocket's ability in maneuvering its payload size.

A larger payload of rockets would require an additional nineteen, twenty, or more aircraft to do what a single fighter aircraft might possibly be able to accomplish with the use of its own missiles. No one on Earth knew the many faulty sensory devices installed on all the missiles including the small missiles inside the many nosecones activated themselves when the massive spec-sized meteor shower covered the outer atmosphere around the earth hitting these many rockets, causing electrical short-circuits to take place within the many rockets.

With their time clocks ticking, these deadly clusters of rockets were just waiting to depart from the nose cones to descend down to earth and seek out their supposedly intended targets. A hard sudden jar in reentry could trigger the many sensitive altimeter detonators on reentry because they were designed so poorly.

The longer the missiles lay in wait in space the better so the soviets could detonate them there, but they were zooming in toward the earth faster now, and it would only be a matter of seconds before it was too late to detonate them in their once space orbit, and save the world from eminent disaster.

Lt. Richard Nixon, flying with the Royal Canadian Air Force, was the first lucky unlucky flying ace to lock his radar guiding laser heat seeking missiles onto one of the deadly neutron rockets carrying the missiles. He spotted it as it broke down through a high cloud cover

over the country of Canada just above the city of Toronto. He and his squadron witnessed it descending rapidly down from space to deploy its deadly payload in rockets onto the heavily populated city and its surrounding area.

He could see the nose cone of the rocket had already peeled away its covering displaying the multiple assembly of twenty or more already activated nuclear neutron rocket missiles it held secure inside its heavily armed nose. He swiftly turned his squadron around locking his aircrafts laser firing radar onto the rocket, and fired two destructive laser heat-seeking missiles from his aircraft to destroy the first multi headed rocket descending back towards the earth below.

Fire one, and fire two. It was the last communication ever heard from the squadron leader of flying aces. The other pilots in the squadron all listened and watched as their noble leader locked his radar guided missiles onto its pray in front of them, and fired the killing rockets from his aircraft, all squadron pilots watching as the two missile went to do the job they were intended to do.

The many massive smaller explosions in front of their squadron leaders aircraft did not look very bad to any of them behind him as they veered their aircraft away from the initial explosion trying not to hit any debris floating around in the air in front of them from the exploding missiles.

The pilots felt several small shockwaves flying through the cloud left by the explosion that did not seem to be bad. Although the massive neutron field generated from the many smaller exploding war heads penetrated their frail bodies like a zillion silent machine gun bullets that didn't hurt their outer bodies, but sent the deadly array of neutrons throughout every pilot in the squadron.

It caused them instantly to go into involuntary convulsions, rendering the entire squadron of Canadian pilots dead. None of the pilots ever knew what hit them it happened so fast, so unexpectedly. These pilots were instantly lost, due to the rapid release of the overactive payloads of deadly neutrons filling the air around them, and sucking their bodies dry of any life supporting electrical energy they possessed.

The instant absorption of all the pilots' internal electrical impulses from their bodies over function control of the heart rate and movement, left them sizzling and smoking in their cockpit seats.

Control over their aircraft was gone, as was their ability to live. What little electrical impulses they once had in their brains and nervous system vanished instantly.

CHAPTER SIXTEEN

The Eye in the Sky

Several dozen Soviet cosmonauts along with two German astronauts living aboard the International Space Station witnessed the spectacular view of the many missiles all activated at the very same time. They watched as the earth in its day of devastation took place from above in their safe orbit a few hundred miles away from the destruction.

They all had heard from their own mission control space compound in Kazakhstan, Russia as well as from the Houston Command Station located in Texas that they, along with the crew of the Twitchel, might become victims of this awful unforeseen disaster in order to save the many lives of their loved ones and other inhabitants around the earth.

The crew knew when told by the Americans that they would not be safe if it take place in space. They watched, fearing for their lives, as the many missiles penetrated back through the ionosphere and into the earth's atmosphere back toward the earth and away from them.

The eye in the sky saw everything taking place within its viewing vision as the space station passed over the earth in their orbit. The crew aboard the laboratory, some sitting and others floating in weightlessness, watched the several television monitors in the space station, as the Canadian fighter squadron's leader locked his radar guided missiles onto the first rocket to reenter the sky over Canada. They were able to keep an eye on the chase as the five fighter aircraft followed in close pursuit in perfect formation after their enemy missile and watched as the two laser guided missiles sought out their kill and did their job. The first explosion destroyed the main rocket as the second missile ignited all the other mini nuclear missiles into a massive explosion of released neutrons. Three of the payload that the main rocket had been carrying had already departed the nosecone from the main rocket, and were on their separate ways to targets of dismay somewhere over Canada.

The squadron seemed to be in hot pursuit of these last three missiles as the five aircraft followed in close pursuit thereof until the very end. The space station was listening in on the emergency airwaves countries agreed to listen in on during this time of trouble. Each pilot wanted to know when and where the next missile was about to mysteriously show up out of the deadly skies. The eye in the sky watched as squadron after squadron of fighter jets flew through the blast area of the exploding missiles after their initial killings on them. The cosmonauts from above cheered for the many pilots below. It looked as if the fighter pilots on earth would win the horrendous battle against these deadly missiles and save the earth's people and animal life from extinction.

Little did the crew aboard the space station know there would be heroes departed in their fearless efforts of battle! They watched as three Canadian Air Force fighter jets nosed downward into high-speed dives straight toward the earth, burying the three deep in the earth's crust below. The two remaining Canadian fighter jets looked as if they were in hot pursuit and going in for the kill on the three remaining missiles getting away seeking out their designated targets. Suddenly the two aircraft in hot pursuit went into similar high-speed straight downward spiraling dives as had the other three aircraft crashing nose first into the surface of the earth in two big puffs of heavy white and then harrowing black billowing smoke.

The radioman aboard the International Space Center tried in vain several times over to communicate back to earth what they had just witnessed. Finally, after several attempts, he was able to transmit their radio signal back to an observatory station located in New Zealand. He explained to them just what had taken place in the air over Canada.

The warning message sent to earth from the space immediately transmitted the message to Houston control, Cape Canaveral, the

Pentagon, and to the many leaders around the world listening in on the special frequency line.

The new Soviet leaders knew they were in great trouble for the horrendous folly they had caused to materialize in their governing control over Russia and their time in history. They had now became caught up in their own schemes of things to prove their supremacy to all on earth, and now very vulnerable to their own deadly forces of power of destruction that they caused from above as were the rest of the world. Their damn star wars game had gone array on them and backfired! The poor quality put into the supreme guiding systems implanted in the missiles proved faulty, for the missiles flying in from outer space had no justifiable reasoning in their courses of directions they took for their intended targeted positions where they were supposed to be tracking to.

The Soviets true course of avenue to prove and show their own supremacy to the world was now a true blunder. It had failed and now proved deadly against the ones who had created this deadly monster in the first place.

With several missile sightings by pilots of reentering missiles into the earth's atmosphere taking place, the many fighter pilots in the skies over the earth set off after them. They, too, met their premature deaths as did the first sighting proved deadly to the squadron pilots who were in hot pursuit of their enemy. The demand to end this damn invasion by their own missiles came to the new Soviet leaders loud and clear as this enemy to all they had created for their own destructive weaponry arsenal was now slaying their own pilots by the droves.

It did not matter anymore. No matter what was to happen to the many astronauts in outer space. The Soviets knew someone had to push the damn panic button now and destroy this out of control advancing enemy from outer space. It was already too late for the many that had already died a senseless useless death because of the greedy ones.

If the panic button was to be pushed previous to any stray missiles reentered the earth's atmosphere, none would have suffered except maybe the astronauts. Again it was a very poor judgment call in timing on the scared Soviet leader's part in destroying their own advancing fleet of attacking missiles. By this time in history, every missile carrying their death wish had been safely in orbit, prior to receiving the signals from the many other activated missiles. All this caused by the passing of many small comet fragments of ice and stone particles activating just a few number of rockets, and they all in turn activated all the rest. Every one of them had already reentered back into the earth's atmosphere prior the button being pushed, readying themselves to deploy their already armed and deadly cargos to their predetermined points that were anywhere now.

It would have been less deadly to the citizens around the globe having exploded the hundreds of missiles loaded with mass destruction in outer space in a much more timely fashion, than to have waited for so long in doing so.

They chose to push the panic button after the fact when all the warheads were all now flying around in the earth's atmosphere again, and then pushed it to destroy them all at once.

CHAPTER SEVENTEEN

The Big Flash

Watching as the missiles broke through the earth's atmosphere from outer space, the crewmembers aboard both the international space station and the crew members aboard the space shuttle Twitchel, witnessed a most spectacular seen unfold before their very eyes in the skies that surrounding the earth below, their home.

Pushing the button to destroy the masses of descending missiles proved to be as deadly to some as if they had been sitting right on top the bombing devices themselves as they exploded. They did not die directly from the explosions of the many bomb-laced missiles or from the massive doses of neutrons produced by them all exploding at once. They died from the destructive resulting forces the trillions upon trillions of activated neutralizing neutrons had on all the electrically operated equipment known to man in the world.

It was similar to the sun having a huge solar storm flare up on its surface causing titanic sized black spots that caused massive power outages of electricity around the world. The astronauts aloft observed as whole rockets with their activated cargo stores exploded along with hundreds of smaller already deployed neutron missile bombs on their way to their predetermined destinations all exploding in midflight all at once.

The shock wave of the sudden release of neutrons from the many missiles both large and small hitting the earth was immense, and overly destructive in so many other ways. There were storms of lightning and neutron induced colors of the rainbow engulfing the air of the earth, causing huge storms to develop in the sky around the globe, the likes no man had ever witnessed before, except he saw an atomic bomb explode from a distance.

The many colors of a rainbow; reds, violets, browns, greens, and others danced among the newly developed clouds above the earth, and caused lights to fill the air as bright as someone welding steel together or using a cutting torch to cut some steel in half.

The many astronauts above watched in awe. They could not believe what was taking place on the planet of their homeland below. The earth suddenly became a large orange glistening ball of haze, drifting alone in space below them like a fluorescent orange ball. The sky above the earth was gone. It looked as though someone or something had just painted the atmosphere of the earth with a mist of orange paint, and none could see below its thick surface of color. The haze of orange blocked out any chance of seeing any landmasses or sizable continents of noticeable size. It looked like the earth had vaporized right in front of them while they all watched it disappear. The earth now looked more like the planet Jupiter, totally covered in its dusty storm clouds. The earth had no rings around it, but it was impossible to see if it was still there or if it had really vaporized the way it sure looked like it had.

The once happy hearts of all in space, sunk to the bottom of happiness with fret, fear and concern for the welfare of their loved ones beneath the orange mist. The two space vehicles could hear one another trying desperately in vein to raise a friendly voice from anyone, far below them on earth that could answer them back. After an hour of trying to no avail, the two crews decided to talk to one another.

What was the Twitchel to do now? She had enough emergency food, oxygen, and water supply onboard for the crew to survive in orbit for two weeks and then they would have to attempt a return trip to back to earth, or die from lack of life support supplies and functional necessities to keep them all alive in space.

In talking to the commander of the space laboratory, Commander Ivan Khrushchev and Commander Colonel Nelson Anderson in charge of the Twitchel decided it best for the welfare of all to rendezvous with each other, to hook up their crafts together, and wait out what was happening below. The space station needed a vehicle for transport if anything went wrong aboard it in the near future, and the Twitchel's crew needed a safe place to call home until it was safe to return back home to the earth.

The International Space Station laboratory was equipped with an experimental oxygen producing system, made up of natural plant life and mechanical re-breathers. The original design in the oxygen system's capacity limited the number of crewmembers the space station could carry at one given time, which would allow them to live within the laboratory's chambers for a long time to come. With the space station filled to capacity with astronauts, another several astronauts added to the system would put a strain on the delicate balance and ability of the system to support more life for a greater time than a year or less. Within that time period, the two crews hoped the earth would be back to normal, if not lost forever.

They had outfitted the space laboratory with its own extended winged cubicle-styled garden growing facility, a special ultraviolet lighting system powered by exterior solar powered electrical panels for ultraviolet light for plant life growing purposes and to produce a limited amount of fresh food to eat aboard the space station.

The cubicle also was capable of recycling human waste into usable fertilizer to help in plant life growth after the sterilization took place in one of the laboratory's many solar powered sterilizing mechanisms along with a large supply of fresh and recaptured filtered wastewater used daily for fresh chilled water to use for bathing, drinking, and cooking.

The International Space Station was a self-sufficient floating city all alone in space with intentions that it might live on in space forever. Its only exception was that it needed recharging once in a while with new filters for purification to its life support systems, and now would have numbers beyond its original design living aboard it that would tax it beyond its limitations.

The linking up of the two space vehicles proved to be very beneficial for the crew of the Twitchel and the space station crew. The sky above the earth was now covered with a nontransparent sheen of orange greenish glowing mist so the occupants of the space station and crew from aboard the shuttle could not see what was really taking place on the ground below or in the skies above the earth. The horrendous effect on the earth from the many neutron bombs exploding all at the same time in its atmosphere had a devastating crippling outcome on the human occupants, as well as all the animal life on the planet. The massive scattered explosions of condensed neutrons let loose in the atmosphere, neutralized the abilities of power plants worldwide to mass-produce electricity, earth lost without power.

The earth became a huge celestial ball void of electrical power lost in space. It was similar to a huge round junk pile littered with nothing but dead machinery scattered around its surface as useless scrap heaps of metal and plastic standing whole, but dead empty without any life supporting blood of electrical current flowing freely through any of its many wired veins for its life.

The earth below the space station was lost without power to communicate to them or to the earth as well. The earth as man once knew it became a neutralized planet. There were no more strong negative or positive charges left on the face of the earth to deal with, to produce any type of electrical power they once knew, and so well enjoyed. Gravitation upon the earth became less with polar caps slightly neutralized. The electric power around the earth had been absorbed by the massive release of the many neutrons all being released at the same precise time. Man had finally invented and set off a weapon of destruction around the earth that the earth could not reclaim in just a matter of a few quick seconds, days or months ahead.

The highly condensed neutron bomb proved to be the ultimate of all situations which the earth could not handle naturally, or was it man who couldn't handle what he had invented and caused? The magnets of the world would not counteract with each other in opposing fields

strong enough to produce electricity without becoming glazed over in a mass of greenish orange slime, then became almost instantly oxidized, rendering them useless for man to try to produce electricity with them.

CHAPTER EIGHTEEN

Devastation in the Air

All commercial airliners around the planet with their many passengers of fare in flight that day or night, depending upon what time zone they were flying at the time were subject to doom. All electronic and electrically operated controls onboard them required to fly the large airliners along with the internal lights flickered and went instantly dead in midflight.

Only a small handful of lucky people flying their aircraft in daylight around the earth were lucky enough to have survived the big blast. With manually operated flight controls and not flying very high up in the air, they were able to glide their aircrafts to a safe landing area if there was a safe place to land them in sight, had the masses in neutrons not already taken the lives of the ones onboard the aircraft most especially the pilots. Helicopter pilots and other poor souls in their crafts fell from the sky. Planes flying at night lost all concepts of visual and artificial horizons making instruments in their cockpits useless due to the mist of orange sheen that covered the earth, blocking out the true horizon with it illuminated by the bright moon from above.

Many airplanes fell from the sky for the lack of the pilot's ability to see where they were safely going to land because of darkness and the misty orange green sheen they were in, if they were still alive. Many pilots experienced severe vertigo for the very first time in their years of flying long hours that they were very accustomed to flying. Only the lucky people sitting in airliners on the airport tarmac waiting for other commercial airplanes in front of them to taxi out onto the runways for takeoff were the lucky ones.

The poor people on any aircraft that had just barely taken off from the ground and had become air born fell like rocks from the sky, scattering aircraft parts, people, luggage, and debris all over the ground beneath them. The small number of fortunate pilots were able to save themselves, lucky to make a safe landing amounted to less than the number of fingers on a person's single hand.

All others in flight that horrible day perished mostly from being instantly sucked dry of every flicker of natural electrical impulse generated in their nervous systems. Emergency lighting equipment in all buildings around the world flickered for a split second and then went instantly dead. All other electrically powered equipment within the confined structures of manmade edifices followed suit. Escalators came to a sudden stop. Tall building having elevators with mechanical brakes suddenly jolted to a sudden stop as they started to plummet towards the bottom of their shafts. Elevators with electrically operated magnets for stopping mechanisms for brakes sank quickly to the bottoms of high-rise buildings at great speeds, demolishing the elevator cars while mutilating everyone riding inside of them.

People with artificial hearts that ran on battery packs for power slumped quietly in their seats as others fell dead to the ground where they were walking. People with battery power operated defibrillators were sucked dry of electricity, as their own electrical impulses were rendered useless.

Emergency-generating generators never had a chance to start up because of their highly charged starting batteries went instantly dead, sucked dry of their readily charged electrical power.

Cars, busses, trucks, trains, planes, ships, and more, became idle as if they all had had an electrical heart attack all at the same precise time in history.

The only operable equipment still running on the face of the earth were but a few diesel powered engines, not requiring the need of electricity to operate them or to keep them running.

Diesel powered trucks with faulty electrically operated air shut off solenoid valves remained running, and would only shut down when the driver closed the breather flap on the engine manually. That is, if the drivers of those vehicles were lucky enough to live through the horrendous invasion of the massive neutron attack, depending on the elevation of the highways they were driving over at the time.

Truck drivers going over the Great Divide in the Western hemisphere of the United States, along with everyone else on the mountain roads that day, died from being sucked dry of their life giving natural electrical charges they needed to survive.

The entire different categories in transportation-alamode in equipment around the world came to an abrupt halt. Cars engines on thoroughfares stopped running as millions of drivers pulled their lifeless vehicles off to the sides of the roadways, if they were still alive to do so.

Some vehicles just pulled up to a dead stop in the middle of some roadways with their almost dead drivers and passengers thrashing about in massive convulsions behind the steering wheels and in seats of the vehicles.

Trucks, cars, aircraft, busses, and the like ceased to operate that day, as did many millions upon millions of lives that were lost in a matter of only a few tormented seconds, minutes, and hours depending where they were when the Russian leaders pushed the panic button.

Some diesel engines in emergency power generating plants that were unfortunately running, using electrically operated computer sensors to govern their speed controls, went from a dead stop idle, to running as fast they could without a governor to slow them down. These engines ran full speed till they either ran out of diesel fuel they needed to operate or until they exploded from running in excessive revolutions per seconds beyond their capabilities of running, as parts from these

engines went flying everywhere when their crankshafts, pistons and other movable parts from within all came apart from exploding.

Death to thousands of individuals that day, their many livestock and pets, along with many species of birds in the air, and other flighty creatures living in the sky were instantly crucified in an untimely misfortune that took place around the globe.

Citizens of the earth died trapped in elevators while others died just out taking their little pet dogs for walks, their pets succumbing right along with their owners on that sunny afternoon in parts of the world, as did thousands of other people on operating tables in hospital operating rooms.

Hundreds upon thousands of ill-fated people died falling from out the skies in aircrafts over the globe in the many doomed commercial airliners as did thousands of unfortunate military pilots trying their damnedest to save the world from a horrific catastrophe about to take place, but all failed.

Innocent campers and their families out in the wilderness of nature enjoying the nice quiet of the day died, along with millions of office workers in high-rise buildings trying to flee. Every one of them died trying to escape the horrific approaching disaster.

Young new mothers in higher elevations died in their homes while nursing their young babies. Some babies were lucky enough to have died right along with their mothers, or they would starve to death while lying in the still of their dead mother's quiet lap and arms of their deceased mothers. Some babies were not as fortunate as others.

Simple electrical communications around the globe came to an abrupt end. The masses of computers, telephone lines, radios, shortwave signaling devices, teletype machines, and countless more electric communication devices around the planet came to a threatening end to all of the inhabitants of the world in a matter of split seconds.

Thousands of coalminers along with other types of miners died deep down in coalmines along with hundreds of people caught down inside traffic tunnels on highways. Thousands drowned from rising floodwaters pouring in and from asphyxiation. Electricity required

to run powerful water pumps to keep the mines and tunnels below ground dry and to pump in fresh oxygen down to them from above ground in order for them to work in the desolate depths of the earth's vast mines, suddenly ended.

Large numbers of innocent lives both young and old were lost around the globe that day, along with many species of creature becoming extinct.

CHAPTER NINETEEN

The Lucky Ones

A very small few from the earth's large population became lucky that day or became the not so lucky ones that day. They were the ones experiencing all the luxurious benefits made possible by electricity that day, as they drifted hopelessly around the planet earth in orbit above.

Everything looked pretty bleak below to the ones in space, as they all hoped someday in the near future they might all be lucky enough to return back home to the earth they once knew. If they were able or could not return, they surely would be doomed to die a different kind of death in space. If the earth that they once knew was an uninhabitable globe without an atmosphere, unfit for man to survive on or in by the massive invasion of highly condensed neutrons in the heavy water, they were all doomed. Not able to see through the orangey mist surrounding the earth, their hopes were all but gone if anyone below could have survived such a thing, all without hope they would ever see a loved below ever again.

The effects of the neutralization of the planet below wore heavy on the ones still left alive after the detonation of the neutrons bombs paraded around the globe in a flash. The paradox of destruction surrounded the globe in an instant within milliseconds from the time of detonation when all of the weaponry self-destructed. The remaining human inhabitants and animals that were still left alive all became instantly sick. Most living creatures partially drained of their once enjoyable energy they thrived on prior to the massive blast, because of their many assorted body functions needed to run properly by the minute electrically generated impulses from the brain throughout their nervous systems had been rendered weak.

The previously sick populace of the world would soon lose their fighting battles to the simplest of diseases known to man, such as mild colds and simple headaches could cause the natural electrical charges in the nervous system to come to a complete stop, and they would all die.

Inhabitants of once friendly countries around the globe turned sour and vicious toward one another. They soon became aggressively hostile, rebellious toward people of other lands who seemed to have plenty of everything that they did not have. World chaos started to crop up immediately surrounding the devastated planet. New hostile societies formed with greedy people at their helms no better than the ones who had started this mess in the first place.

All this anger was generated by a few uncaring people just like the few who were to blame for this catastrophic dilemma. These few selfish people did not give a damn about anyone but themselves, whether the innocent of the world lived or died, just as long as they were in charge.

The several ones who originally organized this deadly invasion were no longer alive, destroyed by the paramount of their own greedy making, having mass-produced all these deadly weapons in the first place. The star wars program was to make them the greatest all time leaders around the world, and yet it destroyed them in their own demise dying in agony as one of the hundreds of missiles detonated right above them when they pushed the panic button, the way they should have died before this horrendous event ever took place.

The immense loss of life around the globe triggered by the unfortunate mishap was more devastating than if the two super powers of the world had launched a full scale, blown out nuclear war against one another, using up their entire arsenal of nuclear weaponry. The total loss of life of creature and humans alike was horrifying and uncountable, and all because of a few greedy individuals with the want for power.

There was little of any available resources for reporting the magnitude of the tragic events or activities taking place around the world. The innocent people around the planet were in darkness to any important news unless they were a good horseback rider like an old out-west pony express rider. Luck being with you if your horse had not cruelly been taken away from you as it roamed your back pastureland.

Doctors, still alive after the invasion, did their best in helping the extremely sick and needy populous of the world with what they had left of useful medical supplies and medicines. The doctors left alive could not take the enormous medical demand placed upon them in the chaotic cities or in the immediate suburbs. The doctors who could, took their entire families including aunts, uncles and parents away from the humble jumble of the crowded metropolitan districts and tried to escape into the quietness of the countryside. There they found the same medical demands placed upon them as everywhere else around the country.

A number of doctors who had lost their wives and children, used the best sedatives they had available to them to stop the severe heart throbbing pain of loss they felt within, and took their own lives so they would not have to live with all of the grief they were experiencing.

Life on earth had become an instant living hell for most, including the rich and famous of the world, where money did not mean a damn thing to them anymore, compared to their once healthy life they had before they became sick from the many neutrons surrounding everyone. No matter how much money they offered the doctors or anyone else around to make them feel better, it did them no good, for everyone was in the same boat, and would stay sick for a long, long time to come.

CHAPTER TWENTY

Empty Skies over Earth

Countless vast great air forces and powerful nations around the world were completely wiped out, and did not exist any longer. Most all capable fighter pilots went down that day along with their ill-fated aircraft. Only a small number of pilots were able to jettison out of their ill-fated aircraft, and thought they could parachute down to land safety, not knowing they were going to be falling, and drifting slowly down through the massive neutron bombardment of deathly microwave rays to the ground below. In the air, they would die a horrific death before ever hitting the ground. Strapped to their escape parachutes, they dangled about thrashing in involuntary convulsions. Their bodies giving off a strange gracious phosgene odor all looking like large greenish orange snowmen descending down to earth dressed in costumes for a Halloween party. Not a single pilot who ejected from their aircraft survived the descending flight down through the massive neutron cloud without giving up their life or their minds. The ones who died in decent were the lucky ones, as the ones who survived the descent down became as dense in mind as vegetables.

Many freighters and pleasure cruise ships afloat the salty waters around the world, stopped dead in the middle of the seas. The vessels' engines all stopped as they lay dormant while bobbing and drifting helplessly up and down in the middle of the oceans they were upon like corks on a fish line.

The luckiest people of all left alive in the world after the big blast were the many simple living people. Self-sufficient farmers and tribe's people living off the land in the backcountry were the lucky ones. They did not have any of the modern day conveniences nor could they afford the luxuries of those who had once lived in the crowded cities in the so-called rich civilized metropolises area around the world. These lucky minorities were the lucky poor farmers around the earth. The ones who did not mind getting their two hands dirty slaughtering some of their home-raised animals for food. The lucky ones were those who did not mind chasing around inside a chicken coop to collect eggs or mind milking a cow for its milk, and living off the land at the time of the blast. These were the lucky people of planet earth now. The starving populous of big cities tried desperately to imitate the farmer in the ways they lived.

Native tribes living in desolate back lands on islands, or in the middle of vast jungles of the world, were now considered the lucky citizens on the desolate planet earth, for they did not know any better than to live the simple way in their lives they were all taught to live and were living well.

They were all accustomed to living off the land. These poor native tribal people did not understand why so many of their loved ones perished out in the openness of the lands. They had not been sick in anyway, until they were all found dead, along with many of their native animals lying dead around them, as well as so many foul from the air that had fallen dead to the ground.

They thought the many gods around their world must have become angry with them, along with all the dead animals, for what they had done, or had not done to please the gods that day. The remaining tribe's members not affected by the neutrons, vowed to care for the unlucky ones who had become simple minded from the sudden loss of some natural electrical impulses generated by their brains to think, and move about.

Many inhabitants of the new earth became instantly simpleminded like tiny children in all of their actions. It had everything to do with their approximant closeness to the neutron bombs themselves when they all exploded, sucking away any electrical impulses that could be taken away, without leaving them dead, but would have been more humane if it had. People of the planet who worked the land for its nourishments became the supreme powers over the land, but they did not know it or understand it.

The highly overeducated people of the planet knew the different fields generated in high tech computers, but not fields of the land. These highly educated people know and understand how one bank of a computer field works with another computer field of banks. These people know diddily-squat about planting a field of corn, one of potatoes, one of beans, or any other vegetable stables as a source of food in helping to keep their family's fed and alive, or how to keep them safe without stealing food from others.

These highly educated people became lost. They became the lost souls of planet Earth when it came time for them to earn their keep out in Mother Nature's raw straw fields of the simple ways of life in survival. Many would find it hard, but the ones with integrity and love for their families would learn the ways of many new fields for the happiness and survival of their loving families. Life on earth would change for most everyone, and become as life on the old planet earth, before they invented electricity.

CHAPTER TWENTY-ONE

The Clearing Sheen

With the first few weeks with the Twitchel docked to the space station, time passed slowly by for everyone at a snail's pace for the two space crews stranded in outer space.

The earth below remained covered with a bright colored sheen in a luminous blush, making it impossible for them to see anything below it. They could only guess what might be taking place on the world they once knew.

The mysterious greenish orange blush color covering the earth was caused they thought, by the sudden influx in mixture with the Earth's atmosphere of oxygen, nitrogen, and the restructuring molecules of gases released with the sudden influx of highly concentrated defiantly charged neutrons activating with the dense heavy water with their sudden release.

It all reflected back to the Sun's ultraviolet rays of light, setting off a chain reaction in the atmosphere that made the earth look like a huge ball of florescent-orange glowing wildly in the dark of space like a bright star.

On the sixteenth day after the invasion of the destructive rockets, the orange sheen overcast surrounding the earth began to dissipate and fade away, giving the crew aboard the space station a hazy, cloudy view of the changed world below, that the astronaut's once thought they knew.

The three different nationalities of astronauts aboard the International Spaces Station, the two Germans, the many Russians, and the six Americans, all attempted ineffectively a numerous amount of times' a day, to contact any friendly voice from the quiet planet below wanting to hear a voice in return?

The radios aboard both spacecraft were filled with aggressive violent static each time they mike-d up their communications radios between each other, but nothing was being broadcast from any radio from down below.

Nothing worked, no matter how hard they tried to reach a friendly voice from below that might want to talk to them from earth. Not a single voice was found anywhere around the dials on the many different frequencies they tried on their radios?

The astronauts above could vaguely see the planet through the misty sheen, as the mysterious orange sheen slowly dissipated. Its blue of sky began to clear. It was if the world below had ceased to exist, as they had once known it. Another week passed away before the orbiting international laboratory could use their high-density telescope to observe anything moving or taking place on the ground of the earth below. They had no word or contact from anyone below by the radio, no matter how many times a day someone attempted to awaken and raise someone's friendly voice from below to speak too.

The distinguished outlines of the large continents below began to emerge slowly through the fading orange sheen, as the sky became more-clear surrounding the covered planet. The space station was passing over Sydney Australia when they first attempted to put the onboard telescope on their craft into its first real test of operation in searching out answers to what had taken place below.

"Commander, Commander Ivan!" "What is it lieutenant?" "Come take a look-see at this Commander! There is something very strange taking place down their sir." The telescope placed on the space laboratory was so powerful, that the one designated in using it could practically make out the faces of the people on Earth they were observing from the eye in the sky, some two hundred, and some odd miles more above the earth.

The lieutenant in charge of the telescope was shaking his head back and forth, as he looked down on the city of Sydney. He could not or did not want to believe what his two eyes were seeing to be true, and neither could Commander Khrushchev believe what he was witnessing at that time! There was not a single category of any vehicle moving anywhere on the roadways below, or anywhere else around Sydney moving for that matter.

There looked to be hundreds of cars, and trucks scattered all along the many stretches of highways, and roadways sitting idle, not going anywhere. All the vehicles looked abandoned. There stood a long, long far stretched out train with many boxcars attached to three locomotives pulling it not moving in either direction, just sitting dead idle on the tracks below not far outside the city proper of Sydney.

The train's switching station in Sydney looked filled to capacity with idle locomotive engines pullers, passenger cars, and boxcars scattered everywhere along its many assorted tracks. The international airport on the outskirts of Sydney looked like a horrid idle mess of aircraft without any activity going on. There looked like a numerous number of commercial airliners scattered all about the airport's tarmac.

There were several sitting idle on the taxiways of the airport in total disarray. Some were still whole, as a couple of others looked tangled and damaged, for they had crashed into each other as they sat on the tarmac of the airport looking like they had been readily waiting in line for takeoff.

They could see where a couple of airliners had crashed and were scattered around the outskirts of the city. One at the end of the runway as if it had just taken off and crashed, and another one approaching the runway, which looked like they had just fallen straight out of the blue and had crashed where they lay. The airport looked deserted with no one walking around it. It looked like no one was getting ready to fly anywhere, yet every parking lot looked to be filled to capacity with many cars with no one standing around them or walking too or fro anywhere about.

It appeared there were many people just lying all about around the grounds asleep or dead whatever the circumstance might have been at the time? The strangest thing of all was the absence of the many bustling people moving in and about the city itself. There had always been countless people in and around the city of Sydney in the past always looking busy this time of day.

The eye in the sky telescope showed the once busy city idle, just like the many cars and trucks on its highways, without anyone moving around in it at all. It was as if a tsunami of poisonous gasses had flowed over the land, and taken all life away from the city and the surrounding countryside with it.

To look down and not see anyone, not a single person moving around was unbelievable. It looked as if life on Earth was over with for its inhabitants, and the commander of the space station not wanting to tell anyone aboard what he thought.

Commander Ivan moved the huge telescoping arm to get a better look around the city and countryside. He was able to identify other significant sightings of what looked to be impact crash locations. He thought from their appearances they may have possibly been other aircraft that had fallen straight out from the sky and crashed.

There was not a single solitary aircraft flying anywhere in the skies over the land, or sea, not even a single helicopter which really made him think something very strange was taking place below.

The awesome impact of the many missiles exploding over Sydney must have had a most devastating effect on all life, he thought briefly to himself. The speedy orbit of the space station quickly carried the space station out over the ocean, and away from the city.

Out over the ocean Commander Ivan observed a lonely single three-mast sailboat heading toward the port of Sydney under full sails. In the harbor of Sydney, he had observed several merchant ships along with a few pleasure craft all moored up wresting against the dock, while there were others scattered about the harbor bobbing up and down on the

waters along its shorelines. A few of the ships and pleasure crafts along the shoreline of Australia were on their sides or floating freely in the waves and currents of the sea. Something very strange was taking place below. Something very wrong had occurred to the world below, and it wasn't anything he was going to discuss with anyone onboard the space station yet, not until he had a chance to see what was going on, on the other side of the world later on that day.

The space station passed from the light side of the Earth around to its dark side. The millions of flickering night lights around the big cities and many small towns around the globe were silent, and not lit up to take away the darkness. Not one flicker of a single lamp could be seen anywhere below lighting up the tall buildings now in total darkness.

The space crews could see absolutely nothing but the pitch black of night, except for an occasional campfire ablaze, lit by someone living in the backcountry to keep he, or she warm and to cook their meals upon the commander assumed.

It turned out to be an overpoweringly ghastly sight in dismay for everyone who looked down through the telescope.

To observe their world below, that once shown bright with its many bright lights glittering up the darkness of night showing off big city after big city, and small town, after small town. The once brilliant lights of the night on earth were now down to just a few measly scattered campers' fires, flaming aglow in the darkness, separated by miles away from each other.

The sudden instant effects the neutron bombs had on earth, did not affect anything above the earth's Ionosphere, for the vast cavity, the void of space protected the crews of the Twitchel, along with the crew of the International Space Station. The void they were in protected them from experiencing any of the ill-fated effects the invasive neutrons had had on the planet Earth at the time of the explosion.

The once pure aqua blue atmosphere surrounding the earth with its clean clear looking color of purity, now looked more a dirty rusty wishy-washy looking brownish aqua blue, than the purity it once shown.

Dumbfounded, the stranded astronauts did not quite know what to think about what they were observing below. Everything aboard the space station seemed to be working quite well, but the earth below seemed to be a powerless space ball floating helplessly in space without electricity to bring its dark nights back aglow. There were no signs of streetlights, neon signs, or sporting arena lights of any kind, that once lit up the dark night skies to be found anywhere around the globe. The lack of electricity on earth was the strangest of all occurrences to them, so they thought.

One would think there should be at least one single bright shining streetlight somewhere around the earth, on at least one of the many continents, but there was not even one single aglow of an electric bulb anywhere below that they could see. What could have been so drastic to eliminate all the electricity-producing qualities of the earth? The thought of it behooved those trapped in space. None could imagine such a thing'

The space travelers were amiss, thinking and hoping the world would be as it had always been before when the orange mist dissipated, but it was not. They continued observing the newly changed Earth, while they passed innocently overhead, everyone knowing the Earth they once knew as home, had gone through a living hell of an immense disaster.

Their planet had gone from being a bright pretty aqua soothing blue colored ball in space to a now brownish looking worthless dirty sheen ridden ball of light dirty orange and a poor blue in color.

The astronauts wondered if planet Earth had lost all of its life supporting systems of oxygen producing life of plants as well, at the time of the explosion below the cloud cover. They also wondered if anyone below the orange sheen could survive the deadly looking gasses it looked to produce when the blast occur if all were dead or possibly some had survived.

Passing above continent after continent as the time of day changed around the world, they could see the world had gone through a hellish nightmare. There definitely were fewer living humans, animals, or foul of the air living on earth or flying in its skies than there had been before the great catastrophe took place.

There were thousands upon thousands of idle cars, trucks, planes, and trains sitting motionlessly dead idle where they must have been when the big bang happened.

In every country they were able to look down into, they could see commercial aircraft crash scenes scattered everywhere around the global airports of the world.

In cities, towns, and rural suburbia alike, they could see the dead bodies of men, women, children, animals, and foul of the air scattered about the countryside, littering the ground like dead locus after a heavy frost. Every country the space station passed overhead had been affected one way or another from the big blast that had changed the world they once knew forever. They witnessed some people moving around, and it brought to them a little ray of hope.

CHAPTER TWENTY-TWO

The Gruesome Sight

The efforts by the ones left alive below, were busy covering and burying up the many dead bodies of humans and creatures scattered around the open land. The stench of death on earth must have been truly great on the select few doing this type of gruesome work trying to protect the world from an outbreak of disease the world had never seen before caused by so many decaying carcasses of animals, and creatures of the once thriving animal kingdom around planet Earth.

It became even more than strange to the space capsule crew no one from planet Earth had tried to reach them in the last few weeks. Everything still looked intact around the many compounds of space-agency observatories all around the globe the eye in the sky could see from the telescopes operator's position in the space station. Kazakhstan rocket facilities in Russia looked secure with a space rocket on its launching pad looking ready for flight, with no one moving around the grounds at the site.

It was different at Cape Canaveral in Florida, where there were many people busily moving around the facilities. Still, there was no communications from them to their NASA friends in space. It was as if everyone down below had forgotten all about the ones lost in space floating around helplessly, not knowing what to do next.

They did, however, observe a very limited number of vehicles starting to move to, and fro over the roadways around the earth, after several long weeks of observing none moving around at all. These few vehicles moving on the many deserted highways were a limited number in freight trucks and cars, and a tractor or two busy out in some farmer's fields.

It seemed very strange seeing so few vehicles in motion around the globe, with so many more of them all sitting idle where they initially stopped, dotting the roadways around the Earth as litter thrown away.

Strange things were taking shape on Earth no one onboard the space station could fathom in one's mind what it was, especially way out there without any transmitted information from below broadcast to them in order to make any sense out of what was really taking place on the planet.

Weeks living in space seemed to pass ever so slowly for most all astronauts held captive there by their own desire to stay alive and live until whenever they could or could not return back home.

The two Germans and the many Russian crew of the space station with the crew of the U. S. Twitchel had no place pressing to go too. Most all the astronauts were there of their own free will and accord. Willing to go there when each volunteered for the space duty presented them for their new assignment aboard the space station, except for the Americans. The American astronauts were the ones trapped in space as prisoners not of their own free will and accord for the next year or more, whether they wanted to be or not. If things did not improve below, they may find themselves never able to returns back home, and become a space casualty caused by the neutron mishap along with everyone else. If things below did not improve or radio contact reconnected to the ones in charge of their recovery, they might be doomed anyway.

The situation on the space station was somber least for the ones who thought about home all the while. Everyone onboard the space station knew the day of reckoning would probably come sooner than later and much sooner than they all wanted it to come. When the end of life might come to them aboard the Space station when their precious food and other supplies would run out for them.

The long passing days on the space station, turned into weeks, and they into months, as time passed ever so slowly for the crews of astronauts. The six-member crew from the Twitchel, pitched in to help do whatever they could do in helping the Soviet Cosmonauts, and two Germans aboard the space station in completing their assigned responsibilities, in setting up their many experiments into completion.

The space travelers aboard the space station all took turns in keeping a watchful eye on the inhabitants of the earth below. Many keeping a constant vigil with earphones attached to ones ear in hopes of possibly hearing the tiniest on radio voices sending out a message to them. Hoping some caring individual back home on earth might really try to contact them, but no sound of anything ever came to them. It mostly worried everyone for there were no music stations playing anywhere on any frequency playing songs any more that they use to like to listen to, to make the time aboard the laboratory pass more smoothly, and wake them up in the morning to cheerful sounds. Now everything was deaf-still to the eardrums except for their own conversations of what might be happening down below on Earth.

CHAPTER TWENTY-THREE

Eyes toward the Heavens

Many a caring inhabitant left alive on earth, sat out at night on their front piazzas around their homes with eyes glued towards the heavens above.

Some were hopefully looking and watching for the brightness from the bright beacons shining above them from the still electrified space station with its many bright blinking lights to pass overhead in the southern most skies of the United States.

Lieutenant Ann's family looked night after night for a glimpse of the space station to pass overhead along with the many smaller satellites aloft giving off any electrical illumination at all.

Stargazing youngsters and oldsters alike daydreaming nightly, wishing they had been among the fortunate lucky ones privileged to having been living aboard the space station in space when all hell broke loose on Planet Earth below.

If only the movie Star Trek was a true to life adventure. Then Dr. Spock and his faithful crew aboard the Enterprise would be able to come to the rescue of the citizens living on planet Earth now, and all would become well and better off for everyone. They would be able to right the many wrongs the greedy dead Russian leaders had caused to happen and repair the Earth back to normalcy.

CHAPTER TWENTY-FOUR

A Prayer for a Daughter, a Mother, a Wife

There was one particular family living in upstate Vermont who had great concerns for one of the many astronauts living aboard the space station they hoped with all their heart.

Her husband Ben, her two children Sarah and Amber, along with her mother and father, praying his wife, their mother, and their daughter was safe and well living onboard the International Space Station above them in space.

They all prayed for her nightly and for the others up there as well that they would not be lost forever in space drifting around the planet dead, and entombed forever in a crippled space shuttle having been doomed to a horrid fate of death, as so many others on earth had become victim to. A misfortune caused by selfish power seeking fools who themselves had destroyed each other and their own families in their quest for greed, wealth, and power.

Over time and months, more vehicles began to appear on the many roadways below. They began moving one here and there over the vast highways around earth. The abandoned cars, busses, and trucks sitting abandoned aside the roadways were being pushed aside to make room for the few trucks, busses, and cars that were starting to frequent the roadways more often. Time looked to be marching slowly forward for the ones below. Everything on Earth looked to be getting back to normalcy, more now than before at the onset of the unfortunate mishap. Whatever normalcy was now?

CHAPTER TWENTY-FIVE

Decaying Death March

With shovels in hand, along with picks, hoes and whatever else one might find for useful tools for digging. People in large groups around the world started burying the countless hundreds and thousands of dead bodies of people and their dead slaughtered animals lying dead all over the earth, along with the millions in dead carcasses of the thousands of many different species in wild animals and birds alike. Some very lucky individuals were able to use backhoes and bulldozers to do their sickly jobs more quickly.

Only a certain few strong willed individuals aboard the space station had strong enough stomachs to withstand the surveillance of the ones burying so many unsightly individuals using the eye in the sky telescope to watch, and see this unnecessary necessity, taking place below. Commander Anderson having a strong stomach, witnessed many bloated, some exploded bodies of men, woman, and children from the fermentation of their innards sticking of them, and sick looking carcasses of animals alike spewing out their guts from the hot sun of the day, in different location they were found around the globe.

It appeared there was more damage done in some countries more than in others. Australia and Russia looked to have taken the brunt of the many missile blasts, while other countries around the planet had some direct hits of the neutron bombs in scattered places near cities, and larger towns, but not so out in the countryside. Most backland in

high places around the planet paid the price of the many wild neutrons spreading out over the land causing death to many creatures and simplicity to some minds leaving adult humans and animals like with the thinking ability of a three or four-year-old child.

CHAPTER TWENTY-SIX

The Light of Night

Streetlights around the planet began to appear below in the dark of night illuminating a few dark streets and alleyways in cities and towns around the globe. A number of vehicles began appearing on roadways at night, running around with headlamps affixed to them, shinning bright as they drove along the roadways as they had before. The astronauts above thought it a wonderful thing the world was getting back to normal as they gazed down from their captive prison in space. Everything was more as it was before, getting back to normalcy once again, until they zoomed in with their high-powered telescope onto one of the vehicles headlamps on a vehicle moving along a dark roadway in the night.

They observed the vehicles headlamps were not an electrically operated headlamp at all. They were both kerosene oil fired style lanterns taken out of retirement from years past, with reflective mirrored crystals affixed to them for better illumination of the roadways in front of the vehicles for night travel. Many of the new streetlights around the world were the old style oil wicker burning lamps or piped in gas-fired lanterns illuminating a vast amount of buildings and streets below. The old ways of illuminating the night appeared to be coming back improving the quality of life below, but was it really getting better for its inhabitants. Were all these new improvements a necessity in the times at hand, for electricity looked to be a pleasure from their past.

The many crewmembers aboard the space station began to wonder what had happened to all the electrical producing power-generating plants around the earth. The Hoover Dam along with all the other power-producing damns around the world were still left intact, but there seemed to be no power being produced from any of them.

It behooved the ones in space why none of the generating plants on earth were incapable of producing the lifeline of electricity the people on earth had become so accustomed and dependent on.

Were all these people who knew anything about electricity or how to produce its great power by using these huge generating power plants all killed in the initial big bang, or were the power producing generating plants all internally destroyed somehow by the initial blast?

The situation in darkness surrounding the globe behooved the people of the earth even more than it did the ones who were living in outer space. The electrical engineers of huge power plants had no power even when the generators they were tending too were turning at their fullest high speeds.

The unfortunate thing about all these generating plants around earth was, when someone attempted firing up any water turbine never or used to generate electricity, a huge electrical absorbing force in an orange sheen would appear.

The devil in the sky "the creature" as it had become known would come shooting out of the air from nowhere and snuff out the lives of those whoever they were who were attempting to produce the forbidden force of electrical power the monster above hated.

For some strange reason, a sudden surge of electrical power would summons large numbers of wild powerful neutrons from out of nowhere, and cause the sudden neutralization of all electrical impulses around the area, including the small electrically generated impulses of the human brain and nervous system.

The earth's population began calling this opposing force of electrical power in the air and sky above "THE THING, THE EVIL NEUTRON CREATURE FROM OUT OF THE AIR AND ABOVE".

It became ever more frightening to the cosmonauts and astronauts living onboard the space station as to what was really occurring on their homeland sphere below. The world they once knew had drastically changed for them all in only a matter of seconds that dreadful day almost a year ago now.

CHAPTER TWENTY-SEVEN

A Long Hard Year

There had been no radio communications from their homeland or from anyone on Earth for almost an entire year now. The life supporting supplies stored in the space station lockers was quickly being used up and dwindling away because of the extra load of six extra mouths to feed from having the Twitchel's crew aboard using up the limited oxygen supply everyone was so quickly using up in record numbers as time quickly passed away.

Every experiment onboard for producing different varieties in foods and ways in producing oxygen had been very successful, while everything was being over taxed daily having so many participants taking advantage of its limited usefulness, and soon the extra consumption of everything aboard the space station would put everyone onboard in jeopardy of extinction.

The two commanders, Commander Colonel Nelson Anderson from the Twitchel, and Commander Colonel Ivan Khrushchev from the International Space Station having seen so many once very active herds in cattle all dead, destroyed out in open fields on the earth below, along with the farmers who owned them lying dead beside them.

Witnessing the many dead bodies around the planet laying exposed to the elements of Mother Nature's wicked force everywhere upon the face of the earth this last year didn't want to see the same thing happen to their supportive crews aboard the space station. Especially the ones who had so unselfishly risked their own lives in helping Commander Anderson's crew in need of nurturing them to stay alive for the last slow long tedious year. They did not want the space station to become like the so many small cities and towns below they had sadly observed from above gone by the wayside.

Desolate little dead ghost towns, with many dead bodies of people and animals still scattered everywhere around, after a year of exposure to the elements of Mother Nature with only their skeletal remains still lying out on the ground. Slain and annihilated by the multitude of neutrons where they stood, when the many rockets in the air exploded with the push of a single button.

The cumulative poor circumstances of life on earth below lie beyond the scope of human imagination. It all seemed worse than going to a theater to watch a good horror movie one could not forget after leaving the theater. This was a true to life show, as it all unveiled right in front of a live audience who took turns watching the deteriorating earth through the eye in the sky telescope, watching the Earth in real live action. Everything happening on earth was real, and not a make believe screen set. The many distasteful scenes below, they were not able to wash away and out their minds with a good night's sleep, for it would be there again as they reawaked in the morning.

The situation aboard the space station was slowly becoming a very critical one, as the two commanders discussed in private conversation away from their people not to upset the two crews what the next best thing would be for them all to do. The several extra mouths onboard the space station to feed was dwindling down the reserve oxygen and food supply to a very critical point, and it wouldn't last but a mere three or four more months more for everyone the way things were being depleted so rapidly.

The situation onboard did not look too favorable for anyone, even if nothing bad was to happen to his or her new experiment of food plants that seemed to be doing a fine job of supplying everything, but minimally.

It was not keeping up with the high demand placed on the space stations source with its life supporting supplies capabilities. Drastic steps had to be forthcoming straightaway. A critical decision had to made sooner than later in order to save the crew aboard the space station from starvation and suffocation, along with the crew of the Twitchel.

Commander of the Twitchel, Commander Colonel Nelson Anderson gave a direct order to the shuttle's crew. "Pack it up ladies and gentlemen. We are to prepare our ship the Twitchel for our return trip back home to earth. Whatever and wherever that might be," he added.

It was time to take their very, very, very slim chances against this evil demon they were to face back on earth in and around its deadly skies above.

They were going to meet this evil demon head to head and face it when they reentered the earth's troubled atmosphere, and may God help them all when they do!

There had not been a single sighting of any type of airplane or other form of aircraft flying in the skies around the earth below, that they were able to observe over the last year. There had been a group of Canadian geese they watched migrate back north after a long winters stay in the south. There were other birds, not many, flying in the skies these days as well, and one of the observers on the telescope said she had seen a single hot air balloonist on one occasion drifting along over Earth. She could not tell if the pilot was still alive or dead because of the attitude of the telescopes ability to twist and turn, but the balloon looked to be under good control all the while she had the opportunity to watch it ascend up into the sky above the ground.

Commander Anderson's only hope for his crew of the Twitchel was that whatever it had been that had stopped so many vehicles on the ground and prevented all the airplanes in the sky from flying in its heavens, wouldn't be able to stop he and his crew from safely returning home in the Twitchel back to Earth.

He hoped to land their big bird safely back down at the Florida landing site from where they had first taken flight from. They all knew the high risks in whatever had happened to the other aircraft in the sky that terrible day just might happen to them, or they could all stay up in the space station and die a slow suffering death along with everyone else.

After lengthy discussions of openly discussing their slim chances in space, talking it over for the last several days, they all came to the same final agreement and conclusion that it was time to take their chances, and try for a safe trip back home to earth. They would at least all be back home on Earth one way or another. This way they stood a slight chance of a burial in separate graves by their loved ones, if not all buried together in one large crater made by their bird should the shuttle go straight into the ground without them able to land as the many other aircraft seemed to have done that horrific day.

It would be one hell of a rush going into the ground at that fast a rate of speed, and the haste of death would come so fast to them not a one onboard would ever experience the pain of it.

The almost fifty Soviet cosmonauts with the two German astronauts, and the several American astronauts, had all become very close friends during their year-long stint of living together in outer space, aboard the International Space Station.

Had it been by sheer coincidence, or was it purposely done by the would be world leaders of Russia, that the International Space Station at that precise time of the disaster was to be manned by so many Soviet cosmonauts and had added the two German astronauts to satisfy NASA for the time being. A few cosmonauts were now going on their second year aboard the International Space Station. Trapped and isolated in outer space ever since their replacements were not able to be sent up, they were not able to return back home to Earth to their loved ones without a replacement team's vehicle for their transportation safely back to Earth. Now their future still looked very bleak for them all.

CHAPTER TWENTY-EIGHT

Preparing the Twitchel for Flight

For the following next two weeks, the crew of the Shuttle Twitchel crawled inside her fuselage, out over her tiles, and below her outer skin, checking for any damaged heat shielding tiles. The crew checked her inner fuselage for any loose wiring in her electrical harnesses, and practiced to preflight her daily to the best of their abilities in her cockpit for not having flown her in over an entire year or better. They checked out her manually hand and foot operated hydraulics equipment in order to fly her, and safely land her should her electrical system fail them on her reentry back into the Earth's atmosphere.

Commander Anderson did not want to leave a single square inch of his majestic bird unchecked in these last several days of continual checking and rechecking her stability, and flying abilities. He knew if her onboard computers failed them when they reentered the earth's atmosphere as he suspected they most likely would, along with the backup computers. He wanted to be able to control the flight path of the shuttle manually, by using the heavy hands on means and strong feet operation by using brute leg strength and force on her rudder and braking controls.

He had little faith in their decision to return, but it was time to deal with the downward life situation aboard the space station, in its life and death circumstances that was staring them all in the face.

The Twitchel crew would have to muster up an extra amount in pure adrenalin strength during reentry in order for them to activate the manual hydraulic controls of the shuttle.

Now in their weakened state of muscle after living in space without the benefit of having gravity pull constantly down on them to keep their body's muscles properly toned. The extended period in space had weakened them extensively even after keeping a regimented schedule in an exercising program in the space station's gym during their long stay.

What would be their chances of landing the Twitchel without her electrical back up computer system working, and in place? Not a very good one, if none at all, and they all knew it.

They double checked all of her hydraulic override equipment twice, and then sometimes three times, just to make sure it all worked properly, for if it didn't work, they just might as well blast off into the far depths of outer space, and die. Some of the crew second-guessed themselves, not once, but twice and three times as did the others of the crew just to make sure their craft was safe, and ready.

The crew of the Twitchel pulled at all of her many levers to see just how easy they would be to operate, or not operate, and at that time, they all operated quite easily. The only exception to their ease of operation was that they were under no strain or outside pressure of gravity or wind resistance on them, as the Twitchel sat motionlessly attached to the mooring of the space station. When the shuttle reentered the earth's atmosphere, things would become much different when the true test would come in light of her ease, or not so ease of her operation, and the fluidness of her controls against the Earths atmospherics outside forces of gravity and air against her could cause great difficulty.

According to their solar-powered clock and calendar onboard the space station during their stay in space, they would be reentering the earth's atmosphere at approximately 0900 hours on Friday the thirteenth of May. What a day to try to land their craft they laughed. The shuttle crew might just as well crash and burn in hell on that day. As any other day of the month, reaffirming suspicions believers in the world, that Friday the thirteenth day of May or any other thirteenth day of the month of any year as a forbidden day to do anything that was important, for it was sure to become a failure.

The Twitchel were all for setting sail into the dark unknown events on that day. Why not the Thirteenth day of May they bolstered in cheerful unison? They had been away from their loved ones too darn long, and enough time away was now long enough. It was time to try their chances at returning backs home to their loved ones waiting patiently back home for them they hoped. They all prayed to God silently for a safe return home.

In general, when people separate from each other for long periods of time strange things happen to their relationships. The Twitchel's navigator, Lieutenant Ann Mitchell, was extremely happy, maybe overly excited, about at least attempting a return trip back home, and to be reunited with her two children, her husband, her mother and her aging father at their home where they all lived in upstate Vermont.

Her daughter Sarah was only 15 months old when she ventured out on this supposedly short mission of retrieval which was supposed to last only a couple of days or more away, and had now turned into a year-long struggle of survival of her wits and soul searching madness. Amber had been three at the time, and now they were both a whole year plus days older.

Ann wondered if her two beautiful, wonderful precious children would still remember their mommy when and if she returns back home to them, or if any of them were still alive to go back home to after the catastrophe which took place on the planet.

The other crew members of the Twitchel also had wives and children waiting for them back home as well, or at least they all hoped and prayed the same as Ann, that they, too, were all still alive and doing well. Without any radio contact for over a year, there was little any of them knew about the earth back home except for what they all could see through the telescopic eye in the sky.

They never drifted or flew over upstate Vermont close enough, so Ann never had the opportunity to look down and see if her husband, her children, or her mother and father were alive out in the fields of their Vermont farm with their cattle and crops.

If anything was to happen to her on this mission, her husband, Ben, had promised to take himself, along with their two children and her mother and father's farm in upstate Vermont to live and grow up. She wanted her children to experience the tranquility and atmosphere provided them that she had experienced in growing up in Lunenburg, Vermont.

CHAPTER TWENTY-NINE

Returning Home

0400 HOURS A.M. as planned, the Twitchel's crew released the docking security blocking mechanism with a flick of a hand switch on their computer. Their bird was free from her once secured birthing platform firmly attached to the space station's docking platform, and was now drifting slowly backwards out and away from the huge space station's laboratory air lock docking station.

There had been many, many friendly loving hugs and kisses given each other prior to the sad departure by the two very caring crews of the space station, along with the very nervous crew of the Twitchel. There were many true tears of sadness flowing, along with the overall concern for safety exchanged by the parting friends. There was no bitterness shown between the different nations living aboard the space station between its occupants. They were true friends brought together by a most unpleasant tragedy, then bound together by an everlasting friendship only one could share with others of a close family such as siblings.

A decision had long been decided prior the Twitchel departing, that if the Twitchel's crew made it safely back to Earth and were able to land at Cape Canaveral, the few lucky candidates who were able to, and had been chosen after all the food and oxygen were to run out aboard the space-station, would then land their Soviet-made landing space capsule at the spaces programs central headquarters in Florida if at all possible.

It was a very sad goodbye when the airlocks between the two space-vessels was securely sealed shut, as everyone in space mused over the fact they might not never see one another ever again. The space station maintained a constant radio frequency open with the Twitchel until the spacecraft broke through the earth's outer ionosphere and down into the Earth's atmosphere. Soon as the Twitchel passed down into the Earth's atmosphere, everything on that channel turned to instant static, as had all frequencies when any spacecraft went through the dead zone on reentry.

It was the same static coming in over the radio, just like when the space station tried talking to anyone on earth over the last year. The view from the space station's watchful telescope watching the Twitchel returning to earth was like sitting down in the front row seat of a movie theater watching a picture show.

The crew aboard the space station lowered the high power telescopes strength to minimal power. Then transferred its camera's image to the many smaller television monitors positioned throughout the different cubicles within the space station, so the entire crew might keep in constant visual contact with their friends aboard the Twitchel. Everyone aboard the space station was concerned for the ship as the craft and its crew made their daring decent back toward Earth.

The Twitchel's reentry back through into the earth's atmosphere was a picture perfect reentry, according to the television monitors positioned within the space station. A white streak followed the Twitchel's tail section as the ceramic protective heat shielding tiles became red-hot absorbing the heat of friction caused by the atmosphere during reentry. Suddenly, as the space station crew all watched on their monitors, disaster struck the Twitchel.

It began to wildly shimmy and shake, and then it tumbled through the air a couple of hard times it looked on the several monitors they were all watching. The crew aboard the space station thought for sure the day, Friday the thirteenth was as evil day for the crew of the Twitchel as it was religiously held in belief by many self-proclaimed witches worldwide.

As the shuttle parted away the docking platform drifting away from the space station, the Twitchel's crew seemed very nervous and anxious, and extremely happy all at the same time. Lieutenant Ann Mitchell with very high hopes in seeing her precious family once again, but with tight reservation imbedded deep down in the pit of her stomach and mind. She thought about what might be waiting for her upon her return home to Earth, were both happy and sad times to be-had by all.

The other crewmembers in the Twitchel had their own dreams in seeing their loved ones, once again. Everyone aboard the Twitchel knew it would be a slim not fat chance, a snowball's chance in hell of not melting if they were to all make it all the way back home safely to earth in one piece. Everyone felt his or her chances in making a clean reentry back into the earth's atmosphere was slim to nil to nothing, and felt sure they would meet their maker soon.

It would be almost impossible to maneuver their big bird during reentry handling the heavy weight of her, or to control her in a level path of flight, should she lose her computerized flight navigating control systems on their reentry into the earth's atmosphere.

Five long hours quickly passed for the crew of the Twitchel, as the crew aboard the craft fired her retro rockets to slow their craft down and position it into a reentry flight mode for their safe reentry into the Earth's atmosphere without burning up their ship. Both computers, both the main and auxiliary computers, were gone over twice and checked again and then triple checked for their proper operation.

Their course and latitudes checked as were the manually operated hydraulic levers for their flight control. Everyone knowing very well when the computers went down, if they did, they would be going down as well, hoping they would be able to maintain control over the Twitchel, and not literally be going down to their doom in a blazing flame of glory. Everything checked out in perfect optimal operating conditions.

The Commander hoped his crew would be in a strong and operable condition to control the beast when that special time came. The time had come to switch on the reentry booster rockets manually they

thought for their safe reentry into the earth's atmosphere, and did not let the onboard computers do their designed job.

With the computers sitting idle, they were flying by the seats of their pants, a smart way to handle their attempt at making a safe landing back on Earth, the commander hoped anyway

"Fire the boosters." The command was given by Commander Anderson as the booster rockets came to life thrusting the Twitchel from the outer most limits of the Ionospheres, and down into and through the atmosphere's most outer skin.

Down through the broken up Ozone layer and into the unstable saturated neutron atmosphere surrounding the earth. Suddenly all hell broke loose with the Twitchel, with everything all happening at once. Commander Colonel Anderson had just switched the electrical power of the shuttles main power to the off position, as the Twitchel reentered the earth's atmosphere and the craft began to shimmy and shake. They should have waited a few more seconds, and let the onboard computers do their designed jobs, but he did not wait long enough in not wanting to find out why the earth had no power, and become another statistic of the devil creature that lurked in and around the world's atmosphere at the time.

The g-force exerted upon the crew inside the Twitchel became intolerable for the crew as they tumbled once, then twice and then a third time, twisting in their craft in the air over the earth.

All happy thoughts about reuniting with their loved ones, friends, and families suddenly vanished, turning happy thoughts to timid despair instantly. All knew the worst was yet to come in their frantic situation, as bodies and minds lay hard pressed in their seats, their flab and muscles beneath their outer skin stretched. Everyone's flesh trying hard to dislodge itself from the skeletal frames so lightly attached, and slip away from them disintegrating within their own flight suits.

Everyone aboard the Twitchel was about to pass out from the extreme G-force being exerted upon the men, and Ann in their troubled moment of tumbling. Living in outer space for over a year long without the benefit of gravity had weakened them all extensively.

Colonel Anderson reached forward with all of the built up might he had left in his weakening body and hit the switch to the main computers back on. It was a long shot. A shot in the dark, but the only hope they had for the moment, and it worked.

Miraculously the main computer came instantly back to life sensing the problem immediately, and fired off two recovery retro rockets, enabling the Twitchel to place herself back into a new thirty-degree controlled pitched descending dive, downwards towards the landing site many miles below.

Colonel Anderson placed his two hands firmly onto the main controls and flew along with the autopilot being controlled by the computer to get the feel of flying the shuttle once again as his head spun round, and round in circles from being spun like a top in his seat.

The computer opened the forward shields covering the shuttles windshield, and slid them back out of the way along the two hand rods connected to the slides along the top panel of the controls.

The Florida panhandle first came into view as they made their turn towards their landing site.

The crew hollered out in joyous revelation. The crew all sickened from their horrendous experience a short few minuets' or hours past. They did not care for they were with great joy in their hearts for not crashing. They tried their radios to contact the Kennedy command center without any response from them.

Oh, there was a response all right! The thing in the atmosphere, the neutralizing creature made up of massive neutrons followed the radio signaling beacons radio waves up from the ground or wherever it suddenly came from out of nowhere to the spacecraft, engulfing the Twitchel in a bright orange sheen of green, orange and dark brown making everything inside the Twitchel black.

The eye in the sky aboard the space station lost visual contact with the Twitchel behind a cloud for a couple of split seconds they thought as the neutron creature living in the earth's atmosphere engulfed the Twitchel.

It instantly absorbed every positively charged electron out of all the active electrolytes from the hearts of its main control battery banks and wind generating electrical banks. It rendered the electrical controls aboard the Twitchel useless.

The Twitchel was a dead bird gliding through the sky over the Earth without any electronics onboard to help her fly, except for her manually operable abilities to control her flight hydraulically, and a wind operated pressurized speed control affixed to her control panel as an indicator.

The Twitchel's navigator, Lieutenant Ann Mitchell, tried in vain to arouse someone on the ground who might hear her desperate calls for help. She was hoping someone from the landing site might hear her, but to no avail. All she could do now was to hope someone had heard their plight in the MAYDAY message sent before they lost their power. They were about to land their bird hard, and needed help if by chance they crash landed. Not knowingly so, the many many repeated messages she tried to broadcast during their landing fell upon deaf ears.

Colonel Anderson tried switching from the main controlled power banks to the backup auxiliary power systems soon as the main system went dead, but the auxiliary system was as dead and drained as the main power packs were. He had suspected it would be right from the beginning.

They definitely did not have any electronics on board the Twitchel to fly her on any longer. It would now be up to the crewmembers to bring their ailing craft down to a safe landing manually, if it were at all possible to do so.

Colonel Anderson had been holding firm the controls of the Twitchel with both his hands this time, should a sudden loss in power were to happen again, and it did.

He hollered out to his crewmembers. "Harry, you, Bill, and Dave get down in the damn aft hold and forward wheel well hold compartments. Start cranking the hell out those damned landing gears. Get them down right now. Ann! You stand by the hatch and let me know when they are down there and in position to act. We have only but one shot at this landing so the damn landing gears had better be working for us or we are doomed to end up out in the drink and damn well drown."

Colonel Anderson didn't want to set the landing gear down to early, not until the final minute, or seconds prior landing in fear the drag of air exerted upon the aircraft caused by the landing gear might act more like air brakes and could slow them down too drastically slow and make them fall short of the intended runway.

It seemed like an hour had slowly passed by to the men in the hole of the Twitchel when the order from Commander Anderson came down to crank down hard on the landing gears. "Lower the landing gears, NOW!" Ann yelled out to the men down below in the Twitchel's lower fuselage. "Lower the gears NOW, guys." The three men in the Twitchel's belly positioned themselves one each at a set of landing gear wheel cranks and began cranking their hearts out on the three sets of landing gear gearboxes.

The three crewmembers had never worked this hard ever, never in their entire lives together as team members, it seemed. Their weakened bodies produced extreme pain in them as they cranked and cranked, and cranked until they felt such pain in their arms they did not want to crank another turn on the shaft they were turning, but they did.

The three men knew if the landing gears and wheels were not all the way down, and locked into position when it came time to land the Twitchel, they would be the ones at fault, the ones who blew the mission in returning safely back home to Earth.

Therefore, they continued to crank with cramped hands and arms until they could crank no more, and then cranked some more and some more.

Slowly the landing gears emerged from out the underbelly beneath the Twitchel, until all the landing gear looked fully extended downward and all three locked into their landing positions.

"Are they down yet, Ann?" Colonial Anderson was getting jittery for he was having a hard time keeping the big bird aloft and flying level in their rapid descending approach toward the long runway below.

It was taking more his strength and effort than he had ever thought possible or imagined it would take to fly this big hunk, this hulk of steel in the air. "Damn it guy's. I need those wheels down now! She is coming in real fast men, too damn fast. Strap yourselves in men.

Steve, give me some flaps right now, but slowly." The Twitchel fought Colonel Anderson hard when he had her winged flaps extended out by Steve. The flaps slid down into position holding back a solid mass in air beneath her belly from her long sweeping wings accumulating a cushion in mixed air below her, accompanying the frictional drag in air extended out from the landing gear producing a slower air speed for his craft.

"Steve, get ready to help me with these damn brakes. I don't think I can handle them all by myself. I don't have enough strength left. I just do not have it in me anymore.

Lieutenant Mitchell, get ready to deplore the drag chute cable. I think we should give ourselves a quick silent prayer people. We need all the damn help we can muster up right now. What do you think people? Doesn't that old runway look beautiful?"

"I can't ever remember being this happy, to have ever seen a runway that looked this beautiful before, Colonel." "We are not home safe yet Steve! There is a whole hell of a lot of ocean out ahead us there should we miss this damn landing.

I do not see any type of emergency vessels lining the runway to help us if we miss this landing.

You aren't scared, are you, Major?"

"Yes, your damn right tooting I am scared, Colonel! I am half scared to death, and if we make it back home alive in one piece, I am never going to step another foot in any kind of flying machine never ever again! I have had it with all these flying gigs. I do not know about the rest of you people, but I saw my whole life flash away right in front of me up there.

It was kind of like a rapid slow motion picture clip, frame by frame of my whole life, just like a movie of my life up there on that damn reentry. As far as I am concerned, and I am sure, I am not all alone in this. No more missions for this lucky kid, and I do feel lucky, a little bit anyway!"

"Brace your selves gentleman, and you too Ann! Here she comes! She is coming up quickly people. A little more flaps, Steve, a little more flaps. Give all the flaps. Give all the flaps right now Steve! It's going to be a hard one!"

Colonel Anderson pulled back as hard and as firmly he could on the flight control gears in his hands with all the strength he could muster up with his cold frigid hands and weakened arms to set the Twitchel down on the runway.

He was trying to make it as soft a landing he possibly could without the help of the onboard computers. The Twitchel came in soft as could be without any calamity in her landing at all.

Ok, Steve, give her some soft braking with me. Lieutenant Mitchell, let go of the braking drag chutes, Lieutenant. A little more brake tension Steve, a little more. Damn it guys, we sure are good, aren't we? Home, sweet home, good old terra-firma", Colonel Anderson yelled out screaming at the top of his voice, as they joyfully rolled down the runway.

The Twitchel came to a slow rolling stop, out on the tarmac. Close to the far end of the longest Kennedy runway. Soon as they stopped, Ann broke down and cried uncontrollably.

She began her blubbering while still sitting in her station, she was so damn relieved and happy to be back home again on earth.

She got the rest of the crew joyfully crying right along with her as well, with their eyes filling up with happy joyful tears of bliss running down everyone's cheeks.

Bill jumped down to the ground from the last rung on the dropped down emergency-chained escape ladder, and kissed the good old terra-firma tarmac of the paved runway, and surface of good old Mother Earth beneath his feet.

He yelled out with joy in his heart. "I am not ever going to leave you ever again baby! I am not ever go to leave you again!"

He yelled out at the top of his lungs joyfully, so loud everyone for miles around, if there were anyone, could have heard him loud and clear proclaim to the world he would never fly again, no matter what the circumstance might be, for he was done with it for good.

CHAPTER THIRTY

Did They or Didn't They

The crew aboard the space station wouldn't know for several days if their friends aboard the Twitchel ever made it back home alive, or not?

They watched from above as the Twitchel broke through the earth's atmosphere, and began to tumble out of control. Then they saw their friends regain control over their Starship, just prior the speedy orbit the space station was in that took them out of range of visual contact out over the ocean.

None of the two crafts tried talking to one another after the Twitchel broke radio contact going through the dead zone of the atmosphere to see if everything was going to be all right, for if they had the neutron mass would have struck all that much sooner seeking out the source of the radio signal.

Every crewmember aboard the space station were too busy, being half scared to death for themselves, and for the safety of their friends descending back towards the Earth, not wanting to bother them in this critical time they were going through. They knew their friends were in serious trouble for that split second, and all they could do was sit back, watch, pray, and wait holding their breaths until the Twitchel righted herself again in flight.

The peninsula of Florida's east side coast faded quickly out of sight, as did their valued view of the returning Twitchel as a thick foggy cloudbank aloft came rolling in over the land from the ocean, drifting westward. It would truly be a miracle, if anyone onboard the space shuttle could have survived the wicked tumbling act the Twitchel looked like it had gone through, never mind the integrity or condition of the craft itself after such an encounter. For the next couple of days, the space center at Cape Canaveral remained overcast.

The sky above the cape stayed covered by a low white misty cloudbank that prevented anyone from above viewing anything below, every time the space station passed overhead of the Florida compound. The entire space station crew had their own doubts about their friend's fate of having made it back home safely, never mind alive.

The space station crew searched the path of ground the Twitchel would have had to have flown over to see if they might spot a crater made by the Shuttle in the ground, had it fallen out of the sky short of its intended target, like so many other aircraft seemed to have done when the big blast hit.

Like new expectant fathers, sisters and anxious grandparents were waiting on word of their first newborn son, daughter, or grandchild to arrive, who anxiously walk back and forth in a hospitals corridors or waiting room

The crew aboard the space station anxiously walked with magnetic shoes, floated around, or crawled around back and forth. All worried sick at different intervals of the day and night. Back and forth and then back and forth inside their confined cubicles and stations inside the space station.

Each nervously waiting for the cloud bank covering the cape to lift, so they might at least catch a simple glimpse of something down there to see if their dear friends had made it back home alive and safe in one piece, or not.

Not one aboard expected down deep in their caring hearts to see what they witnessed below, for they were all so sure they're friends aboard the Twitchel were all dead after seeing the horrible tumbling act they had all gone through.

It was early morning on the fourth day after the Twitchel departure the space station when the space laboratory station passed directly

overhead of the safely landed Twitchel. It still looked very much dark over the cape and rather misty down there in the early dawn of day. Daylight was just barely breaking out over Florida.

The shuttle looked to have landed to the one using telescope. It looked to be on the ground at the far end of the runway, but in total disarray according to the view presented through the early morning mist. It looked to him like the craft had crashed along the runway, with many parts scattered out in the front of it, as well as parts of it in the back of the craft.

Another couple long tedious nerve-racking hours passed before the crew of the space station would know for sure if the craft had landed safely, or had crashed the way it looked to the operator of the telescope.

His heart sank swiftly to his feet in sudden heartfelt sadness filled with depression, along with several other sad looking faces among the laboratory's crewmembers. They hated in having to wait another few long tense hours before viewing the Twitchel waiting for their next pass over the Florida landing sight. On the very-next pass over the sight, the Sun of a most-perfect day, was shining brightly down on the Twitchel below.

For the first time the crew aboard the space station looked down to a most beautiful sight, with an American flag spread out in front the Twitchel, and a huge Russian flag spread out to the rear behind the craft.

There was a message painted on the runway behind the Russian flag in big bold white letters. All back home. Everyone safe in good health, thank you! Thank you comrades very much. Hope to see you soon. Will send messages to all your families everything is ok with all.

It was the thank you very much and "hope to see you all soon in the message painted on the runway that caused not a dry eye in any of the cubicles where they were watching the monitors from, causing everyone aboard the space station to get all misty eyed, including Commander Ivan. Instant jubilation range out in happy joy among the many laboratory crewmembers, for they were all incredibly happy, and somewhat jealous, that their comrade American friends had all made it back home to Earth safe.

The men and woman aboard the Twitchel were all incredibly surprised themselves, just after landing. A new diesel-fuel powered mini bus came rolling right out from the command center and down the runway to great them. It picked them all up for the short ride back to the Kennedy Command Center, and its debriefing facilities.

Back at the command centers medical facilities everyone received a clean bill of good health. Everyone examined by the space agency's two medical doctors who examined them one by one for having lived in space for such a long extended period of time. Everyone aboard had broken all American records of living in outer space for such a long stint in time.

Everyone felt extremely nauseous being back home on earth, and it was not from their extended stay away from home, or living in outer space that was the culprit causing the horrible feelings they were all experiencing.

One by one during their private physical exams the doctor told them to get accustomed to these new light-headed sickly feelings they were now experiencing. They would become accustomed to them soon, for this was the new way of life for everyone still alive and living on earth. It was not fatigue from being in outer space for so long that they all thought was to blame for it, or from the horrific tumbling act, they had all experienced during their reentry.

These new sickly feelings were in all animals around the earth.

The cause was due to the new irrational conditions existing upon the planet at the time. Every one of these sick feelings was being generated by the lack of positive charged particles in the air, and a change in gravitational pull on their bodies. Everything now was surrounded by low negatively charged electrons, resulting from the many billions upon billions and trillions of wild free-floating neutrons floating freely and wildly in and around the earth's atmosphere.

Most all the massive neutrons invisibly drifting in the air close to the Earth's surface, reminiscent a deadly gas viper-snake laying readily in

wait to strike out at its next victim at any given moment. It could strike out at anyone, anywhere, except in the shallow depths of the Earth's crust, fifteen or better feet below the ground's surface.

The uncontrolled explosions of all the missiles happening simultaneously were to blame for so many unnatural changes taking place on and around the surface of the earth. These overcharged underdeveloped weapons of mass destruction were not thought out properly, or understood by anyone of the Russians before they made them and placed them into orbit.

No one knew the long lasting effects or the outcome of so many exploding neutron bombs all taking place at the same time.

The hurriedly Russian execution in sending all these mismanaged war headed missiles aloft into outer space, and then followed up by the faulty unforeseen neutron invasion from its own weaponry put the world everyone was accustomed to into total turmoil.

It set up a scene of confusion, placing all creatures on earth in a living hell of eminent danger for every living creature on the surface of the earth. The foul of the air and insects trying to live in its atmosphere would constantly turn out to be in harm's way. The normal human food supply chain for the populations around the planet fell to an extreme low critical short food supply to feed everyone. Thousands upon thousands of innocent people began to starve to death globally, because of the neutron missile crisis. Thousands more unhappy citizens around the planet began committing suicide because of the death of loved ones taken place around them.

Many of the planet's citizens did not understand what had happened or knew how to deal with such a crisis placed on them, while thousands more of innocent beings existed as stupefied vegetables in human life form roamed the planet as living zombies. This unnatural invasion of so many neutrons into their bodies all at once left them with an intelligence of a two or three year old child forever, or less should they die of starvation. All these unnatural happenings resulting from the wild effect the massive invasion of neutrons had upon the bodies and minds of many.

The simplification of so many minds had become a pitiful situation affecting most every nation around the globe, and it was getting worse. These people were helpless, more than babies, for babies had mothers, and these poor people had no one to take care of them.

The earth had no electrical power on or above its surface. Anything twenty feet or so beneath the earth's surface was still capable of using, or making electrical power. Even then, it was unsafe to use it openly without caution because of the "Neutron Creature" in the atmosphere above.

This new man-made monster will try searching for it. It would travel down open corridors, down tunnels, airshafts, or through any opening or slightly cracked window or door, and travel down stairwells in seeking out and destroying the electrical power source. It would also destroy the people around it, who were using it, and the ones trying to make any would perish as well, a most horrendous death of involuntary convulsions and stink a horrendous smell of phosgene gas. Electrical power flows sparingly below ground, in order not to cause the creature in the atmosphere with its evil powerful force to come looking for its source.

This new invisible creature always wants to upset the positively charged electrons and protons with its multitude of neutrons causing an instant reaction with each other like a high voltage power line falling down into a crowded swimming pool and killing all the innocent people therein.

The earth changed drastically in a matter of seconds from coast to coast, and everywhere else with the invasion of these wild neutrons released around the world. The timing of the astronauts return from space to Earth was not getting any better for the worst of it. The world had changed drastically, and there is nothing anyone can do at this time to change it back to its natural way of being.

Whenever this new creature claims another one of its victims, an orange greenish blue gaseous fume of phosgene vapors would rise up off the body of the victim or victims and into the air in a great stench.

It did not matter the victim be it a human or an animal alike from the attacks upon them, the strong non-electrical force that surrounded these victims, would bleed them totally or mostly dry of any electrical impulse they once had leaving them dead or in a vegetation state they all wishing they were dead knowing its outcome.

CHAPTER THIRTY-ONE

The Loss of Thunder in the Skies

Planet Earth had not had a good old thunder boomer of an electrical rainstorm ever since the catastrophe of the neutron invasion took place. Torrential rainstorms still fill the skies around the Earth with a floating cover over the earth during bad weather.

Every rainstorm it seemed brought along a dirty orangey blue light with them. The dirty colored light would shoot around in streaks throughout and around the stormy clouds. The orangey bright-lighted vapor will shoot from cloud to cloud looking similar to an exhaust vapor from a rocket's exhaust, trailing through the clouds, and sometimes shooting down to the earth below without making any kind of sound with it. The situation is very strange to watch, and not hear anything when it takes place. It leaves whatever it strikes in its travels colored in an orangey mess of toothpick-sized splinters or an animal all wrinkled up with dried out withered skin, whether it is an animal or a human being, it doesn't really matter as long it is a live living victim at the time.

It was a truly remarkable unsightly event to witness, especially if one were witnessing an attack on a dear friend or relative by this unforeseen silent creature of death. A sighting taking placed looks horrifying to watch, and there is absolutely nothing anyone around can do about it, or have yet found a way to stop it from attacking when it happened!

One would have to wear an airtight rubber lined, totally enclosed self-contained breathing apparatus, a hazmat suit, all the time outside while out of doors to protect oneself from this creature living in the atmosphere.

CHAPTER THIRTY-TWO

Tried to Reach Out

We have continually over the last several months, attempted many times to get in touch with the space station, ever since you were lost out there. Our many observatories around the planet have kept us well informed of your situation best they could without power to run their high-powered telescopic equipment, and the slowness of our ancient stile communication systems we have now.

The space observatories around the world had informed NASA about the Twitchel, for she had hooked up with the space station after the deadly explosions of missiles down here.

We knew at the time it was the only true option you people aboard the Twitchel had that early time in the disaster. You really did not have much of a choice if any at all nor a snowball's chance in hell, of landing your spacecraft back here on earth safely through that thick cloud of mist, and that creature living and lurking in our atmosphere.

In the first few days after the blast with the wild neutrons all freely floating around the earth, it would have been plain suicide to attempt such a landing with your craft down through the cloud. You could probably see the immense cloud cover we had over the earth, if the earth was still visible from up there.

It was a good thing you did what you did commander, and hooked the shuttle up with the space laboratory as your first choice of a safe haven, for now look at all of you, your all back home on earth safe and sound.

If you had tried to return backs to Earth any time during those first few weeks, the immense force in all the neutralizing neutrons in the air would have surely attacked the Twitchel on reentry and would have killed you all instantly. The neutrons would have attacked the electrical charges in all your bodies at that time, your nervous systems, as well as the shuttles main power, and backup power sources.

There were but a small handful of the thousands upon thousands of military, commercial airline pilots, and solo civilian pilots flying that day, which did not lose their lives, that lived to tell about it, and even they are troubled some with the simple mind syndrome effect that affected so many people around the world.

There were some pilots who ejected themselves from their ill-fated aircrafts to live, but did not live to tell about it. These few pilots became the unfortunate ones who were able to eject from their ill-fated aircraft trying to survive. These unfortunate few all floated down to earth as if placed inside a running microwave oven while up in the air with all the wild neutralizing neutrons attacking their bodies. The wild neutrons sizzling, and burning the poor souls all the way down to the ground's surface as they floated down through its cloud of death.

Some of these pilots after reaching the ground looked like little Sun burnt orange aliens all wrinkled up and dried out like a sun-dried raisin where they came to rest. Some pilots landed in fields still attached to their tattered parachutes. There were some lucky ones the ones who had survived the attack, and then there were the poor many hundreds or thousands we don't know who had barely survived but who are now out roaming the fields and forests of the earth trying to survive like mutated mindless lost animals scrounging around for scraps of food. It would have been more humane to euthanize them all than let them suffer the way they do.

Any pilot that did survive the attack of the creature, and we only know of a couple that did that ejected very close to the ground are among those mindless lost souls.

It has been truly a sad demoralizing time for man and the animal kingdoms around the world! These once very intelligent military pilots and civilian pilots alike, have become vegetables of simplicity, joining the many thousands upon thousands of unfortunate simple-minded populous around the world, out roaming the streets and back roads. They eat dead animals, or anything they can possibly scrounge up for food as staples just to survive. They all walk around like lost little zombie children, as we have all come to know them around here.

We try helping these simple people as best we can with limited recourses and supplies we have until we can bring back the big crops of food we once had to feed everyone.

NASA knew the time was soon approaching, for some very drastic measure to take place up there onboard the space station for the survival of everyone. Either everyone on board the space station were already dead, or the experimental laboratory was about to run out of the necessary equipment of supplies to maintain any type of healthy lifestyle out there with so many people onboard the tiny station to take care of.

The many telescopes in our worldwide observatory systems require electricity to power up and we have no electrical power to beget their telescopic abilities. This has not allowed anyone to use them to see close enough to or capture any type of movement whatsoever onboard the space station from without.

If we could have scrounged up but a mere smidgen of electricity to fuel up the high powered telescopes, we could have all been peeping Toms from down here, and could have looked directly inside through one of the side portholes of the station to see if there was some sort of movement inside, but we couldn't.

Everyone down here were all quite concerned, and worried sick from the on start with this whole mess, that you and the others up there may have perished in the explosion right from the get go. After the sheen around us cleared away, we could see all the external lights and beacons continually remained lit up all the while around the spacecraft. We figured the neutron monster in our atmosphere did not or could not attack anything outside the Earth's atmosphere.

We have no working knowledge or opinion of the full extent or impairment these senseless neutron bombs have had other than here on earth. We did not know at the time if some or any of the damn missiles detonated outside the earth's atmosphere, and if they had exploded out there, how much damage they would have caused or could have caused in the imbalance of things in the solar system.

We all presumed seeing the flickering strobe lights of the space station at night all aglow, these massive neutron fields did not reach or affect anything outside the earth's atmosphere where air is void of materials or elements to carry any neutrons.

Without any molecules of substance in its makeup, space acted as an insulator of adsorption and protector for everyone outside the huge ring of the ozone layer from the creature's power.

CHAPTER THIRTY-THREE

The Big Question

"If there isn't any electricity on earth, sir, then how do all the busses, trucks, and farm tractors we observed from space running around then?"

"All the vehicles you have been seeing running around down here, run on diesel powered engines. Out of necessity, we have had to install the old-fashioned high-pressurized air regulator styled turbo starters on all these diesel engines, making them all capable of starting on their own.

When any driver wants to start his or her new turbine outfitted vehicles, they must first release a lever on the floor between two high-pressurized air tanks. This air pressure activates the turbine induced air starter affixed to the diesel engines flywheel and the spinning turbine comes to life for a split second or two of high-pressured turbulent spinning air power to turn over the lifeless engines.

They work quite similar to that of an electric starter, but without the need for electricity to start the engines. The starters are noisy as hell, with a loud whistling sound that is almost deafening. The only real problem anyone has had with these new air turbine starters so far is generally in very cold weather. If the engine doesn't start the first try, and sometimes a second attempt if one is lucky enough to have enough spare air reserve of thrust power built up in their air tanks, enabling them to give it another try in an attempt to start the engine a second time. Some use a small amount of starting fluid to make sure their engines start the first time.

One generally only has the single chance at starting his or her vehicles less they push them down the road to get them started. All the vehicles you saw running around down here use the standard shift driver transmissions and clutch method.

We do not use any automatic transmissions as of yet, for they will not start your vehicle even when you push them as fast as fast can be. Everyone who owns a vehicle these days that runs, owns a standard shift driver transmission for their own, and everyone else's convenience of starting engines by pushing and rolling the vehicles along, and popping the clutch while in gear if necessary to get their units started.

Some smart people have learned to leave their vehicles parked on hills, if there are any, just so they can start the vehicle if their starters fail them the first attempt, especially those ones not lucky enough to own an air-induced motor starter yet.

When the operators of these vehicles want to or need to shut their engines down to turn them off, they must do so by closing off the fresh air intake manifolds flapper on the engines air inlet side, and the lack of fresh air shuts the engine down straight away. Most all vehicles have small air compressors affixed to their engines now, so the air tanks affixed to them will fill themselves up automatically with the extra needed high-pressured air supply the air turbine starters need, in starting the diesel engines up for them. We have come a real long way down here in just over a year's time gentlemen, and you too, Ann."

"When will we all be able to see our spouses, children, and families Sir?" Ann blurted out anxiously and loudly! "You will see them soon Lieutenant, very soon. When we observed a couple of the crew members out crawling around the outer skin of the Twitchel, looking like you were getting your craft ready to fly again, we figured, in anticipation of your return, in notified all the families of the Twitchel's crew.

They were all ecstatic to hear you were preparing her, or at least looking like you were getting her ready to come on home. Some of your families are already here in our accommodation sections Ann, while others of your families are on their way here as we speak. Not a one of you will see any of his or her families until tomorrow or the next day though.

Everyone has to have enough time to readjust to the earth's atmosphere and gravity before you are able to see any just in case you all become ill for a short period of time do to the lack of gravity you have all gone through out there. The two medical doctors from the flight surgeons office, are in total agreement with each other about this, so please have patients with them and us in reintroducing you back to your kinfolk.

For the ones who could not come to be with us! We will do our best in getting you back home to them as soon as we possibly can. You have our word on that, but until then you all must learn to have patients with our decisions. You may roam around the facilities freely, but please no contact with your relatives, not just yet, thank you!"

"Boy, have we, boy, have we learned how to have patients, right crew? Commander Anderson spoke up with a smile on his aging face, as everyone in the room nodded their heads up and down laughing and grinning at one another.

"Slow communications is the number one factor in all our everyday lives now a days. Our mail is still our most first-rate way in staying in touch leisurely with anyone around the globe, and we do have some operable phone lines buried far enough below the earth's surface and waters between the cities of our planet so we can still communicate with one another for the purposes of emergencies, should they arise. There are telephone crews out there working around the clock as we speak, trying to connect all the cities and small towns of this country, and around the world, trying to reconnect everyone together again by underground wire harnesses for the safety of the people still alive in this world of ours."

"Gee! We use to laugh about the old comic strips, the city of Atlantis beneath the deep-blue sea. These fantasy lost cities that use to exist beneath the planet's soil and the ones under our seas. Look at us now for they are all really happening. We once laughed at Jules Vern for writing about spaceships soaring out into outer space from our planet once, and then we built them. Almost to the same exact specifications that he had written in his books. I guess the lives of our comic book heroes are always coming true for us these days, thank God for the comics.

Getting back to your question, Lieutenant, your family is on their way down here from Vermont as we speak. I would say you would be able to see them by tomorrow or the next day after that. I would guess if the medics say it is all right with all of your medical conditions, that is.

It is a long way down here from upstate northern Vermont to good old sunny Florida you know, especially by bus transit these days with all those many stops in between they have to make along the way!"

Ann's deep blue eyes swelled up with happy tears of joy as she broke out in a happy grin from ear to ear with tears running down her happy cheeks hearing her loved ones were on their way there to meet her. She was so happy she could not help but show her bubbling feelings of being overjoyed in front of everyone in the debriefing room.

"Major! Would you mind going with Captain Trainer to the next debriefing room, please? He has an important message for you, Bill! Captain Trainer has something of great significance to talk over with you alone in the other room, Major!" Bill's eyes widened like large dinner plates, swelling up with instant tears of anguish, putting on a total look of pure white fear which swept over his sudden lost happy face with fright like a hard frost in winter. He knew whatever needed being said to him in private by Chaplin Captain Trainer in the room next door with him was not good. Why could his space family members not hear the words meant for everyone's ears? He knew deep down inside whatever the important massage was to be, he sure as hell did not want to hear any word about it from Chaplin Captain Trainer. He turned a true white the color of pale white mist as the ghosts of white on a Halloween costume.

He slightly staggered, limping helplessly across the main conference room floor, not hiding the deep sad bad news and predictable pain he was about to hear from the others when he exited the room with

Captain Trainer. Dr. Captain Trainer was known to everyone around the facilities as the base's psychotherapy doctor, specializing in traumatic behavior experience analysis. He was trained in smoothing over one's loss, be it in life experienced by one military personnel's friend, family or crewmember. No one in the debriefing room wanted to trade shoes with Major Bill, no matter what the private news was he was about to receive from down the hall in doctor Trainer's office.

Ann felt a huge sad lump of sorrow develop suddenly in her throat for Bill as did everyone else in the room, feeling instantly sorrowful for him. They all hoped the bad news would not be too devastating for him, for he was such a nice friend and loveable human being.

He, like the rest of the crew, could not wait to get back home to his wife and children. The remaining crewmembers in the debriefing room had the same exact mystified looks of horror instantly embellish on their own faces as he had when he left the room. Especially when they were all told the sad tragic story about the incident that had occurred to Major Bill's immediate family after he had left for space once he had left the conference room.

His wife, his little daughter, and his infant son of only a few months old, fell victim to the horrific blast felt around the world that day on their flight home from the cape when the massive neutron blasts occurred. Like so many other innocent victims in the world that day who were flying here or there that cheerless day, when the destruction of these many innocent beings and unsuspecting animals around the world, along with just about every kind of flighty creature in the air died that horrific day.

Most the planes in the air that day crashed, while there were no recorded survivors listed on any of them. Some fighter pilots felt very lucky at the time to have ejected out of their disabled aircraft. However, everyone knows the fatal outcome to what had happened to them, and they would have been just as well off, to have had all perished in their aircrafts, instead their living through convulsions all the way down to the ground to perish. The others, having become one of the many simple minded acting androids roaming helplessly around the planet in search of food and handouts to sustain their simple-minded lives.

"Gentlemen, and you too, Ann, I hope you will excuse me for saying gentleman all of the time." "It's okay, Sir, you can call me anything you would darn well like to now that I am back home here safe and sound on earth!" Everyone had a go laugh. "Good then, well gentlemen! We lost, and I do mean lost, most of all the qualified people on the face of the world that day that could fly. We lost all the best pilots around the world except for a very few that did not fly that day. There are but a very few of us old flying bucks left, and let's not forget the good old gals still alive that can fly as well." He winked at Ann and smiled before he went on with his speech.

"We do have a very few newly outfitted aircraft ready to try and fly again. Our navy is almost back up to full speed with their old battle ships taken out of mothballs and we do have a very few aircraft carriers back in port being outfitted today with other newly high standards of old time war-faring abilities.

There is not a navy out there anywhere in the world that have regrouped the way we have here in this country, but this is only for our countries security.

By the way gentlemen, all the information I am telling you right now is all top-secret information, and I give it to you strict in charge, you are not at liberty to discuss this, and I do mean this info cannot, I repeat, cannot go anywhere outside of this conference room. Agreed? Good."

"Our modern day nuclear fleet of submarines can still operate when beneath the water's surface of our seas. They are unable to deploy any of their long range missiles because the creature in the sky is a leach to their payloads, and sucks the very power out of their battery operated guiding power battery supplies and lines in communications in their guiding systems as soon as any the missiles enters the airspace above the water's surface. The missiles could go anywhere they damn well pleased then, and destroy our own homeland if we are not careful in using them.

It just is not safe to deplore any of the electronically controlled warheads until we can further figure out a new and more accurate way of guiding them safely to their intended locations or targets. We have taken a couple of our old diesel operated submarines out of mothballs and installed air-turbine starters in them to start them according to intelligence. We are now ready to defend our country against any enemy. We just thought we should add that little tidbit of information, to make you all feel a little more secure in your all being back home here with us.

When you all are reunited with your loved ones, you are not at liberty, as I have said before, to discuss any of the private matters we are discussing here in this room with any of them. Not your mother, your father, your sisters or brothers, especially your children, understood?" "Yes, understood, Sir". "Good then dismissed."

Major Bill never returned to the debriefing room that afternoon, and everyone knew very well why. Each crewmember were led away to their own awaiting sleeping quarters to change into their new uniforms they had just been measured up for just prior to going into the debriefing room meeting after landing. Every crewmember one by one checked out physically by the two attending flight surgeons.

Ann had had an attending flight nurse in the room with her during her return physical, but could have cared less if one were in the room with her or not. She was just damned glad to be back home, and had all the faith in these doctors there on the base, for the attending doctor she had, had given her, her flight physical just over a year past before her last mission, and the attending flight nurse was the same also.

Ann drew herself an extra-large bathing tub full of warm almost too hot, of hot warm bathing water, while adding more than enough bubble bath treatment solution of pure floral fragrance to relax in. The lavender fragrant soap filled the tub almost overflowing with the lovely smelling bubbles of Lavender meant to relax her, and it sure as hell did. She lay soaking in the bathtub until the water in it turned cool, almost cold. It all felt so good to be in a tub of water after so many months of only being able to take sponge baths. She used old recycled body wipes to refresh herself with after exercising in the space stations gym to maintain her physical outer and inner appearance of healthy mind and body.

She became lost in the comfort of her soothing warm bath, when suddenly a hard firm fisted knocking came at her new quarter's door, catching her totally off guard, taking her back by complete surprise. She had been totally lost in daydreaming relaxed awe in the frothy tub of slowly dissolving, slowly popping bubbles of delight and relaxation.

She flew out in a flash from the tub of white foamy water, grabbing for the soft terrycloth bathrobe she had hanging on the back of the bathroom door. Hastily without thinking, she loosely wrapped the robe quickly around herself, and headed for the locked entrance door. She had been very quick in wrapping the loose fitting robe around her wet naked body. She opened the door and stood standing there dripping wet looking like a little old beautiful dripping ragamuffin. Her long grown-out brown hair hung down on her slender body, dripping water droplets all the way down her bathrobe down onto the floor below, and suddenly realized the front of her robe was half-open, displaying half her womanhood.

Commander Anderson looked down at her and smiled as she fumbled with her loose robe. She turned a crimsoned red with embarrassment as she tucked her collar in around her neck to hide her womanhood. She was an attractive young woman to look at, he thought, even though he was old enough to be her father and almost her grandfather's age.

"You know, Lieutenant, you get more beautiful with every passing day that I see you. Your husband is one very lucky man to have you to hold." She turned as bright as a freshly ripened red-hot tomato.

"The crew, Lieutenant, I mean I, would like to take you and the crew out for a very special dinner this evening to celebrate. Lieutenant, would you like to join us for a goodbye meal to celebrate our returning home, and a farewell from each other this evening, Lieutenant?"

"It would be my pleasure, Commander. I couldn't think of anyone except my other family that I would like very much to share a great meal with right now, Sir."

"Why, that is quite understandable, Lieutenant." "Would you like to come in and wait for me while I get dressed, or should I meet you and the crew somewhere?" "It isn't that I wouldn't like to come in,

Lieutenant, but I just think it would be a little more appropriate to meet you and the others downstairs in the main lobby. I shall go round up the others while you get yourself dressed Lieutenant, or may I call you Ann?"

"Of course, you can call me Ann, Commander. I wouldn't want it any other way." "We shall see you at 1900 hours then, Lieutenant, I mean Ann". "Yes, Commander, 1900 hours it is in the lobby, Sir", as she closed the door behind her.

"Please Lord, please let Amber, Sarah, and Ben get here by tomorrow. I miss them all so very much, I can't stand it, and don't want to wait another second to see them either."

Commander Anderson along with the rest of the Twitchel crew except for Major Bill, were all seated and waiting in the lobby of their accommodations building when Ann came sleekly descending down the winding staircase dressed like a modern day model showing off a new line of wardrobe.

The crew all looked greatly refreshed, well groomed, and looking wonderful to her. They all had clean-shaven faces and were now dressed up in clean dress military uniforms. Most of all she noticed the fresh stylish haircuts they had performed on them before refreshing themselves up in the showers. What a handsome bunch of guys they all were, Ann thought to herself. All the crew in dress uniform appeared very handsome to Ann, and she in return looked like a million dollar babe to them all. She looked like a Hollywood model descending a model's walkway, coming down the staircase in her new sleek-line high heel shoes with a touch of special makeup on, and the lovely dress she was wearing showed off her most lovely figure. She glowed on her insides with a very warm heart, feeling the beauty she bore on the outside to kill, feeling so beautiful out of her drab old stinky military flight suit. She could have been the ugliest woman in the entire world coming down that staircase, and she would have still felt the same way, but she was not, and the goodness of it showed.

The sad part about her was that she did not even realize or sense the beautiful looking woman she was, just feeling refreshed in life after her lovely soothing bath, and feeling damned well pleased to be back home on earth once again.

Her fellow crewmembers, watching her come gracefully down the staircase, had never looked at Ann in any other way other than an equal astronaut officer working right along with them in the space program until tonight. Tonight she was not just one of the other persons onboard anymore. Tonight she was a most beautiful specimen of young womanhood, and each one of the crew wanted to treat her as the person she really deserved to be treated. Ann had become more a young sister to all the men over the course of the last long trying year aloft held prisoner in space against their wills. She was the one they all turned to at one time or another in conversing about their strong hurtful feelings of loneliness, and wanted to talk to her about their families whom they had all so dreadfully missed, including Commander Anderson on a couple of rare occasions. She was able to give them all the close feeling of strength and closeness to family they needed, even though she was not part of their own real family, but she really had been.

"Lieutenant, you look absolutely ravishing this evening, absolutely ravishing indeed," said Commander Anderson to his first lieutenant."

Ann had prudently curled, put her hair up in a lovely looking French twist, and was not wearing the typical NASA looking military uniform they were all so accustomed to seeing her in over the last long year.

She wanted to look differently nice for herself this first night back on Earth. She had put on a most beautiful red sleek lined civilian evening dress showing off her slender lovely womanhood, the youthful beautiful and ravishing young woman she was as she descended down the stairs and off the last step to the stairs. She walked ever so graciously up to her fellow comrades who were waiting in the lobby for her.

"Was this dinner, Sir, supposed to be in full military dress uniform?" Ann asked Commander Anderson. "No, Sir, Lieutenant, I mean Ann. It was not. It is real nice to see you all dressed up that a way, and not looking like some old mechanical robotic android all dressed up in your old flight gear Ann."

The crewmembers except for Major Bill all traveled from the main housing barracks to the military officers club in the adjacent compound to spend their evening together. The crewmembers kept away from their immediate families and friends intentionally by orders until the next day. The two medical flight surgeons from the bases medical facilities along with their wives and a nurse accompanied the returning flight crew to the officers club that night. They stayed a safe distance away from the crew just to observe and keep an eye on them being back so they might enjoy themselves together one last time as a space family before separating from one another when all would go their separate ways in life after such a trying ordeal they had all gone through together.

Everyone around the dining table ordered the same exact meal from their menus, of clawless southern equator waters lobster tails as a side dish, to go along with a medium rare tenderloin soft cooked steak for their main course in small proportions. They had had their options of fish, clams, shrimp, veil, and an assortment of other fancy dishes along with as many desserts that they wanted. They enjoyed the pleasure of a drink or two of their favorite beverages getting almost tipsy on the first drink after not having any alcoholic beverages in such a long time.

Real food for a change that really looked extremely appealing to everyone with excited roaming eyes, all having to eat it in very small increments and bites of appropriate portions so no one would become severely ill from over eating.

The clubs food was rich in high protein and many carbohydrates for their first real evening meal together. They all knew better, and none wanted to act like gluttons and get themselves sick in front of one another on their first day back from space.

Most of the meals they were accustomed to in space had been small meals, mostly vacuum wrapped in freezer dried meal packets. These along with the bare minimal of fresh produce mostly leafy lettuce and a hand full in green bean sprouts which easily grew in the experimental gardens flourishing in the space stations west wing garden. There, the bright sun would shine through the craft's portals half the day to bring the gardens plants their needed sunshine to assist in helping the plants flourish with life. The sun's rays enhanced by arranged mirrors along with the use of solar powered sun lamps to assist the plants when the craft drifted in its orbital course back around the Earth's dark side, and away from the sun half the time in their orbit.

The experiment in growing assorted plant life aboard the space station was twofold, supposed to generate oxygen for their life support systems as well as some food for stables. A variety in uneatable plants were also living there in the west wing to produce oxygen for the sole purpose in extracting carbon dioxide produced by the astronauts out the air in the space station and produce it back into usable oxygen by the plant life through photosynthesis.

The water they all had to drink toward the end was becoming bland and had an awful tasting substance to it. It all having been reused so many times over and reprocessed through the huge distilling and charcoal filtering system onboard the space station which supported their lives for so long out there in space. The reuse water system not been designed to support as many for so long a period in time along with their many friends onboard the earthly situation held prisoner in outer space.

No one knew for sure just how long their imprisoned friends of space would last out there without any further fresh supplies sent to them from someone down on earth. Possibly a few more months or possibly less. No one really knew for sure, but it would not be for eternity that was for sure.

The spectacular new officer's nightclub had been barely finished being built beneath the ground like a castle with all the provisions of a palace. It had all the necessary blood flowing supply of electricity alive in its wired veins. With all its many electrical wires encased in thick PVC insulated piping to protect the inner flow of the precious flow in electricity from the Dracula like electricity sucking creature living in the atmosphere.

The neutron-saturated atmosphere of the earth did not seem to affect electricity buried in cables below twenty feet in the earth and encased in plastic as an insulator. All the water and sewer piping inside and outside the facilities seemed to be doing a fine job in sustaining life well below ground grade. The facilities did a fine job in protecting the individuals down in its structure out of harm's way.

The crewmembers of the Twitchel including Commander Anderson took their turns at dancing with Ann. She was a good sport about it too, and it was a wonder she did not pass out from total exhaustion from all of the dancing they put her through that night. But it was a fun filled night for her enjoying all the fuss and attention. She felt like a brand new young woman again. They all thought of Ann as a sister and not that of a sex symbol, but tonight she sure as hell looked beautiful enough to excite the hell out of any of them.

The bonding together they all had established between them in outer space was like that of twin babies living together in their mother's womb. Everyone having established some kind of bonding only siblings would have had for one another. They all knew this night was the end of a long last beginning. Their once well-established closeness as a unified family's nucleus of all living together as close friends had finally come to its end.

They would not be living together as a single-family unit never again, and that was all right with most of them, especially Ann. She had her family to return to and couldn't wait to see them all again as a unit.

With only one more minute to wait for her loved ones was just too long a wait, but she had no choice in the matter. She would have to wait at least one more day until they could get there on the next day's or the following day's bus.

The year-long stay for them trapped together in space created a closeness a family tie for them none would ever be able to replicate or want to ever forget but now being back home on planet earth, they each were all going in their own separate, and various directions around the country to be with close family, and friends. They had all talked of their loved ones in simple happy conversation, while at the dining room table at the officers club, knowing happily well, some of their relatives were already waiting for them at the Florida facilities.

How anxious everyone was to be back on earth and able to be going home and seeing their loved ones the next day. Throughout the night, the crew carried on in serious happy conversation about their many close and other friends still stuck in space. All hoping one day they too would all be as lucky as this crew had been and be able to once again return back home to Mother Earth.

To be with their loved ones someday, except for Bill who had already lost the closest family members he had to him. He was not in attendance at the club with them to say his goodbyes to their new old family ties. Each astronaut wished he or she could help him in a way to make things better, but did not know quite what or how to go about helping him cope.

As their wonderful evening together wound down and soon coming to its end, so did the good times they were all sharing with one another being the separate family they all were. In parting company in the main lobby of the Kennedy Space Center's living quarters, not a single eye among them was dry. Every one of the men, including Commander Anderson who was supposed to be the alpha male among the crew, was reaching down into his rear pants pocket for his handkerchief. Ann pulled out a white tissue from her black sleek purse she was carrying as the others all pulled out a clean cloth to wipe their own weeping eyes as well. Ann felt the worst about the ending of their yearlong relationship or at least she showed her emotions the most. She soaked down everyone's dry shoulders with her sad parting tears of sorrow, as she rained down tears on everyone from her free flowing misty weeping tear canals. She kissed everyone on their already red sad cheeks like siblings do, while squeezing them tight as a clamp on a fire trucks hose before she would let them go one by one. She only wished Bill could have been there with them to share in their happy, but sad time of farewell.

Ann saved her saying goodbyes to Commander Anderson lastly, and when she had finished hugging him the tightest and longest of them all, she bolted up along the tall stairway crying heavily. She ran sobbing into her tissue not wanting to look back on the family of friends she knew she would miss so dearly knowing very well that they were all standing there in the lobby looking up, watching her bolt her way up the stairs crying like a little baby. She fumbled feverishly in her purse for the damn door key to her bedroom quarter's door, and then tried unlocking the damn foolish thing. The damn key just would not fit properly into the slot. She was attempting it upside down, as she tried several times, with her eyes flowing out a misty stream of tears, clouding her vision in seeing what she was doing wrong. Turning the key over the right way, she finally managed to get the door opened, and threw herself on the bed weeping.

She could not help but to think about poor Major Bill somewhere in the compound trying to sleep alone and suffering emotionally, with him stewing over his own unbearable heartfelt grief that very moment. She cried a couple of very hard sad heartfelt tears for his demise. She felt extremely guilty for not going to him in his living quarters, and trying to comfort him as best a true friend might, at a time in his life he could get no lower in his feelings of guilt for abandoning them.

Probably blaming himself for being on that mission in the first place, for if he had not gone, his wife and his two little ones would not have been on that plane that went down and would not have died.

Ann's logic said better to leave him well enough alone for him to grieve by himself in peace and solitude. Bill's other close crewmembers from the Twitchel felt as Ann did about his situation, wondering about the saddened condition he must be in, as they all slowly rambled back to their own rooms. Thinking quietly to themselves about everything that had just transpired in their lives over the last year, and years before, when they were not in the military. They wondered what their lives would be now without the space program, for that was what they had all dreamed about ever since they were all small and had read about John Glenn, and the first ones on the Moon, and all wanted to be a bigger part of space exploration when the time came, and now it was gone.

It was as though they all had mental telepathy thinking the same thoughts at the same time along with thinking about this very emotional last goodbye of the evening. They were all sorry in their own way to have to say goodbye to their friends and the space program.

CHAPTER THIRTY-FOUR

The Long Wait

Saturday morning came suddenly for Ann and slowly went away longingly for her as well. Most the other crewmembers' families had all arrived at the cape to be with their loved ones. Ann guessed she would just have to wait yet another day before seeing her loving family.

It seemed to Ann all day Saturday that Sunday morning seemed to have some brakes applied to it. The hours of the night before Sunday morning went by like someone or something was making the coiled up spring in her Big Ben alarm clock turn its tiny hands ever slowly for her as she watched it clicked out each second, wishing for time to fly by more quickly.

She lay awake most all night long worrying about the arrival of her family, wide eye opened on her bed wondering if the younger of the two girls, Sarah, would even remember her mommy. She fretted over and over and over in her countless thoughts of the night if her other little girl, Amber, would run up to her with arms stretched wide open or hide behind her daddy's legs cowering for protection from this horrible looking stranger standing there before them as their mommy.

"Could it possibly have been that Ben was one of the unfortunate many thousands of human beings left simple minded as a two-year old child from the neurotic caustic results of the many wild neutrons had on him. Could it possibly be Ben or one or both of her children might possibly need someone's care around the clock to guide him or them around by his or her hands like a puppy dog on a leash. Was that why this was taking so damn much time, so long for them to get her family down there to her from all the way up from Vermont? Maybe they had to send a chaperone along with him and the children just to watch out for her poor Ben, and what about the children? What if they, too, were simple minded?" Ann had to stop her constantly negative thinking about everything for she was driving herself absolutely mad.

Saturday evening for Ann turned into a frightful anxious time of nightmares. When she did finally fall off to sleep, it was into a restless thrashing quick hour or less of fidgety sleep. All night she lay mostly awake thinking and dreaming about her husband Ben and how she was going to cope with him in this sort of condition. If he or the children are in such a poor simplemindedness condition, her swift speculative mind of imagination was working overtime. Her mind was trying to reveal the truth to her in coping with him and what about her two poor little girls and their conditions.

Ann thought for sure she had been gone away from earth too long. If he was still sane and mentally stable, surely he would have gone off and found himself someone else, some other beautiful woman to have and to hold, to love him during her long unforeseeable stay away from him. He surely had all the right in the world to do it if he had the need. The night turned into a living hellhole of fantasizing bad dreams and nightmares of her own making, and doubts of what to expect when everyone came together again for the first time.

When morning arrived, Ann lay awake on her disheveled bed in her nightclothes soaked from nervously perspiring with worry she experienced of her own making all night long thinking the worst of everything. Someone would have had to have told her by now if something happened to one of her family members, the same as it had to Bill's family, or would they?

She was perplexed about the situation she being the only female aboard the Twitchel. Maybe they thought she would not be able to handle it until one of her family members showed up with him. She was driving herself insane, trying to figure out what might be if anything was and why, doing absolutely nothing good for her mentally, or physically concentrating on this matter. Ann did not want to be that stranger from long ago coming back into her family's life. The dreams of that night had frightened her to the point of madcap with anxiety she was feeling down deep inside her mind and were almost overwhelmingly intolerable.

The light of the new Sunday morning sun's rays shining through Ann's window stirred her awake after finally having falling asleep late into the next morning. It was almost 0900 hours, 9 a.m., in the morning when she awoke. "9 a.m." Ann shouted out at her Big Ben alarm clock on the night stand. She bolted from her soft down-filled bed to take a quick shower without hardly touching the floor. She developed goosebumps the size of ostrich eggs it seemed to her being so excited forming all over her tired body, her stomach churning wildly like a butter churn, full of soured cream, as if she were again pregnant and experiencing morning sickness from being pregnant a third time, but she was not.

The strange feeling in her stomach was most likely caused by the rich food of lobster, steak, and sea food soup she ate the night before or possibly by the two strong Bloody Mary's she had.

Every time she thought about seeing Ben and he girls for the first time, her stomach would churn wildly, almost to the point of making her want to vomit. All the while, more goose bumps would form all over her, even though she was now standing in the soothing flow of very warm almost steaming hot shower water, trying to calm her anxious nerves from jumping out of control. It did not seem to matter how hot she turned the shower up to, the goose bumps the size of ostrich eggs still formed all over her body.

Before the chilling nervousness cooled her down, she thought she was beginning to have a nervous breakdown or was she developing lung or body disorders of some sort do to the massive assembly of many neutrons surrounding her. Being back on earth was wonderful, but the experience of having so many people around her again was nerve wracking. She was beginning to think she was a candidate for going to see Chaplin Captain Trainer.

Ann made herself a lukewarm coffee from the warm hot water spigot from her sink. She slowly walked toward the curtains and peeked her head out of her bedroom quarters' window located in the front of the building so she could watch as the people came and went from the facilities. She then began pacing back and forth across her bedroom floor with her coffee cup in hand thinking with anticipation of the consequences this day might bring either good or bad, and she hoped only for the good.

It was a beautiful summer's day outside it looked to Ann anyway. The sun was shining brightly down over the salty seawaters across the bay reflecting its brightness back into her beautiful eyes with its bright rays of light.

She thought about the many frightening things about earth now and its people told to her and the crew all while sitting in the debriefing room just two days ago. God it seemed like months with Colonel Fretters rambling on and on at the podium with such horrific sounding information about how the earth was then and how it is today. She questioned everything about anything. What was she to expect from herself thrown into this madcap new distraught world she was so unaccustomed to living in, and was now ruthlessly dumped down into it and had to learn to survive in it all over again.

Were all these new changes that had taken place to the earth as bad as everyone was trying to make them all out to be, or had they all really become this awkward in way of life over a period in time? Would a simple chore like going to the local store to pick up a few groceries or an article of clothing changed? Would all these simple little chores still be as pleasurable an outing she once enjoyed doing with Ben and the kids or turned into an unpleasable experience for everyone? What if the ones she loved doing it with were gone not physically but mentally and her life was about to turn into a nightmare from hell when everybody showed up that morning?

There was no more television to watch from the comforts in one's home on a Saturday night. There were no more radios to listen to in order to cut through the boredom of a long restless day, along with no more modern electrically operated conveniences in toasters, irons, or anything to help her or anyone else with around the house to make life just that little more simpler in everyday chores.

She could not imagine it being so even though it was the new way of life on earth now, and this really bothered her. This being the new way of life on earth, unless one lived well beneath the hard surfaced crust below the earth's outer skin where all was the same as before, except that everything was now underground. The entire civilization of the world had been put back in time a couple of hundred or better years, living the old fashion way of days gone by without any of the modern conveniences of using electricity to make their lives that much easier to cope with.

Ann drifted more slowly from her quick walking down into a sauntering back and forth across the room thinking about the day and then slowly turned into the bathroom. She proceeded to wash more and make herself more beautiful than she had looked the night before, if that was at all possible.

This was Ann's big day, her special day like her wedding day was a few years in the past. Today she would be seeing her two little precious girls and her most wonderful husband for the first time in such a very, very long lonely time away.

When 1200 hours came to Cape Canaveral, it found Ann prancing again back and forth nervously across the main lobby in the guests' compound. She continually snapped her fingers in progression with her marching back and forth across the lobby as if she was on guard duty if front of the main door of the facility securing it in secrecy from anyone in anticipation of her hopefully soon to be arriving family.

Commander Anderson and his wife, seeing Ann looking a little pale and nervous in her ways, stopped by for a moment to talk to her as they were getting ready to leave on their journey home on the bus which was supposed to be stopping momentarily out front of the facility for their departure.

"A little bit nervous, Lieutenant Mitchell?" "Yes, Sir, Commander Anderson. One hell of a lot nervous Sir, pardon my mouth Mrs. Anderson. This feels like I am here to meet some strange guy for the

first time in my life and going out on a blind with him, and then, well the children."

Commander Anderson's wife spoke up to Ann with a light soft voice to ease her anxiety. "I hear you have two beautiful little girls who just cannot hardly wait to see you, dear. I mean you are waiting to see them aren't you?"

"Yes, ma'am, I sure am. I am more nervous than an old wet hen caught out in the middle of the barnyard in a driving rainstorm next to the chicken coop with its doors locked with an old hungry fox snapping its jaws at her tail feathers with hunger. Maybe even a high wire performer doing his or her first walk across the high wire. I sure hope the girls remember me when they get here."

"I am quite sure they all will my dear, I am sure they will." Commander Anderson broke out with a great big smile across his mostly stern face as he quickly glanced over Ann's head, looking toward the main door to the lobby.

CHAPTER THIRTY-FIVE

The Reunion

"MOMMY, MOMMY, a little voice came echoing over to Ann from behind her from across the main lobby from a little girl who was just barely squeezing out into the main lobby from the rotating door.

Ann had not noticed the passenger bus that had just barely arrived out front of the building or the sound of the opening of the lobby door spinning that squeaked a little when it rotated around on its base.

Ann's oldest girl, Amber, came running at her like a racecar flat out at high speed running across the main lobby toward her mommy who had been away so long from her reach. Ann turned hearing the little voice call out to her with welling up tears of joy in her bright blue eyes, as Amber jumped right up into her unsuspecting mother's arms as Ann bent down to great her, almost knocking Ann over from having weary muscles from being in space so long without gravity.

Ben walked swiftly across the lobby floor toward his lovely wife while carrying shy little Sarah. She was holding her daddy very tight around his neck with her in his loving arms both smiling at Ann with pleasure written all over their happy looking faces. Ann wept profusely with happy tears seeing them there, having great feelings of joy rise up in her long aching heart for their closeness, along with tears of joy flowing profusely from her eyes for having her family back together once again as a whole.

"What is the matter Mommy," asked her daughter Amber. "Why are you crying Mommy?" "Your mommy is crying happy tears. That is why your mommy is crying, sweetheart. I am all so very happy inside." Ann held onto Amber squeezing her lovingly tight with emotion, and swiftly walked over to be with Ben and Sarah. She and Amber met them halfway across the floor toward the rotating door. First she kissed Ben, then Sarah, then Amber, then Ben, Sarah, and then Amber again. She could not have been happier than a little girl getting her very first new pony all her very own on her 6th birthday, or her first new puppy, kitten, or bunny rabbit for her very own.

Ben looked as good to her as did her two little children. Ben began at once to lovingly bust Ann about her short mission into outer space she had left them for a little over a year ago. "Boy, this was the shortest couple of day's mission you have ever gone away on Ann!" Ann laughed a hearty laugh then burst into streaming tears of joy again, as she hugged Ben, Amber and Sara tight as she could holding Amber tight as she could without hurting her in her arms of joyful love.

"Why is mommy crying daddy? Is she all right daddy? Does she still love us the way you said she would?" "She is better than all right, sweetheart. I think your mommy loves you even more now than she did before she left. She loves you just like Daddy, Grammy, and Grandpa said she would. We are all right now, sweetheart. We are all just fine."

They didn't talk to one another again for about fifteen minutes it seemed. They just kissed holding onto each other tight for the longest time, smelling each other's body perfumes of love they were emitting.

Commander Anderson and his wife, Becky, just happily stared over at the young loving family's reunion from a distance, seeing and sensing the love that was flowing freely between Ann and her caring family. Ann composed herself just long enough to talk without crying. "Sorry guys. You must all be extremely tired from the many long hours' journey you just finished traveling all that way down here from Vermont. So very far and such a long ride especially for you, Ben. You must be extremely exhausted from watching over these two little angels."

"Not really, Ann. The children have been excellent all the way down here. They took turns looking out the windows of the bus and slept most of the rest of the time. Amber is a sweetheart. She has been like a little mother to Sarah and kept her busy playing with her when she got bored with all of the traveling. You should be very proud of her. The trip down from Vermont wasn't as bad as you might think it could have been."

"How about something good to eat, guys?" Ann asked. "What would you three like to have for lunch? We can go over and down into the officer's club and lounge for a treat for you three. You can have anything on the chef's menu your little hearts' desire. Oh, how wonderful it feels to have the three of you back in these tired arms once again! It has been way too long! Way, way, way too long!"

The reunion with her family went much better than she had imagined it could have possibly gone. Sarah was a little reluctant to go to her mother at first, but when she finally realized who Ann really was, she broke out into the biggest widest smile Ann could ever remember her having on her cute little face. She instantly put her little hands out to Ann, once again united as one big happy family.

Just prior to commander and his wife leaving for the bus, Ann introduced Ben to Commander Anderson and his wife Becky. She caught them just as they were about ready to leave out the revolving front doorway for home aboard the awaiting bus parked outside. The same bus Ben and their two children had just arrived on.

Sitting down and enjoying themselves together at last in the officers' club's dining hall, the two adults talked of the many experiences they both had gone through in the several long lonely past months of the last year gone by. Little talk about everything came hard at first, and mostly consisted of talk about the children's welfare, then proceeded to get around to Ann's parents. Ben finally talked about how everyone had all handled her being gone for such a long period of time and not so very well at times. Ben told Ann he and her family were all very sick, and worried she might never be able to come back home to them ever, if not never. He told her how the children would sit in their grandfather's lap for hours, and he would tell them stories about her when she was just as little a girl like them and how stubborn she turned out to be as an adult teenager. He always laughed hearty right out loud when he told the two little ones stories of when she use to feed the little piglets, and how she would push them with her tiny hinny out of the way when she went to feed them their grub. She would sometimes jump up on one of their backs to ride them around the pigpen like little ponies as they grew bigger and bigger out in the pigpen. He always kept your interest in their little hearts every night.

NASA, along with the Air Force had informed Ann's family that the Shuttle Twitchel had safely coupled itself up with the International Space Station, but that was all they were able to tell them about anyone's wellbeing.

They had no idea had anyone onboard the Twitchel was seriously injured by the big blast or not from the sudden infusion of massive neutrons into the atmosphere that shook the world, and possibly might have affected them in space.

Reinforced repeatedly by all around them, they told Ann's children that someday in the near future, their loving mother would safely return back home to them. But as time marched on, and days swiftly passed away turning days into weeks and weeks into months, they became harder and harder to convince their loving mommy was still alive, never mind ever coming back home to be with them again. Their many lonely days of missing their mother, turned into saddened weeks of loneliness for the girls, and their sad, sad weeks soon found their way into long doubtful months.

Too much precious time away from their precious mother had lapsed away especially for Amber, who would ask her father the question repeatedly over and over again like a broken record. When would her mommy finally be coming home? Day after day, she would ask repeatedly until that very special day. Even on the bus trip down to Florida to see her, she asked again. She was full of doubt and would not stop asking the question until the time she felt herself snuggled tightly in her mother's arms once again.

Looking up from across the table at his little girl, Ben could see it in Amber's face that she was the happiest little girl on the face of the planet he had ever seen. She continually gazed over at her mommy sitting across from her with glistening reflections of her love in her eyes and donning the biggest glimmering little shiny smile that could melt the Arctic Polar Cap!

It seemed to Ben that everything would soon be back to normal for them or almost back to normal. Their lives as normal as they could be now, for the world had changed and it would be their new world. The norm of normalcy was not the norm, nor was not the normal of norms the norm anymore on planet Earth.

Lying comfortably together in a bed that night for the first time in many a long and lonely anticipated night, the conversation between them drifted from a joyful conversation in reunion of their family to one of seriousness between the two. Ann's military time of full duty was nearing its end, and her time was nearly there for her to re-up, and reenlist with the Air Force. The space agency network of science and research team, in their exploration in experiments into deep space which had now become the underground laboratories of the world.

Ben was worried sick. Ann would be ready and way too willing to want to reenlist up in the military for another stint of four more years of service to her country and stay with NASA no matter what. He yearned for her final answer of either a yes or a no, right then and there, as they lay in their bed together before she said another word to him about anything. With the girls both fast asleep, Ann did not give a damn about what he wanted to hear for she did not want to think another thought about anything in the world for the next few minutes but them making love together. With a glistening smile, and love shining in her beautiful eyes, Ann gently placed her soft petite hand up over Ben's babbling mouth to quiet him as she threw her naked needy body up over and on top of his nakedness. Like a cat in heat on a hot tin roof, she was ready for him. It had been well over a year since being held tight in the arms of the man she loved, especially in as romantic setting as this furnished room was, never mind having been able to make love to the one she so dearly loved.

Both Ann and Ben went off happily into their own sound happy sleep for the first time in a very, very long time. They fell fast asleep contentedly snuggled tight in each other's loving arms not having been able to do so in such a very long time. The two of them slept the night together like babies in a crib holding each other tight in a warm passionate sleeping way as if they had just taken sleeping pills to quiet their every need.

The next couple of days, Ann and her family spent it at the command center reintroducing themselves to one another, making their reunion a truly joyful and blissful one for Ann, Ben, Amber, and Sarah.

On the third day, Ann, Sarah, Amber, and Ben, boarded a northbound passenger bus like Commander Anderson and his wife had done just days before. This would bring Ann and her family all the way back home to Lunenburg, Vermont. Then Ben would drive them up to her father's farm where her parents were patiently, or not so patiently, awaiting her return. They would have liked the safe return of their only daughter back to them well over a year ago. They were both anxiously waiting to hold her again in their loving arms once again.

The second bus ride home for the children proved to be a worse one for their attitudes of sweet calmness as had the first one been down to Florida.

It had only been a very short three long days since they had last spent those many long hour on the bus trip south from Vermont. They had had something very important to look forward to back then on their first long trip, but had nothing quite as exciting for this trip back home as seeing their mommy back home.

Ann was extremely concerned for the children's wellbeing and comfort as it weighted heavily on her mind while watching the two little babies of hers becoming more restless and sadder with the thought of the long journey back home. She told them how excited Grammy and Grandpa were for them to be back home with them to quiet them down.

She tried playing silly little games of counting different animals along the way which soon became old hat to them by not seeing animals the way things once were on planet Earth. The slow tedious bus ride back home for her family, showed Ann just how different life on planet Earth had become since she left over a year ago. Not that all of these changes had come from being gone so long, but had changed the way people lived their everyday lives because of the disaster that had taken place. The invasion of neutrons had changed just about everything that had been modern on the face of the earth at the time, especially the way Ann remembered it being before she left on her mission.

This new way of life she was hearing about of people living underground was becoming the new way of life for most people who still wanted to enjoy the many comforts of life like before. These lucky few people had enjoyed the many comforts of electrically operated equipment at their ready fingertips all their lives, and with many still lucky enough to have wealth, could afford the extreme pleasures of building these new dream homes beneath the crust of the earth, and living down there like kings and queens. The remaining worldly inhabitants, not affording these types of electrical suitable homes confined to the surface of earth, went without and would have to survive the best way they knew how to in their new environment.

Enjoying any night out on the town in these new days, people spent most their time underground in facilities permitting people to enjoy the modern-day conveniences of an old style life. The new life style above ground now spent like days of old, modern-day pioneers living out of doors in the countryside, enjoying the pleasures of open fires. Using the fire to see at night and to cook their meals the old fashioned way, with wood burning stoves, whilst lighting up the dark of nightlife with oil fired lanterns, along with coal fired stoves and wood burning furnaces for their winter's heat, along with hurricane candle units for some light to read bye.

Many lights around the world already converted back to their old original old-fashioned oil and gas fired lanterns in lighting up the dark of night in streets and buildings alike. New old fashion ways of old, for all had been used in lighting up the dark over a hundred and fifty years or so ago, using Whale oil for fuel, but now with the convinces of copper, steel, and plastic piping, they piped in natural gas.

People of the new modern day today are using gas to cook with, to light up the dark, and heat their homes. These are among the few conveniences these lucky people today's modern-day conveniences have in not needing electricity to run them. All they had to do was install gas-fired lights in their homes for lighting in the nighttime. The unfortunate others of the world have to use old messy oil fired lanterns with messy wicks that make soot stains on everyone's walls and ceilings. Many people of the day started using soot free candles instead for their oil lights at night, making breathing easier for most, especially the ones who have experienced breathing problems.

All along the long way home, Ann watched as southern farmers were out in their fields plowing, harrowing, while most used their horses doing what gas powered tractors use to do. The lucky farmers were the ones previously out-fitted with their own diesel-powered tractors who are now the elite farmers of modern day farmers. Some unlucky farmers were the ones out in the fields with their cows, goats, donkeys, and their children doing what a horse should have been doing out there instead. They also spotted hundreds of people out in fields along the way with hoes and shovels in hand, plowing the soil of the earth for survival. Others were planting seeds for food for their very needy families.

Things sure were different on planet Earth now than they had been before or at least they sure as hell seemed to be to her. Ann was just caught up in a state of awe looking at the differences that had taken place in just over a year. The roadways were almost vacant of any vehicles of any kind, compared to the last time she traveled along the busy highways on the earth.

All the hustle and bustle of traffic of cars trucks and busses was gone, with only a very few trucks on the roads hauling needy goods of wares and food from city to city and across the country. The railroad systems across the country were slowly improving and getting back to normal as normal could be at this time.

Huge diesel power driven locomotive engines driving big electrical turbines to generate enormous amounts of electricity to drive the trains' truck unit forward and backward were history. Some of these

trains the railroads outfitted with some sort of direct drive reduction, geared down truck units with clutches to push the big trains along using their diesel engines. These new trains are not as powerful as the old ones, but they still do their jobs. It just takes a little longer for them to commute from point a to point b, especially some of the old time steam locomotives of yesterday year that had to be put back into service from the many tour train attractions around the country.

The many skyscrapers of this new old modern time of yesterday year were yet another part of the new cultures downfall on the earth, now rendered mostly useless by the big neutron blast, now nearly vacant compared to just over a year ago. The many huge skyscrapers around the planet became death traps for many hundreds if not for the thousands of working staff and inhabitants who remained in them at the time of the disaster. The instant atmospheric saturation and penetration of wild neutrons wiped out everyone working on or above the first fifteen floors in most all tall buildings. The mighty mishap took great numbers in those still on the lower floors as well turning many of these people into thoughtless walking zombies. In most buildings right along with all the other people not having the chance to descend down to the basement floor where most survived, except for the few who were trampled to death in the great exodus in people fleeing, trying to save themselves from disaster.

The tall skyscrapers of the planet had now become mostly tall edifices of tall useless spaces especially without their precious blood flow of electricity flowing through their wired veins of life to keep these structures alive. Great metropolitan areas were evolving in depths down in the earth below the earth's surface where electricity was still functional. The correct depth below ground allowed the magical electric juice to flow lucratively in its wire veins of life. It was not dead as above the earth's crust where the neutron fields saturated the earth's atmosphere. Up there it sought out and destroyed any source of electrically generated power.

Sometimes it would include minuscule impulses generated by some poor animal's nervous system, destroying whatever was in its path trying to seek out the generating source of power whether it is an animal organism committed to the ground, or a foul, or insect of the air.

This neutron monster took away innocent lives from people who barely scuffed their stocking dry feet across a positively charged wall-to-wall carpeted floor with static electricity in it or from being on a wool scatter rug thrown down for neatness. They were all killed dead, wiped out instantly rendering them useless for just scuffing their feet nonchalantly across anything that caused them to generate a mere impulse in static electricity around them.

The thing, this creature from out of the air in the world, would come right out of nowhere and suck the life out of every electrical impulse generated, whether it is from a statically charged rug, or the minutest of electrical impulses generated in their bodies when touching things that would cause a spark generated. It was best to keep yourself static free in order to live and survive in this newly evolving world with the Thing of death floating freely everywhere above. The invisible neutron field of death was the most dreaded creature of all times by everyone living on the face of the earth now.

The northward bound bus made its first overnight stop of its trip to Vermont with its foursome, the only passengers on it at the time, at the Grand Colonial Trader Hotel. The mere nostalgia of the building along with its fascinating dressed staff were quite interesting to say the least, especially in these poor times of great despair. The Grand Colonial Hotel seemed to be putting on the dog for all of its many guests and visitors. The entire staff members were all dressed up in garb of colonial time dress of yesterday year. The halls and walkways around the hotel were all lit up with old time traditional colonial style gas generate lights and lanterns of a hundred or better years ago.

The entryway into the huge reception hall had a magnificent gas fired crystal chandelier hanging from the ceiling greeting everyone with its beauty and awe who entered there in. The distinctiveness of this building had been a preplanned structure of beauty, to represent a great nostalgic mansion of grand southern hospitality from the past by its original owners and planners.

It had been previously preplanned a long time ago to be built this way long before the big blast of missiles came to the area, and had been planned to go into full operational service the following week just after the horrible tragedy that had struck upon the earth in which case the hotel didn't open on time. Its grand opening delayed to a few months later, when the appropriate time would happen for the likes of such a unique building of its time came.

With having the luck of the Irish, the new building sat close to the capital of the country. The new hotel flourished immediately the second it opened its doors for business, frequented by state representatives and foreign dignitaries frequenting the Washington D.C. area doing their jobs representing their lands and states in Washington.

Everything in the hotel operated by hand naturally or by bottled gas, so it read on an informational bulletin hung as they entered the building. This bothered the hell right out of Ann considerably. Everything inside the Colonial Grand Hotel looked very antique yet wonderful, the way it was supposed to look over a hundred years ago.

The gas fixtures reminded Ann as a very small girl visiting her grandparents' home down in South Lunenburg, Vermont of a bad experienced she had being around her grandmother's propane gas cooking stove, and it was not a very happy remembrance either. She was having a grand old time in helping her grandmother cook an apple pie. She was helping her grandmother and turned on the gas to the oven for cooking the apple pie, then went to the counter to fetch the match without having it readily in her hand with her when she first turned it on. When she opened the oven door and lit the match, the built up gas in the oven exploded right in her face, singeing the hair on her head, burning her eyebrows and eyelashes off, and leaving her looking like a dirty scorched red tomato with soot all over her head. It was a wonder she did not have second and third degree burns all over her face and her arms now, for she was almost de-haired from the exploding burning gas that melting the hair off her head.

She went around for the longest time sporting the awful looking sunburned skin with several awful looking pealed blotches of skin around her head and arms to follow this horrible experience. No wonder she hated the thought of sleeping in a building that was fully operated by gas. Ever since that incident, any kind of gas has definitely not been one of her more favorite devices of use for anything using it. She has all ways shied away from any gas appliances that used natural gas or bottled propane for their source of heat or power.

Ann would rather have liked the old modern conveniences of electrically operated appliances back in her life. She felt the world around her just was not going to be the same again, for she could sense it. She knew things would be a whole hell of a lot different now that she and her family walked through the main doors of the Colonial Trader to rest their tired bodies from sitting so long on that damn bus, bumping along the highway for most of the day. Most all the big hotels and more the small motels along the way remained closed or boarded up along the deserted roadways. The owners of the Grand Colonial Trader were lucky, for if their fancy hotel was located anywhere else but where built outside the country's capital, it too would have probably not been open for business and all boarded up like so many the others.

A handful of lucky hotels and motels along the roads leading back home to Vermont remained open for business. Mostly for their prime locations built so close to large metropolitan areas barely busy enough to afford them staying open, having the conveniences in gas appliances maintaining their life from the beginning, and helping to keep them alive.

The Mitchell family, shortly after checking into the Grand Colonial Trader, sat down in its elegant dining hall and ordered their evening meals. The children after sitting for just a short while, became rather rambunctious, having been trapped in their rolling playpen with seats for so long having nowhere to run or play all day to rid themselves of their built up youthful energy.

They were sick and tired of having to behave themselves for as long a time they had had to especially after having done the same exact trip just four short days earlier. The excitement in having their mommy back home with them and taking the very long bus trip down to Florida was becoming just too much for two little children to endure, and they were letting it be known to everyone around them, especially Ann and Ben.

Both were very thankful the dining room remained almost empty of any guests at the time. The children managed to quiet down when their meals came lastly to them.

After eating a few mouths full, Amber fell fast asleep in her booster seat as the littlest one Sarah fell fast asleep in her high chair before dessert came. Ann picked up Sarah out the high chair while Ben took Amber in his arms. They carried their two children up the stairs to their room for a quiet night's rest, Ann hoped. They tucked their two children into the king size bed set up beside theirs for the night. Ann instantly began feeling sad about what she had been missing daily held hostage in space away from them for so long. She was excited in having the experience of carrying Sarah up the stairs and merely tucking her into her bed even though it was not their home.

When they first entered into their sleeping accommodations for the night after dinner, they saw a pushcart in the middle of the floor with a bottle of Baltic's finest champagne tonic on ice on it. The cart held a fancy clear lead crystal ice bucket filled with ice and sitting alongside the ice bucket were two very elegant tall stem champagne glasses along with two long stem roses stretched out on the cart beside each glass. Ann glanced over in Ben's direction and said in a low voice mouthing the words, "You shouldn't have Ben." "I didn't." Ben replied whispering. "I think whoever did it got the wrong room, but I wish it had been my idea."

After putting the children into their bed for the night someone knocked gently at their door. "See, Ann, I told you they must have gotten the wrong room number. I was not telling you a story when I said I didn't order them. Someone is here to retrieve the champagne tray and bring it to where ever it should go. Sometimes mistakes do happen you know even in fancy places like this one." Ben went over and answered the knock at the door. Upon opening the door quickly not to awake the children, they saw a young lad standing in the hallway with a spray of beautiful flowers held tight in his right hand. "I am truly sorry miss, sir, as I forgot to place these lovely flowers on the cart with the champagne." "Are you sure you have the right room, sir? Neither I, nor my husband remember ordering any champagne or flowers for this room."

"Ah miss, are you Lieutenant Ann Mitchell, miss?" "Yes, Yes I am." "Well then, miss, I have the right room then ma-am. These flowers are for you miss." The door boy handed Ann a beautiful spray of assorted roses and flowers with a card attached to them.

Ben reached into his pocket, and preceded to hand the young lad a tip for his services. "That won't be necessary, sir. Your short or long stay here with us at the Colonial Grand Trader Hotel is paid in full for the entire family's stay here with us. Here is your money back from your evening meal with us, thank you. Everything is on the house for you and your family during your stay at the Grand Colonial Trader, miss."

The young lad quickly made an about face and swiftly walked away. Ann and Ben just stood there looking at one another with joyful looks of bewilderment upon their happy faces. Someone special was lurking in hidden shadows of the night and was definitely looking out for their welfare, for it pleased Ann to no end and bewildered the hell out of Ben.

The flowers, the champagne, their meals, and stay at the Grand Colonial Trader Hotel was printed upon the thank you card attached to the bouquet of beautiful flowers, was complimentary to Ann and her family from the nations around the world, especially the citizens of the United States, signed the President of the United States.

With a note also attached to the card that read on as such. "Happy to have your recovery team safely back home with us, Lieutenant. It took great courage on your part to volunteer for such a dangerous mission in trying to help save the world and the people in it from such an outrageous menace lurking in our midst. Sorry you became one of the tragic sufferers that day Ann, but in a total different manner. It must have been a very difficult time going through what the crew aboard the Twitchel went through, especially you being the only woman onboard the craft. A year of not knowing one way or another if your family was safe or not especially your children, if one or both were still alive or dead must have taken quite the toll on your motherly mind.

Glad to have you all back home safe and sound. Would like very much for you and your family to come to the White House tomorrow a.m. for a quick visit with the First Lady and I, Lieutenant. Your short stay while in the Washington D.C. area at the Grand Colonial Trader Hotel is complimentary, provided by the good people of the United States, with whom so many prayed for you each and every day I am sure for your safe return back home to us. We are more than delighted to provide you your every need while you are here in the Washington D.C. area, and thank you again very much, Lieutenant, for your heroism. We hope you will decide to come. We shall send an escort for you and yours first thing tomorrow morning at 9 a.m. sharp." Sincerely, President Stallman.

CHAPTER THIRTY-SIX

The White House

Outside the Grand Colonial Trader, a diesel powered luxury sport utility limo pulled up out front at precisely 0900 hours sharp. It displayed the usual White House's emblems of the United States of America seal attached to its two front doors. The military driver jumped out and opened the side doors to the limo for Ann so she and her family might climb inside for their short but long limo ride to the White House.

White House security had tripled itself with many more soldiers surrounding its perimeter than it had usually had in the past. Today there were no electronic security devices or systems in place to protect the president because of the lack of electricity on Earth to operate the devices should someone try to breach the grounds of the capital or any of its many buildings. The same held true for the pentagon and its secured establishments. Ben was more excited in his being able to meet President Stallman than Ann. She truly did not care one way or another in meeting him. She did not want to waste any more precious time away from her mom and dad, for all she wanted to do at that time and moment was to get back onto that wonderful bus that was being held over for them back at the Colonial Grand Trader and get going back home to Vermont. She could not wait to spend quality time with her aging parents. The two of them being elderly and all made Ann fret all the more about being gone for so long, and now another day wasted

almost fried her rump to the sizzling point, but she would do it for her country and for Ben.

How many, many times had she hoped and prayed at night and during those long lonely days away been able to see and hold both of her parents alive just one more time again, and in a good state of health. All she wanted to do was to put her arms around the two of them one at a time and tell them just how much she loved them and had missed the two of them so much. She had never felt a need like this before, but now knew how they must feel seeing how much she had missed her own children for so long, and this unexpected visit to the White House made her fret about her parents all that much more.

Ann looked the picture of a perfect military poster model, posing for an Uncle Sam's I Want You poster. When she awoke, she dressed herself up in her freshly pressed military dress Air Force blues after having the in-house service press them for her after she read the note from the president. When they stepped out of the escort vehicle in front of the White House, the secret service men immediately escorted Ann, Ben and the two children off to the oval office where President Stallman and the First Lady were having tea. The two happily greeted the four of them with open arms. President Stallman shook Ann's hand and introduced her to his lovely wife, Pat, and then Ann introduced her family to them.

"Welcome my dears, welcome. Oh, my-my-my, oh you poor dear, lieutenant. You trapped up there in space all by your lonesome without these two little precious darlings with you. Oh my, oh my. What a pity it must have been. It must have been real hard on you not knowing whether these two little precious ones were still alive or not especially for over a whole long year."

"Yes ma-am it was." "Well, you certainly deserve some sort of heroic decoration, a medal, or something for that, doesn't she, dear?" The first lady turned toward her husband expecting some sort of an instant reply from the president immediately. President Stallman saw the need in his wife's request and shook his head up and down in total agreement with the First Lady, while Ann smiled back a crimsoned colored grin of total embarrassment.

The thoughtfulness of the First Lady was nice, but Ann had other things on her mind. All Ann wanted to do at that point in time was to be on that damn bus going home with her family, and not stuck there in Washington D.C. being flattered over for having been stuck up in outer space for so long. She was sick of being gone away from home for so long.

It was not that she was not grateful for all the attention she was receiving, but she was very homesick, more now than she had ever been before while stuck up in the space station this past year. She knew at that time there was no possibility of her getting back home, but now she was so close to it that it made her more sick to think she had to wait yet another day before she could get to see her folks.

She made the best of the day visiting with the President and the First Lady. The First Lady took a great liking especially to Ann's two little girls, while President Stallman wanted to know every little damn detail from Ann on how she was or was not treated onboard the International Space Station being the only American woman onboard. Some of his questions were quite personal of how she managed with so many men alone, and Ben's ears were listening with great interest with wide-open ears to hear and see what he might learn of what her last year's life aloft had been like. President Stallman did not pull any punches in his questioning either, and wanted to know precisely down to the last gory detail of just how well the large Russian staff aboard the space station had treated her along with the rest of Commander Anderson's crew.

He wanted to know in very much detail the crew's treatment and just how well they all had survived in such a little capsule trapped in space, and what did they all do to pass the time away for fun, and not so much fun for a year, etc. When Ann had finally satisfied the president's appetite with the stupefaction of space, he turned his conversation to the many horrible happenings that had occurred down here below and had taken place on Earth that past deadly day along with all the mixed offensive days that followed.

When the president began his lengthy conversation and speech, it was mostly about the grief the Russian leaders had caused who had ordered the scores of unsafe missiles launched into space and the grief it caused their own people. One quarter of the entire Russian population annihilated by the faulty weaponry their so wonderful leaders at the time, mandated into hurried fruition. Their new greedy leaders all died along with many others around the earth when those damn rockets all returned back to the Earth. By the time they pushed that damn panic button it was already too late for the innocent people down here.

The emergency button exploded them all in our atmosphere. Too bad all the self-installed Russian leaders died that day along with so many innocent Russians. It would have served them right to have lived long enough to see what they had done to their own people. All the missiles had reentered the atmosphere, he said, and set out their weaponry of destruction when the final decision came to destroy them. If they were to have been detonated in space, nothing would have happened down here on the earth, and he explained how she would have possibly not have been standing there along with them that instant.

The world would never be the same he inferred, and it would take at least another ten or twenty years or more before the people of the world would get accustomed to this new way of life they had all been thrown into. The strong willed people around the world he said, would survive the many inconveniences of the neutron invasion, and the frail people with internal vises of unworthiness would dominate their weaknesses into enslaving themselves for others of the world as it has been since the beginning of time.

President Stallman was really beginning to start and frighten the hell out of Ann with everything he was describing in detail, and she knew what he was saying to be the truth, but she almost did not want to hear it. Ben was lost in awe with his every word and did want him to stop talking, but Ann had had enough and was ready to leave before she even got there. When they left for the Grand Colonial Trader Hotel again, she was overwhelmingly pleased to be getting back to her journey going home.

After having finally arrived back at the Grand Colonial Trader, with the children fed and safely tucked into their beds asleep, Ann wanted to talk more openly about everything that had transpired since she had been gone. She wanted to know just how life had been changed so on the Earth for the past several months for him and the rest of his and her family's. She asked him flat out without any sugar coating applied to the question just how hard life had been on everyone.

"Are people on Earth different now, Ben, and how different are they? Are they hot one day like a firecracker and cold the next like ice? Have things really changed as much as the President Stallman and the First Lady say they have? I want to know, Ben, I want to know right now."

"Everything on Earth is wearisome Ann, and downright frightful as hell to say the very least sweetheart. This creature, this thing occupying the air of our universe, in the life air we inhale lurking somewhere or everywhere like a devil in our skies over the earth, is our worst enemy. The Neutron force is an enemy to this world and to every last and all living creatures living on the face of this Earth and in its Sky. You or anyone could be just sitting lazily around for instance. Someone out in front of their house on the lawn just minding their own damned business, just trying to get a suntan, or just out watching the beauty of the stars on a warm summers night with a gentle breeze softly blowing. When suddenly from out of nowhere, this thing, this damn invisible creature from the heavens comes out of the sky striking whomever it damn well pleases or wants to, and thumps the life right out of them, and kills whatever other creatures it chooses."

"What do you mean it comes from nowhere and strikes you dead?" "Oh, it is as if lightning strikes someone but it really is not electricity. No one knows for sure what it really is or where this creature comes from. This invisible thing whatever it is just comes right out of nowhere and strikes its victims like millions of killer bees, and then they are gone."

"What do you mean they are gone? What do you mean, Ben, they just up and disappear, vanish, or die, or what do you mean?" "What I mean, sweetheart, you die, you pass away brutally in pain I guess. The scientists and doctors around the world are blaming it mostly on heart failure. That is all we hear, but most think that is a crock of bullshit.

They all say that anyone who has ever been struck by this creature from the sky have all died from heart failure, but we know better, and so do they. They just don't want to panic the whole damn world, but the ordinary people around this planet are just a damn bit smarter than to listen to those hypercritical suns-a-bitching lying bunch of bastards."

"You sure have changed the way you talk, Ben, and I am glad the girls are asleep, or at least I hope they are asleep anyway. Ann reached over and gave Ben a sweet peck on his cheek before he could continue on about the happenings taking place on the earth since the change. Well any way, Ann, everyone around the planet is starting to get street smart to this damn menacing creature of the universe. People everywhere are all starting to get wise to when and where this creature, if you want to call it a creature, might strike out at them.

Myself as well as all the rest of the people around Lunenburg and the world even though we are not in the military or are studied scientists, are starting to learn and figure out this creature thing all on our own. We figured it out without the damned help of our government, who aren't willing to help anyone anyway, it seems.

I wanted to ask President Stallman just why the hell he didn't care about the people of our country any longer, but I decided it not a good time to ask, and didn't want to ruffle his aging feathers any for he seemed so caring when he spoke, but I saw right through that crap."

"What thing, up where, Ben? What do you mean killed by a creature living in our heavens?" "That is what I am trying to explain to you, Ann. Please listen! Life on earth has been like living in a bubble pushed up from hell ever since you and the others left from here.

CHAPTER THIRTY-SEVEN

Substitute Duty

I was required to be your substitute, ordered by our own supposedly caring government, to go out and bury many of our thousands of dead citizens, along with the millions if not billions it seemed, of the dead animals around both wild and domestic by the thousands, after the devastation of those damn missiles.

Whole towns around this country and the world completely wiped out, Ann, by all those Soviet missiles being all blown up at the same exact time. Not a single building anywhere was hurt or destroyed by the multitude of explosions, only the poor people and their animals, along with a whole bunch of the earth's large bird population flying in the sky that day were also killed, along with every electrical producing field the earth had ever had.

It seemed everything within the blast zone above the earth's surface thirty or more feet or better above the surface of the ground completely wiped clean of life. Not a single moth or butterfly up in the air that day survived. It was just like living in a live episode of a Flash Gordon comic strip, or a Twilight Zone Movie, but this was the real thing, real to life for everyone living in it on the face of the earth that day. Everyone wishing it was nothing but a bad damn dream they were having, and were about to wake up from it all but we are not, and neither are we dreaming it.

It was like an alien monster from outer space came sailing into our world that day and was going around from town to town to town, zapping everything in its sights with their death destroying ray guns of grief leaving nothing alive in the wake of things.

It was horrifying and devastating to so many people, Ann. Remember when President Stallman said to you, you were a hero? Not that you are not one and all that, but, you were probably one of the more blessed lucky ones to have been safe and sound out there in space with your crony friends in the Twitchel, and not stuck back here on Earth with the rest of us.

Military Police from the damn airbase came around knocking door to door on every home throughout base housing, and took a bunch of us along with them. They even took Jeff, our retired sergeant neighbor. The bastards took gents young and old alike out of base housing along with us as volunteers. We were all very unwilling volunteers at the time. Those damned M.P.'s said we were considered as willing volunteers in their eyes having to help in the horrendous clean up in the several surrounding townships in the area.

They said the several towns we had to help clean up were just outside surrounding the base, the lying bastards. None of us had a say in it if they wanted to help or not one way or another. They never asked whether they wanted to go as willing volunteers or objective volunteers and could stay at home with their or our kids.

You being in the military and all, they said it was our duty, our civil obligation to fill in for you and yours in your absence. Fill your shoes or something stupid like that, and took me away, right along with a whole bunch the other not so happy civilians who I am sure didn't want to leave their families as well, including the woman who didn't have children just like me who didn't want to leave our girls, but was made to do so anyway!

You remember Sally next door, don't you?" "Yes." "Well anyway she took the two kids, I mean the girls while I was gone and watched over them for the four months that I was away. Those damn lying M.P. bastards told us it was just going to be for a few days helping in the cleaning up of some of the towns outside the main base gates. It turned out to be a whole hell of a lot longer than just a couple of days for us, and more than just the few towns outside the base the way they described it was going be.

Many of us have been all over this country burying people and animals of all kinds, including zoo animals, birds, and the likes. We all began feeling like the satin's morbid undertakers from hell doing all this crap. We had to bury little innocent children along with their parents and grandparents that all died in the same house. It has been like living in a hell of death on the earth since that day, Ann. I really did feel like the morbid mortician from hell, most the time, as I was out in the field helping in the cleanup of the wretchedness' scattered around this country.

We should have lit all the houses and barns on fire. They could have let Mother Nature take care her own dead and then gone on to the next house and farm along the way and done the same to them. They would not let us do that so we had to carry all the victims out of the houses or barns including the decaying stinking animals and bury them too.

We put dead bodies and corpses into body bags until we ran out of bags, and then we just started flopping dead bodies upon dead bodies along with their dead animals laying them all out along side of each other in the hand dug ditches and trenches and buried them all together. It was horrid absolutely horrid carrying decomposing corpses that fell apart in your hands because of them decaying on the bone and the stench was something none will ever get out of their nostrils no matter how long they are to live. Unbelievable! Hundreds of the dead bodies along with thousands of carcasses of dead animals had all bloated up from the hot heat of the day and some had already exploded into mounds of rotting stench and piles of guts. Maggots from common houseflies and other insects had already commenced thriving on the exposed corpses. It was horrifying to look at all those damn bodies of young and old alike dead and rotting away. It was horrendous!

Some bodies were so far gone, their eyeballs were missing and their brains were starting to bloat and swell out through their eyeball sockets. The bomb that caused this mess did not wipe out all the fly population though. Good old Mother Nature did come along and start her messy recovery clean up job by having all her little maggot friends start doing their jobs. The worst part of the job was up to people who had to do the dirty work for her.

You do remember Sally's husband, the "Sergeant" don't you?" "Yes," well you remember what I said about the thing the monster living up in the sky striking out at someone from nowhere no matter what the condition of the day or weather?" "Yes." "Well I was just about twenty or twenty-five feet away from him I'd say give or take a little filling in a ditch we had already filled with bodies. When suddenly I heard him start to moan and groan wildly. When we turned to see what the matter with him was he was already on the ground thrashing and bouncing around on the ground bouncing up and then down like a damn basketball. He must have died a most horrid death from what I could see and when the officer in charge of our detail bent down and took his pulse reluctantly after a short while, not wanting to get too close to him at first he was gone.

The other men around just pushed him into the dugout pit right along with all the other assorted dead corpses and we buried him just like the others, after the officer in charge reached down and tore the dog tags from off his neck and his wallet from his pants.

He had a distinct orange sheen and wicked stench about his whole body. It was worse than any ordinary hard working body odor of sweat as he lie thrashing around on the ground, so we knew it was that thing from the sky that took his life that day. I had an extremely hard time adjusting to life as a father after that when we returned back home from burying so many dead people, especially so many little children around who did not deserve to die the way they did.

I took Sergeant's dog tags from the officer in charge who had yanked them from off his neck, then took the Sergeant's wallet they had also taken from him before they pushed him into the trench along with all the others. There were so many damn dead bodies another one in the trench didn't make a bit of difference. It could have just as easily have been me that creature had taken out that day. The weather was clear, and sunny, not a cloud in the sky anywhere around. When we finally got back home, I had to break the sad news to Sally about her loving husband. Sally knew there was something very much amiss as soon as I knocked on her front door. I was standing there all by my lonesome out front without the Sergeant standing right there next to me. The Sergeant and I had left together and as we were leaving he said we would be back together soon. So in my book, that meant the two of us would be returning back home together. At least that was what she had figured in her own mind and when I showed up all by my lonesome, she knew right up front probably from the look of sadness in my eyes, that there was something very dreadfully amiss like there was.

The sergeant would not have taken the time as I had to knock on the damn front door. He would have just opened the damn thing up and barged right in like the big kid he always was. Just like a young cowpoke riding a Brahma bull for the very first time in a rodeo hooting and hollering madly, getting the kids all fired up and ready to play hard like he always did when he first got back home for the day, but not this time. Sally did not say anything. She did not say one single solitary word to me when she first opened the door wide with a big happy smile on her face. When she saw me standing there all by my lonesome, she just put her arms out around me and began to cry like a little baby. She knew the Sergeant was gone and was never going to be coming back home to her or for the kids again!

The girls were bitterly cold toward me when they first saw me like I was dirt on snow or ice or something bad like that when I returned back home to them from being taken away from them against my will. They probably thought that you and I had deserted them altogether, and had both gone away forever. I did not even have the chance to say goodbye to the girls properly when I had to leave it was done so fast when they took us, the Sergeant and me away. I have been constantly reinforcing them that you would one day soon be coming home to them. I have tried explaining to them why you were not home yet. I do not think they understood. I would show them where you were at night up in the heavens when we caught a glimpse or a glimmer in the southern sky of what I thought was the orbit of the space station going overhead.

Amber thought it very cool and awesome you being way up there in the heavens with God helping his angles do their work in the sky. When she told us that I had a big lump come up right up into my throat, as sad tears filled my lonely eyes. It was a good thing it was fully dark outside when she said that, so she could not see I was crying. I carefully wiped away any tears from my eyes hoping neither of the girls would see me doing so.

I really hoped you wouldn't get the same cold shoulder I got, like they didn't love me anymore, when I first came back home to them, even though I probably deserved it for leaving them without saying goodbye. I must have become a very cold individual for doing what I had to do even the way I treated myself for what I had gone through. I guess the whole thing still bothers the hell right out of me on occasion. No, most of the time.

It was like heaven to me to see each their little faces staring back up at me once again, but I guess I was too cold of heart, to see them the way they saw me as their father. I guess they could sense something very wrong with me, when Sally hugged me tight, and began to cry like a baby in my arms. I guess the girls thought it rather strange I was hugging someone other than you, and I did not bring you back with me when I returned. They just could not understand why Sally was in my arms crying so, and would not let me go for quite some time. Finally she invited me in and the girls were still cold to me after that, even though I tried to hug and hold them tight to show them how much I had missed them. It has taken one hell of a long time to win their confidence back. Amber seemed to have smiled a little bit at first right after Sally finally composed herself. Sarah on the other hand has not smiled yet or at least not until she saw you for the first time the other day.

She sensed something very much amiss with me, I am sure of it. She felt something bad had happened to you and she had it in her mind she was not going to smile again until her mommy could hold her tight in her arms once more like you did. Now she smiles with a meaning of glimmering hope in her eyes as her tiny cheeks all wrinkle up with her cute little dimples and her teeth shining bright through her tiny lips with a great big smile.

Well, back to the story of this thing here on earth, this creature thing, this monster living in our skies. My theory is this with that creature monster living in the sky, Ann. The creature thing took the earth's energy away from it for its food supply so it might live on in our atmosphere.

Well, it took the earth's energy away from her surface and sky anyway, and now the earth is trying its hardest to reclaim what man tried to take away from her. It's a wonder the earth didn't right up and explode from the horrendous imbalance of electrons, neutrons, protons, atoms, and whatever the hell else there was up there running and floating around bumping into one another in the damned atmosphere that day.

Well anyway, anybody or animals, or other creatures living in this world can become a conductor for the earth to use in its quest to regain its power back from that creature, its super power back from that thing up there. People are zapped to death out walking along an old county road or pathway on a bright sunny day. Any animal out in the wild minding its own business, or say one or more of a farmer's cows out in his pasture just grazing away minding their own business, might just become and do become victims of this monster, this thing living up in our sky.

I think they become victims, murdered by the earth in its frustrating attempts to try to regain some power back from that creature, or the creature trying to keep the earth at bay all the time. I really do not know what in the hell is really going on. The general population and animals of the world become like a hot fuse link in a wire circuit shorting out, when too much electricity is applied to the fuse. They become a direct grounding link between the massive loads of neutrons when any creature encounters it or are around it when it strikes out.

I know this sounds a little strange maybe a whole hell of a lot strange, but that is my theory, Ann. The Earth is trying to regain back its control from this over imposed imbalance in nature caused by man for man, and is killing off man and his animals. That is how I see it, Ann."

"What does it do, Ben? For goodness sakes man can you not explain yourself a little better than that, would you please! How does that monster in the sky you call it, this thing up there, kill people? I am sorry, Ben." Ben could see she was getting frustrated not understanding a thing he was saying.

"I didn't mean to yell at you, Ben. It's just been one hell of a long trying year for me stuck way the hell up there in space without you and the girls around me. Now this, this thing I come home to. This corroborated story of a monster lurking in the heavens of our planet trying to kill our people. That really puts the frosting on the cake, Ben, doesn't it? You do know what I mean don't you? How do we go about protecting our little Amber and Sarah from this creature thing, ourselves, our lives, my parents, or anyone else's life for that matter from this horrible monster lurking in our heavens above?"

"You can't protect yourself or anyone else from it unless you or they become a mole, an ant, or a worm, and live underground for the rest of your life. What a life that would be, huh? The thing doesn't penetrate too deep down below the surface of the earth, and the magnetic fields of the Earth seem to be fighting it off now or at least trying to attack it every once in a while.

I just do not know how to explain it any better than that, Ann. It does not affect any plant life that I know of, only air breathing creatures, or creatures that generate any amount even the smallest insignificant amounts of electrical impulses generated from their insignificant nervous systems enabling them to think, and otherwise move around. I just don't know."

"Well where the hell does that leave us, Ben?" "What do you mean, Ann?" What I mean is just this. Where do we go from here to live with our girls to protect them and us from this creature thing, this invisible creature thing lurking in the sky?"

"There is nowhere here on earth to run or hide with our children Ann. That creature thing is everywhere. Rumor has it that it is even worse over the Ukraine in Russia, as it damn well should be. If it weren't for those stupid egotistical sons of bitches, this whole thing wouldn't have ever have had to happen to the earth."

"The Russian people are not all that bad, Ben. If it were not for those few Russian cosmonauts onboard the space station, I would not be standing here with you right now. They could have just as easily blocked the docking platform and airlocks on the space station, and that would have left us out in the cold in space to die from suffocation or starvation without any oxygen, or food to survive. You just cannot go around judging a whole country because of a few egotistical bastards that are power hungry. It just isn't fair to the rest of the good people of Russia."

"I know it isn't fair honey, but it does take all kinds of people to make this world of ours go round, including the sour apples on this planet. I just hope they were some of the first people to go, when they first pushed that foolish button of theirs. No I do not, not really. I hope some of them suns-a-bitches are still around, whether they are simple minded or not, so they can see just what they have gone and done to this once nice world of ours we had. I would love to be able to point out to them just what their greedy little minds did to so many innocent people around the world, including what they did to their own fellow citizens. I hope some of those bastards found themselves in the middle of this damn mess just like everyone else around the globe. It would serve them bastards right if they were, and I hope some are still alive and experiencing it! I wish no harm to anyone in the world, but I do hope the ones who did this receive it in the end what justice is due them bastards. It would serve them right to suffer right along with the rest of the others who are suffering dearly from all this!"

They were warned by their own scientific people not to make or launch these damned rockets until they were perfected beyond a reasonable doubt. Being so impatiently egotistical, they did not have enough brains to listen or take heed from their own scientific people. Now look at what those greedy bastards have done to our world, a planet in pure despair and there is not a thing anyone can do to correct or rectify their freaking mistake. This world is full of smart people all right, people able to mess up everything worldwide for everyone, but

not smart enough to straighten out what they have so unconscionably caused."

"How are Mom and Dad doing with all this happening around them, Ben?" "They both are doing just fine, Ann. They would have loved to have come down to Florida and welcomed you back home as well for they were both invited too, but this trip down here would have been just too much for the two of them to endure at their age.

They did not want to upset the apple cart, so they decided for their own good health and wellbeing, that staying home in Vermont was a great deal smarter for them than coming way down here to Florida, and getting themselves all excited, worn out, and sick. They are both doing just fine, super fine in fact."

"Good, and I just cannot wait to see the two of them again. You just cannot imagine how I have missed everyone down here so much while I was stuck up there. I just cannot wait to get back home to the farm and sample some of mom's special homemade cooked meals. Then I will know I am home and can enjoy them and myself. If there is one thing you are definitely not going to get in outer space is one of a home cooked meal like the ones Mom cooks up in her kitchen. I just cannot stand it anymore, Ben. I do not want to have to wait any longer before I can just put my arms around the two of them and squeeze them tight with a good old tight loving Vermont bear hug. I never knew how anyone could possibly miss other people the way I have missed you Ben, the kids, and my parents.

It is hard to explain just how painful it feels, and how hard it really is being stuck way out there, unable to be with the ones you love so dearly, and not able to talk to any of them, or to know just what is happening to anyone below. Everyday locked up out there in that steel capsule, seemed more like a week to me, and every week a month, and every month an entire eternity. Oh, how I missed the lot of you guys so much. There were so many nights I just lay awake in my cubical, silently crying with tears flowing from my eyes thinking of you and the kids, and every once in a while my folks. I could not help it but I thought of you and the girls most the time and cried for days.

I especially cried for the first few days away, and the twelve days just prior to Christmas, as well as the days when you and the girls all had your birthdays. I even cried at Easter for crying out loud, and on the Fourth of July, too. There were just so many nights I lay awake wanting to be in your arms again and have you tell me everything was going to be all right with everything. Did you miss me, Ben? I mean did you really miss me?"

"Honey, there hasn't been a single solitary day gone by with that I haven't missed you or thought about you in one way or another. I was recruited to help dispose of all those decaying bodies before I knew if you were dead or alive, or had a chance to be alive. I spent four lousy long hard long hours-less tiring months out traveling around this country. From town, to town we traveled, burying people and animal carcasses for miles around the south before I found out the Twitchel had safely rendezvoused and linked up with the space station.

Even then I did not know if anyone were dead or alive onboard. All they would tell us, or could tell us at that time, was that the shuttle had linked up and docked itself to the space station. No one down here knew for sure one way or the other; they just presumed you were all safe and doing well at the time.

They did inform us, however, that one day in the future that the limited supplies onboard the craft needed to survive in space would run out for everyone, and you would either have to come back home to earth, or perish out there for lack of food and oxygen. They predicted it would take about six, eight, ten, or more months before something as drastic as that would take place, if you were ever to come back home, or at least give it a try to come back home then.

I just knew it or felt it in my heart that you and the others had all perished out there! The four months I spent out in the field with the Sergeant just about killed me, thinking mostly about you all of the while stuck up there dead in that shuttle with the others, especially when the Sergeant was struck down and died I almost wanted to die myself. The only reason I did not give up on life myself was for our wonder little girl's sake.

I knew they needed at least one of us to come back home to be with them, even if it was only myself. Losing one parent would have been shocking enough for them to experience in their little lives, and I could not see them two losing the two of us.

Personally I felt inside as if I had died within my own being out in the field with all those dead bodies scattered out all over the countryside Ann. The only two things that kept me going day after long day were our two beautiful little precious girls. I knew I had to return back home to them as soon as I could just for their sake, and not my own. That was if that damn thing in the air hadn't taken them away from me, or us by the time I was able to return back home to them.

I too have had to have a lot of courage, Ann, to be strong for the two of them while I was out there in the field, and it made me all that much stronger for it I guess. It made me a survivor Ann, a real survivor of the times and in what I was doing, going through, and where I would go when it was all over and done with.

You just cannot imagine what it was like when I had to help bury the hundreds of little children out there that we had too Ann. I cried for every one of them. It was just like burying one of my own children, I mean our own children every time I came across another dead child in a house, barn, or out in a field. I was truly astonished and surprised I had any tears left in my little head too cry after a while, but the tears just kept on a coming, and coming, and coming.

I just could not help but to think about all the good happy times these poor little children were going to miss out on in life with their folks, which we were burying right along with them in those retched ditches. I cannot imagine being a funeral director and having to prepare a small child for the grave. I just cannot imagine people doing that for a living. I would have nightmares about it all of the time, and would have to give that profession up. I still have nightmares about burying people and their little ones.

Did I miss you, Ann? You're damned right I missed you Ann. I have missed you from the tips of my littlest toes, to the longest strands and tips of the longest hairs on my head.

I missed you so much I could taste the hurt of loneliness in my wanting mouth for a kiss from you. That is exactly, how much I have missed you so much, and so did the girls along with your parents, as well as everyone else that knows you down here.

This country has missed you and the others because of those few damned pig headed unconscionable fools that wanted to show the rest of the world just how big and important they thought they all were, and now don't even exist anymore the bastards.

My wish other than getting you back alive was to have all those idiots suffer the way I saw so many people and their families out there were suffering, or had suffered during that awful attack of theirs. Whether intentional or not intended to happen, the whole thing just was not fair, not fair at all to the good people of this world. I sure hope there is at least one of those miserable bastards left alive to pay the price for this.

When I was finally notified the Twitchel had made it and safely docked with the space station, my painful throbbing heart stopped hurting quite so bad. I knew there was at least a little spark of hope for you, a wee light at the end of the tunnel that you could possibly still be alive out there. I just couldn't help but to think of you trapped up there with all those men, not knowing what was going on, and you not able to come back home. Did I think of you, Ann? You're damn tooting I thought of you, and I missed you just as dearly as one needs food to live on and air to breath. If you did not come back home to me soon, I think a broken heart might have overcome me. That is how much I have missed you, Ann, and I will never let you go out of my sight ever again, except with your mom or the girls.

I was getting pretty desperate for you in the end. I wanted to see if any of you especially you Ann were still alive up there, and needed some kind of special help. I wanted to go to Washington personally too make our Government send a rocket with a special capsule on its nosecone up there for your safe return, but you came back home to me first safe and sound without their help.

I really do not know what I would have done if I had I lost you. My only hope and prayers are this, we will never have to be-separated ever again as we were. Being separated from you for just one day right now would be way-too much for my aching heart to bear. Now that we are together again, I can become a stronger father and the manly person I once was. I tried to be the best parent that I could possibly be, but without you by my side I was but half of a real person, and really only half of a father that I should have been to the girls. It has been a real living hell here on earth trying to be both mommy and daddy and sole support provider for the girls and your parents. They need their real Mommy and daughter around to be happy, Ann! I just cannot work the way I use to work.

Taking care of your folks, their farm, the children, and worrying about you all the time has driven me almost insane. Almost to the state of madcap. I have worried so much about you and everything else in the world I do not hardly sleep at night. I was just about to lose my mind any time real soon, when word came to us from Cape Canaveral, from the space center that you and the others were home safe. Did I miss you, Ann? You tell me.

Look deep down into my eyes and see who I really am now. Did I miss you? You're damned right I did!

I know your time to reenlist in the Air Force as a NASA officer will soon be arriving in another month or so, but if you do not take that damn oath of reenlistment, and swear yourself back into the military, it will suit me just fine, and everyone else around here in your life. I know it has always been your dream and career, but now it is time to think of your family, and a career as a mother and homemaker. I cannot stand the thought with you gone and us alone ever again any longer.

I am asking you please do not reenlist again Ann, for me, for the children, your folks, and for our relationship. I am begging you not to reenlist Ann. I am not demanding it but, please, please, please for our sake, for mine sake Ann, please do not sign up again for God's sake, Ann.

Think of the children this time, and please think of me. Did I miss you? You're damn right I missed you, and so did the girls right along with everyone else around here. You'll damn well see what I mean when we get back home to the farm and to Lunenburg!"

CHAPTER THIRTY-EIGHT

The Arrival Home

Dave Silsbee turned to see who might be departing or arriving on the midday bus arriving from Saint Johnsbury, before getting into and closing the door to his diesel fired pickup truck. He had just purchased some supplies at the hilltop general store, and post office by the common. He had been watching the bus come up the U.S. Route 2 hill, the road leading in from St. Johnsbury as it pulled up to its bus stop to let Ann, Ben, and the kids out from their long journey home from Florida.

"Hey, Dave," Ben yelled out from across the road! "Wouldn't mind giving old Betsy here a push to fire her up for me would you, Dave? Sure thing, Ben, glad to hear everything is working out good for you folks. Glad to see you home safe and sound Missy." "Thank you, Dave", Ann hollered back.

"Hear you had a real hard time of it stuck up there all by your lonesome self in space with a bunch of them their crazy male Russian cosmonauts. I sure hope they all had some good manners, and treated you all right." "They sure did Dave. They were a great bunch of good guys and gals up there." "Girls, too? Heck I thought there were only a bunch of Russian men up there with you missy, and you being the only gal up there and all."

"No, Dave! There were about two woman cosmonauts to every male onboard." Ann said that to diffuse any rumors going around. "Damn! I should have been one of them there lucky cosmonauts myself, I guess. Two to one you say?" "Yes sir, Dave. Two women to every man up there. Boy what a bunch of lucky men they all were, huh, Dave?"

Ann smiled, as Dave hit the air lever to his automatic air starter, to fire up his diesel engine pickup truck. The starter whistled out a loud whirring shrill deafening rush of air noise from its exhaust, as the diesel engine in his pickup truck fired up without any delay.

"You are going to have to put yourself in one of these here fancy air starters Ben. They sure come in real handy at times. Don't know what I would do without it now Ben?" "I guess you're right, Dave. Thanks again for the push, pal." "You are welcome. Glad to have you home Missy". "Glad to be back home." "See you all in church Sunday morning." "Thank you, Dave. Say high to the misses for us Dave." "I will Missy. You have to come to church on Sunday morning Missy. I hear everyone in the whole town is a going to come out to welcome you back home you know. See you all on Sunday." Ann and Ben waved as Dave drove away down the South road towards his farm in South Lunenburg.

"I guess we all have to go to church on Sunday morning right Ben?" Ann asked Ben turning towards him with a funny smile on her face. "I told you I wasn't the only one who missed you around these parts Ann. When everyone found out you were back on earth safe' and sound. Father Michael after having a prayer in his morning worship for you and the other astronauts every Sunday morning wanted to have a day of thanksgiving in your honor, and Sunday was chosen for your return party. I told you, you would be surprised when we got back home, to just how many people around did miss you when you were gone. Now you will see for yourself just how everyone around Lunenburg missed you, and Sunday will be the day."

Ann's mother heard Ben's loud diesel pickup truck come roar howling, clap-pity-clap the engine valves singing out as the diesel engine barked, racing up the road and dirt driveway. "Pa! Pa! Ann is home, Pa! Come quickly," Ann's mother, hollered out in excitement. Ann's father came running out through the front door of the farmhouse and onto the front piazza to great their only daughter, his only child. He moved with great speed, gliding easily for the ailments of his old age. From sitting in his favorite maple rocker in the front parlor to the front porch, he shot in a flash.

He was so ecstatic to hear the good news about his little girl being home, he went running to the door instead of his usual stiff hobbling along. He held his old Hickory cane in his left hand while bracing off the furniture with his right hand as he hustled along. Today he was like an Eagle in hot pursuit of a swift fish in a stream or a rabbit on a dead run across a field. Ann's parent's eyes became blurry eyed, filled with happy tears of loving joy for a change, instead of their usual worried sick looks. Their returning daughter Ann ran up to the front porch to great them standing there, with happy joyful tears of her own streaming down her face as she saw their happy aging faces. Throwing out both her arms she grabbed the two of them together as one, and cried happy joyful tears right along with the two of them. She hugged and squeezed the two of them almost half to death she was so happy to be home and seeing them still alive.

"I missed you two guys so much. I love you Mom. I love you Dad. I just love you two to pieces," she said without taking a breath, with a frogeye, half-clogged low happy sounding joyful voice. "How are you two doing anyway, you two look so grand." "We are doing just fine, Ann, much better now thank you dear especially now that you are back home with us safe and sound here at the farm.

The question is, dear, how are you doing? That is all that is important to us right now, sweetheart. We did not know if you were dead or alive up there in the heavens aloft. We have been worried sick for months over you dear. Everyone worried for you up there all alone without Ben, and the two girls! How are you doing?"

"I am doing just fine, thank you! I could not be doing any better if I tried. The question is, how are you doing, Dad?" "Real good Pumpkin. Damn good, and you look pretty good to me too young lady. I am doing better than good now. I am doing great, Ann. Especially now that you have gotten yourself back home to us, safe, and sound from off up yonder in that damned flying machine of yours.

Damn those high fall luting flying machines anyway, and you had to go off and pick one that goes up in to outer space, you damn fool child. I am good now honey. Glad to have you back home safe and sound with us! You aren't going to go off and do that dang flying machine thing to us again are you Ann?"

"No Pa, not if I can help it, I am not. My life of high flying machines into outer space is over, Pa. I do not have an inkling in me to take it up again, if I can help it that is. Maybe a hot air balloon ride or something like that someday that doesn't go quite so high, just for the fun of it." They all laughed in unison, as Ann laughed while making the comment.

"Isn't any good to try and fly any those flying gadget things these days anyway child? I hear a guy down Springfield way went up in his hot air balloon, and was killed by that monster thing living in the sky when one of his ties down lines dragged along the ground, and the monster turned the man and his balloon orange. Then the balloon crashed and burned with him still inside the balloon's basket. I sure hope you are not a going to go and try something stupid like that, are you?" "No way, no more flying for me, Pa."

"Your Ben here Ann, has been a great big help since you've been gone, dear. Came all the way up here from Florida to live with us, shortly after he got back from doing that God awful job they made him go off to do. Came all this way he did, way up here to Vermont with your two wonderful girls to help us out here on the farm, and to live up here with us.

Your pa needed someone desperately to help him out after that bomb went off. Old Howard our old hired hand went off and got himself killed by that horrible monster thing from the Sky. He was off up in the back forty acre field, fixing some bad fences the cows had broken though, when suddenly that thing lit up the sky with orange over the farm. That monster thing took half our herd of cattle too up there, right along with him, when it took poor old Howard away.

It's a good thing we had old Dixie out in the barn in her stall or we would have all been in an awful fix without her! Not a darn thing would start up for us, not even our faithful old tractor. It would not even try to turn over when we turned the danged key to start it. The old tractor had died, the new car would not start, and neither would the old pickup truck. Everything went dead all at the very same time. The earth has not had a lick of electrical power on it or around it ever since that day.

Your pa hitched up old Dixie to the hay wagon, and then he and I went out to look for old Howard. The world looked frightfully awful outside, the sky all orange and all, and we did not want to leave poor old Howard out there all by his lonesome alone in the awful storm that looked to be brewing.

Your pa had taken him up there earlier in the day to do some fencing repairs. We could do nothing for the poor chap by the time your pa and I reached him. He looked a real mess like something or someone awful had painted him a burnt orange color like a bad rotting Halloween pumpkin and the odor he gave off was wow, he smelled the high heavens with such an unpleasant odor about him you just could not stand being anywhere near him. He smelt as if someone had emptied an entire jug of burning ammonia all over him in flames or had urinated on an open campfire or something that smelled all bad like that, and he looked an awful mess.

Your pa had to put him in the back of the hay wagon all by himself, and then drove him over to Dick's place for him to take care of the arrangements for his funeral before he went over to tell Florence his wife about what had happened to him. Poor old Florence the poor old girl. When your pa stopped by to tell her about old Howard, he could not believe his eyes. She was dead, too. He found her out back by her clothesline looking the same burnt orange, and smelling just like poor old Howard. A couple of hundred folk around these parts lost their lives that dreadful day. Your pa and I were some of the lucky ones, around here I guess.

We were down in the vegetable bin down in the cellar I guess when all hell broke loose outside. Sounded like a million or more angry killer honeybees were just flying around outside the house mad as hell, as if someone had just opened up their hives without smoking them first to calm them all down. Never heard such a horrid racket in all my life, and never want to hear that sound again. Good thing you were way up there in that space machine when that damn thing hit us down here. Guess no one flying around that day ever lived to tell about it either. I heard about a whole bunch of bad news about people flying that day that went down with their air-o-planes.

Well old Dick the undertaker kept busy for one heck of a long time after that. Too busy if you asks me my dear, and old Doc Roberts was right out straight, and is still trying to help people cope with this disaster. Lots of folk he couldn't help though, they just stood around in big groups like dumb old cattle grazing in a field, all looking and acting all dopey and lost, as many still do today. Never can remember seeing so many simple minded acting people around never in my lifetime.

Some of these people use to be real smart, too, like Mr. Thompson's daughter the librarian. She cannot even tie her own shoelaces anymore by herself or get dressed no more. She is simple minded like a toddler. Everything around here has really gone array ever since you went away. Glad to have you back, Ann!

Your Ben here has been doing the work of ten men, never mind one dear. Works harder than most, fingers to the bone every day dear, and does not complain one bit. I could tell by his eyes how he missed you dearly, every time I looked into his eyes. They almost bleed with pain and compassion for you my dear. He has been an awesome father to the girls too, and a very good provider for us all Ann. He has been running the farm, and working his hands raw.

You sure could not have married yourself a better man than that there Ben of yours Ann! Now that your pa is all laid up and all, Ben has to do all the work around here 99% of it all by himself. We just cannot seem to be able to hire anyone else either, seeing there just is not anyone else left around these parts to hire. Every farmer for miles around is all in the same boat and predicament as we are around here, except we have Ben to take care of the load for us.

Folk around here have been trying to run their farms without any help at all, except each other chipping in when they need a helping hand. Some folk around here will not even come out of doors anymore, because they are all afraid of that thing up in the sky. They think if they go out in the open fields to work their crops, that the thing will come right out of nowhere from the sky and snuff out their lives just like it did to poor old Howard.

Damn shame what them fool Russians went and did to us, and the rest of the world, isn't that right sweaty? How have you been, Ann? You're pa and I have been worried sick over you ever since you left, and that bomb went off." "I've been OK I guess guys. I am just glad to be back home with you two again!"

"Ben kept on telling us, you were all right and all, but seeing you here in the flesh is better than just believing what he was saying to just keep us happy. He is a right nice man. Ben here use to tell your Ma and I to just look up into the southern sky late at night, and wave to you when the lights of that there space station would go flickering on bye for a split second over the top of the horizon. He kept on telling us you were waving down at us when we were waving up at you all at the same time, and after a while we all began believing you were. Were you Ann? Were you really waving down at us when we were waving up at you?" "I sure was pa, more times than you can count."

"Ben had all kinds of faith in your returning back home to us and so did we, I guess? He use to rock Sarah on his lap out on the front piazza at night in the old rocking chair looking up into the heavens, and kept on telling her and Amber where you were. He said that you would soon be coming back home to them, soon as you possibly could. He sounded very convincing at the time too. We use to pray very hard at night before bed that God would keep a watchful eye out for you, and I guess our prayers were all answered. Here you are now all the more beautiful and all, and home here safe and sound with us thank goodness."

With another grizzly bear type hard squeezing hug by Ann's frail father, he told her he was more than glad she was back home with them. He wore great tears of joy in his eyes she had made it home safe and sound, then let her go to stand and listen to her some more.

"Your Ben here Ann is and has been a real good provider. You should be downright proud as a peacock with him the way he has handled everything around here and in the town as well. He has been a good Johnny on the spot here on the farm, and in helping all the other farmers around the area. He went and made up a windmill to help run the water pump out in the well, and made a water holding tank out in the barn so we could have running water all of the time. He hooked up the old diesel engine out of the old White-milk tanker truck left out back that still ran to run the air compressors for the milking machines, and all the other air operated equipment around here. He is one handy individual to have around, and you should be downright proud of him, that Ben of yours. He should have the old pickup trucks new air starter in her shortly, and then everything round here should be very good again for a change.

I guess he plans to dig a huge crater out back and building us a home down in the ground so we can be sure we are safe from that thing, and have the conveniences of some electricity back again, using solar power or something like that, I do not really know, or understand how it works. He is just full of great ideas, Ann. Could not have asked for a better son in-law than that-there Ben husband of yours you married.

Glad you roped him when you did! If it weren't for Ben here, half the farmers around Lunenburg and Lancaster, NH would have lost their crops of hay this year. Your hubby Ben has been right out straight helping every farmer around the northeast kingdom of Vermont. They have all pitched in to helping one another out getting in their crops of hay.

Old Dave Silsbee has been using his old diesel powered equipment right along with everyone else in the region, and between him and your Ben here, all the cows of Lunenburg should be able to eat good this winter. Right smart ambitious lad that Ben of yours Ann, glad we have him for our son-in-law."

For the next couple of days, everyone kept busy doing chores around the farm that had been neglected while Ben was away, and at night telling their tales of what the last year had meant to everyone since

the big blast that created the monster in the sky, that now inhabits the earth's once friendly atmosphere.

There were more horror stories being spread around about the creature, than there were of the good old happy times of old being talked about. Ann could not believe her ears, hearing all these awful things of change that had taken place on and around the globe that had taken place and become the norm since the big blast. It was as if she was waking up into a nightmare, instead of waking up from one.

Ann's farther went on talking about several stories of the blast and how things were, and might become to pass in the future. "One of Ann's cousins lost his life that dreaded day, right along with about a hundred or better more. All caught up in the situation these poor innocence people operating or riding along on the Cog railroad steam engine line, almost on top Mount Washington on their way to its summit. That was when the big blast took place.

Some tourists at the base station of the mountain became extremely sick as well, but the ones so high up on the mountain died a suffocating, twisting, and jolted death it looked from all being so heavily exposed to all those wild free floating neutrons, that quickly massed out all around them, all at the same time.

All the animals half way up the mountain or above died the same horrific deaths as did the people there along with the wild fouls of the air that dropped out of the sky like rain. Everyone atop the mountain died that horrific day except for one very lucky young man. The rangers in all their ranger huts, and the other ones stationed around the mountain died in shelters and outside their stations died.

All the hikers half way up or better on the mountain-top died as well, including all the weathermen and rangers stationed at top camp died an awful twisted death, except for a young electrician named Sammy Robinson. He was able to live, protected from the neutron exposure down inside the concrete foundation and rocks surrounding the basement of the weather laboratory. He was better than twenty-five feet beneath the surface below the tower section of the observatory, inside its stone lined cellar trying to repair a shorted out transmitter lead wire for the weather stations Doppler radar transmitter that had failed earlier that day, around 4 a.m. in the morning, and had just arrived to begin his repairing of it.

Suddenly every lighting fixture in the subterranean vault of the laboratory went out leaving Sammy in the black of darkness including his trusty flashlight that had a strange odor about it when he picked it up. He was truly amazed at all that had suddenly transpired around him, leaving him in total darkness, making him quite upset and queasy to his stomach.

He was very upset with his flashlight, for he had just replaced the old batteries in his flashlight, and had put in two brand new supposedly super charged nickel cadmium rechargeable batteries into it from their charger on the wall of his garage earlier that morning. The charger had read fully charged and he had just tested it earlier before descended down into the basement of the Mount Washington's Top Camp Weather Station's observatory.

Sam figured the flashlights bulb must have blown out from the strong surge of power from the new batteries, but it did not even flicker when he pushed the button. He should have taken a spare light bulb for it down along with him, but he did not give it a second thought, that the bulb would blow out at the same time the electrical power of the station would fail.

He stood there in the dark in total dismay, everything electrical had failed on him, all at once. The pitch-black darkness really ticked him off. Completely upset that the new emergency lighting system that he had so recently installed into the basement of the building he had serviced failed him. It flickered for less than a split second, and then went instantly black.

A sudden feeling of instant nausea and dizziness struck him as if he had just come down with an instant case of the flu. His ears began to ring loudly with an awful buzzing noise inside them that made him more the dizzier from the vibration. He was going to scream at the damn idiots who sold him this faulty equipment, only a couple of weeks earlier, who had said the new emergency lighting system was the best of the line in their newly improved emergency lighting equipment on the market.

In only a matter of a short few seconds, Sammy managed to get hisself turned around down in the basement. He managed to lose his way a couple of several times in the basement of the observatory, for it was totally pitch black down there. All he had to go on in finding his way out of the structure was his feeling around in the pitch-blackness of the cellar with his feet and hands to guide his way out the maze inside the building.

It took him two and a half, almost three hours to find his way out the maze of tunnels, air ducts, and loose wiring conduit left scattered around on the floor of the blacked out basement. He tried hard not to kill himself stumbling over old equipment, and other scattered unknown equipment left scattered all over the cellar floor down in the laboratory by the sloppy personnel working for the weather station, and other personnel who worked there before him.

He had to step over some discarded old scattered equipment in the basement trying hard not to break his damn fool neck. This mess use to bug the hell out of him before when he could see it with light every time he visited the facilities. Now this blackout really bugged the hell out of him, falling over everything beneath his feet.

He decided when he got out of this hell hole, he was going to give whoever the lazy bastard was who was supposed to be in charge of keeping the place clean, and really give him a piece of his mind about the disgusting situation down there. How could anyone leave such a mess, and have to walk over it once or twice a day when they themselves had to go down there to take readings from some of their special weather equipment. It just did not make any sense to him.

Sam was really upset with himself, for just a couple of days prior to this he had given up smoking cigarettes for good, after having tried several times in the past to do so. He was pissed off at himself for his damned cigarette lighter was out in his service truck about a hundred or better feet above and away from him outside in the parking lot, and it couldn't help him to see in the dark now.

He surmised the top camp weather station had probably lost its power lines due to the extreme winds they sometimes experience up there. The emergency generator in the furnace room failed to kick in when it was supposed to start on its own. Who in the hell knew what was going on up there, he thought, for he was as mad as hell that this was happening to him.

The day had started off real bad for him in the first place with a flat tire on his service van when he first went outside to leave for the mountain. Now this blackout was the straw that broke the camel's back. Every damn time he came to this God-forsaken place on top of Mount Washington something strange seemed to happen to him, and this left him feeling this place was nothing but a jinx to him somehow.

When this year's contract with the weather station in keeping their equipment up and running was up, so was he with this damned place. He was not going to climb over the junk they left around down there anymore, and maybe just maybe his damn tires would not go flat on his vehicles anymore. When he was finally able to reach the top of the stairway, he felt like he was walking out into a battlefield when he emerged from the cellar of the weather station and into its lobby finding everyone smelling of deadly phosgene gas, all dead, and looking a disgusting color of burnt orange. He felt like he had emerged into the twilight zone of hell, feeling sicker all the while, not knowing it was from all the many neutrons floating wildly all around him.

Outside the mountain's laboratory, everyone there were also dead. The cog railway steam engine and its cars were all lined up tight against the emergency stopping barrier at the top end of the railed track with a trickle of smoke still coming up out the engines stack pipe with all its passengers, and its engineer laying scattered every which way in the cars and engine, also dead.

All he could think about was someone had dropped an atomic bomb, some-where close by the mountain. The sky looked a bright orange sheen in color from a nuclear blast he thought, and the bright of blue of the morning sky was gone. He figured it would be a matter of seconds or minutes before he would die from the saturation of radiation penetrating his body, for he felt miserable from so many neutrons

surrounding him in the air. He thought this feeling was radiation causing him to feel this awful way, but it was not and he did not die.

He suffered more and more from the extreme amount of massive neutrons surrounding him and trying to attack his nervous system all at the same time. But the working jump suit he had on and his protective leather lined hard hat was protecting him. He tried to start his service van to descend back down the mountain road, but his van would not start. It was as dead as a doornail. There were a couple dead bodies on the ground behind his van he would have to move or run over them to get it out.

He was in a war zone, and he knew it. He went to a car parked next to the road's exit leading down the mountain to see if there were keys in it, and there were. There were also a couple of dead people in it, and when he opened up the door to see if it would start, an horrific odor met his nostrils almost making him instantly vomit. He took a mountain bike someone had ridden up to the top of the mountain and had no use for it any longer for the cyclist was lying dead on the ground beside the bike. He righted the bike from the ground and swiftly proceeded in descending back down the mountain road.

There were cars scattered off the roadway everywhere that had been coming up the mountain, and several very severe car wrecks going down the mountain. There were bikers of all kinds, motorcyclist, and pedal bikers alike, hikers of all ages were strewn all over the roadway like fallen dominos. The landscape of the mountain was a nauseating mess covered with dead birds of all kinds scattered everywhere along with all the dead bodies.

Around the world, a vast assortment in species of fowl from the air rained down from the heavens dead in record numbers, drained of any electrical impulses they once had. Millions of birds, insects, bats and other species around the planet instantly died along with the hundreds in air planes falling from the skies filled with thousands of innocent people that came raining down.

Half way down the mountain at the ranger station, he saw many people scattered around on the ground dead, while others just lay there shaking from immense seizures from the massive invasion of neutrons that were almost dead. Sam thought at first that he had crossed over into the twilight zone from hell or that he was in an Alfred Hitchcock movie's live set of a still set production before he made it all the way down to the mountain's base camp at the end of the mountain roadway. When he finally reached the bottom, he found the situation similar to that at the half way mark except for all of the dead people. Instead he saw people just walking around lost as if they had all been at the ranger's station halfway up the mountain. They were in total disarray, lost to what was happening and taking place around them. The world had instantly transformed into a world of chaos. Some of the people had the hoods to their cars and pickup trucks opened wondering why the engines to their vehicles would not start or had quit running. There were no longer any more cell phone communication systems anywhere. Radios around the world didn't work any longer as there was no more electricity available to anyone to operate them. The once bright blue color of the sky above had turned a pale orangey watery foggy color of dirty green.

Sam rode the borrowed mountain bike and had to ride it thirty-five miles away to his home. Along the several roads, he came upon more horrifying accidents from the many neutronically induced deaths. The higher in terrain he rode, the more tragedy he found along the roadways.

When Sam finally arrived back home, he was cheerful, relieved and very fortunate because his lovely wife and two beautiful little children were secure away from any harm inside their modest home. Their lives had been spared, but would never be the same from that day forward.

He would find tragedy had felled many of his friends, relatives, and neighbors living in the surrounding higher terrain area that day as did so many in the world. It was a very good thing, that Sam had a small farm he worked and lived on for his hobby and was able to work the land to his benefit and enable him to help his family survive in the hard times that were to come. He, too, would become a helper of friends and neighbors in dire need and of the local farmers in the region who relied on each other to work their fields and to help the many others less fortunate in need of survival.

The sky and air above the earth was much less crowded now with so many fewer birds to occupy its vast space. Some species of birds and insects had become instantly extinct because the effects of the neutron blast. Some wildlife species around the globe were mostly wiped out, but with a very few still remained to carry on their breed of life.

It would take years to rebuild the population of birds, insects, and other wild life in the world back to where they had been before the blasts occurred around the globe.

CHAPTER THIRTY-NINE

Daring Pilots

Not many daring souls had tried to face this creature in the heavens by flying since the big blast. A couple enthusiastic balloonists figured it was now safe to fly their hot air balloons again. Not using any electrical power in flying their balloons, they figured it would be safe to fly them. They as well met their untimely deaths when the hot air balloon tie down ropes hanging from the gondola acted as a static electrical conductor dragging along the ground. They, along with their daring guests aboard their air ships, glowed an orange sheen of smoke in the air like a bright light bulb, dying almost instantly as the masses of killer neutrons surrounded them. The monster in the sky sucked the smallest of electrical impulses of life out from their frail bodies before returning back into the quiet heavens. The so-called smart balloonists all figured it would be safe to fly as they had nothing of electrical power onboard their craft, but had forgotten to take into account the possibility of static electricity generated by the tie down ropes possibly skipping loosely along the surface of the earth, might cause such a thing to happen.

The Twitchel had been the only aircraft known to fly successfully ever since the neutron bomb incident. Maybe it would be safe to try to fly her once again, but nobody knew for sure. There had been several people around the planet that everyone knew about who had died trying to fly.

In Ann's father's prediction was more than a 100% correct when he said someone would be foolish enough to try to start to fly the deadly skies once again real soon.

The Air Force itself was preparing to try and test flight a newly outfitted flying machine. The space craft Twitchel was being stripped out and re-outfitted as they talked to try to fly back into outer space for another mission. It would be a mission of mercy to bring more food, oxygen, and supplies to the unlucky ones still stuck out there in space. NASA knew time was running out for the crew if no one did anything real soon as they would all mostly perish. The time was soon approaching when only a mere half dozen citizens of the world would have a slim chance of returning back home to the earth as the others in outer space would all perish a slow if not agonizing death of misery starving to death, or suffocating for lack of oxygen to breath.

Ann did not know it at the time, but in the near-off future she would be asked to preflight the newly re-fabricated space shuttle Twitchel. She would be asked in the near future by NASA to join her old crew in an attempted rescue mission to go back into the unknown of new space travel to bring oxygen and desperately needed survival supplies back to the space station circling the earth above.

Whenever Ann spoke about her last year living above, she would always talk very highly about all the very nice people still held captive against their wills, and were not able to return home to Earth from aboard the space station. How desperately she worried about the ones who had helped save her life with being out there without any means of retuning back to the earth without the help of others.

CHAPTER FORTY

Sunday Morning Mass

Most the town's people around Lunenburg, Vermont all went to church that next Sunday morning for worship. Some just turned out to meet their home town hero, and celebrate Ann's successful return back home to Earth. The church instantly overfilled. All the town's people, along with many people from surrounding towns, had come out to see their hero who returned from space. Many had to stand inside and outside the jammed doors of the church listening to the mass and sermon.

Ann was given the podium just prior the early morning sermon and was asked by the clergyman of the church to give a short oration of her experience before the regular sermon began. She talked shortly about the ordeal she and the others first went through when the shower of comet dust and dry ice activated all the deadly missiles. She then went on about being aboard the space station, and how the ones up there, the Russians mostly, and the two Germans in space had helped save the Twitchel's crew along with herself from dying a horrendous death in space. With no place to go that looked safe for them floating helplessly above a world that at the time looked like a huge floating orange basketball, the space station crew opened their doors to them so they accepted the invitation with delight at the time. Everyone on the space station prayed for the ones on earth hoping they could return one day to be with their loved ones back home.

Ann took questions from all the children and a few of the adults. She then handed the podium back over to the cleric for his Sunday morning sermon that was short but to the point. It was all about the Good Samaritan who had come along the roadway to find a beaten and robbed person, and helped the one in need. He went on to say how everyone should give a helping hand to the ones less fortunate than they, especially now in these times of need. The ones aboard the space station in his sermon were the Good Samaritans, and the crewmembers aboard the Twitchel pointed out the less fortunate ones in need of the helping hand. The sermon was short, and the people all seemed to get something out it this day including Ann and her family.

Everyone greeted Ann as she disembarked out through the front doors of the church heading for the town's common on the hill where the big gathering was to take place. There some of the women folk asked Ann what she planned on doing now that she was back home on Earth safe and sound.

Ann had a most wonderful reply, Ben thought. She told everyone she was going to settle down and become a good mother to her two beautiful little girls and a good wife to her husband now that she was back. She had had just about enough of space travel and was ready to stay put helping Ben out taking care of the farm, her folks, and the children. Her answer both delighted her parents and Ben to tears after hearing her say that. Maybe she was getting sensible after all, her father thought quietly to himself, and was going to settle down and stop all those foolish damn dreams of hers about visiting the other planets of Mars, Jupiter, and any other of the celestial heavenly bodies that so intrigued her young fancy mind to venture off into the great unknown of space. Maybe her imagination had had an inspired reality check starting to get some common sense knocked into that real thick skull of hers, he thought.

Fun and games filled the warm sunny cloudless afternoon with the great assortment of foods and fond conversation. Ann was becoming hoarse by the end of the day from talking so much. She stood there in high spirits while being back home in the little town of Lunenburg, Vermont surrounded with so many friends and family.

She could not help but to reflect back all afternoon on the sermon of the cleric from the morning as she went about being happily home and having fun with family and friends. The sermon really touched her deep down inside her soul as it reflected back on the space station and all the wonderful people who had helped save her life and got her through that most terrible time. The crew up there certainly deserved better than being stuck up there with only one space capsule onboard that could only save a very small handful of them when the critical time came for some of them to leave the space station and return back home to the earth.

It would be unfair to leave all the others out there to perish in space, and probably wouldn't die a very pleasant death when the time came. The thoughts of them in the space station kept reflecting back and forth through her mind all afternoon as she glanced around at all the wonderful people who were out celebrating her safe return back home to Earth. What were their families and friends thinking about, after hearing about the successful return of the Twitchel back to Earth?

At the conclusion of a most joyful day, Ann felt more like a politician running for a state representative's office or other higher government office. She felt more than a celebrity astronaut hero returning back home from outer space, for she wasn't a John Glenn or anyone like that, she was just another astronaut in another point in time and in a different situation of space.

Instead of being the first astronaut to circle the globe in space, she might very well have been one of the last astronauts to be in space, for she thought at the time that the space program everyone knew had come to an abrupt end. The monster up in the atmosphere had remained still and quiet all afternoon leaving everyone enjoying the towns crowded common enjoy themselves, but could have at any unsuspecting moment taken someone from them.

The crowd felt extremely uneasy having so many people all crowded together in one location as everyone held their jittery breaths. They spoke to one another in total anticipation of the monster's arrival at any given second all during the afternoon. The number of deaths the monster had been causing regularly snuffing out innocent people and animals on a daily bases was beginning to dwindle more and more with each and every passing day as time marched on.

Either the earth was silently winning its war against this monster, or the neutron monster living in the sky was getting ready to destroy humanity for eternity. Only precious time would tell, and everyone could only surmise what would next take place. The earth seemed to be getting back to normal these past few weeks except that there was still no way to produce electricity without severe consequences. This was when the neutron monster would come out from its hiding place invisible in the air and snuff out whoever was brave enough or foolish enough to try to produce electricity for their own or someone else's use and benefit.

CHAPTER FORTY-ONE

The Visitor

Ann finally settled in to her new way of life as a full-time mother, chief cook and bottle washer, house cleaner, homemaker, nurse, and parental councilor. She found herself becoming extremely happy while being busy this new way. Working hard every day helping Ben out with doing the many hard chores a farmer's wife would normally perform. She helped out the neighbors by doing chores as they were all so short-handed and everyone had so much they had to get accomplished before winter was upon them. She was getting tired from working so hard all of the time, but was enjoying every last moment spent with Ben, the girls, and her mom and dad. Ann felt she could adjust to any of these new circumstances thrown at her that might arise as long as she had Ben, the kids, and her parents around to keep her mind off the other things in life that bothered the hell out of her. She was becoming a typical seasoned farmer's wife, whether she wanted to or not.

It was an early Tuesday morning several weeks after Ann had arrived back home, and someone came knocking at the front door of the farmhouse. When she went to see who was at the front door she was quite pleased and surprised to see Commander Anderson standing there all dressed prim and proper in his dressed military blue attire.

"Good morning, sir!" Ann said with enthusiasm. "Won't you please come in Commander? What a pleasant surprise to see you so soon.

Would you like to have the misses come in with you for a cup of hot tea or a coffee and a bun with us, sir?"

"Sorry Lieutenant! She is not with me today. I am here on official business only from the Pentagon, the Air Force, and of course from the people of NASA. Here are your new orders Lieutenant."

"But Commander," Ann said with trepidation written all over her face. "I am due out of the military in just a couple of more weeks. I thought we had come to an agreement back at Cape Canaveral before I returned back here to the farm. Personnel told me that I did not have to report to anyone or anywhere anymore. They told me that my time spent in space had accumulated enough time to fulfil the remainder of my stint of service sir. My time of military obligation of my enlisted contract with the government is over. I really do not want to reenlist again, sir. All I want to do now is to be a devoted mother to my children, a good wife to Ben, and take care of my aging mom and dad for the remainder of their lives." Ann's voice was becoming louder and more stern as she talked on, almost yelling at the Commander, with her eyes starting to mist up and almost cry from her instant nervousness.

"May I come in, lieutenant?"

"Why of course, sir, come right in."

"What's all that blasted noise about out there? Did someone get hurt or something? What is going on? Is there something wrong, Ann?" "No Pa, there is nothing wrong." "What the hell is it then?" "Nothing is wrong, Pa. This is Commander Anderson. He was my captain and was my commanding officer while I was aboard the Twitchel."

Suddenly Ann broke down and did cry. "What in the hell is the matter, Ann? No one comes into my house and makes my little girl cry for nothing. What in the hell is going on?"

"Could we be alone for just one moment please, Mr. Hamlin?" No you certainly cannot. Not in my damned house. You cannot be alone especially when whatever it is has something to do with my little girl Ann here. No you damn well cannot. Whatever it is you got to tell her, you get to tell me as well."

"It is ok, Pa. I have spent an entire whole year up in outer space with Commander Anderson. He is really a real nice man." "Are you sure Ann?" "Yes, I am quite sure and am positively absolutely sure of it. Could you please put some water on the stove for us to have some coffee please Pa? Maybe Commander Anderson would like to have a cup of coffee with us." "That would be very nice, thank you. I am truly sorry, Ann. I had these orders drawn up for you myself, and I can have them cancelled just as fast as I had them made out."

"I am very sorry, Commander Anderson. It has been a real hard time for me to readjust these last few weeks back here to all this new way of life for me, sir. I am just barely getting used to being around my family again and what it is like being a mother to my children again, as you can well imagine."

"Well, Lieutenant, family is what these orders are all about."

"Sir", Ann spoke with bewilderment in her voice and on her face as well. "I don't quite understand what you mean family, sir?" "Well Lieutenant, its meaning is explained explicitly inside this envelope. Open up the envelope Lieutenant, and see for yourself. These orders are all about family, Ann, maybe not your immediate family down here on earth, but is about your extended other family in another world if you would want to call it that in space."

CHAPTER FORTY-TWO

Orders To Fly Again

Ann read her new orders: "Promote Lieutenant Ann Mitchell to the rank of Captain. Extend time of enlistment for the purpose of one rescue and relief mission only. The mission's purpose is to deliver much needed life support supplies to the International Space Station in outer space. This special mission is to deliver desperately needed oxygen, food, carbon mixture for water supply systems, medical supplies, and transportation of as many Russian cosmonauts as possible back to Earth to Cape Canaveral. Welcome aboard the rescue mission, Captain. President of the United States, President Stallman. P.S. This mission holds with it a sizable reenlistment package that will take care of your family should something ever go amiss with this mission. Glad to have you aboard, Captain."

"I wouldn't have asked for you directly, Ann, if I didn't have full faith in you, especially your qualified abilities to make this mission a success. I do have to tell you a couple of things about this mission though before you agree to it. First, I think this mission will work quite well with you onboard to help me. Secondly, if it does not work, none of us will ever be coming back home this time. Third and foremost, if we don't try this mission, all the crew aboard the space station will perish out there except for a very few lucky ones that will fit into that damn relic of a space capsule they have with them out there. Six lucky ones will make it, but that's all that will be able to return home to Earth.

Consequently, according to new figures just out back from NASA, calculating everything we used up as an added load on the supplies and equipment, the space station has maybe a mere few weeks or less of usable oxygen and supplies left onboard for them to survive if NASA's calculations are correct and Commander Ivan's were wrong. I guess Commander Ivan and I did not calculate the added load on everything correctly using the amounts of supplies needed when we decided it was time for the Twitchel to pack it up and leave a few weeks ago for their safety.

We used up way more of their oxygen supply than we had previously calculated because we didn't take into account a couple of determining factors in our calculations when we did the math together, and they will die soon if we don't return the favor of life to them that they extended to us. I just thought that you, being one of the lucky ones to have used up some of their supplies, might like to help us on this mission of mercy if possible, Captain Ann. I just thought we had an obligation to them that is all."

"You know my answer, Commander Anderson! I just did not think, well I tried to put that idea out of my head completely, about their needs. In the back of my mind, I have been scared to death for them all. I felt that somehow they would all survive one way or another. I just did not think it would have to be up to us again to be the ones sent back up there to help save and rescue them. I figured their own government would take enough pride in themselves to send someone up there to try and save their own people for goodness sake. Pardon my attitude, Sir."

"That's quite all right, Captain. I along with several other dignitaries from NASA tried in vain to talk to the newly installed Russian Parliament. They would like to help, but cannot do a thing soon enough to help anyone out up there. If we don't do it soon, they will all perish. I will feel personally responsible if they all die for my part in it as I am sure you would too, Ann?"

Commander Anderson really knew how to make Ann feel real guilty, and he sure did one hell of a good job of it. He felt the mission would be a flop without her, and would try to say anything to convince her to help them. If he had her going on the mission he was sure he could and would convince the others of the old crew to go along with him also.

"Here is your danged cup of coffee, Mr. commanding officer, sir. Now what in the tarnation was all that damned crying about out here in the first place? What did you go and tell my little Ann to get her all fired up like she was anyway?"

"Well Mr. Hamilton, I guess I will have to let Ann tell you all about it. Mmmm, how did you make this wonderful cup of coffee taste so delicious? Thank you, Mr. Hamilton." "I used my own natural sugar for it, that's how. I put a little of my extra honey in it for the sweetener. That old monster thing in the sky did not wipe out all the honeybee hives, thank goodness. Took half our cows though, but it didn't get any of the chickens, our faithful old horse Dixie, or the pigs or goats out in the barn either. I guess we been pretty lucky round the farm here compared to most folk and farmers livestock around these parts. Guess we have been good and lucky is all I have to say, sir. Damn good and lucky our family is. Anyway, Ann, what did this here Commander, this Commander Anderson say to you, to get you all fired up and crying that a way?"

"Where is Mom, Pa?" "She is upstairs in the bathroom, dear." "Ok, well I will be right back down then." Ann turned around and went out the archway toward the stairs.

"Ann is the sweetest little girl in the world you have their Mr. Hamilton. She is a real sweetheart, and the nicest little girl I have ever met in my days. Wish I had a daughter just like her."

"Have you got any children of your own, Commander?" "I have, sir. I have four pretty good boys of my own, sir. The likes of having a daughter like your Ann would have surely made our family complete. My boys are all grown up and gone out on their own now, but having a girl would have been a real nice treat.

How many children do you have, Mr. Hamilton?" "Just my one little girl is all we have, Commander, Ann is our only child. Has a stubborn damn fool mind all her own too, that dang-nabbed little filly of ours. She went off to school all by herself looking for a better way to spend her life and did not give a hoot about us at the time. She just didn't want to be a plain old Jane like the rest the nice girls around these parts. Met up with that there Ben guy one day at school, and got herself hitched up to a stranger to us back then.

Came home one day and wanted to sleep in our house in the same bedroom with a strange man, she did. I did not like that idea one bit, but what in the hell was I to do about it, it was her husband. Always wanted to fly them no good for nothing flying machines, too. God would have put a good set of wings on our backs if he intended for any of us to fly, I always said. I cannot tell that thick-headed girl a thing, not a dang blasted thing. When she gets her fool head set what she wants to go off and do, there just is not a dang thing anyone in the whole-wide world is going to do to turn her fool mind around any other way. Dang fool girl is going to go off and get herself killed one of these days if she doesn't settle down real soon."

"Come in here, Mom. Sit yourself down beside Pa. I have something very important I have to tell the two of you." Ann's mother began to cry. "What the hell did you tell your ma, Ann? Holy cow girl, for crying out loud Ann, why did you not go and tell me first. Couldn't you at least have had the common decency to have waited and tell the two of us together, couldn't you have?"

"Ann didn't tell me anything, Pa. Every darn time she gets the two of us to sit down together, she always tells us something we just do not want to hear. Just like when she wanted to go off to that college school of hers, and we both were against it. We both knew we were going to miss her terribly, and then fool girl came home with Ben, and then went off to fly those airplanes. I just know it is a going to be something awful she is a going to tell us, Pa. Go ahead dear, your pa and I are waiting and a listening for whatever it is."

"Well, Commander Anderson here wants me to help him out for a little while." "What do you mean he wants you to help him out for a little while?" Ann's father asked. "He wants me to help him on a mission to help save the lives of those people still stuck on the space station."

"NO! DAMN IT ANN, YOU ARE NOT GOING! You are not going to help him out this time. I damn well forbid it, Ann! It is ludicrous and crazy, Ann. I read it in the paper, Ann. If you fly, you die. You go and tell him no. You are not going to help him save those blasted Russians that caused this damn mess to happen in the first place. I forbid it. You hear me **ANN. I FORBID IT!** You tell him **NO!** You are not going to help him out this time, and I mean it, Ann!"

"I am truly sorry you feel that way Pa, for there are two innocent German astronauts up there as well. They did not do anything wrong to anyone and neither did the Russian cosmonauts that are stuck up there against their own will. If it was not for them, I would not be standing here alive today and arguing with you about going there or not. I cannot just sit down here all happy and idle and not do something to help them if I am capable to do so. I have to try to save them, don't you understand, or I wouldn't be able to live with myself, and I wouldn't be a very good human being for it, if I didn't try, either."

Ann's father broke down and shed tears right along with Ann's mother. "Damn fool girl anyway." Her father said. "You still don't have any damn brains left up in your head, do you, Ann? Can't our government find someone else to take her place, Commander?" "We gave it a lot of thought Mr. and Mrs. Hamilton. We could not come up with anyone quite as well qualified as Ann. She is the only one in our command center unit that knows how to navigate the Twitchel or any other one of our shuttles properly. We had one person in training just as the big blast came, and he is still with us, but hasn't had hands-on training like Ann has, and we have no simulator for him to practice in now. All the other ones who were well qualified to take her place all died trying to blast those foolish neutron rockets with bombs out of the sky that awful day. She is the only one left around the world that I can really count on to have a successful mission. Without her onboard, I am afraid our chances are about one in a thousand, if not less."

Ben then came in from the field carrying Amber on his back after letting the cows out of the barn to graze, while Sarah was fast asleep on the sofa in the den after playing hard before breakfast, and did not awake to the entire commotion taking place in the next room.

"What is going on, Ann? Why are both Mom and Dad sniffling and wiping tears away from their eyes?" "I have to go away again, Ben, for just a few weeks or maybe longer, I don't know how long this time."

"Why? You said you were never going to go away ever again. You said you were giving up the military life for good. What in the hell is more important to you than your own family, Ann, the Military or us? Did you not make a promise to us, to me, Ann? You said you were never ever going to leave us again and be here for us forever." "Yes I did, Ben, and I meant it too, but right now the people who helped me stay alive all the while I was gone for over a year in space are in desperate need of supplies and oxygen. I have to help them stay alive if I can, and if I don't, they will all die."

"How the hell do you even know if they are still alive now? No one can even talk to them. Maybe they are all dead as we speak. You cannot do this to me again, Ann, I cannot live another day without you in it. You do not really know what it has been like for me these last few months without you with me. I am asking you not to go, damn it. I am begging you for my sake and for the kid's sake of happiness along with the good of your mom and dad's sake. Please. Ann, for God's sake, Ann, please don't go!"

"I have to go, Ben. Does anyone of you care enough about what happens to those poor people up there? I have to go. They saved our lives when we were in need of them, and they could have just as easily have said no to our crew and me. I just have to go this one last time and help save my friends if I can. They are more than just friends to me, Ben, they are like all of you, they are my family, too, and I love them. I love them like I love the lot of you too, and I am going to help save the ones who saved my life, and that is that! I am going, and nothing anyone says or does is going to change anything."

With heartfelt tears streaming down her cheeks while sobbing, Ann abruptly turned in place and ran upstairs to pack her few military clothing still left hanging loosely in the closet. Her heart was aching as it had never hurt before. She really did not want to leave her family this time, but felt as deeply about not going as going. She would have felt torn between two worlds in any decision she would have to make, but felt very strong that this choice was the more ethical choice at a time like this, besides there were other lives that counted on her than just the four at the farm.

Tears were steadily streaming down from her swollen eyes as Ben approached the open doorway to their bedroom, and he could see her body shake as she cried. He stood quietly, standing in the doorway watching her in pain as she wept, throwing her loose clothing from the bed and into her trunk and duffle bag. She did it with a frustrated force while she shed tear after tear of pain from being torn apart in her decision making.

Ben felt his pain and could feel the extreme pain she was going through as well, realizing what she must be going through in having to have made the unselfish choice of hers. She was breaking her promise he knew she never would have ever intended to break. He could sense her bitter grief growing deep inside her and see the torment she was going through as she put every item of clothing away with at least several tears for each item of clothing as she put it away into her bag.

He knew down deep inside she did not truly want to leave but had too, for it was her Christian duty to help those trapped above. She was to be the Good Samaritan. She looked to be in total divided torment with herself in her final decisions to leave her family on the farm for the short haul, and it was truly wearing on her. She did not want to leave him anymore than he wanted her not to stay.

Ben slowly walked up behind her gently putting his loving arms around her waist and gave her a soft kiss on the top of her aching throbbing head. He could feel her uncontrollable trembling inside and could feel her pain right through his own arms that mixed with his. She turned and they both embraced each other without saying a word to one another crying in each other's arms, feeling the pain of missing each other until they could be as one again.

Ben had had it with her, and was going to her in leaps and bounds ascending the stairs three steps at a time in his own self-imposed rage. He was going to tell Ann he was done with her for good this time, forever! He was going to leave her and the kids, and the farm to start a new life all his own with someone new. With someone who cared for him the way it should be and would never leave him again, one that would love him for what he really was. He was going to find someone who would not just up and leave him all of the time at the drop of a damn pin. He was feeling betrayed by her career for her career meant more to her than him, like she was cheating on him with another man. He could not take this uncertainty in his life of not knowing if she would live or die each time she stepped out the damn doorway and went away. It was driving him absolutely crazy inside, and he had had enough.

Stopping short watching her from the doorway. Ben could see and sense that Ann was in agony. Her pain seemed more intense for her than the pain he was feeling in his hostility for himself. For a split moment after Ann said she was leaving them again for space, Ben had second thoughts about all the loving things she had said to him previously about not ever going to leave him or the children never again. They were nothing but a bunch of damn lies he thought until he witnessed her in heartfelt agony over her decision, and was crying her heart out as she packed.

When they each let go the other from their long emotionally weeping embrace, Ben stood back from her. He stretched out his arms placing his hands upon her shoulders. With a tender voice he asked her to be real careful and to please be safe for him and for the sake of their children. He never wanted anything bad to happen to her. He was going to miss the hell out of her more now for just the next few days or weeks than he had had all the rest of the time she had been away before.

Ben really felt this time looking down the length of his long arms that he would never ever see this lovely woman his wife Ann ever again. He could only hope and pray by some miraculous miracle that she would one day in the near off future return to them one more time unscathed, safe and sound. He had his doubts and what in the hell could he tell the kids this time? She was going anyway and if he made her feel terrible now she might not think clearly in her job, and he did not want it to be on his shoulders that is was he who caused her never to return. He could not live with that, and wished her luck.

Downstairs, Commander Anderson was going over everything with Ann's mother and father about the shuttle's next mission. He was trying to put the two of them at as much ease with what they were going to attempt to accomplish with this mission. He proceeded to explain how safe this mission would be; and if he did not think it safe, he would not have asked their only daughter to be a part of it. He told them what a wonderful girl she was and how talented she was in navigating such a wonderful piece of equipment such as the shuttle that could ascend itself way up into the high heavens. He explained how she was a fabulous pilot, probably the best pilot and navigator he had ever seen or flown with just as they said she had always wanted to be. They listened intently but frankly did not give a damn about any poor Russian bastard still trapped above in out space or liked the idea she was leaving them again, especially to fly off into outer space one more time.

He tried to ease their worried faces and minds by telling them this mission would be a piece of cake, much easier than the first mission was. They were definitely not going to be flying off into the unknown dark of space trying to snag any stray missiles this time that might turn around and attack anyone. There were no missiles left in space to descend back to Earth and attack the rest of the world as they had before.

Commander Anderson could tell by the sick worried looks and grief written all over their senior aging faces that his valiant efforts were coming across fruitlessly. Knowing he was not very convincing, he sat back quiet in his chair and waited for them to ask him a question or two about the mission, but they did not. Ann's mother and father just sat there looking worried all the while staring into one another's eyes feeling pain for the absence that was to come again of their only daughter being gone for a second time.

When Ann and Ben finally emerged back down the stairs from their bedroom, he was carrying her suitcase in one hand and her duffle bag slung over his other shoulder. Everyone in the parlor could tell both had been crying profusely. Commander Anderson understood as he had gone through the same damn thing with his wife only a few days ago, along with a good chewing out his children gave him back home when he informed them all what he was to be doing next. They like Ann's mother, father, and Ben tried to convince him otherwise not to go, but their words fell upon deaf ears.

Ann, much like Commander Anderson, had free spirits and willing souls of their own. They would do whatever they thought and felt was right. No one in the world would ever change their minds once they made them up to do something, especially when it was this important a decision in saving those who had helped save them.

The trip back to the space agency was a constant session of questions and answers fired off between both Commander Anderson and by Ann. She went over the flight plan with Commander Anderson over and over again. She didn't want to leave a nut, bolt, or tiny wire tie on this mission unturned in her mind during preflight. She wanted to know all the in's, and out's of the new manual controls that were installed on the Twitchel.

She had some very important input necessary for the Twitchel to make this mercy mission a safe flight. Commander Anderson knew Ann would have some very interesting direct dissecting answers to some very important parts of questions that needed addressing before the flight, such as the dry battery banks in the blast off phase of the mission. She addressed the necessities of not adding the electrolyte activating acid to the batteries until well after the Twitchel was far safe outside of the earth's atmosphere and in a secured orbit aligned up with hitching up to the space station.

For the next two long days' travel back to Florida, just about every time one of them opened up their mouths, something new and important about the mission would come floating out of one. On occasion they would break away from the serious conversation about the mission, and reminisce about one's own family's affairs and how each family was coping with this new life style they all had to adapt to now.

Some of the other crewmembers had already arrived at the cape and were now training and going over all the necessities to make this mission a successful one. They all had volunteered and hoped Ann would too

once Commander Anderson stressed the need for her abilities to her. Without her, this mission could be a very pressing and hard job to succeed.

Major Bill was the first of the old crew of the Twitchel to come out and greet Ann when she and Commander Anderson showed up at the launch sight facilities. Bill had finally, after several long hard lonely weeks of grieving, come out of his shell of lonely hurt and grieving, and was ready to help his fellow crew members take on the challenge of helping save the crewmembers of the International Space Station. Bill still felt the pain for his loss, but was convinced his wife and children would want him to help those who had helped save his life. This was the beginning of a great healing process for him to go through, and now it was time for him to get on with the remainder of his life.

Commander Anderson was not very reassuring to his crew about the Twitchel's initial takeoff and its first stage section of the flight. These new solid-fuel rockets attached to the Twitchel's fuselage had to be ignited by hand, and if only one of the two rockets were to fire and not the other, they would be spun around the launch site like a wild boomerang out of control and crash. The newly installed acid-activated battery banks had to have been installed because the old ones had been totally destroyed by the massive attack of the many neutrons on them.

The new batteries would each have to have their individual empty cells filled with automobile sulfuric acid, the agent used to activate the batteries after the shuttle was in orbit. They did not know if the neutron bomb explosions contaminated the activating sulfuric acid stored in the several small plastic drums or would adhere to the lead plates in the new batteries. With no accurate way of testing the acid solution for the batteries that was supposed to be tested before going into them when on Earth, they would have to wait until they were well into their new orbit and test them then.

If any electrical wires had been damage in reentry, they would have to find them and repair them aloft before they continued in their mission to the space station. Everything about this mission had been place in the hands of a couple of real good rocket scientists and this crew had to put their full faith in them and their abilities and their knowledge of

flight in themselves as a crew, and a little help from the good man from above to make this mission a successful one.

Suddenly the entire crew, for no reason at all, began conversing with one another about their sole obligation to their many friends aboard the space station. It was their moral obligation to help, or the crew of the space station would all die except for a couple of lucky ones who might or might not survive. Seeing no one had returned to earth yet from the space station, all they could do was surmise everyone aboard had survived this long and all alive and doing well. Should the solid rockets fail during lift off, then what? They had no electrical back up to control the ignition. Without any electrical back up control, they would all be doomed to die. What if the electrical system didn't work once they inserted the acid into the batteries when aloft, then what? They would all be lost in outer space, and the Twitchel would become a multiple tomb for them all. The chances were slim to none if anything would go wrong, but there was always the slimmest possibility that something might not work.

The risk of this mission was worth it. Commander Anderson was encouraged for the entire crew was all in favor of giving it their best to try to help rescue their comrades trapped in the space station. Commander Anderson ordered the Twitchel's crew to attention from their conversations and were almost out of control expressing their own inner emotions and feelings about their obligations to their friends aloft. "Attention!" The flight crew became instantly quiet as they all came to order. They all turned around to address whomever Commander Anderson was calling them to attention for.

"Men, please be seated. This is Dr. Smothers. Please give him your full undivided attention please." "This is going to be the most dangerous of any mission you have ever participated in gentlemen", said Dr. Smothers, "you, too, miss. We believe everything is in proper order for you for a very successful flight. It is unfortunate that we do not have at our disposal all of the conveniences of modern day technology we once had at our fingertips. Technology everyone is so accustomed to having a little while ago, but you will have it, once you have reached the outer limits of our stratosphere.

This "neutron thing", this monster in the sky everyone calls it here on earth, consists of an overabundance of manmade condensed neutrons taken from the earth's own natural waters and has mixed itself with all the natural neutrons floating freely in our atmosphere, causing things to happen here on earth no man would have ever expected to happen. It is not effective at high altitudes above our atmosphere yet, we hope. According to Commander Anderson, and your navigator, Captain Ann Mitchell, the neutron field didn't affect the Twitchel's electrical system until you all reached a height of about seventy-five to fifty -five thousand feet when you all had reentered the atmosphere on your return flight to Earth several weeks ago.

The Twitchel's cargo bay has been partially filled with a maximum number in oxygen bottles to replenish the space station's air supply. The rest of the cargo bay is almost filled to capacity with food and other supplies for their garden experiment which I hear was doing just fine when all of you were aboard, and had helped all of you to survive. It is also filled with the station's stores of other necessary supplies to extend their stay in space.

There has been a special cargo container filled with the lifeblood supply of sulfuric acid, safely stored away in the cargo bay for use in the main battery banks power system aboard the Twitchel. You must carefully install and fill the battery banks with it once you are in orbit. I am quite sure Commander Anderson can fill you in on all the other details necessary for a safe flight.

The new solid fueled rockets have all been simultaneously preflight tested on a small-scale model of the shuttle and all pre-flight data has gone quite satisfactorily to our calculations. Everything on the scaled down models worked according to all the reduced measurements and scaled down weights and measures of the payload as planned. The only real problem that anyone can come up with is the proper flight path the Twitchel shall follow in order to place you all in a proper path to link you up with the orbiting space station. This work you will all accomplished once you have reached your proper orbiting height. This will happen when you all break out of the earth's gravitational field and start to orbit around the earth in free flight.

When the g-force of flight releases you, you will have limited time in quickly activating the electrical supply to the ship's mainframe computers. The time in speed will help secure your safe projectile and help you dock with the space station in a timely fashion. If you fail in this quickly required procedure, it may take you over a week or more for your projectile paths to realign again for your rendezvous.

According to our records, the crew of the space station will have already have used up or could have breathed in the last of their precious oxygen supply and would have already passed away. If you fail in your attempt to activate the electrical life line system of your craft, you all may be lost in an orbit that will allow you to travel out of your intended orbit, and spend the rest of your short lived days alive traveling deeper and deeper into the outer spaces void. It is extremely pertinent that you fill the battery banks quickly and get your power banks up and started as soon as possible. Let me now turn this meeting over to Commander Anderson. He will instruct you all on the changes we have made to the Twitchel for your conveyance of flight and safety. Commander Anderson."

"Gentlemen, Captain Mitchell, there have been a few new systems in controls added to the Twitchel. There are a couple of new portal holes been drilled and cables added to her for controlling the projected travel course in her flight into outer space. The portal openings need sealing up once we rendezvoused with the space station. Once we make it that far, and I am sure we will. If we fail to seal these portals with heat shielding reflective tiles after docking, it may cause us to burn up on our reentry try back into the Earth's atmosphere on our return trip back home to earth.

To get that far and forget a simple crucial task such as that would be a shame. Let that be the responsibility of us all to make sure these new tiles installed in place before we returning. I know I make this mission sound doubtful, but it really is not. All I want to do is instill in each and everyone of your minds, the importance in every detail about this mission. I want to instruct each and everyone of you to be looking out for your fellow astronauts. Let us cover each other's backs just in case one or more of us do make a simple little deadly mistake that might

cause this mission to fail. If we don't, then we would have done all of this work for not. For the next few days, we will work hard at trying to perfect simple little tasks that sound so primitive but worked for Orville and Wilber Wright. Only they just flew for a few hundred feet above the ground for a very short period in time where we will be soaring many thousands of feet and miles above, and orbiting around the globe. We will start at 0600 hours sharp, tomorrow morning, men. I know you all would like to have your very own aircraft to practice on for this mission as I would myself, but we do not have one to do this with. This mission will be like flying by the seats of our britches, so the saying goes. It will be just like a want to be pilot getting into an unfamiliar airplane taking off for the first time in it and wanting to fly. This flight will be similar to a test pilot's job. If he is lucky, he will be able to handle the new aircraft and land it safely back down with bouncing only once or twice. If he is not lucky, he might crash and burn. Let us be the lucky test pilot that takes his aircraft up and succeeds. Let us fly our bird successfully, and land this bird without getting her skived to pieces. This is my wish and prayers for us men. Let us fly our bird, and bring her home safely.

CHAPTER FORTY-THREE

Early Morning Exercise

Early, 0600 hours, Commander Anderson found the crew of the Twitchel ready. They had all assembled in the flight room ready to get to work, as Commander Anderson began calling out for everyone to participate in calisthenics. One two three, one two three, one two three, Commander Anderson called out as they all did jumping jacks in place. Come on men, you cannot all be in that bad a shape, can you. It has only been a very few short weeks since we all did this in place aboard the space station, do you remember? One two three, one two three, one two three, is anyone getting tired yet?" "No, sir, Commander, not tired yet" every one called out in unison as they all panted for a deep breath of fresh air to breath. Whew, I am", said Commander Anderson. "I guess I am out of shape as well", and they all laughed. "Let's get some grub."

"Not so fast men. They will serve our meals to us in the bird today while we practice. We don't have much time left to practice for this mission and need to make every second count. Let's not let our comrades down up there that are counting on us to help them. Of course they have no idea what we are up to, but let's not let them down anyway."

Walking for breakfast, the crew all laughed and joked to each other how mean Commander Anderson was to them for making them all exercise so hard before breakfast. The commander had been right about not having any breaks after eating their breakfast. 2000 hours came fast as the day flew by faster and faster than the speed of sound could travel. The next morning found the crew again exercising in the flight crew room at 0600 hours like the day before. "Boy, the last few weeks we have really let ourselves get a little lazy, and might I say a little plumper in the middle as well." The crew knew better than to argue with the commander because they knew he was right for the most part anyway. He led them out the door for a three-mile run, and then back to the chow hall for a leisurely breakfast this morning. He was right about not having any breaks again in their long hard days of practice aboard the Twitchel. Every day seemed to fly by faster than the previous one.

The levers that were added to the Twitchel were very challenging to pull on to add the extra strength needed to control the ailerons and tail section while in flight without hydraulic assistance. The mechanical ignition activators for in flight ignition of the second stage rockets were also stiff in their operation. When they were underway and in flight, the force of air and speed levied against the hand controls would be a hundred times greater than they were when the craft was sitting idle on the launching pad.

The days were long and the practices intense. Commander Anderson wanted his crew to be in tiptop shape with everything they had to do without the slightest chance of a glitch occurring anytime during this mission. He worked everyone hard until the crew could not take it anymore, and then worked them all some more. They knew what he was doing was right, and not a one disputed his every command, whatever he asked them to do. He was doing it all for them, and they knew it.

A couple the older Twitchel's crewmembers had recently retired from the U.S. Air force and NASA with full pay and military benefits. Even so, they were back and ready to help this mission for their own personal satisfaction in helping out the good people above and off the space station that had so unselfishly helped them out in a desperate time of need.

The Twitchel's crew practiced pumping acid into practice batteries while submerged in tanks of water held floating with tie lines making it similar to them floating in space. The crewmembers equipment dangled from supports in the water-filled tanks as they in full space gear practiced putting on all the gear needed to protect them and the other crewmembers from the sulfurous acid while using special mats to absorb any residue that might escape the pumping in the dangerous procedure.

The days were long and hard as hard as the Commander was tough on them. At the end of the day if he asked them if they were ready for another hour or more of calisthenics, they would all be ready even if they were not, and he knew it. He had a crew that he could count on no matter how tough the job was before them or how much he expected from them.

He figured Ann would be one of the first to break and weaken, but she hung in there extremely tough like the rest of the crew. She in fact faced and withstood things better than most the crew with the daily pressures. It was probably from doing so much work back home at the farm helping with all the chores, and was in better shape physically and mentally than most the men of the crew were now.

"0600 hours crew," "Yes, sir, 0600 hours, sir!" They all hollered out in unison. "0600 hours, sir." Commander Anderson smiled. It was now 1700 hours and Commander Anderson let everyone off early for the day. Prior to dismissing everyone, he joked with them and asked them if they were ready for an hour of calisthenics and a three-mile run. The look on their faces said it all as they all yelled out "yes, sir". They had been working very hard all week, and he wanted to let them enjoy themselves a little before the next day's hard workout began. Even he was feeling the strain of the heavy workload he had been putting on them and what they all had gone through, but they were not complainers. It would be a night to eat chow early, relax a little bit, and hit the sack early for them, and they all would.

The crew appreciated the extra rest as their minds and bodies rested. 0600 hours seemed but a blink of an eye away for most of the crew when the early morning came. There never was any time to go off gallivanting to the officers' club and have a night out on the town so to speak, as everyone needed to be tiptop for this mission. Everyone including Steven, the little social bug of the crew, was fast asleep way before 2000 hours arrived that night. He knew the importance of a good night's sleep, and what having a clear head meant when one wakes up in the early morning hours.

He had learned a very good lesson over a year ago before they were unsuspectedly trapped in space for the year. He had had a couple of real bad days of training in the water tank with a massive hang over, and a couple of hours spent in the aircraft when they did their high-speed dives that gave everyone the sense of weightlessness. He would now save the partying for the nights when he didn't have to work the next day or have to fly for a couple of days. They were hard lessons learned, but well remembered. He was fast asleep even before the others were. His time for razing holy hell and party hearty in time would be later, much later after the accomplishment of this very special mission.

0600hours found Commander Anderson's crew well rested and outside doing their final pre-flight inspection walk around. The Twitchel was standing majestically tall like a skyscraper, ready for launch on her launching pad, looking like she could not wait to get going. She looked like she stood two football fields tall, like the Statue of Liberty on Stratton Island in New York City's main harbor. She looked so beautiful standing there all alone like an eagle on her perch getting ready for flight with determination written all over her. The moment of truth would soon come to them as it sent large goose bump size chills up and down most everyone's spines. Ann could not wait to be back in the air and up into space aboard the Twitchel. This would probably be her last chance to fly in her again, and she wanted the moment to last for a lifetime. She had made Ben a promise, soon to be broken again but she had been up front with him about it. She had to do this one last mission, and then it would be the end of her career for good.

She just hoped it would not really be the end for them all. Today she and Major Bill would be learning all the new controls installed in her in order to get the eagle up and into outer space safely. Sitting in an old dilapidated retrofitted shuttles cockpit simulator in the main hanger at the launch compound, Commander Anderson, Captain Ann, and

Major Bill were busy at learning the new mechanical aspects of the Twitchel's strategic flight control mechanisms.

Dr. Smothers was standing in the midst of the three of them giving explicit instructions to the trio on just what to look for and how to fly the Twitchel by using hand levered cable pulls and spring loaded wind up release triggers to make different things happen at different intervals during the ascending flight into outer space. He emphasized extreme concentration on explicit instructions of how important it was to this mission everyone onboard to be absolutely, positively certain, that all the external cavities of these new flight devices installed removed and their breached holes filled in with heat retardant material after the Twitchel made its final docking with the space station.

If any one of the several little holes in her outer heat shield body covering made of special material not repaired, she would burn up along with her crew and come apart during her reentry. This was a most important concern for the doctor, fearing the flight to the space station would be a success. The return trip back home to Earth would become a catastrophic disaster due to some simple little hole in the Twitchel's outer side not protected. One little human error could cost them their lives, and everyone onboard had to be responsible to double-check each other's work to make sure this mission was as safe as possible.

"Commander," Dr. Smothers said. "These two foot levers are for keeping the Twitchel's flight path a true and accurate one, correct?" "We realize you will be under a great g-force up there, so we hooked these levers up by your feet to control them because of the g-force factor. We calculated it would take all of your strength to hold onto your seats with your hands and be able to operate the flight control levers with your feet. We hope you will not have to use them at all, and if you do, very sparingly. You will be flying this bird by the seats of your pants respectfully, and the slightest wrong correction will put all of you in great danger of failing this mission. This foot levered paddle on your right will adjust the Twitchel's path to the left, and this one to your left like the ones in your aircraft will adjust her path to the right. By using, the two of them simultaneously will help you fly her straight up and into her intended path to break through the atmosphere and out into an exact orbit you want to be in.

The g-force's place will determine just how able you are to cope with these new mechanisms. The pulley blocks and cables assembled within her fuselage will help you overcome any external wind forces placed upon her. They are to be used simultaneously just prior the earth releasing you out of her grip and her airspace to adjust your attitude in attack for your proper orbital rendezvous.

You will have to rely mostly on your horizon indicator instruments and magnetic field direction indicators for you proper projector. Do not cut yourselves short by prejudging your orbital path, Commander. It will be much better to overshoot your intended orbital target at first rather than undershooting it.

If you, by unforeseen chance do undershoot your orbit, you will fall back to the earth and have nowhere to land your bird except in the middle of the Atlantic Ocean, and that would be catastrophic for all of you. The Twitchel does not like to float, and you would sink like a lead weight on a fishing line before you could safely escape the hatch from the cockpit. There also would not be any rescue vessels or aircraft available to fly out to your craft after landing. All of you would probably drown anyway or die awaiting rescue by a passing sailing vessel that day or some day in the far off future, and it would be by chance only. As I was saying, it is always better to overshoot your intended orbital target than to undershoot it.

When you reach your orbit, you can energize the dry battery cell packs and have full power almost immediately. You will be able to fly your bird by the computer then and come back to your intended orbit with ease. Remember Commander, overshooting is always better, and never undershoot your intended targeted orbit when entering outer space.

"Captain Mitchell, these two levers when pulled extremely hard and together in unison, will activate your second stage booster rockets.

They are to be pulled simultaneously and never just one lever at a time. When the first stage rockets fail, we hope together, you must first pull these two first sets of levers to blow the main stage rockets away from your aircraft. You do not want any extra baggage attached to the Twitchel that will keep you from gaining your place in orbit. Should just one of your main rockets fail before the other, you will have to activate the release activator blasters immediately to release them both for your safety.

One main rocket burning by itself will turn your aircraft, and send you way off course and possibly back to Earth. This could be a very poor situation if that was to happen, then you would have to pull this fourth set of levers to blow away the second stage rockets, which would allow Commander Anderson and Major Bill here to bring the Twitchel back around to Earth safely. One might only hope and pray you had enough altitude so you and your crew could safely return to the landing site, which is highly unlikely or as close to land as possible. We truly do not want to think that happening, or for it to go that way do we? With the second stage rockets activated, they will put you into an original orbital path lined up with the space station, and bring you up to her before you have to release them before docking. I know there are a lot of things to think about on this mission, but they are the only way this mission will be successful."

Major Bill was listening with open ears while watching every move Dr. Smothers preformed with his hands while listening intently to every instruction given to Commander Anderson and Captain Mitchell. If something drastic was to happen to either one of them, then it would be up to him to take over their controls and to fulfill their every duty. He had more to think about than the two of them put together, and that was why Commander Anderson was thrilled when he came forward and volunteered for this special mission. He was probably the most valued crewmember aboard the spacecraft other than Captain Ann.

The next few days of training were extremely intense for the crew of the Twitchel as they went over and over every last detail necessary to make this attempt at saving the ailing space station a happy success.

Ann carefully listened with her imagination racing, pretending to be feeling and hearing as the main rockets failed and then she pulled the levers to release them. She would count out a ten-second count

mentally to clear the Twitchel from the first stage rockets. This method trying to feel to simulate to her that they had released themselves. Then she would pull the next set of levers to activate the second stage rockets, and then wait a while and make believe Commander Anderson had given her orders to release the second stage rockets. She would then pull the third set of levers as was planned. Everyone went over his and her duties in performing many times over in order to make everything work like clockwork.

1700 hours came quickly as usual on the last day of training before the big day. It found the crew of the Twitchel sitting in the debriefing room with Commander Anderson getting ready to talk to his very talented crew. "Men, the time has come for us to put our last couple of weeks of intense training into practice. I appreciate the diligence you have all shown to me, and I can only hope it all pays off for us and the crew of the space station. I do not know about the rest of you, but I am afraid I might make a mistake up there and screw something up. I can only ask those of you who feel confident enough about this mission to go along with me tomorrow. I personally asked to have every one of you on my team this time because of what we have all gone through together before. I have total confidence in all of you, but am doubtful of myself."

"Excuse me, sir, Colonel! May I say a word or two, please?" "Why yes, major, go ahead." "The commander brought us all home safe and sound the last time we flew didn't he, and I for one am very confident in his abilities he should do it for us one more time. You all know how I feel about flying these days or getting up over two inches high off the ground. It scares the hell right out of me. It scared me half to death to fly the last time, but not with him. I would be the first one to drop out of this mission if I did not have the kind of faith I have in Commander Anderson. I just found out a day or two ago from my unit that this mission was totally voluntary and was not mandatory for me. I guess it was anyway right from the beginning and am always the last one to find these things out." They all laughed.

"Some of you have known it right along from the beginning, right Ann?" Major Bill looked over at Ann and smiled. She was the one who had told him she was there volunteering her services out of the kindness of her heart, and that this mission was strictly voluntary.

"I for one will back him to the ends of the heavens, no pun intended. We owe our lives to those unlucky cosmonauts stuck up there to at least try our best to help them out." "Sir, may I speak?" "Yes, Captain Mitchell." "Major Bill is right Commander. My enlistment duties had ended just over a week or so ago now except for this short stint of time I have voluntarily reenlisted to help out Commander Anderson accomplish this very special mission. I would not be here if it was not for Commander Anderson and all of you volunteering, and of course we cannot forget our friends in space.

Let us put the Twitchel to a real test this time, and ride her as if a craving cowboy rides a raging bull. The recrafted Twitchel bird is ready to ride. Even though she does not have any electricity flowing in her veins yet. She is our lifeless Frankenstein here on earth, but let us rejuvenate her back into shape. Let us be the ones to give her life back to her when we get her back into space, and save some lives in doing it. Let us go save our friends aloft. Let's put the Twitchel to another test, and may she never fail us."

"Commander, sir?" "No more questions please. The chow hall opens up for us at exactly 0400 hours in the morning men. Be here in the briefing room in full flight gear by 0530 hours and ready to fly. Eat light as usual before any flight, and get plenty of sleep and rest tonight. Heaven knows we all need the rest. Remember, men, 0530 hours for a quick departure, not a minute after that. Don't be late!

The crane will lift the platform up on a preset time to enable us to climb aboard our bird for as early a departure as possible. Remember 0530 hours men, dismissed.

CHAPTER FORTY-FOUR

The Night Before Takeoff

The activities surrounding the flight crewmembers during the evening were writing letters back home to their loved ones. All crewmembers were instructed by Commander Anderson to write two letters. The first letter incase their mission became a failure in which case they could console their loved ones for the choices they had all made.

Whatever they wrote wouldn't help soothe the pain, but might help heal the healing process their loved ones knowing they knew the risks of this venture. They all were at hand and willing to take that chance, to sacrifice themselves if need be in order to help save the ones that had showed them so much compassion in the first place, and saved them when in need. They had had the chance to come back home for a little visit that the others would never have the opportunity to do, and they were all thankful for that.

The second letter written told their families of the extensive training they had all been going through, and how demanding Commander Anderson was upon all of them including himself. He was a great man to serve under, and they were all very confident and happy to have the chance to serve under his command once again. They wrote of their love for their families that they would all be coming home soon, and not to worry. Everything was going to be all right. These letters were to be mailed the minute the Twitchel was safely in her orbit with the space station.

The rest of the evening and late into the night was spent contemplating over their many duties and thinking how very experimental this whole flight idea would turn out to be. It was similar to the flight of Wilber and his brother Orville's first flight at Kitty Hawk. Only the crew of the Twitchel all hoped that this flight would last a whole hell of a lot longer than just those three short minutes the Wright brothers aircraft flew. Everything would be over in just a matter of seconds if anything were to go wrong during their risky take off.

All knowing very well that it was all very possible, more likely than not with this creature lurking in the shadows of the sky in the bright of day, and invisible to the naked eye. This damn deadly creature hiding in waiting and seeking out to destroy anything within its environmental grasp with the minutest of an electrical charge attached.

Ann laid back on her bed talking aloud to her two daughters Sarah and Amber. She talked to them along with Ben as if they were right there in the room with her and could hear her every word. She lay there between the sheets crying her little heart out. She was worrying about everything, especially the next day's mission. She had not finished writing her two letters yet. Writing while crying and rolling back and forth on her bed as if she was in severe pain trying to compose herself so she could complete the letters.

She had had second thoughts about the safety of the mission and would have loved to have backed out that very instant, but knew deep down inside her skills were needed in order to make this as successful a flight as possible. Anyway, there were fifty-seven, no fifty-six people counting on her. No! There were fifty-seven people counting on her. She was forgetting to count everyone and needed to count on herself for a safe mission to and from the space station so she could return back home to her loving family safe. She knew everyone was praying for her safe return back home again, right along with the many town's people in her congregation. She forged ahead with dismay writing her last letter to her loved ones back home.

Her letter to Ben had quite a few noticeable teardrops stain marks on the paper, along with a couple of ink smudges on the wet paper she was trying to write on. In her letter to Ben, she wrote to be the best father he could possibly be to their two children in case she would die. She said she must do this for them, the ones who first saved her life. Then she fell fast asleep while lying between the sheets crying.

Her Big Ben alarm clock startled her awake when it went off at the stroke of 0300 hrs. It awoke her from a dream she was having with her girls and Ben. They had been out at the town common with the other town's people enjoying a day of games and food. She wondered if such a happy time would ever take place again in her lifetime. She jumped from her bed. She lit up the oil-fired lamp beside her bed, and then she picked up the pad of paper and ink-pen still lying beside her on her bed. She quickly finished writing her last letter to her family, put it into the two envelopes with their address on it, and sealed them tight. She would drop them off in the lobby for mailing when she went downstairs to meet the others for breakfast. She did not really feel like eating, but knew she had better eat something to keep her energy level up so she would be able to help the others fly the shuttle into its orbit.

CHAPTER FORTY-FIVE

The Time To Fly

"Good morning, Steve." "Good morning, Ann." "Have you seen any of the crew up and about yet, Steve?" "The Commander and the Major just went in, that's all I have seen so far. I don't know if anyone else went in or not."

The entire crew except for Steve and Ann were all sitting down at the table when the two walked in together through the door to the mess hall. The cook was ready to prepare any meal their little appetites so desired. He had a variety of steaks, top of the line cuts for the red meat eaters, lobsters and fish of all kinds for the ocean meal lovers, and anything imaginable for any type of meal the Twitchel crew would like for their last meal on earth before they departed for the space lab aloft in the heavens. They felt as if they were all prisoners on death row, and this was going to be their last requested meal, their special choice in food they all desired before their execution at sunrise. Was this a bad omen, or was it not?

Ann felt uncomfortable knowing they could have anything their little hearts desired, and felt as the other crew members did. The thought of it took all their appetites away like trying to drink a glass of extremely soured and curdled up milk or a glass filled with seawater.

"Ladies before gentlemen, guys." Ann blushed as the crew all laughed. "Captain Mitchell. What will be your pleasure for breakfast ma-am?"

"A single poached egg on a slice of dry rye and a very small cup of grape fruit sections on the side with a cup of orange juice, please."

"Ok, ok. Wouldn't you like something different like a lobster tail, steak tips, or anything, anything else at all?" "No thank you, Cookie, just the single poached egg, a slice of dry rye toast, and some grapefruit sections please". "Ok, I got that one. Commander Anderson your pleasure, sir"? "I will have the same as Captain Mitchell please." Every crewmember in the room ordered the same exact meal for their breakfast as Captain Ann did for her breakfast meal. "Come on you guys! Don't any of you want a lobsters tail, or a shrimp cocktail, or anything special like that this morning?" Every one shook their heads no and said "no thank you, Cookie".

The cook went off sputtering to himself saying poached eggs, a toast, grapefruit sections, and orange juice. I just cannot believe it. I went out of my way to get all this and got them everything possible to eat I could think of for this special occasion, and all they want are poached eggs, toast, grapefruit sections and a damned cup of orange juice, I just can't believe it. The cook had been told by his superiors to have everything and anything imaginable available on hand to eat for this crew of astronauts just in case any member of the crew wanted something extra special for their last meal here on Earth before departing on this very treacherous mission above. The head cook wanted to make sure everyone had whatever he or she all wanted to eat. He, too, was thinking it could possibly be his or her last meal. He hoped it would not be but wanted them to enjoy whatever their little hearts and appetites desired this day.

It was precisely 0515 hours when everyone was assembled in the preflight addressing conference room when Commander Anderson came waltzing in fully dressed in his flight gear. Everyone else in the room was already dressed and ready in theirs. They all came to attention as best they could all dressed up in their protective flight suits.

"At ease, please gentlemen! It is time to test our new but old bird for flight. Are we all ready to give her flight this morning?" "Yes, sir, Commander." They all shouted out in joyful sounding unison. "Then let's get started, but before we do, I would like to ask one simple little question of you. Is there anyone among you who has any doubts about this mission? If you do, this is the time to speak your peace of mind, not ten miles up into our mission where it will be too damn late to do so. Does anyone of you have any doubts about anyone sitting next to you, including him or herself?" He looked directly at Ann when he spoke.

This would have been an easy way out for any of the crew if they did have doubts about themselves or anyone else going along with them, and would have been a good easy way out for them to back out of the mission and save face for themselves."

The entire crew just stood there saying nothing, nothing at all. Not a one looked to the left, or right, or around that might show they had any doubt in their minds about themselves, or anyone else in the room for the mission. "Good then. Let us get this bird in the air and give her hell.

Outside the command post sat a small diesel powered shuttle bus waiting ready and running just for the crew's arrival so it could take them off down the roadway leading to the launching pad where their big bird was waiting ready they hoped. When they pulled up to the launching pad, the crane was already warmed up and prepared to lift them to the Twitchel's top hatch landing platform in order for them to climb aboard their bird safely, and take their designated positions inside of her cramped cabin with cables, peddles, and pulleys.

An attendant stood ready to help the crew onto the railed off platform, and to assist them on their way up to the top of the Twitchel. Ann was a little uneasy during the accent to the landing platform of the Twitchel. Flying in an aircraft never bothered her before, but to be out on an open platform a couple of hundred feet up in the air bothered the hell out of her to no end. She felt the same way in a helicopter that had a clear-bubbled cockpit. In it she could see down to the ground through its clear glass bubbled floor. Ann, Commander Anderson, and Major Bill were the last of the crew to climb aboard the star ship, and strap themselves into their designated seats. Ann looked anxiously at the many cable pulls and the assorted number of wooden handled levers at her station she was supposed to pull on at different inflexible times in their flight, as their platform associate helped everyone over the assortment of cables to their seats to sit everyone in their own particular capsule spaces.

Commander Anderson and Major Bill felt the same as Ann about her tangled web of fear. They all looked at the massive number of cables and levered handles scattered about the cockpit cabin that looked more like a large spiders web of tangled cables, hoping whoever was in charge of using them would know which cable to yank on when the precise time in their flight came to pull on them.

"Are we ready, gentlemen?" Commander Anderson asked his excited crewmembers. "Yes sir, ready for flight." Commander Anderson dropped the weighted green signal flag out the opened side port window, immediately closing and securing it tight with its own mechanical hand operated locking mechanism. The crew closed their helmeted facemasks of their flight suits, and turned on their individual oxygen supply lines.

They had a fifteen-minute countdown window to check and recheck everything at their stations before the initial ignition of the main solid rockets took place. A bright red stop streamer flag that they could drop anytime within the first fifteen-minute period to abort the mission if anyone decided they did not want to participate or there were any other wrong procedures of circumstance discovered in the cockpit in the last few seconds before ignition.

It turned out to be a long tedious last fifteen nervous minutes filled with wild emotions floating wildly among the crewmembers hoping this was not the very last mistake of their lives they would ever have the opportunity to make.

CHAPTER FORTY-SIX

The Final Countdown

Four, Three, Two, One, Zero. The ground crew was ready to fire off the solid fueled rockets. They waited until the very last exact second as preplanned and may-be even a couple of extra-long seconds beyond the original ignition schedule according to Commander Anderson's watch. Just in case there would be a red flag thrown out the cockpit and was on its way down to the ground that they did not quite see yet before lighting the booster rocket igniters.

With no red flag in sight, no abort signal dropped. Ignition, the ground crew set fire to the igniters attached below the Twitchel's two first main stage solid fuel booster rockets. Quickly they jumped into their armored heat shielded vehicles and drove slowly away pulling the protective safety shields around the towering shuttles platforms away with them. As the safety shields opened up beneath the rockets exposing the solid fueled rockets to the open intense fire below them, the rockets at first slowly came to life. The two rockets looked at first like a couple of huge sparklers on the 4th of July spitting out a small amount of white hot sparks, and then became a couple of huge Roman candled blow torches filled with thrust. The Space Shuttle Twitchel left the security of her safe and sound birthing, shooting skyward like the beautiful eagle she was.

The ground crew did their jobs well as they watched in awe especially at this magnificent bird ascending toward the heavens above. Everyone on the ground had his or her own special doubts as to why this bird would not make it into outer space and into a perfect orbit, never mind accomplish this very special mission.

Without the aid of computer control along with its back up secondary computers, this bird had many strikes against it before it ever left the security of the launching pad on the ground. Inside the cockpit of the Twitchel, all were wet with nervous perspiration as the fifteen minutes slowly passed away for them. They would glance occasionally at one another looking for a smile of confidence, which everyone seemed to have. It made them all feel one hell of a lot, or at least a little bit better knowing or feeling that everyone around them was still confident that this mission would be a safe one, even if it was not to be.

It sure would have been a whole lot nicer to have had the electrically operated liquid cooling circulating fan and pumps running to help keep everyone cooled down and comfortable for them, but it did not, and it was hot as hell in there. It felt like it must have been 110 or more degrees inside their flight suits.

They could feel the Twitchel shake and shudder for a split second, as her main thruster rockets were coming to life. Vibration after vibration vibrated everyone in his and her seats. Suddenly the solid rocket fueled rockets exploded with immense thrust. It squeezed every one of the crewmembers back into their seats almost instantly as she took flight toward the heavens.

No one had flown successfully into outer space since the big blast that had tried, or was able to come back and talk about it, except for Ann and the rest of the Twitchel crew. Now they were going to try another attempt at doing it once again. Sitting in the cockpit of the Twitchel before takeoff, the different crewmembers were thinking about the stories they had all heard about the hot air balloonists who had tried and failed. The balloon and gondola rose successfully, but the pilots and their passengers all died as the result of the neutron mass snuffing out their lives instantly from them. Then there was the back yard pilot who made a diesel-powered aircraft that flew, but he had had the same deadly results happen to him, as did the hot air balloonists.

The sky above the earth had become so saturated with electrically attacking neutrons, that its immense strength took down a flock of migrating Canadian Geese flying south for the winter a couple of weeks after the big blast. It attacked and drained the insignificant amount of electrical impulses generated by the migrating birds small brains, generated in its thinking abilities and instincts.

The thrust generated from the solid fueled rockets was greater than the usual thrust generally created by the liquid fired main rockets used that could be electronically controlled and adjusted in their flight. There was no governing of this big beast. The g-force was immense as they lifted up off the launching platform. No one had ever experienced such g-force before, not even in the rocket sleds they used to practice with for their missions into outer space. Their eyeballs felt to them as being forced back into the eyeball sockets of their skulls as their flesh felt as if it were going to be torn right off their skeletal frames at any given second as they shot skyward toward the heavens above.

The initial force of the g-force lessoned the higher and faster they flew. Commander Anderson and Major Bill anticipated having to take over and release the flight controls locked securely into place, for the initial take off. The g-force exerted upon them was so great they could not have taken over the Twitchel's flight controls even if they had had to.

If only one of the main rockets had fired, they would have had to take control of the shuttle, but with such force applied to their bodies at the time, it would have been highly unlikely anyone could have done so. If only a single rocket had fired, they would have shot up into the sky in a half circle, and would have come crashing back down to earth for they would not have been able to do anything about it.

Ann thought for sure during the initial takeoff that she was going to pass out at any given moment. She like the rest of the crew on board had luckily blown up their flight suits to maximum pressure to keep their blood from migrating down to their legs causing them to pass-out during the initial takeoff. They inflated their suits in anticipation of the extra g-force mentioned to them in the briefing room that was going to be on them using the solid fuel rockets. She hurt so damned bad during liftoff she thought for sure her insides were going to come right out her rectum and vagina at any given moment, as did the others about their rectums.

Ann knew if necessary, she would have to blow away the main rockets attached the Twitchel during takeoff if a rocket failed to ignite. She knew it would not be possible for her to do her job for the state they were all in, and it scared her half to death thinking about it. She sat squashed at her station in her seat listening intently for a glitch in their take off and kept feeling for that mental command from her inner senses that something was amiss and going wrong, as they continued to soar skyward.

Anticipation bothered Ann in her having to release the main rockets from the Twitchel when they reached their maximum altitude for their usefulness or if one or both failed after using up their full fuel supply.

Relieved when the g-forces exerted upon them lessened as she was now able to at least reach forward with her tight heavy limped arms feeling like steel, and take hold the crucial release levers attached to the explosive devices attached to each end of their cables, if they were still attached to anything after such force had been exerted upon them.

These explosives would release the first main stage thruster rockets from beneath the Twitchel's belly, she hoped. The great g-force exerted upon them was becoming less and less. The time was quickly passing when she would have to perform her first duty of the mission, and yank hard on the first set of levers. Ann held onto the levers of the detonators as tight as she could in anticipation of the rockets faltering at any given moment. Finally, the entire crew felt one rocker falter and then the other rocket almost simultaneously. The powerless clinging rockets became like air brakes as the Twitchel slowed in her accent to the heavens.

Ann yanked hard on the levers in her hands firmly, she thought, hoping to release the main rockets from their bird, but nothing happened. She wondered had she grabbed the wrong levers by being so nervous. She sat back in her seat and with a quick glance knew she had the right levers in her hands all along as the Twitchel continued to slow down. She yanked as hard as she could once and then twice on the levers, and then finally she heard the explosion and felt the Twitchel shake from the releasing rockets falling away from the shuttles side.

Ann grabbed at the other set of levers in front of her having her adrenalin level at maximum strength now flowing through her veins from having yanked at the first set of levers several times, and gave the next set of levers as hard a yank as she could possibly give them. The lever in her right hand broke right off in her hand. She turned as white as a ghost fallen into a freshly fallen snow pile, almost passing out from fright of it that she had caused the mission to fail, and cost everyone their lives including her own. Thoughts of not seeing her children ever again ran quickly through her head. Suddenly the secondary stage booster rockets came to life a couple of seconds later, and the Twitchel shot forward under her own power once again. Ann slouched back into her station's seat and sighed a great sigh of relief as the color of her skin started to come back into her very white face. The g-force suddenly returned to the crew, but nothing any greater than that of taking off in a fighter jet from off the ground or off the deck of an aircraft carrier.

Commander Anderson reached forward with his right hand and released the locked-in flight controls, as Major Bill held tight the controls in a smooth flight pattern with his feet.

Soon the bright of light blue sky gave way to a dark blue almost black canopy exhibiting a million or more beautiful bright brilliant sparkly twinkling stars as they passed out of the earth's atmosphere and into the beginning of their orbital path with the space station.

Their projected course could not have been any better even if they had been flying with the computers on board guiding them. In the far off distance above the earth's round horizon, the lights aboard the space station were barely visible in its orbit traveling around the earth.

Commander Anderson turned to Ann and ordered her to release the second stage rockets. Ann yanked firm and hard on a third set of levers, and the second stage booster rockets blew off without incident shooting them off into outer space, leaving the Twitchel in orbit all by her lonesome except for the space station several hundred or better

miles ahead of them. A bright green light lit up miraculously on the instrument panel. Commander Anderson thought and could not believe it. The light was a reflection of the sun's bright brilliant rays shining through the windshield of the Twitchel reflecting back off the glass of the light bulb's panel. He knew the electrical system of the craft was totally dead and all batteries aboard had to be activated by filling the dry battery banks with sulfuric acid stimulating the electrolytes in them and lead shields within their cells to produce electricity. The solar panels needed connecting in series with the batteries so they would start producing electrical power back to the main cells as well.

David, Chuck, and Steven quickly unharnessed themselves from their seats and headed as fast they could as they floated in the cabin's air space toward the hatch of the cargo bay in the rear of the cockpit to do their jobs. They quickly unlatched the cargo bay door and went to work on the dry battery system to fill it and energize it with the sulfuric acid held safe in there secured containers.

The International Space Station's lights were quickly disappearing out of sight of the Twitchel as its speed was just a little greater than was theirs. Commander Anderson had had Ann release their secondary stage booster rockets way too soon. Their orbit was correct, but their speed to overtake the space station was definitely too slow and wrong.

Commander Anderson had too soon anticipated their speed, and had figured they would drift toward the space station and be under full computer control by the time they reached her, but his hurried calculations were definitely wrong. The Twitchel was drifting further and further away from its original orbit as planned.

"DAMN IT. Damn it. Damn it. DAMN IT. I just cannot believe I just did that. How damn stupid of me, how damn stupid can one be?"

Captain Morris, can you estimate a time for arrival when the space station will catch up with us in this orbit it is in now?" "No, sir, Commander, I cannot. Not until I know our calculated travel speed sir and not without the computers up and running at their fullest potential, sir.

A wild guess would be twenty eight or maybe even thirty six days?" "They definitely will not last another thirty-six damn days, not according to Command Center. Not even if their rebreathers are performing properly. I sure as hell hope their oxygen supplement experiment is still operating perfectly. I sure screwed up this time when I told Captain Mitchell to release those damn boosters when I did. Why did I not listen to my subconscious? I think it was trying to tell me something just before I nodded my fool head."

"Secondary battery bank systems charged, sir. Working on the main battery bank system now, sir." "Why didn't you fill the main battery system bank first Lieutenant?" "We were told to fill the secondary batteries first, sir, and then the main battery banks last, so not to overcharge any electrical systems that might have been left on and possibly blow out any computer links, sir. Something about too much electrical surge in the mainframe if we do the main battery banks first and the secondary system last, sir." "OK! OK!" "This way you can run your preliminary testing to preflight her, sir." "OK, Lieutenant, as you were.

Get a damn move on then men. Get that main battery system up and running as soon as you can." "Yes, sir, Commander Anderson!" "Major turn on the secondary power switches. Let's preflight this bird anyway and hope for the best."

Commander Anderson was truly beside himself for making such a hasty ill-fated fool command and now there was not a single thing he nor anyone else onboard could do to correct his poor judgment call of their location and speed. "Secondary power switches on, Commander.

We have some power now, sir." "Open up all solar shield protectors, Major, and expose the solar shield energizers to maximum swing. We need all the electric power we can muster up, right away!"

Everyone knew Commander Anderson was now browbeating himself up over the way he was beginning to say damn, damn it, or damn every other word he used to get his messages across, for it was not like him to do that. Commander Anderson usually came across in a very calm cool good natured control over most all difficult situations, but not this poor situation he got them into after making it this far into their rescue mission. This bothered the hell out of him, especially if he was the one to have cost the cosmonauts onboard the space station their lives because of a very foolish mistake he had just made.

"Solar shields open wide, Commander. Solar panels absorbing power from the sun at maximum power, sir."

"Very good, major, can we bring up the radio to communicate with the space station yet? I need to know the status of those onboard the space station, Lieutenant! The main battery banks men, how are they coming along? Can you guys go a little faster?"

"Time wise, sir, at least another thirty minutes before they're up and running to capacity."

"Well, get a damned move on then would you, Lieutenant?"

"Yes, sir. Commander, right away."

"Major, what is the verdict on those radios?"

"Radios are all static and clatter. I can't seem to broadcast or receive a thing from them, sir?"

"How are those damned battery banks coming along, Lieutenant?"
"Getting there sir, getting there."

Everyone knew the commander had made a bad judgement call in releasing the second stage rockets, and was now taking it to heart that he had made such a miserable mistake in releasing the rockets too soon. Everyone knew he would never forgive himself if he let anyone down, never mind let them all die. He had never really made a bad decision that anyone had ever known about, but this one was a doozy.

"Commander, I hear something on the radio now. It must be the space station lab, sir. I can just barely hear them and can't make out what they are trying to say, sir. Whoever it is surely sounds very weak and sick to me, sir."

"Amplify the radio signal from them, Major, and turn that damn volume up to maximum."

"I can't sir, as that part of the radio system is powered by the main power systems. I cannot amplify the signal or turn up the volume without the main battery banks up and running, sir."

"How are those damn battery banks coming along, Lieutenant?"

"The auxiliary jaytoe bottles are full, are they not, major? We have not used any of them as of yet, have we Captain Mitchell?"

"No, sir, Commander." "Well, what do you think, major? Will they work?"

"Yes, sir, Commander, they should, but what is the concept of the jay-to bottles use, Commander?"

"Are we in the proper orbit with the space station, Captain, and not off course?"

"Yes, sir. We are on course, Commander."

"Precisely what I am getting at, Major. If we turn the shields and fire the two jaytoe bottles together, they will propel us forward and toward the space station, correct?"

"Yes, sir, they should. I guess so, sir. It is a very long shot, but I guess it will work. There probably isn't enough propellant in them to do the full job, sir, but they will help."

"Turn those shields around, Major, and fire the jaytoe bottles on my command, Bill."

"How are those battery banks coming along, Lieutenant?"

"A couple more minutes, sir, just a couple more minutes."

"Well get a move on then will you, Lieutenant, we need those damn batteries up and running now." Damn fool that I am anyway. Why did I release those boosters in the first place? When will I ever learn?"

"Finished, sir. Main power battery banks are fully charged with acid in them, sir."

"Strap yourselves gents, we are going to use the jaytoe bottles to boost our speed. Fire away. Major." The commander was right. The Twitchel did move forward as planned. Not very fast for a spacecraft, but it did pick up speed heading toward the space station at a snail's pace.

"How long for the jaytoe bottles to burn, sir, one, two, three or more minutes to burn, sir?" "Until the damn bottles run themselves dry Major. When there is no more propellant left in them to burn."

"Until they are completely empty, sir?"

"Yes, until they are completely empty Major. "Main power is on full power, sir. All cabin panel lighting and instrument panel lighting is up and running, sir."

Finally the Twitchel had her lifeline of blood flowing with the life of electricity running through her many veins of wires again. "Switch off the auxiliary power, Major. This bird is A-OK, and well alive again. Let us fire up the main rockets now Captain Mitchell; we have a rendezvous with a space station to make."

Ann checked the paneled display for the power locking device indicator light. "Commander, there is no power to the rear thrusters, sir?" "Double check it again, Captain. Do that damn shutdown start up sequence of the craft's electrical system once again, just the same way you would in your fighter jet when you lose your thrusters."

"Yes, sir, right away, sir." Ann shut down the entire electrical display board of controls in front of her at her workstation. Then she did as previously instructed in her training by turning them all back on, one by one. She carefully brought back every switch back in its proper order to the on position and its light-lit back to life. She then switched on the main booster rocket switch at the end of her sequence, but that particular indicator light did not light up as it had not previously done.

"Sorry, sir, still no electrical power indicated to the main rear booster rocket panel firing mechanism light, sir."

"Maybe it is just a damn burnt out bulb or a loose one. Captain Mitchell, fire those damn main boosters on the count of three anyway, and let's get the hell out of here."

"Yes, sir, Commander. Fire thrusters on the count of three. One, two, three." Ann threw the switch to activate the rear main boosters, but to no avail, nothing happened and neither did any light come on as it should have to indicate power to the rear main thrusters.

Dead silence filled the cabin, not a sound nor any vibration from the main thrusters. The rear main boosters remained perfectly quiet, not trying to ignite. Just then, the jaytoe bottles ran out of their solid propulsion fuel as Commander Anderson was having yet another fit for himself over yet another unbearable situation in the second stage of this important mission.

"There has to be a break in one of the wires or connectors somewhere between the panel's control switch and the firing mechanism, sir. It could be as simple as a harness has come apart somewhere out in the cargo bay area sir."

"Do it again Captain, and fire that damn thing one more time! You must have missed something when you brought that damn control panel back to life, Ann."

"Yes, sir, Commander." Ann ran through the sequence one more time of shutting down the entire electrical panel board and all its many switches in the proper sequence of shutdown mode before bringing them all back to life the way she was supposed to do it. She very well knew she had followed the correct procedure in the manual's specified sequence the last two times she had gone through the startup procedure, but still to no avail. She would do it again as ordered. "Sorry, Commander, but there is still no power to the rear main boosters, sir. There is no ignition power sensor light on either, sir. There has just got to be a loose connector or broken wire in one of the connector panels out in the cargo bay or somewhere in my panel here at my work station, sir.

"The space station has come back into view, Commander, with its strobe lights flashing in the darkness."

"Captain, damn it, Jim, how long is it going to be before you can get this damn glitch fixed?"

"I do not know for sure, sir. I will do my best, Commander."

"Lieutenant, break out the tool kits from beneath the station's seats." Steven jumped right to it and took them out for Captain Morris. Ann moved away from her post so the captain could get started on his work. He wanted to make sure the control panel was not to blame for the

mishap before he ventured out to the electrical panels located out back of the cabin in the now almost filled to capacity cargo bay. It would definitely be a whole hell of a lot easier a fix in the control panel with a little luck, but he did not have the luck of the Irish with him at that moment when he opened it up. The break of wire or problem with this particular control switch circuit was as he was afraid it would be; somewhere out in the almost full to capacity cargo bay somewhere behind or under the pallets of dehydrated foods, water containers, and the oxygen cylinders strapped to the floor and sidewalls of the Twitchel.

The work of repairing the shuttle thruster's ignition system was proceeding along way too slow for Commander Anderson, while Major Bill continually kept trying to talk to the space station. All he could hear were faint soft unclear crackling voices coming in over the radio frequency.

The faint voices worried the hell out of Commander Anderson as all he could imagine in the back of his mind were the good people who had saved them from dying a horrific death by suffocation for lack of oxygen. The very substance he and his crew had used so much of that they so desperately needed right now to survive. He knew he had enough oxygen on board for them to live better than another year; also, enough food and water to go along with it, if only he could get those damned rockets to fire, and get the oxygen to them in enough time before they all succumbed from the lack of it.

"How is that damn repair coming along, Captain?"

"Not very good commander, I am afraid to say, sir. As soon as we get this control panel back together, we are going to go out into the cargo bay and try to find the real problem out there, sir."

"How long will that be Captain?"

"I don't really know, sir, but we are trying our best!"

"I know, Morris, I know!" This is really starting to bug the hell out of me. What in the hell else can go wrong now, I wonder? Maybe the damn fools on the ground forgot to charge the rocket fuel tanks before we left the launch pad. If so, we will be in the same frigging fix the laboratory is in now because I gave orders to use up all the fuel in the jaytoe bottles."

Lieutenant Steven and Captain Morris went directly to the cargo bay as soon as they put the control panel back together at Ann's station. The entire electrical panel assemblies were carefully protected by the installation of the panels within the walls and beneath the cargo floor of all the food, water, filter carbon boxes for retrofitting the fresh water filtering system, and the many pallets holding the oxygen cylinders.

There were several electrical panels that Captain Morris had to open up to view in order to find and correct the problem they were experiencing. The entire crew including Ann went out to the cargo bay to help to move the payload of supplies out of the way from the electrical access panels. Moving the huge containers of supplies was extremely difficult and dangerous. There was hardly little room for one crewmember to move around fully outfitted in their full flight gear suits, never mind the seven of them with re-breathers attached to their backs.

The containers of supplies were heavy and bulky, and once the crew got them to move up and away from their tie downs, they also had to stop the movement of them in order to prevent them from damaging the inside of the cargo bay where they were drifting to. The task was hard, long, and time consuming. Using their hands and feet, they managed somehow to unstrap container after container while in their space suits. Weightlessness definitely had its advantages and disadvantages all at the same time in this situation. Crate after crate They moved away crate after crate from panel after panel, securing the cargo back into its original position before going on to the next panel for its inspection. As luck would have it, they should have started at the very last protective panel first because there was where they found the problem.

The crew wasted most of the day searching for a harness connector that had to have come apart during the Twitchel's reentry better than three months earlier when it rolled and twisted on reentry. The extent of the huge g-force exerted on everything including the crewmembers back then must have loosened the connection, and it was just hanging there freely in the compartment separated.

Captain Morris pushed the two separated plastic harness connectors back together as Ann floated back into her station inside the cockpit to see if everything was back to normal again for the main booster rockets, and it was. The panel lit up like a Christmas tree. "All set, Commander! It was that connector that had come apart all of the time, sir." After securing the electrical panel's cover and getting the cargo bay back into shape with everything in its original places, everyone returned to their flight deck cockpit stations to resume their original flight plans.

What else could go wrong now, Commander Anderson thought?

"On the three count, Captain, one, two, three." (The jaytoe bottles had worked earlier, but the Twitchel was hundreds of miles from its final destination.) The main booster rockets came to life. Commander Anderson's face went from a very concerned frown of dissatisfaction to a more normally relaxed pleasant smile when he heard and felt the main rockets of the Twitchel kick in.

"One long ten-minute burn on both rockets, Captain."

"Yes, sir, ten minutes." Ann set her timer instrument on ten and then sat back and relaxed for the first time since their liftoff.

Everyone onboard had time to relax now for a short time. Everything seemed to be going on as planned, but that could change at any given moment. Commander Anderson sat back in his seat waiting for the best or worst to happen. When the timer reached ten, Ann switched the main rocket boosters off. The space station was getting closer, but not fast enough for Commander Anderson's likings.

"One more hard-long burn, Captain Mitchell, another ten minutes, please. On the three count again Captain, one, two, three. Ann flipped the toggle switch for the main rockets to on and the main booster rockets came to life instantly. Ann set the automatic timing device to a ten-minute burn again.

Things were going too good for comfort this time, something amiss just had to take place. At the ten-minute mark, Ann turned the booster rocket switch to off. The speed of the Twitchel had greatly increased as they were closing in on their target, but it was still a very long way away.

Commander Anderson was still very concerned for the safety of the space station crew, and wanted to be with them right then and not wait another minute of precious time gone by.

Major Bill could still hear the faint voices over the radio, but they seemed ever the more faint and weak to him as they did to Commander Anderson as he listened in on the communications channel, and tried to make out what they were trying to say to them.

"Another ten minute-burn, Captain."

"Yes, sir, Commander, another ten-minute burn, sir."

"On the three count again Captain, one, two, three fire." Ann switched on the main thruster switch, and again the main rocket thrusters came to life. Everything was going way too smooth now. On the ten-minute mark, Ann switched off the thruster switch. This time the Twitchel was closing in real fast on its intended target. It had been a long time since Ann had last fired the main thrusters, and the strobe beacon on the bottom of the space station was becoming bigger and brighter.

"Captain Mitchell?"

"Yes, sir, Commander?"

"Fire the retro for a quick blast. We have to slow this bird down."
"Yes, sir, Commander." Ann fired the retro, and the Twitchel began to slow.

"Another burn, Ann."

"Yes, sir, Commander." Several more retro-rocket blasts and the Twitchel would be ready to dock and couple up with the International Space Station again. Everything about the space station looked exactly as it had the day they uncoupled their craft from it and departed over a few months earlier. The soviet's escape space capsule still lay attached to the side of the space station in its original docking position where it had been since docking it. It was there in case some one or several cosmonauts became desperately sick and had to leave the space station immediately for whatever reason.

The exterior positioning lights on the space station switched on as did the docking lamps when the Twitchel came within a mile of the space station. The radio signal was stronger now but still very staticy as it had been before, but at least they could understand each other more now than they could before.

The Russian crewmembers and the two Germans onboard the space station were ecstatic to hear friendly voices being broadcast to them, no matter how static or scrambled up they all sounded. Time was quickly running out for them, for they were all getting very nervous what was going to take place or to happen to them in their fast dwindling last days aboard the ailing space station. Time for their lives had been running out, as many friends and family aboard would be left to die when only a handful from the station would be able to return home to earth safely, they hoped.

CHAPTER FORTY-SEVEN

The Lottery for Life or Death

The crew aboard the space station watched the earth below for months. They kept hoping and praying day after day looking down to see if anything might come about below that might lead to their rescue. The crewmembers of the space station were becoming almost sick with fear they might all vanish except for six lucky ones.

Everyone on the space lab knew that in the near future they would have to come up with some sort of an innovative life plan to save the few who would survive. A lottery for life of some kind to enable a few to return back home to earth letting the remaining members of their crew stay behind on the doomed space station without food, oxygen, or any of the necessary equipment and sources of survival needed to go on, and would all eventually die an unpleasant death.

It would only be fair that the only two German astronauts onboard the space station other than the Russians would be the first to be chosen to leave the doomed craft and wouldn't have to join in the lottery for life unless they so choose to do so. Had it not been for the Russian's foolish leaders creating this evil device of destruction, they would all have been safe to live. Now the grave situation around the earth below has left them all captive prisoners in space for something their leaders had caused.

The space station's commander, Commander Ivan Khrushchev, being in charge of the laboratory had come up with a fair and equitable

273

solution to pick the four lucky cosmonauts which would be able to leave the laboratory along with the two Germans. This plan was a lottery type drawing, a raffle to save four of their very own comrades and give them a chance at life on earth.

A raffle, for all the crewmembers to play in case the situation on board came down to one of a very drastic measure, would only take place when a final decision had to be handed down and made by Commander Ivan and then to implement a safety procedure for the protection of the four lucky ones drawn. The entire crew of the laboratory was on the verge of giving up, and some were on the verge of committing mutiny unless something very drastic was to occur.

In about a month more or less when their remaining oxygen supply onboard the station would dwindle rapidly to an unsafe level, as the plant life aboard supplementing extra needed oxygen in the space station would not be able to convert the massive amounts in carbon dioxide produced by the fretting crew back into usable oxygen. According to the instrumentation onboard the laboratory, the situation was becoming more critical with each passing day. According to the readings taken every day in accordance with the governing air quality control procedures on board the space station, time for the lottery was soon approaching.

It had been months of continual daily observations of the Soviet launch pad sites from the eye in the sky. No one, not one single solitary person, was doing anything in or around the Soviet launch sites since the horrible missile mishap took place well over a long whole year ago. There had always been a couple of rockets standing at the launch sites from the very beginning of their watch, which in fact looked ready to be launched, but one of them most recently fell over on its side, and split apart. The sight of it lying dead on its side without any ground action taking place around it anywhere took all their wishes and prayers away. There never had in all their time looking down been a sighting of any living sole around any of them except for at the American landing sight.

Down at the American space sites there were always activities going on around them on the ground, even before their friends chanced taking the Twitchel back home to Earth after their long stay with them in space. There had been trucks, busses, tractors, and Jeeps after several months moving around the sight at the cape.

False hope had built in the crew a couple of days after the Twitchel had safely landed back on Earth. They moved the Twitchel from the landing strip runway, and brought it back to a large hanger where they always readied the shuttles for launching again.

Could it be possible that the Americans were getting their craft ready for another mission into outer space? Several days passed on, then several weeks, and then their little ray of hope began to dwindle away from them again.

The oxygen alarms around the laboratory began to sound as sections of the laboratory's outer cubicles needed shutting down to conserve on their expanded use in oxygen. The commander stopped all unnecessary exercise aboard the craft, affecting everyone's daily activities, altered in any way possible to curb and conserve the precious necessities in food, water, and the precious oxygen supply that was in critical short supply.

The time had come to implement the use of the lottery for life for the few that would live and the many that would perish onboard. The time of the lottery for life had come!

"All personnel report to the main assembly cubical at once. I repeat! All personnel please report to the assembly room cubical immediately." Everyone recognized the forceful voice over the intercom system as the voice of the space station's commander, Commander Ivan.

"Ladies and gentlemen, it is time to exercise the departure lottery. Time is of the essence, and if we wait any longer, it will be too late. If there is any, the slightest of hope, or the slimmest of chances in hell that any of us might survive, it will be up to the lucky lottery winners of this lottery to see to it that that takes place as soon as possible. As all onboard know, we are desperately low on our oxygen supply, food, and other necessary supplies for our living welfare. We have about a month or less before we have none left at all, and this mission will be over with at that very critical time.

It will be up to those few lucky lottery winners to secure our needs, and send them back to us if they are lucky enough to survive the ordeal of reentry and make a safe landing in America at the Kennedy Space Center.

If they do not survive the reentry and cannot report our ill-fated situation to the world below to the Americans, then we shall all perish as a group up here. As you all know, the Americans have been able to remove the Twitchel from the runway and place it back into one of its hangers. That is all it looks like they are going to do with that craft for the meantime.

We were all hoping with false hopes at first, I guess. We all figured our good friends the Americans would have explained our plight of this poor situation we are in up here to their superiors. If they had, I guess the information they told them fell upon deaf ears. I guess we should have had a couple of more Americans on this mission, instead of you two Germans, no offence men. Maybe then they would have hustled in sending some sort of relief ship up here to help sustain us, and maybe things would have been a little different.

Commander Anderson from the Twitchel explained to me when the right time came, he did not quite know when that time would come as he and I had miscalculated the amounts of supplies we had onboard when his craft left. He said we should try to land our space capsule on or about the launching sight where they landed, and if Commander Anderson could he would immediately have help sent back up to us if it was at all possible for them to do so.

Well crew, the time has come for us to send our message down to him, and I only hope he can as he said he would if at all possible send a good craft loaded with supplies back up here for us. The time has come comrades, the time has come to play our capsule lottery of who lives and who dies up here. I would very much like to return back to Earth as one of the few crewmembers aboard the lucky capsule, and I could if I so chose to. You all know I have the authority to make this type of decision for myself if I want to, but I will not. I have had a good life, and would like very much for someone younger than I would to enjoy a good life as I have. It has been a very difficult decision for me

to make, but I will not be joining any of you in this lottery for life. I want this lottery to be as fair as possible to everyone onboard this ship.

Therefore, every one of you will have to win the lottery for life five different times and in five different ways to enable yourselves to board the returning capsule. The winners will play against the winners, and the losers will play against the losers. The winners from the losers will play against the winners from the winners, and losers from the winners will play against the losers from the losers until only four of you remain as winners. These will be the lucky ones to board the capsule at a time I so choose for their departure.

If I was to play the lottery along with you, the numbers would not, and I repeat, the numbers would not work out for everyone, and I would have to choose the last lucky person to board the capsule myself. I will not choose whether someone lives or dies. Therefore, as commander of this space station, I order myself ineligible to participate in this very special lottery of life. That is an order, and my proclamation before you all. Now let you, as my good friends, play the lottery for life."

Commander Ivan passed out the many sealed envelopes he had in his makeshift basket to each crewmember except to the two Germans who were not to participate in it. He let each crewmember reach into the basket one by one and take out his or her first envelope as the commander passed the container around in front of them.

Commander Ivan had spent many hours upon long grueling hours, designing and redesigning the extraordinary game of life. His next in command aboard the space station did not know how the lottery for life would work. His crew knew nothing about it during the time he was designing it. Only the commander himself knew how it would work.

The commander mixed up the envelopes so he would not even know who might win in the first round of play or not. He wanted the game of life he designed played in the most honest way, and not like his lost superiors game that had gone and deployed all those damn lethal missiles that cost so many their lives.

Commander Ivan was more than a fair man and would have loved to see his loving children and lovely grandchildren once again. He knew it was the only fair way for him to show his real character to his loved ones back home and to the world below. He wanted it known to everyone on Earth that he was a true martyr of goodwill and honesty. He didn't want to go down in history as his wrongful superiors did. He knew most Russian people were good honest hard-working people of the planet, and he wanted everyone below to know that it took only a few bad apples in the leadership barrel of life to make it look like they had destroyed the whole bunch of honest ones, but they had not.

He stayed up many, many nights worrying and wondering how to go about the rules of this particular lottery in making it work in a fair and just manner. He had spent the many sleepless hours making up the many envelopes, slipping the winners' and losers' slips into every one of them and into the makeshift basket they would be picked from, one by one.

No one, not a one, showed any jubilation or sorrow in winning or losing as the first round of lottery tickets were passed out. Everyone knew that most everyone onboard the doomed space station was going to die, and there wasn't any reason for jubilation to be shown at the first drawing, knowing very well they were just one step closer to living, and one of your many friends would be left behind were that one step closer to dying.

Everyone onboard the space station felt the same way about this damn lottery for life. If they were to win so be it, and if they were to lose and be left behind to die, so be it.

The commander waited for everyone to open their chanced envelopes and had the lucky winners come forward for their next drawing, and did the same for the losing members. The next drawing, he had the winner and loser crewmembers come forward in similar fashion until the lottery was completed, and the four lucky winners were standing there beside him.

Everyone now showed great joy for the ones who had won the lottery with tears of sorrow welling up in their eyes for themselves. Tears shed were either happy ones filled with joy for the winners, or they were more sorrowful sad tears for themselves. Everyone tried to represent themselves as joyful tears for the winner's sake anyway or because their commander had been so strong in showing his heroism. He did not play the lottery or let his commanding powers of authority leave someone of them behind because of greed for life and power over them for himself.

Everyone onboard knew Commander Ivan would designate the time for departure, and that no one else onboard the space station, but he and the lucky four lottery winners along with the two Germans, would know when that special time would come in the near future. It would take place within the next couple or few days or weeks, and no later than two weeks before their oxygen supply was to run very low for them.

The commander had the only access keys to the capsule, and his own newly encoded releasing numbers he had himself entered into the onboard computer to release the capsule and its booster rockets from the space station, memorized by him only in order for the capsule to leave the security of the space station under his power.

He had performed all this security surrounding the space capsule just in case someone onboard the space station tried to steal the capsule and try to return to Earth for his or her own benefit. He knew the situation at hand would cause many minds to wonder. He didn't want anyone onboard falling into the situation of trying to dessert leaving them all behind to die when there was a slim but small chance for some to survive and possibly send back some relief help from Earth for the rest of them. He wanted to send the lucky winners of the lottery off with plenty of time left for the ones left behind onboard to live a little while longer.

They needed to know someone down below cared about them, and the lottery crew could possibly send back some help to them by way of supplies. Whatever they could do to try to help them in their desperate situation aloft knowing it was probably futile, but he had to do something to give himself and the others a little hope, if nothing at all.

The time had come for the lucky six to leave the space station. Time was running out for everyone, and if the four cosmonauts and German astronauts were to leave, it would mean all that much more oxygen for the rest of his crew to have to live on before that horrible time of suffocation or starvation overcame them.

CHAPTER FORTY-EIGHT

Excitement of a Sighting

"Commander Ivan. Report to the laboratory's command center bridge immediately, sir. The space shuttle Twitchel has been brought out of its storage hanger and being brought out to one of the three launching pads below sir!"

Commander Ivan ran floating along in weightlessness along the way as quickly as he possibly could move, stumbling in the air in the space station's corridors, bouncing off everything in sight in his way it seemed. Everything along the way, the walls of the tubes between the cubicles seemed to try to stop him from getting to the large eye in the sky telescope quick enough. He wanted to take a look see for himself before the space station's orbit took them too far away from Florida for him to see what was taking shape below at the cape. He figured the United States was either going to send them some very much needed help or supplies for them to keep alive a while longer or it was just going to send up another shuttle to do more of their own experiments in outer space again.

His hopes were that it was his first thoughts that were about to happen, and not those of his second thoughts that he had had. He had been just about ready to allow the lucky contestants of the lottery for life to prepare themselves to leave the space station in the awaiting space capsule they had the next morning prior to seeing action take place below. He had for some unknown reason held off his final decision for a couple of extra days, almost letting the lottery winners leave just before the Americans showed any signs they were coming to help rescue them from their craft or help them in some other way.

He was delighted the Americans had moved the Twitchel out of her hanger when they did or the lucky lottery winners would have already left and been on their way back to earth.

CHAPTER FORTY-NINE

The Beautiful Launch

Two more time-consuming overwhelming long days passed slowly by for the crew of the International Space Station. The weather around the cape was rather cloudy over the launching sight of Florida as they passed overhead again just before dawn. It did not look like a good day for a launch of any shuttle.

On their next pass over Cape Kennedy, the Twitchel was no longer on her launching pad as the craft was gone. There was a white squiggle cloudy of steamy white smoke twisting itself into the morning sky. The powerful telescope aboard the space station did not pick up the tiny black speck giving off the flume of steam and smoke behind it.

The Twitchel was shooting skyward toward them. Commander Ivan lessened the varying power on the telescope's control panel, drawing in the huge extended lens on it and back into the many powered telescopes varying sections to lessen its huge magnification capabilities.

There she was looking beautiful and everything ascending skyward toward them and the heavens. She looked like she was on a flight path that would line her up in a direct line with them. She was climbing toward them at the 0800 hour position located on his wristwatch.

He watched the craft as her two main thruster launching rockets were ejected from her sides, then several seconds later her second stage booster rockets came to life. She was a beautiful sight to him while he prayed in his own way that the craft he was watching shooting skyward

was coming to bring he and his crew some very much-needed precious food, oxygen, and other supplies they so desperately needed to keep them all alive, but he couldn't be dead nuts sure they were coming for them.

He tried contacting the Twitchel on their once designated NASA radio frequency, but there was no response on that channel. They had not quite come out of the silent quiet radio zone yet he thought, as they were just barely entering the outer edge of the globe's atmosphere's outer edge of the space realm.

The space station quickly lost sight of the ascending shuttlecraft as the telescope's ability to turn and maneuver to follow the ship up was limited in its ability to turn its lenses sideways. The huge telescope onboard was built to follow the smallest in movements upon the earth's surface and into outer space, but not very adjustable to the laboratory's sides or to its rear in order to follow the shuttlecraft any longer.

Commander Ivan ordered the smaller telescope onboard to be switched on at his observation station so that its ability to turn in any direction that he wanted he could use. There she was drifting further and further away from them in her own orbit when he was able to lock onto the craft with the smaller of the two telescopes.

Commander Ivan was very disappointed. He had figured the shuttle just launched would be zooming in at them under full power in order to catch up to them in their orbit if they were on a mercy mission to help save them. He and Commander Anderson had figured wrong about the amount of supplies that were onboard his craft when he and Commander Anderson departed a couple of months before. The two figured the space station would have enough food and oxygen supply to last them about eight or nine more months if used sparingly, and they were totally wrong.

The longer they watched the Twitchel, the further away it drifted back, back, and away from them. After several long hours of disappointment it seemed watching the Twitchel drift further and further away from them and finally disappear out of their sight, the commander of the space station had the four select raffle winners along with the two German astronauts report to his quarters.

"The time has come, gentlemen, for the six of you to prepare to leave your posts. Our mission has truly become a sad one for the rest of your fellow cosmonauts and for me as well. In your case, the many friends I hope you have all come to make over the last countless months together. The hope of being saved by the Americans has dwindles down to nothing now I guess. I was sure of it when I first saw them, sure the shuttle launched was coming for us or at least bringing us some much-needed supplies. I guess they don't really know our plight up here and are just out doing some more outer space experiments of their own, instead of including us in their new program. It is truly a shame. We must now prepare for the worst for the ones left behind, and the best for you six at the same time. Remember comrades, 0600 hours Eastern Time. You will report to the capsule's docking platform in your full flight gear for departure.

If, or should I say when, you make it back to Earth crew, I am quite sure you will try your hardest back on Earth to convince someone to please send some oxygen, at least, and other much-needed supplies immediately back up to us or we shall all perish. We do have enough food and oxygen for a couple of more or less months, and we can still use the filtering systems for our water, even though everything is starting to get a little rancid tasting around here. We desperately need more oxygen to stay alive much longer than the plus or minus months.

Your mission will be a mission of mercy for your fellow comrades. I had my own hopes way too high for the last couple of days while seeing the American shuttle ascend toward us, but now to no avail. Remember 0600 hours, comrades, and don't be late. Everyone other than the seven of us will think this just another practice dry run for your preparation to leave, but it will not be. This will be the actual time of leaving comrades and hope you will all remember the instructions we have been going over and over these last few weeks of practice.

You must enter the earth's atmosphere at exactly a thirty-five degree approaching angle to your downward slope reentry or you will burn up without the bottom of your capsule absorbing the intense heat of going through the atmosphere. Remember comrades, 0600 hours, and do not be late. The trajectory point to land at the U.S. base depends on a quick departure so you will land on target and on time in the daylight hours.

No one will suspect your departure just like this was supposed to be another hour of instruction on how to maneuver the capsule with the positioning rockets for your reentry. Remember 0600 hours and do not be late. Whoever shows up late for the departure will not be going due to the short reentry window available at that time of day. The window for departure is narrow and cannot be missed!"

"Commander Ivan, please report to the control room immediately. Commander Ivan, please report to the main control room immediately."

"What is it Sergeant?" Commander Ivan asked the sergeant at the control board over the intercom system.

"The shuttle has fired four small rockets, sir. It may be heading this way, but I am not certain of it, sir."

The commander hurried along to the main control room again, but not in as much of a hurry as last time. He then sat down to watch what was happening to the shuttle's movement on the live television screen monitor attached to the smaller telescope. He watched as the four additional disposable jaytoe bottles affixed to the shuttle's sides of the craft burned until they emptied themselves of their fuel and their flames went out. "They must have had a radical failure with their positioning system, Sergeant. No one in their right minds would have wasted all there positioning device capabilities like that one unless they were in an improper orbit. A switch must have failed them or malfunctioned to have all four fired off all at the same precise time. I have never seen anything quite like that before. I wonder if they are in trouble, or what they are up to."

He wondered, if they were coming to link up with the space station to help them, then why had the crew released the second stage rockets so soon. Even he knew the indicator's warning lights from the computers would warn them with buzzers if they had a problem if they were to waste the second stages too soon and would have kept them from doing it automatically. Why in the hell had they gone and done such a foolish thing in overriding the computers if their mission was to come to help them. The commander sat there feeling stupefied, watching the shuttle for a couple of more hours as the shuttle drifted a minuscule closer with the passing of time, but hadn't indicate in its actions it was coming to help them in their desperate predicament. He got up from sitting in front of the monitor, and then paced back and forth through the corridors drifting from one corridor to the next. He had finally run out of his strong mental strength in stamina, and had only wished now he had somehow found a way he too could have at least figured out a way that he might have had a fair chance to have been in the raffle of life to enable him a chance to have gone back home to his family as well.

The situation at hand for the moment was poor, and disheartening. He could not do a damn thing about it now except to climb into that damn space capsule by himself and return back home to Earth by himself. He was the commander and chief of this damn space laboratory. He had every damn right and authority to make such a drastic call and return back to Earth all by himself and send help back to his needy crew. Why were these corrupt thoughts now going through his tired mind? Deep down inside, he didn't really feel this way, but his subconscious worried mind kept firing up and telling him all these things to do to save himself. Either the Americans were coming to help them, or they were not coming at all. What in the hell were they up to?

"Commander Ivan, please report to the control room immediately". "What the hell do they want from me now?" He wanted to be left alone to gather his tired thoughts some more, so he would not show any signs of weakness. Ivan pushed off with his feet and drifted toward the control room hoping the Americans were coming this time to help them, but he had his doubts.

"The shuttle has fired her main rockets this time, sir." Then Commander Ivan sat down, and watched carefully this time to see what was taking place with the shuttle should time turn around, and they were coming to help.

"Contact her by radio, Sergeant." "Yes sir commander. She is not responding clearly. All I have is a continuance of garbled-up static coming in over this channel, sir. I cannot, understand any words being communicated, but it sounds as if they are trying to raise us on their radio, sir."

Even thought they could not correspond by radios, the commander's gut feelings told him she was coming for them now, and it was truly a splendid good feeling of relief he had inside himself.

Commander Ivan sent out a happy message out over the intercom system in the space station as everyone flocked to the control room or places where there were monitors to watch the space shuttle on the television monitoring screens. The shuttle was now zooming in toward them as she had been on her first entry into space. The ship looked like the Twitchel, the same ship they had befriended just over a year and some months ago, and it was now coming back to them, for them, or just possibly bringing them some much-needed supplies to save them from disaster. It didn't matter what they were up to as they were coming. At that very moment, that was what mattered the most to any of them.

Tears of happy joy flowed freely from every crewmember at their stations, including Commander Ivan. At least now everyone had a mere smidgen of hope as all shouted with glee. They were so overzealous with emotion seeing the shuttle zooming through space toward them, and the burden on their weary hearts lightened. Many of the Russian women onboard began to cry cheerfully as all of their daily-unanswered prayers seemed to becoming answered for them. A couple of the men openly had misty eyes as the rest of the macho crewmembers hid their feelings behind gritted teeth. Many onboard the space station had been feeling the end to their lives was quickly nearing its final days, all except for the six very lucky ones. Now they all, including the lucky six, stood a very good chance of one day returning back home to their loved ones on Earth. Now if only a small number of them could return with every mission sent to them by the Americans sending supplies, and a small number of them might be able to return with the shuttle when it returns back to Earth.

As the Twitchel fired her retro-rockets, the entire crew of the space station bellowed out with a joyous chorus as they all hugged and made merry, trying to jump up and down as they floated together in the laboratory's sections all together.

The very static sounding voices from the radio became clearer the closer the shuttle approached the orbiting space laboratory. When the Twitchels retro-rockets fired to slow their craft down for final hookup, the voices coming in over the radio cleared right up between the two crafts.

While Commander Ivan watched, he observed the Twitchel firing her maneuvering jaytoe bottles to line their craft up for their docking to the station. Commander Ivan was totally confused because he had witnessed the Twitchel fire what he thought to have been their positioning jaytoe bottles, and wasted their short-lived lives just a couple of hours before. He knew they had, as he had witnessed it with his own two eyes. He did not know the ones they had wasted were their spare auxiliary jaytoe rockets that were hand controlled, and not computerized controlled jaytoe bottles. These were the ones affixed to the shuttle in case the Twitchel's crew was unable to bring life back to the main battery bank systems located in the cargo bay of the Twitchel. The crew would then have to use them by operating the jaytoe bottles by hand to bring the Twitchel back into the earth's gravitational pull properly and safely back to Earth hopefully.

"Close the docking coupler, Captain."

"Contact coupler engaged, sir." The forward jaws of the contractor coupler arm reached out and grabbed its intended target, securing the Twitchel firmly to the space station's main docking ports specially designed for any of the American space shuttles fleet to dock with the space station.

The crew of the Twitchel had tears in their eyes when Ann threw the switch, and they could hear and feel the securing couplers of the two crafts engaging themselves locking the Twitchel firmly to the Space Station Laboratory's airlock locking mechanism. Ann was thrilled to death this time, but with other intentions on her mind than before when they docked to save their own hides, and now was glad to be back for them this time. Happy tears of joy flowed uncontrollably from the crew of the space station, as their ears heard the pleasant sounds of coupling couplers locking the two crafts together with their friends that they all hoped were on board the craft bringing relief back to them.

Ann's happy heart was up in her joyous throat knowing very well and feeling quite wonderful that she had made the appropriate choice back home on her father's farm, when Commander Anderson approached her and asked her to come along on this mission of mercy to help out her friends in need. She knew she didn't have to come along or risk her life for the many unlucky crewmen onboard the space station, and could have just as easily have said no, but now she was extremely high in spirits with the choice she had made. Commander Anderson knew Ann would have probably said no to a stranger if he had sent someone else in his place to ask her; therefore, he went all by himself to see her personally. A stranger could not have preyed so easily on her tender caring heart of emotion the way he did. He knew that for having known her so very well for so very long. A stranger would not have gotten down on his two knees and begged her to go with them, the way he was prepared to do so if she had really said no to him. He knew this mission would have been almost impossible without her expertise's knowledge onboard, and they would have probably failed the mission if she had stayed behind.

Ann could not hold back her emotions any longer or the flowing happy tears of joy she was feeling building up at the time. Three months or so earlier she had left this dying hulk of steel, this albatross of a space station laboratory in the heavens that had been her home, free floating in its orbital space pattern, of which she had hoped never to have to lay her beautiful eyes on the dying beast never again. Ann had returned to this unlikely layover hotel she once called home in outer space to give it a much needed CPR and return its once normal heartbeat gone array, back to a healthy beating one within its inner soul and needy mechanisms of life-supporting systems.

Commander Anderson opened up a small green canister of fresh oxygen he was holding in his hand as he entered the space station first.

The canister was a grand token of their daring journey to space to bring to the needy space station's crew. They also brought with them fresh filters for their re-breathing units, charcoal for their water purification system, food, and other much needed incidental supplies he knew they were so desperate in need of. Everyone cheered on both sides of the airlock as the hatches between the two vessels slowly opened up, as Commander Anderson was the first to emerge from the hatch of the Twitchel.

The mood was set, as many hugs and kisses of brotherly and sibling similar love flowed between the members of the two crews like water flowing over an opened dam on a bright warm summer's day. The scene aboard the space station looked more like a reuniting of a lost child with his or her overly worried family, after the child had been lost out in the woods for a couple or so long lonely days.

Commander Anderson and Commander Ivan hugged as if they were lost brothers lastly reunited after having lost contact with each other for many years instead of the way two professional military men would act when addressing one another. The joyous mood between the two crews carried on for quite some time after the crew of the Twitchel had all entered the space laboratory before all finally settled down to the seriousness of business of the mission at hand.

The thin unraveling thread of life had finally come together once again as a whole, and the lives aboard the space laboratory spared for a short time to come for some and maybe not for some of the others. The worst of life's dreaded news was forthcoming to some onboard the space station, for many lost loved ones back home on Earth, and the sad news for some would be too much a burden for anyone to handle at this critical time, especially if you had been trapped in space like they had been for so long.

It took a couple of days of transferring the life-saving supplies from the Twitchel's huge cargo bay to the space station's supply bay. After each long hard day of work, the two crews spent their relaxing time together chatting with one another about the changes around the earth that they once knew. They explained what they had witnessed and what it was like to live down there now, and it wasn't as pleasant as it had been. Commander Anderson brought a satchel with him of disturbing information that he handed to Commander Ivan for him to go over with his comrades who had lost some of their loved ones.

Commander Ivan, being the leader he was, decided it was best if he should wait until the right opportune time should come about, when the hard work of transferring the much needed supplies between the two crafts had been completed before he would break any of the sad news to his weary crew.

It would be hard enough work transferring the bulky cargo from the shuttle to the space station while everyone pitched in to help in a happy way, never mind a somber unsettled one. As the work in transferring the many supplies became more difficult, the two crews embraced one another with kind words instead of angered ones during the trying times in the laborious task of opening cargo bay doors.

It was dangerous hard work transferring the many huge crates filled with supplies using the boom attached to the shuttles inner bay cargo wall. Commander Ivan did not need or want anyone of his crew going zany before or during the hard demanding chore of this mission was over. Before Commander Ivan broke the sad disturbing news to his fellow crewmembers, the sad news Commander Anderson had brought with him for several of the crewmembers; Major Bill stepped forward to tell his sad tragic story of his own personal close family' fatalities.

Everyone hearing Bill had lost his whole family, his wife, his daughter, and his little son in the big bang, everyone swarmed around him with their closest of condolences for such an enormous loss. It was a good thing that he was strong, or Major Bill would have lost it all over again from the pain of the love shared for him.

Commander Anderson strived to use Bill's personal sad news story as a cleansing tool for the minds of the crew who had lost loved ones before having Commander Ivan break the sad grieving news about some of the close family members of his fellow cosmonauts' families. Major Bill volunteered to pave the way for the display of sad news relayed to the several crewmembers of the space mission felled by their own very tragic news of loss. He knew the real pain of it all and was willing to step forward to help try and ease the sudden shocking news that wouldn't be welcomed very well by any of them onboard the space station at that time.

The news handed over to him from Commander Ivan was worse than had been expected when Major Bill stepped forward and addressed the Soviet crew. The two German astronauts had not lost a one of their family members, as had a few of the Russian cosmonauts onboard which had lost mothers, brothers, sisters, fathers, wives, and children.

Whole families in Russia had been wiped completely out with their own weaponries big bang of massive neutron bomb destruction in the regions of their many homes below. It was a horror story being told to them by a total alienated individual whom they thought once was a friend, but now had other thoughts about him after he finished telling everyone what had happened back on Earth to so many of their families and friends.

Having been marooned in outer space for little under two and some just over two long years for most crewmembers, left a few of them in total denial of what could have had taken place back on Earth to anyone.

It all seemed like a horrid dream to most as not having any radio communication with Earth for so long, and not able to communicate verbally with anyone outside the confines from within the space laboratory itself.

The shocking news took its mental toll on a handful of the crewmembers, and they seemed worse than shell shocked with the news. Those few unfortunate ones were told that they had lost so many close relatives rejected the information immediately as inaccurate information, and suffered instant mental depression as other lost souls fell into limpness floating weeping. One after another they all rose from their limpness to firm footedness as they formed their own self-imposed opinions knowing damn well right the Americans were at an all-out war with their country because of the disaster which took place down there. All this talk about their loved ones' deaths and friends dying was nonsense, nothing but a bunch of hog wash. It was all

American propaganda being told to them by the angered enemy, or at least that was what a couple Soviets were convinced it was in their very own lonely depressed states of mind. They would not accept that any of their immediate family members had perished in the big blast because it happened all around the globe and not over Russia. They would not accept it for they had lost no one, and everyone was still healthy and well back home on Earth. Their leaders would not have been that foolish, and their homeland was well. "You people are the devils from the earth, come to destroy us, and should die!"

The emotions of the few now wobbly trying to stand firmly crying cosmonauts frightened everyone around them. Both commanders tried calming them down and asking their fellow comrades in helping to hold them down for tranquillizers for their own safety. The scene was not a pretty one, and Ann watched as close friends she once had over the past year, turned enemy toward her.

The few devastated cosmonauts were now screaming repulsive dirty accusations toward those who had just risked their lives to come and help rescue some of them and bring them food, oxygen, and other essentials to survive with. The United States, the stressed cosmonauts figured quickly chatting, were trying to weaken any relationship they had with their country, and were now trying to foil the precious mission they were sent to do aboard the space laboratory.

"Why in the hell did you have to come back here?" One screamed, shaking her fist at them! "Why in the hell didn't you just stay the hell away, damn it, and let us all die in peace." She slipped into limpness again, passing out cold from the shocking news of her whole family swallowed up by this neutron invasion that included her mother, father, husband, and her two little sons. She just wanted to die right then and there and could not believe all these bullshit lies could have possibly have happened to her family as if it had not happened to Bill's.

The crew did not want to hear any more about tragedy that had taken place back on the earth! Several crewmembers carried the few sedated cosmonauts away to their sleeping quarters, as Commander Ivan had guards placed with them for when they awoke from their sedatives.

Ivan was sure that one if not more of the crew would try something desperate to end their mentally mind-suffering lives all together, and not want to return home to Earth to face the demon of death by their lonesome.

Commander Ivan had seen and heard quite enough, and was truly convinced that the grieving few crewmembers should be part of the select few that should be picked to be transported back to Earth aboard the Twitchel for everyone's safety, including their own. He would not allow any of them to stay onboard his craft to endanger any of the remaining crewmembers' lives inside the laboratory.

He knew he could not afford to have any life threatening crewmembers still onboard his vessel that might prove dangerous to anyone, or the well-being or reliability of the space station's structures' worthiness. Ivan was quite betwixt and between on what to do next with the emotional ones except to send them all back home to Earth. Back on Earth, their stressed out comrades could be tended to properly and comforted by professional disaster councilors schooled in their profession. It would be best if they returned than left up here by themselves alone in outer space to dwell over and over in their wondering minds about their miserable grief and possibly interfere with the safety of all personnel left behind aboard the failing laboratory.

The unloading the Twitchel's cargo bay completed in less than four long hard-working days. It took another three days to safely repair and prepare the Twitchel for her return trip back home to Earth. The spare jaytoe bottles that they needed to be removed from her two outer sides and the securing of holes created there needed filling in with heat-resistant silicon and tiles for reentry. The securing levers and cables used to get the Twitchel safely into outer space had to be carefully removed, and the holes left in her sides had to be filled in with heat resistant material and dried with electrically operated solar powered warming guns to dry the epoxy applied to her outer skin. As work on retrofitting the Twitchel was underway, the two commanders were busy at work trying to figure out who were best to send back to Earth besides the four cosmonauts who had really taken the sad news of their lost loved ones so harsh.

Commander Ivan went over his list of cosmonauts with his first mate to determine who was fit and not so mentally fit to send along with the others. One by one, they eliminated the strongest link in strong-minded ones over weak-minded comrades. They dwindled the cosmonauts down to the weakest link of the best last candidates, and came up with a list of two rather weak constitutionally-minded cosmonauts who would join the two Germans and six other lucky or not so lucky cosmonauts on their last return trip back home to Earth with the daring crew from the Twitchel. The remaining forty-two members of the laboratory would have to wait another long year more or less until another rescue mission might possibly be attempted.

The Soviet space module would have to stay attached to the space station until then, for safety reasons, in case a message needed to be delivered to Earth earlier for help in case a disaster should occur onboard the space laboratory, and they needed to take action for their own safety. Without radio contact with Earth, the space station module would be their only way of communication back with Earth if it was to become necessary.

Commander Anderson had already set into motion another rescue mission that would bring back to the space laboratory three already built soviet made space modules to help in the rescue of another eighteen cosmonauts, six onboard each, and another eight onboard the shuttle. Twenty-six possibly more should the shuttle be outfitted properly to accommodate the remaining crew aboard the space laboratory at that time. If not, then there would be sixteen left in outer space to be rescued at a much later time in the future, hopefully the last and final rescue attempt of the lost mission in space.

Commander Nelson Anderson, reassured Commander Ivan that he would do everything possible in his military powers to return for them, kept secure in the back of his mind. He was now under extreme pressure to arrange for this particular mission this time. His superiors were not for risking the lives of an American shuttle crew to save a crew of their rivals who had caused this worldly disaster and dilemma to have happen in the first place.

The only single reason they went along with it was for the two remaining Germans still trapped onboard the space station who wouldn't survive up there because none of them cared whether the others made it back safe or not.

The goodbyes and farewells would not be as emotional this time as they were the last. There would be a definite feeling that everything would be all right this time for the remaining crew of the laboratory. The odds of them surviving in outer space for another year were in all their favors now, or were they?

CHAPTER FIFTY

The Departure

When the Twitchel parted company from the space station's docking portal, the radios between the space station and the Twitchel were in perfect working order.

In the unloading of the cargo from the Twitchel cargo bay to the space laboratories storage area, the space-walk workers noticed the aft antenna on the tail section of the Twitchel's rear section had been broken. Lieutenant Steven performed an unsecured space walk without a tethered line attached to either him or the vehicles, using the newly designed jet backpack designed for such repairs in installing the newly repaired antenna link. The antenna somehow broke off during the grounds crew standing the Twitchel upright in the launching pad assembly hanger without notice by any of the grounds crew performing their tasks. If someone from the ground crew had noticed the small antenna was broken, a new one would have been easily installed prior to liftoff.

The two commanders selected eight Russian cosmonauts to return back to earth with the Twitchel crew with the exception for the two Germans. The ones chosen did not seem to be at ease with themselves never mind any of the Twitchel's crew who had risked their lives trying to fly up through the deadly neutron mass into out space to try and save them from a life of doom and gloom.

Timing for the speedy reentry of the Twitchel back through the ionosphere down into the atmosphere was quickly passing by. The Twitchel's crew was in their last critical stages of positioning their craft for the proper reentry angle and decent. The youngest of the weary Soviet cosmonaut onboard the spacecraft who had lost his entire family to the big bang by his fearless leaders, mentally lost it. He suddenly cracked under depressing pressure very quietly after belting himself into his secured seat onboard the Twitchel. He just sat there dead silent in his seat for the next few hours gazing out into outer space in his own little world with glossy eyes, staring at the back of his American enemy's helmet, thinking about all that which he had lost back home on Earth. He hurriedly removed his fastened downed seat belted body harness from its latches, and quickly threw himself forward and onto this enemy in front of him and began attacking the back of the head of the person.

He didn't know who or why he was attacking this person, but all he knew was he had to attack this enemy of his that had killed all of his relatives and friends back home before this person, this American enemy, could kill him and his fellow cosmonauts onboard with them. He didn't know it or understand it at the time, but he was attacking the back of Captain Ann Mitchell's helmet. She at the time was in the process of positioning the Twitchel for their final reentry course down into the atmosphere. She was busy with the flight computer and controls, trying to navigate the spacecraft safely home. Everyone looked the same to Scavonivich. All the American enemies had their bright white shiny helmets on with the enemy logo of the United States flag and a NASA emblem printed on them. All he knew for sure or felt in his very confused mind now was whoever this person was, this was the enemy whom he had to attack to save his life. It did not matter who it may have been, for this enemy was busy pushing these deadly computer buttons, and was turning and adjusting the speed dials of death on the control panel board positioned in front of them. This particular person in front of him was the person trying to execute him and every one of his fellow comrades that were with him onboard this death ship heading back toward the earth, so the enemy might destroy them all when they landed.

He hit Ann with such force in the back of the head it knocked her out cold instantly. She was in her last final stages of calculating and setting the proper reentry procedures into the computers mainframe, trying very hard to position the Twitchel safely down into its final pitch and descent back into the earth's atmosphere softly in its proper angle of descent. She had been knocked out just prior to hitting the reenter button on the onboard computers mainframe keyboard, never to accomplish her final reentry course settings on the computer, and lay slumped over motionless in her control seat. Another Russian cosmonaut quickly uncoupled his seat's harness, and arose to the occasion to try to restrain his fellow comrade, but he was too late in doing so. His comrade had already done the damage, and the Twitchel continued down in the original slow descending orbit not responding to the silence of the program ready to go into its control memory, but lay ready at Ann's fingertips to finish the job.

Commander Nelson heard a muffled unintelligible sound in his headphone earpiece as he tried to talk to Ann. With no immediate response from Ann, he turned his head toward her to make eye contact and for her acknowledgement of their supposedly new course bearings. All he saw was a chaotic situation going on behind him between two of the Russian guests they had brought along with them onboard.

Suddenly, Lieutenant Steven, David, and Chester were climbing all over the two Russian cosmonaut guests punching and pushing at one another all at the same time. He could not imagine what was taking place behind him or what could have triggered such a ruckus. Everyone was getting into the fight in the cockpit except for Major Bill and Ann. She knew nothing about the fight because she was the one knocked out cold at the time, unconscious at her controls.

After securing the madcap cosmonaut who had lost control of his mind and sanity, they placed him back into his seat with restraints. They all returned to their positions at their controls, as Ann finally came back to consciousness. She could not imagine what had just happened to her or why she had passed out as she didn't feel sick, but knew she had a terrific headache. Then Commander Nelson briefed Ann in about what had just transpired and happened to her. Ann went

immediately back to work, trying to reconfigure their next possible attempt at a safe reentry attempt for the day, but it was too late to try another attempt. Darkness was setting in, and without the light of day, they would all perish.

According to her new calculations of re-entry time that she performed on the computer, they would have to wait another several hours until the next morning for their new attempt at reentry, if the weather around the cape permitted them to do so. They had lost their present window of opportunity for reentry for the present time. With no one below knowing the exact time of their reentry when they were planning to return to Earth, the runway would be indistinguishable to identify at sunset or during the dusk hours of daylight without the well-lit runway markers to assist them in their landing.

None of the previous shuttle flights had ever attempted this task before even with runway lights. The chances of landing on an unlit runway at dusk was risky if not deadly because of the sun's reflections off the ocean's waters around Cape Canaveral, especially in the evening hours when everything becomes distorted without computer control of the craft during landing.

During the disturbance, they drifted dangerously close to the most outer inner limits of the earth's most outer atmosphere that could pull them in towards the earth, which would result in their eminent doom if it was to happen. They would probably make the reentry back into the atmosphere safely, but without a safe place to land. Without a runway to land on, it would more than likely cost them their lives. They could be lucky and last in a safe orbit in this position until the next morning, when and if there would be a window of opportunity for reentry should the window reopen for them again. Ann sat at her workstation with a throbbing headache wondering if the chance she took in trying to save her fellow astronauts had been worth volunteering for a chance in ending her own life.

If that lunatic cosmonaut had not flipped his damn lid, they could have all been safely down and on the runway by now, but instead she was now looking at a window in her life that might prematurely close for her and for her to become a loss to her family.

Commander Nelson broke her train of thought, and brought her back to reality. "Captain Morris, how much propellant do we have remaining onboard in the main thruster booster tanks?"

"They are about one-quarter full, sir!" "How much propellant do we need Captain Mitchell for a safe reentry attempt to place this bird safely down into the earth's atmosphere?"

Ann looked at the fuel chart in front of her to make absolutely certain the quantity of fuel they would need for reentry. She knew in her own mind from the many long hours of training she had gone through, but wanted to double check her own thinking. We need at least one-eighth of a tank of propellant, Commander. With less than that, we could very possibly undershoot our reentry course and falter in our only attempt for a good landing. It would be very dangerous to attempt it with less than that amount, sir."

"Major! Prepare to revise the Twitchel's attitude in preparation for increased altitude. Captain Mitchell on the three-count captain, a ten minute blast firing the main rockets".

"Yes, sir, Commander. **One, two, three**, contact." Major Morris turned the dials on the computer in front of his station manually, altering the attitude of the Twitchel. The Twitchel pointed itself back into an outer space attitude away from the deadly gravitational pull of the earth's atmosphere. The ship increased its speed and safely pulled up and away from its low orbit.

Ten minutes into the burn, they were cruising at a much faster and higher safe altitude out of the danger zone from possibly being pulled back toward the earth unexpectedly during the next several hours.

"Captain Morris! What is the quantity status of our propellant now, Captain?"

"Just barely over an eighth of propellant in each tank, sir." All we can do now is just sit back and wait for our next window of opportunity to open up for us tomorrow, if it will," said Commander Anderson.

When they were safe in their new orbit, Commander Anderson made radio contact with the International Space Station. He informed the space station of the situation of what had just evolved onboard the Twitchel with Scavonivich, and was wondering what to expect to happen next. They were now forced to wait for the next window of opportunity to open up which might allow another attempt at trying the following day.

"Space station, this is Commander Anderson of the U.S. Twitchel shuttle calling. Is Commander Ivan Khrushchev available to talk or take a message, please?"

"One moment, please, Commander Anderson, while I send for Commander Ivan, sir." "Commander Anderson, what can I do for you, Nelson?" As you can see, Ivan, we have not reentered the earth's atmosphere as of yet, and cannot try again until a new window opens up for us tomorrow, if one opens up for us at all.

One of your friendly comrades, Makita Scavonivich tried to get us all killed a little while ago, Ivan. He thought my crew of the Twitchel was bringing him and your fellow comrades back to the earth for their immediate execution. He knocked out our navigations officer, Captain Ann Mitchell. He knocked her out cold just prior to when she was about to start our decent down through the outer atmosphere. It was a good thing, if you can call it that. It was a good thing that he knocked her out when he did. If he had gone and done it half way through her final settings of reentry and having the wrong data applied for our reentry maneuvers, it could have killed all of us. He wants to come back to the space station to be with the rest of you, but we are too far away and very low on rocket propellant, Ivan. His request for returning to the space station is impossible or I would bring him back there immediately for you to handle. He has almost convinced a couple of your other fellow comrades that what he is saying is accurate and true. I wish you to talk to your fellow crewmembers with us please Commander, and assure them otherwise, for the best of everyone's safety aboard the Twitchel, please Ivan."

"Nelson, please put your communications on intra-capsule conference channel please, Commander"

"The conference switch is on already, Commander."

"Comrades, this is your commander, Commander Ivan speaking. You will, and I repeat you will all, including you Makita, pay strict attention to your friends the Americans. They are your friends! I repeat! They are our friends. They have come to help every one of us and if any of you interfere with them again, you will all face a Russian court-marshal immediately. That is an order! Do you understand?"

They had all understood Ivan's orders except for Makita Scavonivich. He still felt he was going to be being executed the first thing when they all returned to Earth right along with all his fellow comrades the minute the Twitchel set down on American soil. No one was going to convince him otherwise, including his own soviet Commander, Commander Ivan Khrushchev.

The next several hours waiting for their window to open were very long weary hours for the crew of the Twitchel along with the several guests of Soviets they had onboard. Makita would not shut up. He continually, hour after hour, talked all night long about every one of his comrades killed by the Americans when and if they ever got back to Earth. He rambled on wildly, hardly taking a breath giving everyone onboard a massive headache.

The dark of night seemed to last a life time over Cape Canaveral as the shuttle passed overhead several times during the night waiting for the light of day to come to the area. California looked like a good place to land, but nothing had landed there since the big disaster took place, and several broken up aircraft were still scattered everywhere about that might pose a problem for the shuttle if they were to attempt an emergency landing there.

The weather for the day was cloud covered, covering the cape in dense fog it looked from so high above it, so Commander Nelson gave the word that the Twitchel and its crew would wait another day until the light of day again, and try a landing on the cape then.

If Florida was still socked in on the second day, they would try landing in California or on the Salt Flats near Salt Lake City, Utah. They would land where they could land safely. They were running out of options, and had to land soon to survive themselves for they had no supplies onboard to sustain themselves any longer in orbit. When they had pulled away from the space station, they took almost no extra food or water with them to survive on for longer than a short reentry course that should have only taken them about three hours to accomplish. Commander Anderson wanted to leave behind as much food, water, and supplies as was possible for the remaining crewmembers of the space station. However, just in case of an extra go around in orbit, they took an extra half ration in food for each, to be split up between them all, and a smidgen extra drinking water.

Just by chance had they have to wait out one or two extra passes before reentry, but it surely was not enough extra food or drink for two or three whole days it seemed it could take to make this a safe and final reentry landing.

The little fiasco that took place between Makita and Captain Mitchell had caused just that situation of drastic despair to occur. The window had been clear just prior to the sudden occurrence as Ann was preparing the course and getting the Twitchel ready by typing in the new coordinates into the onboard computer to guide them safely back to Earth, when Makita clobbered her from behind knocking her out. Now the window for the day had closed, and their situation was becoming ever the more critical with every passing moment they had to spend in space.

Ann suddenly experienced dreadful doubts that began floating wildly in her mind about making this bad choice of trying to help her fellow astronauts. She wondered again had she made a wise choice in her decision back home at the farm or had it been a choice of sympathy and apathy that had made up her mind over her friends for her own safety first.

Was this whole thing really worth risking her life for someone else's life? What would she have done if someone or anybody were drowning in a pond or body of water in front of her? Would she have jumped in to save them if she were trained to or would she just throw them a life preserver line, and let them fend for themselves hoping the best for them?

During the long hours of darkness over the cape, Ann had no choice in the matter but to sit at her controls and think over the many difficult and varying situations in lives affected both above and below that were taking place. What would or could she do to help the numerous different victims out of their changeable circumstances if they were in as difficult a situation as her friends were in space?

Night aboard the Twitchel was not quiet enough for anyone to sleep there. The night turned out to be a very long, loud very monotonously dragged out night listening to Scavonivich yelling and scream out over and over again. He constantly babbled on and on about how he and his fellow Soviet crewmember counterparts aboard the Twitchel were all going to be murdered, executed by the no-good Americans they were with when they all finally got back to earth. None onboard the Twitchel could sleep a wink with him carrying on so. Even if one wanted to, they could not. By morning, his once very loud wildly strong voice became a low very weak gravely toned down whispered drone sounding and annoying melancholy chorus in repeated words about execution and murder. His voice had become so hoarse, everyone aboard was hoping and wishing he would soon develop a severe case of laryngitis from it all, but they were not that lucky, and he did not.

He relentlessly fought all nightlong with the several restraints applied him without physically tiring, and then had to be once again restrained even more this time than before for his own good, and the safety and welfare of all. By the next morning he was calling his entire fellow comrades criminal spies of the no good Americans as well. When they all got back to Earth and he was lucky enough to escape the clutches of the American pigs to make it all the way back to the Soviet Kremlin, they would all be prosecuted as smutty little no good American pig spies of their enemies.

Early morning over Cape Canaveral brought with it clouded news everyone had suspected it might bring, for Cape Kennedy looked overcast still. It was still early enough in the early part of the day to make a couple more passes above the intended landing site before the window of the day was to close for them.

If the weather did not break over the cape, they would have no other choice but to land the Twitchel on one of the other designated landing areas in California or on the massive Salt Lake Flats stretched out in Utah. They were quickly running out of time for choices, and it was getting critical in their attempt to return to Earth.

The deep annoying scratchy voice of Scavonivich continually bitching, swearing, and carrying on about death repeatedly was thoroughly starting to get the best of everyone's nerves, all being confined there with him forcing everyone to ponder, wondering what was going to happen next, for what he had caused earlier. Ann had had just about enough of this screeching no-good-sun-of-a-bitching-maniac. With her head throbbing all night long from the concussion she received from the dip-shit he had given to her. The hard blow to the back her head and neck, making her feel incredibly sick to her empty stomach, possibly from not eating a healthy meal in over thirty six long consecutive hours, she had had it with him!

Ann decided it was time. She got up off her lazy ass, she thought, seeing no one else in the damn cockpit would, and shut this babbling bastard up. She had had it with him and would deal with him herself. She unfastened her body harness from her flight station, and commenced to get up from her position to quiet him down herself. When standing and turning to accomplish the eager task she had in mind for him, she was too late. When she turned to quiet him down by her own means, one of his very own crewmates struck him a quieting hard blow upside his helmeted head with forceful meaning in it. The sharp blow to his head put his lights out for a while as Scavonivich's eyes rolled up into the back of his head as he had done to her.

"Good enough for the sun-of-a-bitch", Ann thought to herself quietly. The Russian cosmonaut who had slammed Scavonivich smiled at her with satisfaction written all over his face, as she nodded her head saying "thank you." He returned the same "you're welcome" to her as he sat back down in his seat and buckled up with a happy smile still on his face, as he nodded his head up and down in accomplishment to his fellow comrades, taking pleasure in his well-orchestrated feat.

No one onboard cared if Makita was sitting there knocked out cold or sitting there dead in his seat. He had been the cause of their being stuck in outer space orbiting the earth, and it would be a miracle now if they were all to make it back home to Earth alive.

Ann twisted back around from a half-standing position and eased herself back down into her station at her controls. She began feeling a mere more at ease with the quietness that followed with his mouth silenced for a breather, if not for ever. The golden solitude of silence that followed the incident refreshed everyone in the cabin of the Twitchel, for what was to come next.

"Captain Mitchell! Prepare the Twitchel for reentry!"

"Yes Sir, Commander." The time had come to put their protective helmets back on again, and attempt another reentry try back down into the Earth's atmosphere, if a window of opportunity below became available. The cosmonaut who had clobbered Scavonivich, secured Makita's helmet back to his flight suit for him, then put his own on as everyone else in the cabin put on theirs.

The clouds over the Florida peninsular proved to be a threat to them as they passed over once again the state of Florida. It looked like they were going to have to land in California, taking their chances there on the cluttered runway.

Commander Anderson gave the order to abort the reentry try, sit back, relax, and wait for the next time around in orbit to try again. Removing their helmets, they seriously discussed what their alternatives were going to be. They could try California, but the runway was short, and looked cluttered from where they were. If they tried to land there, they could not afford the least bit of error in making their approach to the runway for there was nowhere else around to land their craft safely down without crashing.

Commander Anderson had never landed there and had only landed a shuttle at the Utah Salt Lake City salt flats, and in Florida. The course they were orbiting now flew them directly over California and Florida. If they wanted to land at the Salt Lake City Salt Flats, they would have to alter their course of orbit. It would require using up a good amount of precious rocket fuel, of which they had none to spare to enable them to alter course and land their bird safely back to Earth on the Salt Flats.

The decision became unanimous among them except for Makita, of course. They would attempt one last reentry try over the cape of Florida, and if they had to abort this time, they would make one last orbit back around to the California landing field and put the Twitchel down there if necessary.

Just their luck the clouds were now rolling in thick as mud from the Pacific Ocean into California's Los Angeles area as they made their way overhead, now heading for their final destination of Florida they hoped.

"Damn it, Damn it. DAMN IT. We should have put this bird down now and not have waited for another damn turn around. How much usable oxygen do we have left in the air tanks Captain Morris?" "Ten hours maximum, sir, give or take a little time if we use it sparingly."

"Where else Captain? Where the hell else can we put this damn bird down now?" "Australia maybe, sir, but remember the situation there commander or Hawaii. If it stays light enough, which it should without any overcasts over the islands to see the runways at the airport, it could be a safe spot there if there is no debris littering them. The runway on the main island of Hawaii should be long enough for us to land safely on it, sir." "Prepare for reentry crew. We are going home one way or another, and I hope it isn't the other."

On with their protective helmets the crew once again preformed in haste. "Look for a clear landing zone, Captain. Don't let us overshoot another window if there is one, Ann?"

"Not if I can help it, sir." Florida looked mostly overcast with clouds they guessed at approximately ten thousand feet or maybe even more.

"What do you think, men? Can we chance it, or do another go around to Australia or Hawaii? What do you guys think, Captain?"

"If the computer would not lose power when we first reentered the damn atmosphere, I would say go for it here, Commander! Once the computer is gone, it is all in your hands, sir. Whatever you say, Commander, I am with you on this one, sir."

The cloud cover over Florida looked more like a huge circus tent's canvas canopy hovering over the state like a mushroom. One side of the cloud cover looked open for people to enter into or exit it. "How long till zero count-down, Captain Mitchell?"

"Zero count-down in three minutes thirty five seconds and still counting, sir."

"Stand by." Commander Nelson looked toward Major Bill. "What do you think, Bill?"

"I don't really know, sir. The cloud cover could be one hell of a lot closer to the ground on the eastern coast than it looks to be on the west coast, Commander. The cloud cover could be at zero-feet ceiling there. Then what in the hell would we do, sir, put her down in the everglades? Without instruments to tell us what to do next in this situation, it could turn out to be a disastrous move for us, sir."

"What the hell are we going to do then guys? Die up here or try something very soon? We have about two minutes left prior to the window closing in on us again gents. Let us make a decision now or later when it is too damn late! Do we or do we not try it, men? I am not going to make this damn decision all by my lonesome up here guys. Who the hell else wants to try this damn window now, other than myself? I think we can make it, but it's up to you guys, too."

Commander Anderson was worried about Australia and Hawaii for the runways there looked to be excessively small and cluttered for them to make a safe landing on them. The tarmac there looked littered with stalled out or smashed up aircraft on it, and the weather there could be as cloudy and socked in as it is over Florida, then what. He did not really want Florida either, but time was running out on the window of opportunity soon as was their precious oxygen.

Scavonivich had been sitting quiet in his seat for quite some time now, and started his silly melancholy yelling and chanting all over again. "He is going to kill us all. He is a mad man. Can you all not see it in him he is the lunatic here? He is a suicidal commander wanting to take us all out with himself. You have to stop him; you have to stop him, for he is the crazy one. Can any you fools see that?"

Three, Two, One, Zero of the window was closing in on them fast. Ann hit the retrorocket booster pa

"Sorry, sir. It is too damn late to stop them now, sir. The computers are set, and we are going in one way or another."

Commander Anderson switched from questioning Ann and turned his full attention to commanding the Twitchel's reentry course.

"Major! Switch the computer to auto pilot scan.

"Captain, full shields up, Captain!"

The only visibility they had quickly disappeared behind the heat shields as they rose up over the canopy of the windshield. The final plotted course of their ship was in the control of the onboard computer now. Captain Morris and Captain Ann synchronized their bearings, speed, and pitch of the Twitchel for a nice smooth reentry bearing back down into the earth's atmosphere.

"Heat is beginning to climb rapidly, sir, 1500 Degrees, 1600 degrees, 1700 degrees, 1800 degrees, 1900 degrees, now 2000 degrees, sir! Commander Anderson punched in an angle of decent pitch change into the computer while trying to communicate with Captain Mitchell and Major Bill to talk them through what he was doing to their programmed reentry settings.

Scavonivich in the background was screaming and hollering at the top of his lungs again so damn loud it became almost impossible for anyone to communicate properly with one another inside the capsule. The crewmembers aboard the Twitchel were having an extreme hard time hearing the readings given out by the different crewmembers as they were going into their last descent into their reentry.

No one knew how long the power to the computers would last this time. Not able to remember when the monster controlling the earth's power fields would suck the life out of their craft as it had the last time. They only hoped like the last time in their reentry, it would not suck any of the life out of anyone onboard the Twitchel when it hit.

Commander Anderson called out for the outside heat shield temperature readings to be read to him again. "Coming down good, sir."

"Major Bill! Lower the outside heat shields when the outside temperature falls to a safe 600 degrees, Bill."

"Yes, sir, Commander."

From then on, Commander Anderson and Major Bill had their hands glued tight to the controls of the Twitchel flight controls like welds applied to a steel beam in a skyscraper. They had decided beforehand they were not going to shut the power off to the main computers controls at all as they had decided they were going to let it happen naturally, whatever naturally meant?

They were going to let the free-floating beast in the atmosphere from the neutrons fusion explosion do whatever it had to do, and they were going to be as ready as they could possibly be whenever it took their precious power from their craft.

Their flight computer onboard would be the last thing they wanted, and hoped the transfer of power was quick as death to happen and not alter the course of their craft by too much in their final approach back to Earth. As the heat shields began retracting away, a reddish green and orange sheen started engulfing the front nose of the Twitchel. This time it was not the normal heat generated by their rapid descent back into the earth's atmosphere either. It was the millions if not billions and trillions of little tiny wild neutrons free floating in the atmosphere surrounding the earth attacking the positively charged spacecraft. Everyone knew what it was. Their trembling voices hollering out instrumental readings to each other waited for the inevitable to happen to their craft and the power systems to instantly fail.

Suddenly, the Twitchel began shimmering and shaking from the external forces exerted upon its fuselage. Many of these wild neutrons instantly attacked the outer shell of the craft like ice buildup on wings of an airplane as it began its tactics of draining any electrical power it could from the vessel and any other form it could possibly drain seeking out all sources of power from within.

Co-pilot, Major Bill's hands, along with Commander Anderson's hands were both glued ridged in place as the color of their skin turned an unseen cold frosty white from their holding onto the flight controls so hard with gloved hands that hurt. They knew the craft was wicked easy to fly with the help of all the electrically operated instruments onboard. Along with the electronically controlled glide flaps and hydraulic landing gears, but the instruments on the instrument panel were soon to become an element of the past and it would be man against this huge weighty beast made from steel flying machine.

They were both going to have to use pure man super strength to fly the Twitchel again as they had before when they first encountered their craft without power. It would be difficult to control the manmade machine that was supposed to be all automatically controlled for them. They had been extremely lucky to do it safely the last time they landed this bird, and were now even more ready for the arduous task that lay ahead of them for landing the Twitchel down one more time safely.

Comparable to a bolt of intense lightning departing the earth's surface during a warm summer's day thunder storm, the orange, green, yellowy patina of fluorescent light shot off the skin of the Twitchel it had immediately encompassed like an outer membrane in a flash, as it faded into the unknown depths of the earth's huge atmosphere, and then dissipated into nothingness into the clear blue of sky.

Forthwith at that specific time, the electric power of the Twitchel went from an instrument panel of vibrant colorful display lights to the dark of silent blackness. Not the simplest of rays of a tiny spark or current of electricity could be seen in any of the dials on any panel in the spacecraft. The only rays of light now were the ones generating down from the sun shining through the canopy of scattered clouds and through the main windshield.

The only workable flight instruments onboard for a safe flight down to earth were the mechanical flight instruments. A weight tube altimeter for the height they were flying at. The mechanical airspeed instrument, which had an outer capillary tube attached to catch the swift volume of air moving past it outside activating a sensitive spring airspeed needle inside the gage along with a mechanical bubble floating horizon indicator.

The horizon indicator would help them keep their craft in a true and level flight path. This instrument would prevent any vertigo to happen as long as they believe their flight instrument readings. The magnetic readings for accurate guidance of the compasses on board were not quite as accurate as they had once been before the neutron blast, for now the polar caps of the earth's magnetic fields had been weekend immensely.

The compasses would work for them most of the time, then on some occasions they would fail giving Commander Anderson a very sick funny feeling of mistrust when their very critical direction of approach to their very valued landing area was miss read. The air speed and pitch applied the Twitchel was their most cared about critical condition in their rapid descent back down through the thick cloud covered overcast as mounting tension engulfed everyone inside the Twitchel not being able to see anything outside their craft but clouds.

Everyone in the cockpit of the Twitchel was feeling the emotional static of deep concern with her crew and the several nervous passengers she was carrying to the point of emotional explosion. Everyone soon hoped Scavonivich would die from talk exhaustion but he continued to live and babble on and on ever the more stringently about death by execution. He was not the main reason of tension between everyone now, but the next in line too it all. Even Commander Anderson was at the point of a nervous mental meltdown because of Scavonivich and his foul flowing mouth of ill repute about everyone breathing their last breaths!

Ann sat at her station silently praying. She now wished she had told Commander Anderson no when he had first approached her to help him in this risky mission, and why in the hell had she gone and fired those damn retro rockets in the first place to reenter them back into the outer atmosphere? Was it in spite of Scavonivich and his misgivings about the commander? Yes it was. No one should have to take that sort of bad mouthing Scavonivich continually directed toward the commander. Commander Nelson Anderson was one of the most gentle men alive she had ever met other than her own husband. Ben would not hurt a lousy damn common housefly or any other stupid little bug for that matter. He would help the most stupid of damn creature out of doors of the house and let them go first, even shooing away a damn mosquito so he would not have to kill it. He would rather have it bite him and suck his blood than kill the darn stupid thing. "Why then why? Why did I hit that damn rocket switch? It was not fair of me to take that decision away from everyone else onboard. I took away everyone's vote whether they all wanted to land elsewhere or not, even the commander's choice. It was a very selfish act for me to have hastily done!"

"What is our air speed, Captain?

"Slowing to a mere 400 air miles an hour, sir!"

"Damn it Bill! We should be breaking though this dense cloudy overcast any minute now. The cloud cover can't be this damn low can it?" "If the ceiling is zero, Nelson, we will never know what hit us anyway!"

Scavonivich screamed out in his own total mental fear for he was still convinced the Americans were out to get him and his fellow Soviets. "He is a mad man! I am telling you all he is mad. He is going to kill us all, going to kill us all!" Commander Anderson wished he had not said what he was thinking, aloud, verbally expressing the situation they were in to Bill.

"Breaking 9000 feet now Commander! Breaking 8000 feet now, sir!" Closing in on 7000 feet rapidly, Commander. They finally broke out through the dense cloud cover over the landing zone with limited visibility.

They could see they were approximately a ¼ mile off course visually looking at the runway off to their far right side swiftly passing by the runway on a serious course that was leading them out towards the sea and out over the Atlantic Ocean.

"Easy hard rudder to the right, Bill, follow through with me now." Steven spoke up.

"How about putting down the landing gear, Commander?"

"I don't think so right now lieutenant. I think we need a prayer right now, if we are going to make it to the runway.

"Do we have a prayer, Lieutenant?" If we lower the landing gear right now, it might slow us to a critical stalling air speed in our attempt to return to the runway and possibly never make it that distance. I really don't think we need them yet." The heavy mist on the cockpit windshield did not help matters either. Everything bellow them looked all out of sorts and array to them as they descended down further and further down out of the heavens through the moist mist and wet cloud cover putting extra drag on the shuttles wings and fuselage.

"What is our air speed, Captain?"

"Airspeed 375 miles an hour now, with speed dropping rapidly, sir. "Ease her down, Bill, with our turn, not too fast.

The shuttle slowly turned and dipped downward from their every command as it shook like a dog trying to shake off a big biting tick from its back in its decent.

"If we lose any more airspeed commander at this height, the Twitchel will fall out of the sky like a huge ball of steel, and crumple up on impact.

"What is our altitude now, Bill?"

"6500 feet and falling rapidly, sir, along with our air speed!" "Captain, stand by the landing gear controls."

Steven and Charles both slid down into the bottom part of the fuselage of the Twitchel getting ready in their position to lower the landing gears with the hand cranks when told to do so.

"Captain Mitchell, stand by for my command!

If I holler abort, get the two of them the hell out of there immediately! They wouldn't stand a snowball's chance in hell down there if we have to put this bird down on her belly." "It's going to be real close Major, real close indeed."

"Her airspeed is dropping rapidly, sir, too rapidly."

"Nose her in just a little bit more, Bill. If we make that runway, it is going to be a freaking miracle.

I wish we had the wipers right now.

I cannot see a thing out there with all that useless mist and light rain we are having right now." "How are we doing, Major"?

"I don't really know, sir. I do think we should chance those landing gears down, sir.

"Right now, Major, or in a little bit, Bill?" The colonel's voice was becoming sterner with serious concern with every word he spoke or yelled out at them! "Right now, sir, let's not wait another second, Commander, or it might be too damn late no matter where we have to put this bird down. Some wheels are better than no wheels at all in most cases, sir. Even if we are a little shy of the runway, Nelson."

"Crank the landing gears down now Captain! Get those damned wheels down now and ready to bring us home."

Ann yelled out to Steven, and Charles. "Crank them down, NOW!"

Charles and Steven began cranking on the jack-screwed mechanisms of the rear landing gears with all of their strength and speed they could muster up. The belly below the Twitchel began slowly opening up, as the rear landing gears began to slowly inch their way out slowly from her belly and into the mist and rain of the damp day.

Captain Morris quickly slid down into the forward compartment of the Twitchel's fuselage and began with all of his might and speed in cranking and cranking down on the forward jackscrew opening device for the forward landing gear wells to secure the forward landing gear down.

He cranked and cranked as hard he could, and then was thrown into the ceiling of the big bird's belly. The screw down crank handle had hit him just above his left eye, and it was bleeding profusely from the wound, down into his left eye. He grabbed the crank again with his hands still bleeding, and started to crank again as fast he could still half dazed.

Again, he was thrown about in the belly of the Twitchel, as the rear landing gear wheels on the big bird touched down for a second time in the sand just short of the runway. The front wheels hit the runway and catapulted the Twitchel back up into the air like a beginner pilot would in making his first attempt at landing an aircraft, and then back down onto the runway again, and again, and again. The Twitchel bounced a couple more real hard times as it quickly sped down the runway at a couple of hundred miles an hour.

"The chutes now, Captain Mitchell, the damn braking chutes." Commander Anderson yelled out to Ann to deplore the braking chutes to slow the Twitchel down. Ann yanked as hard as she could on the levers, and the slowing brake chutes of the craft shot out behind the Twitchel like clockwork. There was a slight tug on the craft at first, and then they began to slow the shuttle down.

"Some brakes, Major, some more brakes, Bill." The craft veered to the left and then to the right. Suddenly the nose gear gave way to fatigue for it had not being fully extended and hammered upon when the Twitchel hit the ground along with the front brakes pulling back on the landing gear all at the same time.

The shuttle veered off from the runway and into the grass mounds along its side plowing a huge furrow in the grassy area and sand as it went. The hard landing had caused the front land gears metal framed lowering unit to bend backwards under the belly of the Twitchel, as the hydraulic shafting rods bent and twisted beneath its heavy weight.

When the craft finally came to a complete stop, it had caused an enormous dust cloud of sand to billow up from the ground and encompassed the craft in a cloud of dust, and sand. Steven, Charles, and Captain Morris were in pretty tough shape when the craft finally came to a full stop.

Charles's arm and collarbone had been broken. Steven was the luckiest of them all. He was beat up pretty good but nothing was broken. Captain Morris on the other hand was in real poor shape. When the landing gear came apart, pieces from it flew up into the wheel well and broke his left hip, leg, and his left arm. He was lucky just to be alive. They were all lucky to be alive.

Commander Anderson and Major Bill went to assist Captain Morris down in the front belly of the Twitchel. Ann and Dick along with a couple of the Russian Cosmonauts went to the aid of Steven and Charles. They managed to pick the two of them up out the narrow passageway leading down into the landing gear compartments. It was hard, being as careful as they could with them, trying not to dislocate Charles's already broken arm and collarbone any more than it was already dislocated and broken.

When upon opening up the emergency escape hatch of the Twitchel, the crew could hear the sounds of horns blasting in the far off distance coming toward them from the command compound area. Diesel trucks were heard screaming out with clatter from their running engines seen coming down across the tarmac toward them from the garage buildings.

Ann pulled the lever on the CO2 escape chute mechanism deploring down the inflated chute to the ground for their safe escape. She then returned to help with Captain Morris who was groaning in dreadful pain. He would scream out in pain no matter where anyone touched him to help him. The medical situation onboard was bad, but help was on its way, they hoped. Returning to the emergency chute exit, Ann beckoned to a medic who was just barely arriving. She screamed to him to bring up some shots of morphine or some other type of oral drugs to help Captain Morris ease the severe pain he was experiencing from his injuries, and to bring her a stretcher for the captain as well.

A fire truck stretched out its aluminum chute and ladder for them to use in their escape from their disabled spacecraft. After the medic had quickly scurried up the ladder, Ann showed him where to go to find Captain Morris. With the forward wheel cavity being so damn thick with dust still in the air, along with sand scattered about in the cramped compartment made it damn near impossible to help the injured man.

The medic gave him a shot that knocked him out cold so they could strap him to a stretcher board for his extraction from the forward compartment, and then down to an awaiting ambulance.

The ambulance to arrive first on scene took away Lieutenant Steven and Charles to the hospital for treatment. They both received non-life threatening injuries, but was Captain Morris going to make it with all his injuries?

Scavonivich had a look upon his face as if he were in complete total blackout shock. He looked to be in a la-la-land state of mind, just staring off into outer space even when he was spoken to. He was in another world all by his lonesome now, and no one could locate him anywhere therein, as they tried to get his attention to unbuckle himself from his seat in the cockpit. He was to leave with the others to an awaiting vehicle to transport them to the compounds medical unit for a health checkup. He became just another statistic of the neutron invasion, an individual who was going to need help to get him through life if he made it that far without taking his own life to end his sorrow and misery of facing life alone.

Commander Anderson was totally blaming himself for making such a lousy choice of landing sites. He now knew he should have made a firm decision back in orbit in their making another go around one more time, and then taken his chances on a clogged runway in California other than chancing his way down through the toxic mix of neutron saturated clouds, rain, and foggy mist the way they had.

"I am sorry I did this to us, sir", Ann spoke out to Commander Anderson.

"You performed just fine, Captain. It is I who owes you an apology Ann. I will take full responsibility for this catastrophic event taking place if it turns out to be that way in the report. I shouldn't have been so damn adamant and indecisive up there in making the simplest of decisions, Captain." We should have tried a dusk landing. I know we could have made it."

Commander Anderson smiled at Ann, trying to make her feel a little more at ease with what she had just been a part of in helping happen, but knew it was all riding on his shoulders now for it was he who was more at fault than hers.

"I shouldn't have slammed on the retro rockets, right, Commander?" "Yes, you should have, Lieutenant, I mean Captain Mitchell. I was about to give you the order to fire them on anyway."

"I guess it was a wrong set of choices chosen by the two of us then I guess, I don't know."

He took Ann by the arm leading her out the hatch and down the aluminum ramp to an awaiting service vehicle that would bring them all back to the compound to be checked out for bumps and bruises they might not know they had being in slight shock from the awful incident.

The next day, Ann felt extremely superb with herself knowing she was now one day closer to be going home to the farm and able to be with her loved ones once again. She was still feeling the ill effects from the roughness of the crash landing from the day before, but she did not really care about her own bruises as she was still much better off than poor Captain Morris, Charles, and even Steven. She did feel sick though, extremely mentally headachy sick. She felt exhausted from not sleeping a whole hell of a lot not even a wink all night long it seemed for all she could do between dozing off once in a great while she would almost instantly wake right back up hearing Scavonivich screaming, "death to everyone death to everyone. The Commander is a mad man! We are all going to die. He is a mad man!"

Ann's sub conscience was working overtime, making her think about everyone who had been onboard the Twitchel, without letting her take a break to sleep for herself. If she had fallen asleep at all, it was short lived, dreaming of the crashing shuttle repeatedly.

She could still hear the frantic screams of pain come echoing up into the cabin into her ears from the belly of the Twitchel below. It was Captain Morris screaming out In excruciating pain and from everyone else in the craft including her own silent sub conscience, unconsciously pleading screams for her want of her children and husband. She watched frantically through the windshield of the shuttle as it tried veering off to the left and then shot off to the right, screeching off the runway into the soft grass and mounds of sand. She watched in slow motion as dirt,

grass, and dust escalated up into the cabin of the Twitchel and around all them. She knew in her short dreams she was going to be killed and die every damn time she dosed off for those few quick seconds, but then she would wake up in a cold wet clammy discomforted sweat, all chilled, crying, and nervously shaking.

Ann thought for sure she was about to experience an intense self-imposed nervous breakdown when suddenly she thought about home, Ben, and the children which calmed her right down almost instantly. The first night back on Earth safe and sound seemed to be the shortest yet longest most trying, strenuous, demanding night of her entire life yet. It had been a more nerve-wracking vicious night of worry worse than the anticipation of giving birth to her two small beautiful precious children. She would have much rather have had a dozen or more babies just like them, then go through anything like the night she had just gone through ever again. "Having a baby" she thought quickly to herself. Ann could not wait to get back home to hold her two little precious baby girls, Sarah and Amber, in her arms once again. She could not wait for Ben to throw his loving arms around her one more time and make her feel safe again as he always did. Especially after she had just promised him she would never leave him or the children ever again before Commander Anderson came knocking at that damned farm house door. That ever so shocked mind riddled morning, not that many weeks ago with that special life heart melting request of his.

She made a firm promise to her weak-minded self then and there after thinking a very short while what the circumstances of this last mission could have meant to her loving family if she were to perish in doing it. She felt her obligation for her life to her friends in orbit was certainly over with now, and she would stay on the farm forever and forever. She would now serve her fellow citizens, her friends, and her family best by being active in the local community, the church, and around the county. She would help rebuild the lives that monster living in the sky filled with massive neutrons had taken away from so many people. Ann's outlook on her life now had changed drastically in just the last long short several hours of her entire life. Her family would now become her calling card by taking care of them the way a loving mother and wife should, according to her father. Her thoughts now about his old-fashioned ways about a woman's' place in the home and their life were finally sinking into her thick skull, she thought for herself.

Ben had never directly deserted his family the way Ann had. He took their children out of Florida back home to her father's farm in Vermont. When he returned back from serving his forced government duty by being her husband, he was now protecting them the best he knew how or could against this object, this monster in the sky. He started by helping her father, his neighbors, and other folk around the community the best he could and was doing everything right according to her folks.

Ben was her hometown hero now, and she was going to take that issue up with him when she gets back home to her parents' farm. Ann wanted to live the simple life now by becoming that wife of a hard working farmer, a real mother this time to her children, and a loving daughter to her love caring parents.

CHAPTER FIFTY-ONE

The Suffering

The inhabitants of the earth had suffered dearly for the corrupt actions of a very small group of inconsiderate people who had wanted to control the universe for themselves. The massive loss of life around the globe turned out to be a catastrophe. The ones who lost their precious lives almost instantly at the onset of the massive invasion from the neutrons were better off dead than the many people who had survived the deadly neutron invasion.

Famine along with the loss of life by starvation had finally overtaken many metropolitan areas around the globe. In the many months to follow the massive neutron blasts, many new hostile gangs formed around the globe everywhere. Groups of them going around neighborhoods beating down doors looking merely for parcels of food they had left on their mostly empty shelves in stores of food, or had hidden in closets or under boards in their household floors so not to starve to death themselves. Many of the inhabitants of the earth were becoming desperate for their own survival. Life without electricity around the globe turned most lives upside down.

Large businesses were lost without the lifeblood of electricity flowing through their many veins of empty wires which had fed their great computer's life or operated their desperately needed elevators for travel to their highest points of skyscrapers, or power to light the dark of night. The millions of structures similar to skyscrapers and other large

blacked-out buildings around the world became empty in cities around the world while food-producing facilities of the world became instantly idle.

Large stores of assorted grains in silos and other accrues of foods lay rotting in their secured bins without anyone able to process them or access them without the help of electrically operated equipment to open and close their massive security doors and chutes.

Many human beings took their own lives by not being able to cope with the many new ways of life they had to experience. There were the ones that were not able to sit and watch their loved ones die from starvation. The ones not willing or able to help their loved ones or themselves in any way to go on in this crazy new changing world.

When the going got tough, the cowards around the earth took the easy way out, and left their loved ones to face the difficult times of life all by their lonesome.

CHAPTER FIFTY-TWO

Back on the Farm

When finally arriving back home at the farm, Ann was welcomed back home with wide-open arms by her loving caring family along with many many a wet joyful happy tear. She solemnly promised Ben, Sarah, Amber, and her two loving parents, she would never leave the farm ever again under any circumstances, no matter who it was that came knocking at the front door this time.

Not even the President of the United States, President Stallman. Not he or anyone else could convince her otherwise now. She would not leave the security of the farm or her loved ones ever again. Her commission was now up, and she was now a civilian to do whatever the best was that suited her and her family. Not even the safety or well-being of her comrades aboard the space station was any more important to her than her immediate family which now stood in front of her at the time.

Even though she prayed daily for their safe return back home to Earth, she had made this new promise to her family never planning to break this one, but who knows what the future might have in store for her.

Sitting around on the front porch of the farm that very next day high on Balch Hill overlooking Lunenburg Common, Ann and her mother sat peeling potatoes getting ready for the family's evening dinner. While looking out over the Connecticut River Valley they watched as dark stormy rainclouds rolled in toward them from the east, northeast corner over New Hampshire drifting westward from Mount Washington.

Soon the mean looking rain clouds overtook their bright sunny day overshadowing Lunenburg proper, as the skies opened up with torrential rains bucketing down on the farm like cats and dogs. In the far off distance of New Hampshire a streak of bright yellowish-red light like the tail of a fired off missile caught Ann's keen eyesight. Minutes later, a faint rumble of thunder or a similar sound could be heard coming toward them from the same direction. Thunder and lightning seemed something of the past not heard of or seen around the earth since the horrendous neutron invasion took place almost two years in the past.

"Was that thunder, Mom," asked Ann?

"It sure did sound a little like it, didn't it Pa?"

"It sure did, sweetie." Ben and Ann's folks could not believe their ears nor what their eyes might have seen. Lightning had not been seen for months nor had thunder been heard by anyone in the region since the big bang took place. There had not been a single death by lightning or electrical power since that dreaded day of long ago. It seemed almost sadistic to hope that soon someone or something would have its life electrically taken away, and not merely snuffed out by the dreaded means and ways of the neutrons dreaded assault of dying. Maybe it was thunder Ann's family had heard, and then again maybe it was not.

CHAPTER FIFTY-THREE

Hope

Maybe there was hope for the earth after all. Maybe the earth would reclaim that which was taken away from her by greedy human hands, and then again maybe not. How long would it take for good old Mother Nature to get her act back together; one more year, two more years, or maybe a period much greater than ten or better years in the future to regain her power over this neutron creature, if ever. No one on earth knew just how long or even if it was possible. When and if it did happen, maybe then just maybe, man might be able once more to start generating electricity on the surface of the globe one more time. If only man could put up with a few more years of learning how to cope with this menace, then maybe just maybe the luxuries of life might return slowly to everyone.

Then in the future there might be born another of the earth's ugly inhabitants that might want to control the earth like the ones who had caused this great catastrophe to occur in the first place.

CHAPTER FIFTY-FOUR

Back Aboard the Space Station

The mood aboard the space station was elated to the degree of great to excellent as the Twitchel disembarked her port of call, moving back away from her docking port. The once good mood soon swung to one of disappointment several hours later when Commander Anderson radioed back to his counterpart, Commander Ivan, the encounter Scavonivich had so brutally taken out on Ann's head as she was about to guide the Twitchel back to Earth with its new bearings she was finishing up on typing into the computer at that time.

It could have been disastrous for everyone onboard the shuttle if he had caused her to push the wrong control mechanism switches at that time. The space stations crew continued to monitor the shuttle visually, and by radio until Ann hit the switch activating the retrorockets, and their radio communications was lost as they reentered the earth's atmosphere through the radio dead zone as was their visual contact when the shuttle descended down into the thick cloud cover of the earth over Florida.

Looking down from space the next day when the cloud cover had finally lifted from the cape, the crew of the space station noticed the Twitchel down on the ground a far long distance from and off the side of the runway at the cape. They knew something drastically had to have gone wrong seeing the very large deep furrowed up earth behind it, caused by the forward broken landing gear when landing. They could see the emergency inflated side slide used for a quick escape in an emergency. There were several ground crew maintenance men surrounding the Twitchel the day after her landing. The craft did not look to be in too bad of a shape from where they were they could see, but something had to be amiss with the entire action-taking place around the craft.

Without radio communication to talk to Earth, it would be a long while before the crew of the space station would ever know what for certain really went wrong with the Twitchel or the safety of the crew and passengers within her. There were no flags or messages this time after landing laid out to indicate anything to them like before. They could only surmise and pray there would or could be another rescue mission sometime in the future.

Commander Khrushchev was very reassuring with his firm control of his stern voice promising his crew all went well for everyone below. The craft on the ground off the runway looked intact. It looked as if nothing major had gone too far amiss. They had probably blown a tire on landing, and veered off the runway because of it.

The time had come to start another year of experimental gardening aboard the space station to insure the safety and survival of everyone aboard. They were now able to grow extra food to sustain themselves; therefore the situation at hand looked very promising to all especially without the other eight cosmonauts' mouths to feed, and the crew of the Twitchel which had lived with them for the year.

Four months before the end of the following year, if supplies were running low for them, they would send their last space capsule to return to Earth and request another space shuttle mission by the Americans to return them all back home to Earth aboard. At least send enough oxygen, food, and other supplies again to sustain the remaining crew until another life mission could possibly take place in the future. They all hoped one day to return to Earth. Commander Ivan assured everyone he would be the last person to leave the space station when the proper time came to abort the mission. In his heart, Commander Ivan felt the pain of untruthfulness flowing from his mouth out to his crew for to him the Twitchel looked a mess with a twisted fuselage from where he was sitting and observing it from the space station. The nosecone of its forward cockpit looked very much dislodged and bent downward toward the ground ready to fall off, and from the furrow behind it, he felt the Twitchel's future was never to be repaired or ready for flight ever again. He felt someone for sure had to have been very seriously hurt and injured in this hideous looking landing wondering if one of his comrades or if any of his American friends had been lost in this mission of mercy.

Returning to his sleeping quarters after addressing his dedicated crew, Commander Khrushchev reflected over in his mind what the next best step taken would be for him to do next for his crew. His country had not attempted in any way or tried to make contact with them never since the big blast. Should he send their last space capsule back home to Russia or to the Americans where their government at least seemed thoughtful enough to care about them more than their own country, he felt the International Space Station circling in this void of nothingness in space around the changed world below, full of friendly love caring Russian cosmonauts without a country who cared enough for them to return back home, too.

CHAPTER FIFTY-FIVE

Survival in Space

For the next several months, the crew of the space station watched tentatively from above for any activities that might take shape on or about their homeland space centers. Nothing had changed except that the other rocket that had looked ready to fly had also fallen over due to strong winds or some other faulty reason, as the other rocket had done several months previously, and it too was broken in half. Railroad lines in Russia had taken their old steam engines out of mothballs that had been sitting idle on railroad sidings left out to the weather getting wet and rusty, and had put some of them back into operable service condition.

Old trains were pulling freight cars along the vast railroad system on tracks spread throughout their country. They had not moved the Twitchel from her crash landing site. She still lay motionless in her original place of landing, a good ways off the runway where she had come to her final resting place on the grass. There were no new activities taking place at Cape Canaveral that would indicate a mission or rescue mission would be taking place, or even thought about for their rescue anytime soon. It looked to them the entire world below had forgotten all about their incarcerated state in the steel orbiting container. Trapped in outer space for life or until death took them away. The only friends they had now in passing were the hundreds upon hundreds of informational satellites they passed each and every day that were sending out thousands upon thousands of informative messages per minute back to earth, with all its weather and other information falling silent upon the many deaf quiet ears of dead radios below.

There were a few military aircraft flying security missions over America and its shorelines now with none anywhere else around the globe. In Russia, they had observed steam engine trains pulling freight cars across Siberia along with the presence of a truck or two once in a great while moving goods along its vast empty roadways. Life seemed to be returning to normal back on Earth, whatever normal meant to them these days.

In Moscow where hundreds of people once scurried daily around the big city going busily to and fro with their many busy scheduled days, now only consists of a mere small hand full of busy people coming and going in the almost deserted streets of Moscow.

The world below as everyone had once known it to be had changed rather drastically, and could be seen practically changing daily as the crew of the space station watched all the new happenings taking place everywhere around the globe from where they could watch. It was as if the entire world below was their own private little ant farm.

The eye in the sky their private looking glass window of opportunity to be watching what new things would take place in everyone's lives as insects instead of people. They studied these creatures below making things happen using old technology and equipment of yesteryear. The ones once controlled by electric power units were now converted over and running off diesel power and water wheels where the need of electricity was no longer available or required to operate them. The crew of the space station felt practically superior to their counterparts living below without electricity.

Like Gods in the heavens above, the crew of the space station watched with little hope as this new style of life was taking shape and developing before their very own eyes on the surface of the world below.

They only wished they did have superior powers above the rest so they might help in generating and enabling the creatures below to advance at a much higher rate of accomplishment than they were and

to help them on their way to a more speedy success of recovery. Their main concern for the quick advancement of the aliens below on Earth was for their own selfish needs and wants. Without the novice creatures down below advancing quicker in life by making leaps and bounds in real life progress real soon, their own future of living was becoming very limited and sure to come to an end real soon.

CHAPTER FIFTY-SIX

The Stay of Time

Time spent in the space station laboratory waiting for their friends from Earth to return for them was taken up by doing harvesting experiments of different kinds on different crops by the crew. They planted vegetables of a variety of plant mixes for a variety of food, oxygen production, and flowering seed plants as a way to relax. Everything from time of waking up until it was time to retire for the evening was performed in a clock-like fashion aboard the station to conserve food, water, and oxygen.

All unnecessary daily exercise came to an immediate halt in order to conserve on the oxygen producing capabilities of their plant life experiments, and their own oxygen supply systems. They calculated If there were four less cosmonauts left living aboard the space station at the time, the crew would be able to last a lifetime till Mother Nature took them without any help from the world below, and they would be able to die from old age and natural causes. At that time in anyone's life there would be absolutely nothing any one could do to stop father time from performing his dastardly deeds of wearing out the body and mind, along with pulling the plug on someone's heart. A dream!

The timing of nature in space with Father Time working diligently on failing the mechanical steel structured of the space vehicle was coming much sooner than later for the unexpected life span of the space laboratory. The time of life expectancy was soon to come in the very near future when the space station would become a dead hulk of useless floating steel helplessly adrift in the vast heavens of space. A tomb made of steel littered with bodies of no one's concern within itself, so thought Commander Khrushchev.

If without a new infusion of fresh food, oxygen, fresh water, and much other needed new equipment to rejuvenate the aging old craft back to at least 80% of its 100% functioning capabilities it would prove fatal, a doom's day soon to happen for his crew.

Commander Ivan Khrushchev, commander of the International Space Station had been doing extremely well with all the critical decisions one is forced to make every day with everyone in mind. It was not hard for him for his crew of cosmonauts had become like family to him during their long hardship and untimely stay in space. He was nondiscriminatory and treated everyone with equal quality in his or her duties aboard his vessel. It did not matter to him that six couples were married, and two of the wives were now pregnant and burden with child. Having run out of birth control pills and measures to help in the prevention of giving birth to babies in outer space, the unborn children were a dear concern to him, as he had children of his own. He had grandchildren and a want for nothing but the best for everyone concerned aboard which was family bound.

Ivan was becoming hard pressed in short order nowadays with all the decision making he had to do for his crew. All he could do in his spare time, which he had little of, was to think of never seeing his loving wife, two married daughters, and his three very beautiful grandchildren never again. Living aboard the space station had become hard toil for all, especially for him. Three very long hard lonely years spent living aboard the space station now in lonely outer space. It was supposed to have been a short tour, a very few short three unflagging months at the beginning before the big mishap. Now having escalated into more a mission as though he and his fellow cosmonauts were destined to die in space, and never to see his or her loving family members ever again.

Commander Ivan had a very ethical choice to make as the commander of the space laboratory. He could very easily leave one of his top officers in charge of the space station if he so chose to return back to earth on the sole space capsule they had attached there if he chose to do so, but would that be fair to any of the others onboard. He had more than just his immediate crew to think about these days, for there would be three very much unexpected arrivals of little lives coming to live aboard the space station that he continually had to think about these last couple of months.

There were two very pregnant cosmonaut woman aboard the space station weighing heavily on his very concerned mind. Could these two young pregnant women along with their three fragile fetuses be able to sustain the harshness of a reentry back through the earth's atmosphere in a cramped module of a space capsule? He wondered medically if it would put an end to both mother and child's life in the six to seven g-forces they would have to endure on reentry placed upon their ever-changing bodies during the return mission. Their untimely coming into a life in this harsh environmentally unfriendly element in space was coming too quick for him to endure, and it was time for him to make a necessary decisions in life very soon.

Was he to give freedom to the two of them, and some four other very lucky deserving cosmonauts, but the crew were all so very deserving to be eligible to return back home to Earth. What was he to do? He did the next best thing he could think of. Commander Ivan called a meeting of all space station personnel to assemble in the main assembly room in the aft quarters of the space station at 1200 hours. He would put it to a vote of the crewmembers which would be eligible to return back home to Earth and the ones who would have to stay on the death ship to the very end.

If there could be no compromise in their decisiveness, he had already developed a plan of attack to the matter to fall back on. He had planned another similar life or death lottery incase no one could decide in a fair and noble manner who would leave and who would stay. The crew when asked the question about a baby's life onboard instantly erupted into heavy sounds of almost frantic survival testing voices. So loud the loudness of their voices vibrated the tile in the room they were in like a beehive of angered honeybees whose nest had just been broken into by a bear, but in this case the commander was checking on the mental stability of everyone's mind onboard.

The men and women aboard the space station were all extremely anxious to leave this hellhole of a paradise with electricity for greener pastures back home. They eyed one another with angered stares, using fright stare gestures similar an alpha wolf would use on his pack of wolves. Some almost showing their teeth as well in seeking out the weakest link in the crew who would best not be eligible in going back home on their way to freedom back to Earth, and the weakest in strength and stamina. They were to choose the ones best left behind to die, they not being so well equipped in their own survival skills, tasks, and talents to survive living back on Earth.

"Please," said Commander Ivan loudly, Quiet please! I see this dreadful event has come about for everyone in a very unpleasant way. I have again prepared a new lottery for everyone onboard to participate in. I feel rather guilty to play in this lottery myself, but in order for the outcome of this lottery to come out fair and square for everyone onboard the station, I must participate in it for the outcome to tally up correctly. Everyone has to win five consecutive times in this drawing just like the first lottery run to enable him or her to win his and her fair ticket on the space module back home to Earth in order to send us help. It will be the same lottery game of luck as the last lottery played except with fewer participants this time. Seeing some of our lucky crewmembers, our comrades have already been fortunate enough to leave for home.

The reason behind the lottery needing be run at this point of time in our mission is crucial to Gina and Krista. If we were to wait any longer, they would not be eligible nor should I say able to participate in this lottery because of their growing fragile conditions. I personally feel they should not have to participate in this lottery of life with being pregnant and all, and should be allowed to leave without playing in it if they so choose to do so."

The room again turned into a busy bee-buzzing beehive. "Commander Ivan, sir!"

"Yes, Gina."

"Krista and I would like to be treated as equals with the rest of the crew, sir. We would like to participate in the lottery just as everyone else has to, sir. We feel it was our own stupidity to have become pregnant in the first place, and no one else should have to suffer because of our own selfless actions. ”

“NO! They should be exempt like the commander said,” yelled Gina’s husband.

“No they shouldn‘t.”

“Yes they should,” shouted someone in the rear of the crowd.

“I will make all the damn decisions around here gentlemen. If the two women choose to participate in the lottery with us then so be it, they shall participate in it. It is their own personal choices, and I give them their own rights in choosing. Gina, Krista, you may do either. Which do you choose to do? Play like the rest of us or be exempt and leave with the lucky ones of the draw?”

They talkatively and openly discussed it in front of the others, and came to their own conclusions. Their loving husbands disliked them in choosing the lottery over not having to play the lottery at all as an equal to their fellow cosmonauts. “We choose to play the lottery, Commander,” said Gina to Commander Ivan.

“The decision has been made then gentlemen. Gina and Krista shall play as equals as the rest of us shall do in the lottery.

CHAPTER FIFTY-SEVEN

Let the Lottery Begin

Commander Ivan took out the first batch of envelopes he had made up from his satchel for the first drawing. He placed the envelopes into the makeshift basket on the tray for his crew to select from, and shook the envelopes mixing them up. Everyone took their separate turn in fetching their first time chance of winning or losing envelopes from the tray. Everyone at first appeared to hesitate in opening up their lottery envelopes in fear, or was it in hopeful anticipation of what was to come for or of them, as they looked around the assembly room at one other. Then they quickly opened the envelopes in their hands to display the good or bad outcome awaiting them from within. "Winners, please go to the right as before, and the not so lucky ones please step to the left." Commander Ivan did not want to say loser to anyone of his crew, even though left out in space to die by their own government made them all losers in this drawing.

Instantaneously losing all happy features, Gina lost the pleasant beaming smile she usually displayed on her all time beaming face of joy, the instant she opened up her first envelope. Her first envelope of luck had contained a blank note indicating she had lost the first drawing in this lottery. Slowly she moved over to the left of the room to assemble with the first set of unlucky drawing personnel.

Krista beamed from ear to ear with a sigh of relief and a smile so big a satellite could have flown right through it as her first drawn envelope contained a lucky enveloped winner. She joyfully floated to the right to be with the few who had drawn their lucky envelopes first. The drawing was far from being over, and everyone knew even the ones who were positioned to their right, still could, and just might end up in the unlucky crowd to the left where Gina was with a sulking looking face when the lottery came to its final fruition.

Commander Ivan's first envelope contained a blank piece of paper, leaving him to be with the crowd to the left with the less hearty heart wrenching few who had lost their first attempt as well. He had lost, and down deep inside hoped he would be one of the unlucky ones of the lottery at first, so one of his younger crewmembers he now stood among like Gina might be able to return to Earth and fulfill her life, along with her unborn child's life to their fullest.

He stood beside Chenco's wife Gina and Chenco, along with Krista's husband, John. Krista's face looked disheartened losing her sudden pleasant smile as she looked over at her husband John standing in the crowd of losers to her left.

After marking down the winners and the losers, Commander Ivan brought forth the second container of envelopes to the table to be opened by all. This time the commander won his first chance to return back home with his envelope, and began instantly daydreaming about how nice it would really be to be back home with his family and friends all gathered around him once again.

Commander Ivan looked over in Gina's direction and for a second time in a row of this lottery for life drawing, Gina was again in the loser's circle unhappy with herself, the commander unsure for her to have chosen to play in this stupid but very necessary game of life and death.

"Damn it", he thought disgruntled to himself! His daughter Britt was just about Gina's age and had two little ones of her own to take care and able to love. Gina deserved to go home on the damn capsule to have her baby or babies back on Earth and look forward to a life full of happiness with them and Chenco. This damn lottery was not about going back home to live or not going back home to live. It was all about life and death.

He had prepared the lottery for life to enable a few to defeat the sting of death in space, and spared the slow agonizing death in running out of food and oxygen when the crucial time came to all. This whole damn lottery thing was just like playing that stupid old foolish Russian fools game of bravery, of Russian-roulette, to prove ones bravery or not, but in this damn lottery it was differently being played without a bullet or a gun. Instead, in this particular game of roulette, they were not using a gun, but instead were using these damn envelopes as their weapons, and the damn blank pieces of paper were their loaded bullets of death.

All that came to Ivan's mind at that very moment was a story about a pirate he remembered reading about when he was a much younger man, a young teenager. It was a story of a man, a sailor, who had received an almost blank piece of paper in an envelope that contained a black spot painted in the middle of the piece of white paper, representing a message that indicated he was about to be a dead man in a short period of time. He was either going to be killed by another sailor and sailors or by some horrific deadly sword wielding spirit. He couldn't quite remember the outcome of the message or the story to which it applied at the time, and it didn't much matter anymore, seeing he stood there holding another parchment of blank colored paper without any writing upon it, and not one with a black spot on it, but it was all the same to him.

He looked sadly around the room to his fellow cosmonauts, looking for that lost jovial smile Gina had once shone brightly on her now so very frowning, enormously saddened face of fear and resentment for having to have been there in the first place, but it had been her very own choice.

He figured it must have been a bad spirit that had done the job of treachery for the black spot in the story, it being responsible for the killing of the victim or victims that carried its message out of fear of dying without hope that had caused them their sudden deaths.

A third loss in a row for Gina, this third loss took a tremendous toll on her, as she dawned the look of sudden death all about her in an extended fearful look of concern for her precious unborn children. In the fourth drawing she drew a winning piece of parchment this time, with a losing envelope going to Krista this time round who now looked as if a death sentence had been dealt to her also. Gina knew the feeling way too well! Gina's expression did not show any change or variation in her facial expression or even the simplest of a detectable smile with the winning parchment paper.

All she could muster up on her face now was a sad look of sickness and loss, even though she still had a very slim chance if you could call it that of winning a spot on the space capsule with the remaining number of drawings left on the table to be drawn. If the numbers of participants did not attain their winning numbers in quick succession, the lottery was made so everyone would have a chance of winning or losing. If a crewmember was extremely lucky, he or she could be a winner in the first five drawings. If they were not, then it might take all twenty drawings to make up the winners' list.

Ivan had put an extreme amount of time into developing this special lottery of life and death game again even though he did not look at it as a death sentence for anyone at the time of creation. Now he felt as if he had made a game of death, and was again not happy with himself.

Commander Ivan looked saddened by the way which his lottery was progressing, and the extreme way its outcome was affecting his once loving crew. They were more mystified now of who would live and who would die, resentful of the ones' who were winning, by the ones who were losing. He was not God for goodness sake, so why had he chosen the way of the lottery to figure out the ones to be saved and who would die aboard the unforgiving God forsaken space station anyway.

All he had had to do was to point his damn index finger at the ones of his crew he wanted to, and hand select the six lucky fellow cosmonauts who were to leave the space station. The ones hopefully who would send back help to the space she station to save them all, and that would have been that. He could have been one of the six lucky ones to leave

with the others if he so chose to, but would not have done so having a heart bigger than the International Space Station itself.

By the looks of it, he was becoming the commander of a death vessel suspended in the twilight zone in outer space. Everyone left there trapped by the deplorability of their own past commanding officials controlling the government force back home on Earth in Russia. The damn fools who had now vanished from the face of the earth, according to the last reports received, and brought to his command by Commander Anderson with the last rescue mission. Ivan could still be one of the six lucky ones to leave if he so wanted to and that would be that.

The excitement of the moment took hold of him as he heard a little voice speak to him from deep within his subconscious. "You are not God, Ivan Khrushchev, for this is the one and only fair way to accomplish this mission. None of the crew can put the blame on you for you have tried in every possible fair way to be fair to them all. This is the only way to help anyone and everyone onboard including yourself if you win. Then, if you do win, what will you do? What in the hell will you do?" The little voice in his head then slipped away and went totally silent leaving his head swimming in doubt about everything he had done to make this damn lottery a just and fair one.

As the lottery slowly progressed forward like a person opening a very special gift, but not wanting the outcome to come to them too quickly and spoil the surprise. The looks of jubilation upon some of the faces of the first lucky winners quickly faded into very saddened looks of total dismay. There were still several more units of envelopes held bound and unopened in the lottery carton on the table, and not a single crewmember had yet clinched the winning number in winning envelopes to claim his or her prize in securing one of the available lottery seats waiting for them on the capsule.

What was going on, what was happening? Only a couple of hours ago, everyone was smiling and joking around about someone going home someday. Now the looks on the faces of his once happy crew made the commander wish he had just chosen the six to leave without this damned life threatening game of cat and mouse. The look of gloom and doom was on everyone all around. The lottery had finally eliminated all but twelve of the contestants who were now almost sick with excitement of winning or losing that one special seat they were just waiting to see come to them by chance of a picked envelope.

The twelve who remained were Gina, Gina's husband Chenco, John, Krista's husband, Krista by chance, the commander, Dominique, and six other crewmembers of the space station. One by one everyone took an envelope from the tray of envelopes on the counter. Each unit contained a different number of winning and losing envelopes, so it made the lottery last a lot longer than the commander had hoped it would take to finalize the mission of this very special winning or losing lottery.

This time Commander Ivan opened his envelope first before the others had a chance to, maybe out the excitement of the hour. He had won fair and square. He won the first seat on the space capsule returning back home to Earth. One of the last twelve contestants left. Everyone cheered for him as he bowed before everyone with a friendly gesture of acceptance, as they cheered happily for him.

He looked in seventh heaven for being the first winner in the lottery without just taking the first seat by his own authority of position as commander. In his mind, he was now one of the luckiest men alive on Earth in space, or at least one of the happiest men alive. He could not wait to see his loving family and have their warm loving arms wrapped once again around his love starving self. He could only imagine in his mind the special welcoming home party he would be receiving from both family and all his many friends on his return to Earth. He could not wait to walk on solid terra firma of good old Mother Earth once more. He could not wait to see and smell the scents of Earth. He longed for the smell of its flowers, trees, and its many assorted grasses and hays once again as if he had never smelt them ever before. He could not wait to smell the difference of the changing seasons from autumn to spring to summer, and back to winter. He longed for the smell of his wife and family members for everyone had their own distinct aroma about them. He could not remember a happier time in his entire life than right now.

Krista looked and sounded relieved as she sounded out a sound of relief when she opened up her last envelope next, and found the second seat on the space capsule to be her own. She could now have her baby born back on Earth in a hospital equipped with all of the most necessary equipment they needed if she were to have her baby by a Cesarean-section birth. Earth, she thought, a place where she could raise her family in peace and comfort, or at least she thought she could at the time of her winnings.

Krista's husband, John, opened his lottery for life envelope next. He instantly began to cry from months of built up emotion with his envelope still clutched between his shaking fingers. Krista grabbed the envelope from his hand as she began to cry happily right along with John as she read the good news. She hugged him with all her might. They both had won the second and third seats aboard the space capsule returning back to earth together as a husband and wife team. They could now have the life they had always dreamed and talked about for so long. They were now given the chance to raise their family together back home on his father's farm in Russia where he had grown up. To have a child on a space station in outer space was not part of their original planned mission now everything was going as previously planned, and right for a change they hoped. To die in outer space along with their new newborn son or daughter was not part of their long-term goal as parents or cosmonauts.

Dominique was next in line to open up her envelope of fate. The expression on her face said it all. Her face went from a frozen hard cold frown of staring out into dark open spaces, to an ever-bright smile in pure confidence. Her beautiful eyes instantly misted up with great joy from the outcome of her draw. It was amazing, four winners in a row! She just knew the next draw from the envelopes had to be one of a loser, but it was not. She, too, as the other three had luckily picked an envelope with the winning element of happiness written on it. She glowed like the dawning of a bright new day when the sun comes cresting up over a darkened mountaintop to bring the freshness of bright new light upon the darkness of a dreaded night from the previous day of gloom. The pure attitude of delightful cheer in her lovely facial expressions glowed full and bright of enchanted gratitude with nothing but happiness adorned all through her pleasant smile. She was the lucky drawer of seat number four on the returning space capsule. The stressed excitement of the lottery churned wildly in her stomach to the point of vomiting, but she held it all back with opening her envelope. She knew her destiny was to die in the scrap metal heap she was living in, and could not believe her winning seat that would change her life forever.

The massive tension of playing the lottery of life was rapidly growing with intensity of leaps and bounds with strength with every passing second. There were only two more lucky seats left available on the craft of freedom available on the counter somewhere. As the contestants readied themselves to open up the last of the remaining envelops, some of the losing crewmembers slowly began to dwindle into the quietness as they slowly walked or floated away from the drawing room in thoughtless gloom. The few lucky ones still in for the long haul of the lottery experienced upset stomachs, almost to the point of wanting to void themselves whatever they had left in their stomachs from their earlier meals. With the first four envelopes already opened and showing winners, everyone knew each envelope from now on would surely be a losing one if the odds stayed the same as the last several stacks of lottery for life envelopes had been for the others.

When Gina opened up her envelope, she saw her entire future life pass before her very eyes. She had second thoughts now about the envelope she was about to pick up. In addition to picking up the losing envelope and eliminating her from the contest, she bickered in her mind to pick up the one envelope to the right of the one she had first wanted to choose. Why had she not slipped her hand just a little further to the right in this last draw? The envelope she left behind just had to have one of the last winning messages held secretly sealed within its folded flap. She sank in limpness to the floor on her knees in a heap and began sobbing openly for everyone to see and hear her cry. She did not mean to make this thoughtless display of sudden grief to take hold of her, but the sadness in her melting heart experiencing one of the last of the losing envelopes caught her totally off guard with the losing draw.

Chenco went to her and bent down putting out his caring arms to surround her, and to comfort her in her loss. She was so upset; she did not even know he was there to comfort her. She was numb to his touch, just knowing she was supposed to be one of the few lucky cosmonauts to be going home before the lottery even took place, or she might have opted for the free pass she and Krista had been offered right up front before the lottery took shape.

Two more cosmonauts drew their envelopes from the tray, and two more loosing envelopes produced two more disheartened souls. There were only a couple seats left available amongst the last five remaining lottery contestants. Sebastian took the envelope to the right that Gina had left behind, and upon opening it was delighted for he had become the next to the last winner in seats on the space capsule. There was only one remaining seat left. Gina had watched as Sebastian took the envelope she had left behind as she began to cry even the harder than before.

Sebastian could not help but to feel very sad for Gina, he had a young wife, too, and two small children back home on Earth that he could not wait to see again. He was truly grateful for this seat of flight on the spacecraft, and an only chance to return to his family from this death trap.

Three more cosmonauts opened envelopes, producing three more losers from the remaining envelopes. Three grown men walked away from the lottery room with tears of sadness filling their watery sad eyes. There was only one last envelope remaining, just lying flat and lonely on the tray on the counter.

"Chenco, you are too going home." Shouted out a voice from across the room. Chenco jumped to his feet from comforting his wife, and proceeded quickly across the room to the awaiting envelope. He quickly opened up his envelope, and then swiftly proceeded back across the room to his wife still sobbing hard on the floor. His eyes were filling with uncontrollable tears as he bent down to tell his wife with the good news held firm in his hand, as he reached out his arms and hugged her.

I won, Gina, I won. I am going home honey, I mean you are going home. You are going to take my place on the capsule, Gina. You are going home. He handed Gina the winning envelope so she could board the space capsule and return back home to Earth with the others.

The remaining crewmembers still in the meeting room gained back their happy attitudes as Chenco handed Gina the winning envelope, and told her she was going home. Gina began to cry a steadier stream of happy tears this time, as she reached for the winning envelope.

"My baby will be born at home," she cried. "Yes, our baby will be born at home," said Chenco holding back his building tears of sadness, ready for them to burst forth from his eyes at any given moment. "What about you Chenco? What about you? What will happen to you?" "I will be home before you know it, Gina. When you get back home, have them send a rescue mission back up here for us. Have a replacement team sent up so I can come home to be with you." "I will, Chenco, I will, I will. I promise, I promise! I promise! I will!"

His nobleness of handing Gina his winning voucher changed everyone's attitude in the assembly room back into one big old happy family type of atmosphere again. They would have all done the same thing for one of their own spouses as well, and all were glad to see the goodness left if not in everyone at least in one noble human being still living and alive aboard the space station.

In the back of the room. Sebastian moved quickly across the floor towards Gina and Chenco nestled lovingly down on the floor beside each other, soothing one another with loving words and hugs of pure devoted affection. He stretched out his hand to Chenco with his winning lottery ticket of freedom so Chenco could travel back home to Earth with his wife. "Here, Chenco. Take my winning voucher for Gina, Chenco!"

"Now wait just wait one damn minute here. I am the commander of this damn vessel and I will say who goes home and who has to stay here according to the rules of my lottery. No one can give anyone his or her lottery vouchers. You all agreed to the rules of this lottery prior to our playing it; therefore, it cannot be done!"

Sebastian felt stunned. He stopped abruptly in his fast track toward the two just short of Chenco's out-reached arm and hand which was ready to receive the lucky ticket Sebastian was so unselfishly willing to unload the winning voucher from his own hand. Sebastian's face turned a bitter cold ripe apple red like a fresh winter's wind full of burning frost attacking a vegetable or flower garden in the fall. He stood there red hot bitter toward this man standing before them all telling him he could not let another human being live in his place. He knew the odds of survival aboard the International Space Station were now nil, if not nearly impossible. Without further help from the Americans, things did not look very promising for anyone of them.

"It took me many days and sleepless nights in designing and making up the rules pertaining to this lottery, and you all agreed to abide by them all no matter the outcome. Isn't that right?" Everyone mumbled and grumbled about it, saying "yes sir," agreeing with Commander Khrushchev's choice of their decision of the rule making done by him, and their acceptance

"You did all agree, am I right?"

"Yes, but?"

"No buts about it. No matter how the outcome came out, you all agreed to what I said about the rules no matter what."

"Yes, sir, Commander".

"There is one very important, special rule I left out at the beginning of this lottery which I would like to inject at this time. This new first rule overrides all other rules of the lottery that I have made up. This rule left out was if the commander of this vessel was to win one of the winning lottery vouchers, it would become his sole right and only his right as a participant in this lottery that he alone by choice can give up his voucher to anyone he so chooses to without detriment to any of the other participant in the lottery without recourse to himself or others. This will in no way affect his position as station commander on this vessel or deter his authority in any way. Is this rule agreeable to everyone?"

"Yes, sir." Commander Ivan float walked over in front of Sebastian reaching out his hand, and handed his winning voucher down to Gina looking up at him with love in her heart for him as a delightful human being. Sebastian's extreme color in his red tormented face returned to a more normal cream color of delightful bright white. His hostile first reaction in pure resentment toward this individual faded quickly with added respect for his commanding officer, as Ivan winked at him with a smile on his face in his turning around to face the crew still wondering what he had just spouted out to them. What was his crazy new rule all about that he just quickly made up in his head, and then had all of them to agree to it.

The Commander turned to Chenco and Sebastian. "You two wouldn't have wanted to have been disqualified from the lottery would you?" In unison they both smiled at him.

"No, sir, Commander Khrushchev. Thank you very much, sir." Commander Ivan turned and faced the lucky winning participants of his lottery for life contestants and smiles.

In just under three hours the International Space Station had gone from being a somberly content inhabitance in space, to a very unsettled status back to being almost content once again. All disturbing attitudes in the crew reflected their feelings based upon the commander and his wanting to be one of the lucky ones to go back home to be with his loved ones. Had he not played in the lottery and won, the attitudes of the crew would have been less timid with the outcome in this very specifically designed game of life and death.

His own deep desires of wanting to go back home was almost the tip of the iceberg for the crew for they all respected him for being their leader in good times and in bad. In his giving up his personal winning voucher in freedom and life to Gina changed many soured attitudes toward him instantly. Their soured attitudes turned back around to where they had always been, knowing he was the same old commander that had lead them threw the last couple of years and months without everyone getting on one another's backs.

When someone did get out of line, which was very seldom, he would quickly get them back on track to a place of congeniality along with the crew very fast. They all knew this, or at least hoped he would do the right thing right from the get go. Deep down inside, Commander Ivan's only hope and wish was if the time would ever come in one of his own daughter's lives that a caring person, an individual with attentiveness like himself would do the same unselfish thing for one of them as he had just done for Gina. His heart beat with great loving affection for doing the right thing.

"You are all dismissed. Return to your stations. Thank you for your participation. I am truly sorry not every one of you could have won, but some of us have to stay up here and keep this bucket of bolts functioning until the next launched mission to this station, and hopefully we will all be able to go back home! You should all write back home to your loved ones. I am sure many of your loved ones would like to hear from you and how well we are all doing up here. Keep them down to only a couple of pages apiece if you would. I know a couple of you could easily write a book or two, but there just isn't going to be very much room for mail onboard seeing we have a couple of extra passenger stowaways hidden safely away within a couple of our young lady cosmonauts' bellies."

Ivan just smiled as he looked toward Gina and Krista. He then half walked and floated back toward the command center in the space station to look down on the sullen earth through the huge telescope in search of any mission readied for launching to them in the heavens by the Americans.

He looked down toward his own country or for anyone else on Earth who might care enough about these lost souls in the heavens in desperate need of help from below. It became quite evident to Ivan right from the start that his own country had forgotten all about the promises he and his comrades were given by them when they had all signed up for this very special assignment on the space station. He still had the secret envelope his new commander and chiefs had given him in case an outbreak of war began on Earth below. He had a bad feeling in his stomach that whatever those orders were at the time did not mean a damn thing to anyone down there below any more now. He thought that he just might have to go and see what in the hell they were all about and had to say to him in their dire condition when ordered. The remaining crewmembers of the space station were very happy for the six winners of the lottery now.

They had a party for the lucky six comrades who were going to be returning back home to Earth soon. They gave each other great big hugs and kisses for all would be missed aboard the space station, and there wouldn't be a better time than now for giving goodbyes because trying to hug or kiss someone in their flight space suits was hard if not damn near impossible to do.

Gina and Chenco personally went to the colonel's living quarters to give their own special thanks to Commander Khrushchev for his most generous gift of life to them with his own personnel lotteries freedom voucher. Ivan did not need any special thanks more than the appreciable appearances of gratitude they had painted across their smiles when he let them into his cramped quarters.

The next day found the lottery crew winners busy at work preparing their vehicle of freedom for its final departure from the space station. They had to make a couple of new changes to the outdated space vehicle they would be traveling in back to Earth. Any electrical force fields or electrical supply stored in their capsule to be drained instantly out the capsule by the millions and billions in wild tiny neutrons floating wildly in the earth's air once they broke through into it. Everyone went around double checking each other's supply lists just in case someone forgot the simplest in supplies when it came down to everyone's safety. They double checked their food supply in case they had to stay aloft a couple of extra days in orbit until a true window of opportunity opened up for them to glide down to earth through safely.

They made sure they had plenty of CO_2 cartridges to fill their life rafts and space suits should they land in water, taking along a couple of hand held compasses, putting them onboard in case they were to land somewhere down below on land and wouldn't keep traveling around in circles in the wilderness lost for days. They opened up and repacked the landing parachutes to make sure the fabric and tether lines were still all intact and ready to be activated when needed for their safe glide and soft landing they all hope for on their final return back home to civilization.

Both Krista and Gina posed a slight problem when preparing for their pre-flight flight suit fitting. Both had to try on several different flight suits in order to accommodate their changing body forms, especially Gina. It was quite evident she was pregnant with twins, she stuck way out more than Krista did in her midsection. Everyone in the station joined in and laughed while watching the two girls go through the antics of trying on several different space suits.

Commander Ivan broke out in hysterical laughter as he watched Gina getting on the final suit she was putting on to wear. She looked more like a little child trying to get dressed for the first time than a cosmonaut trying to suit up for flight. When she finally finished suiting up, she looked like the huge white pumpkin from outer space. Ivan had huge happy tears of laughter forming in both his eyes as he was laughing so hard.

Sleep was problematical to the space capsule crew the night before their departure. 0400 hours came very early to the happy but very scared lottery winners. As they ate their last meal aboard the space station, it seemed like a dream come true to them all.

Commander Ivan sat with them as they ate, and wished them a safe and happy return flight and landing. He said he wished he were going with them, but knew Gina and her twins needed to get back home sooner than he did. Chenco was told to take damn good care of the special cargo aboard the capsule with him. He smiled and confirmed the commander's orders directly at him. Gina hugged Commander Khrushchev with all her dainty might and conviction of tenderness. She gave him a great big caring hug and kiss for good luck on his stay and mission onboard the space station.

She pulled away from him with large welled up happy tears of happy joy in her eyes, and a deep sorrow forming in her tendered heart for him. She would never forget the man who gave her freedom of life over death. She really felt she had given him the kiss of death like one of the twelve disciples had done to their leader in Christianity, Jesus Christ.

He was a good man. No, he was a great man and would be missed by all who knew him or had been lucky enough to have been touched by him in his so many fair and equitable ways of being their commander, father, grandfather, or just a loving caring human being. Commander Ivan wished them all sincere luck and a safe flight back home to Earth as they hurried on their way down toward the flight deck where their ride to freedom was waiting ready for them to depart.

Commander Ivan had sat with them the day before and had decided for them that Cape Canaveral in Florida would be their safest landing site for the crew to land. The Russian space landing locations around Russia all looked abandoned. There were no signs of any activities going on in or around them ever since the big bang. Florida then turned out to be the chosen site for their final destination. At least there, there were people moving around the air base even though they had not dragged the Twitchel off the side of the runway to a hanger for repair yet for another mercy flight. Their chances at Cape Kennedy would prove far greater for them medically if they needed medical attention, they all decided.

Commander Ivan gave them strict orders in hand to land there for their own safety. Chenco pulled the heavy metal door shut behind them securing it tight as he lastly climbed aboard the space capsule in their very cramped seating quarters. With the airlocks securely in place they gave the nervous crew permission to depart the laboratory docking station.

For the past couple of years, the crew onboard the space station had been practicing routinely in the small space stations simulator in operating their capsule. They all knew the day would come for someone to return back to Earth in a hurry. Everyone had to practice the many different methods of escape from their adversary being lost in outer space should something devastating happen to the space station out of their control, and only a very few lucky ones might possibly make the safe escape aboard the capsule. Now if something were to happen aboard the space station, all would be lost to the situation of destruction

of the multi-sectional spacecraft and the remaining crew. Everyone onboard the station had to learn how to maneuver the space capsule for departing the laboratory for reentry into the earth's atmosphere for a safe landing.

Now there were six very lucky individuals or very unlucky cosmonauts aboard the capsule trying to bring its mission of escape from space in flight to fruition in bringing its excited passengers all back home safely to Earth in one peace.

CHAPTER FIFTY-EIGHT

Going Home

FOUR, THREE, TWO, ONE, release securing clamps holding space module. The movement of the space capsule away from the space station felt incredibly peculiar to the cosmonauts inside the space module. No one had experienced any type of movement other than their own movement of floating inside of the halls of the space station in over two long years. Their walking in its corridors with the help of magnetic shoes and floating along without any restraints on them through the space station didn't represent movement to any of them.

Gina felt queasy with a sensation of tickling beginning to develop in the pit of her stomach from the moment as the space module departed her mother ship. It didn't seem to bother Krista or the others, then again Gina was the one who developed morning sickness the instant she became pregnant. Krista never was sick or even queasy ever since the conception of her child. What a lucky women thought Gina about Krista every time she threw up in the cramped lavatory of her living quarters.

Sounds of happy cheers came billowing into the space capsule over the radio as the lottery winners departed the confines of the space station. "Good luck comrades and a safe landing" said Commander Ivan to the departing crew.

Chenco distanced the space capsule away from the space station by using the attached jettison bottles mounted to the capsule's sides and

one both forward and aft for control of pitch and propulsion for reentry. They drifted further and further away from the huge dark phantom looking vessel in making their departure. They were definitely on their way home now all alone. They drifted further and further out away from the safe place they all had called home for so long, having felt quite secure in its steel cavity and their duty while aboard the space station. The safety of the departed ones along with their safe landing back on Earth was the only way, the only hopes and prayers the ones still trapped aboard the space station would have a chance for them all to live. If the six cosmonauts failed in this attempt, no one on Earth would know the critical situation developing in space aboard the steel city of beacons and lights at night that floated helplessly over the earth night after night, and day after day not being noticed but by a small number of family members below of the ones still trapped onboard her in the heavens.

With each breath of oxygen taken by the departing crew, the security of the space station seemed to drift that much further away into the space that had no end. No end at all, they thought until at last the blinking flashing strobe lights of her many beacons could be seen no more.

All minds were thinking similar thoughts as the capsule departed from the space station. "Please send us back some kind of little rays of hope of some sort, please. Send us a signal using Morse code by way of the bright sun's rays. Some cosmonauts enjoyed happy thoughts about a rescue mission having already been planned for them to be rescued as they dreamed, or a rocket ship heavily loaded down to the point of exploding with multiple supplies and additional oxygen and food, and a possible ride home for a few lucky one, to maintain their quickly fading lives with a slight chance of hope attached. Any kind of message would be well appreciated, even if one wasn't sent, but looked like it had been." These were merely messages of wishful thoughts only, for no one had any kind of telepathic powers to broadcast their thoughts to one another anywhere in the universe.

The weather over Cape Canaveral had been okay the day before, but some menacing clouds had been developing and were on the increase ever since they decided to depart and attempt their landing. At least with the space capsule, the weather over the cape could still be a little bad, and they would still probably make a safe and happy landing back on earth by the space center.

Chenco gave the command. "Fire the boosters. Prepare for our reentry." Once they fired the boosters, the module began to slow its speed down and began to drop rapidly down toward the Earth's outer ozone ring and atmosphere. Everyone was beginning to feel the force of gravity for the first real time on his and her bodies in over two long years or better of floating helplessly in outer space in weightlessness. There had been no gravitational pull of any sort on their bodies for so long they didn't know if the slightest gravitational force would break their weakened bone structures or not.

They exercised daily aboard the space station using different strengths of strong elastic resistant straps to keep their strength up. After approaching the critical state in survival, all unnecessary exercise had been stopped by the station's commander in order to conserve food, use of oxygen, and in reprocessing the water from the past couple months, and the flab on the cosmonaut's bodies was beginning to show, especially on the girls.

Now even Krista was beginning to feel a little queasy from the increased gravitational pull of the earth's gravitational force on her or was it from the booster rockets that was causing this discomfort? She gripped the armrests of her station for security as did the others in the space capsule. The lights on the instrument panel began to flicker as Chenco was reading the outside temperature of the capsule's bottom heat shield, for it was gaining in temperatures well above a thousand and better degrees. When he last read twelve hundred degrees. the lights on his instrument panel all went dead, and the inside of the space capsule became as black as black could get.

They were falling helplessly now toward Earth in solid darkness that caused great concern for Chenco. He did not know how high they were, and if he pulled the mechanical lever to fire the parachutes out behind them too soon, it could prove disastrous for everyone. If he were to fire the chutes at a high altitude, they could drift half way across the

Atlantic Ocean ending up in the ocean somewhere between the United States, Great Britain, or even off of Africa. If he fired them too late, they might slam into the earth's crust killing everyone, or merely burn up from the intense heat caused by the friction of the oxygen on the bottom of their space craft.

He was betwixt and between in what to do next. The g-force was beginning to affect both Gina and Krista. Krista's stomach was churning as was Gina's trying to come up and out through her mouth and nostrils all at the very same time. Her twins were being forced up into her chest cavity as they plummeting quickly toward the Earth below. They in turn were forcing her stomach up into her throat, as she was trying desperately hard to breathe without success. She tried swallowing and swallowing several times trying to prevent her stomach acids from reaching her mouth, and in between the shallow swallows she managed to take a wee breath of air with each tiny swallow. A little acid did finally sneak past her flexing throat muscles and flowed out into her mouth burning both her mouth and nostrils to the point she now wished she had stayed onboard the space station. She wondered if this crazy ride she was on was in any way going to affect her or the babies inside her in any way.

She only hoped if it did take their lives that she would go right along with them for putting the poor little dears through such an ordeal as this. This was her second mistake in life, she thought. Her first mistake was getting pregnant in the first place. Would it really be her fault for trying to give her babies a better chance at survival, or would it really be her fault for killing the two of them. She began to shed tears from the miserable pain she felt for them. More acidic bile shot from her stomach and came rushing up her throat to her mouth. Like fresh red hot molting colds fresh out of a campfire, the burning acid was thrust up into her mouth. The pain of it seemed unbearable, and she needed to breathe some fresh oxygen or die. She swallowed very hard so she could breathe again, and took in a very small breath of oxygen at that time. She knew she was about to pass out, but did not want to drown in her own acidic vomit by filling her helmet with pure vomit when she was passed out cold.

A ray of light came blasting though a glass portal, as John manually blasted away its heat shield covering. Chenco could now see the round horizon of the earth's outer ring through the portal, and decided it was time to fire the decent parachutes to slow them down and safely lower them down to the awaiting Earth below.

Suddenly the force Gina and the others were all experiencing went from rushing up into their throats and began pushing everything straight down into their groin area. It felt like someone from outer space had reached out and down and was trying to pull the capsule and its crew back up into outer space again. Then the feeling felt like nothing at all, until again the Earth's gravity caught hold of them letting them know it was still around them, and began to pull down on them once again. Gina went to raise her arms in order to release her face shield from her helmet as the others had already done with her arms feeling like heavy lead weights. She managed with great difficulty to remove her face shield to wipe away the burning acidic vomit from her face and chin. Krista had experienced the same things that Gina had experienced, and was busy wiping away her own face and chin but to a smaller degree because she was not carrying twins.

Sebastian had lost an entire mouthful of stomach fluids up into his helmet, causing him to look more of a mess than the others. His eyes were on fire from his own excretions. His eyes, ears, nose, face, and hair were covered; he was a mess with vomit. He was totally embarrassed from his involuntary actions as were all the others. His own embarrassment quickly faded away when thinking of his loved ones back home on Earth who he was going to be seeing soon, he hoped. He could not wait to see his wife and their children once again. It had been too long of a stay in outer space for him, and he hoped he still had a family to go back home to.

The sun was beaming down shining bright and beautiful through the uncovered portal windshield. Chenco looked to the altimeter for a height bearing and was not pleased at what he was looking at. The reading read fifty-two thousand feet and not falling rapidly, the way it was supposed to be for a clear shot to land at the cape. In fact, it did not seem to be falling at all. That meant the capsule was floating along

in the upper air stream aloft just hanging there and not falling toward their intended target below. He hoped the bottled up oxygen they were using would last until they landed.

He had fired their decent landing parachutes way too soon for their proper landing. The perfect height to let out the chutes would have been twenty-five or thirty thousand feet. He had gone and done what he had feared the most in their reentry sequence. Their altitude was slowly falling, but not fast enough to suit his wants in their very slow descent. The air stream aloft could be taking them anywhere around the globe. It could be taking them up north deeper into another unchartered location of United States, into a southerly direction down over Cuba, or in an easterly direction out to sea toward the Leeward Islands.

The upper airstreams would take them wherever the damn air stream was flowing to and wanted to take them. They had no choice in the matter now. He was exasperated with himself in his haste to discharge the landing chutes ahead of time, but there wasn't a damn thing he could do about it now.

They were caught in the high air stream of the earth, and would eventually land somewhere on Earth's land he hoped, but was that too much to surmise, or was the damn altimeter needle stuck.

As if a feather caught adrift on a gentle breeze, the capsule drifted easterly out and away from their intended landing zone. Their decent was way too slow and everyone aboard knew they were in some sort of trouble for it. The weakness of the polar caps' magnetic fields made it near impossible for them to detect their true bearings with their hand-held compasses they had brought with them while still inside their metal capsule.

Wherever they were going to land, they would have to make the best of it. They were pretty well equipped for most anything on Earth, except for what they were about to enter into down below. The earth had become a hostile planet of forever-changing developments for humanity, and they were about to enter their own twilight zone of horrors. If any of the crew were to survive this cruel happening they were about to enter into would be pure luck, and if they were not to survive, they could count themselves lucky for not having to experience it for very long.

CHAPTER FIFTY-NINE

The Eye of the Storm

They had no idea where below the capsule might be headed as the steel hulk began a more rapid descent down toward the earth below. It seemed to them as if it had been hours of leisurely drifting along, caught in the high air stream currents above the earth before they were let loose from its death grip adrift. Chenco was afraid they were going to run out of oxygen very soon if they stayed aloft much longer. Knowing if they opted for opening up a hatch at such a high altitude for oxygen and fresh air it would not do them any good. Helplessly adrift up in the high atmosphere where there was little oxygen, if not any at all. It would prove an instant death wish to all if they had opened the capsule up because the sudden drop in air pressure alone would have killed them all almost instantly, and they would have frozen to death within a few short seconds.

Down, down, and down they drifted. Down through a swirling cloudbank surrounding them like a huge swirling cotton puff. The altimeter indicated to Chenco they were now descending down very rapidly as they should have been doing at least an hour or better beforehand when their parachutes were first deployed.

Soon they would be on good old terra firma once again, and none could wait to be there. They were all so very anxious and excited. With only minutes left before they touched down, Gina placed her hands and forearms beneath the precious cargo she was holding tight within her womb by placing her hands beneath her belly. She wanted to support her twins as best as she could with her hands, knowing the sudden hard landing was going to be an unpleasant impact for both them and her. Krista did the same imitating what Gina was doing just as a precautionary measure for her own precious cargo.

"Less than five hundred feet before touchdown," Chenco yelled out as he watched the altimeter declining rapidly in numbers. The three large parachutes stretched out wide and high above the capsule in a thick mist, looking quite beautiful to the six lucky cosmonauts held secure in the capsule, as they descended rapidly down through the clouded cover and misty fog they had now encountered in there rapid descent towards the earth.

"Two hundred feet to impact," Chenco yelled out, as the excitement grew within everyone. "One hundred-fifty feet, one hundred feet, fifty feet, twenty-five feet to touchdown. Brace yourselves."

Suddenly something hammered at the capsule sideways just before impact, and then a soft impact followed. They knew they had landed in water somewhere, but had been preparing for a much harder impact thinking they were going to be landing on good old hard solid ground. Gina and Krista were much better off by landing by in the water than landing on solid ground as the water cushioned the impact of the landing greatly. The capsule first landed on top of a huge rolling wave lessening the impact of the capsule all the more as their craft settled down through the rolling waves to the surface of the sea.

The parachutes came down lying to one side fully inflated as gale-force winds atop the surface of the sea dragged the capsule sideways across the top of the raging waters, bouncing the capsule along the top of one rolling wave after another.

Suddenly the capsule quickly submerged beneath the water's surface, dragged along by the inflated parachutes twisting and turning them, as a huge wave broke over the top of them beneath the water's surface, twisting at them even more.

The awkward motion inside the craft caused Gina and Krista great discomfort in their pregnant shape. They became instantly sea sick with the constant motion of twisting and turning inside the capsule. The two screamed as both of their stomachs came bolting up on them. Sebastian, smelling and seeing the secretions from the girls' stomachs brought up, began his own vomiting.

"Release the chutes," yelled out Chenco to John. He couldn't inflate the rubber raft to support the capsule with the parachutes still dragging the craft along, for the force of the pull of the chutes along with the huge waves would tear the inflated raft to smithereens, and they would sink to the bottom of the sea, lake or wherever they were in no time at all. They would all be lost and drowned. They could be crushed to death from the immense pressures deep beneath the water's surface. Water was beginning to seep into their craft while being dragged along continuously beneath the water's surface by the huge parachutes. The capsule was acting like a big fishing lure being dragged along behind a fishing boat attached to a fishing line still tethered to the chutes in the high gale-force winds.

Worse, they were beginning to be dragged deeper down into the depths of the water causing pressure to be exerted upon the outer seals of their space vessel letting in the salty water of the sea even more. They would soon drown if no one did something very soon to release them from this very bad situation.

Chenco released himself from his seat in order to reach and release the parachutes. When released, the capsule began to sink even further down into the rough of the sea. He then slammed out with his hand in the total darkness of the capsule for the raft firing mechanism.

When he hit it, they could hear the sounds of CO_2 cartridges filling the circular rubber raft as the external bottom round shell ring of the capsule exploded out away into the sea, the way it was supposed to have, and the rubber raft quickly inflated itself. The capsule shot upward toward the surface of the water upside down sending Chenco into the ceiling of the capsule as if it were the floor. When the capsule finally reached the surface, it lay suspended upside down in the water with its hatch submerged beneath the surface of the water. The inflated round rubber rafted ring did not allow the capsule to right itself into an upright position the way it was supposed to have.

Hanging there suspended upside down in their stations, the gravity of Mother Nature's natural forces caused everyone's blood to rush up into their upside down heads. This made everyone think their heads were about to explode by feeling the real force of gravity upon them that they had not experienced in such a very long time. One by one, they released themselves from their seats falling downward onto the ceiling of the capsule, now its floor.

The cone shape of the capsule's top caused everyone to lay all twisted together as a can of fishing worms intermingled and stuffed into a small bait can like sardines stuffed into the tightness of a can so close they could hardly move.

Panic, worry, and emotion overtook the girls as everyone inside all tossed back and forth onto each other as the craft tossed from side to side. Then up and down on top the surface of the raging sea, like an irritated animal trying to dislodge a drilling deer tick from its back, or an angered bear trying desperately hard to dislodge a number of stinging bees from its nose.

One of the storage lockers above them beneath a seat suddenly opened up and dropped a huge heavy oxygen tank down onto them. Sebastian took the brunt of the blow to his head, losing consciousness instantly. He slumped down in a heap in the middle of everyone, causing the tight quarters in the capsule to become ever the more unbearable.

The dim light shining through the portal window was small. It was as dim as a small-lit match would give off light in a ten by ten foot dark room on the darkest night of the year. The crew could barely make out their own crewmembers all cramped up in the tight space beside them.

"Take off your flight suits; we have to get the hell out of here", yelled out Chenco over everyone talking and grumbling out of fear. "They will drag you down to your death if you don't get rid of them now. The inflating firing mechanisms are wet, and will not work now. Get rid of the damn things. Where are the life rafts?"

"In locker number two, Chenco," a voice yelled out. "Help me get Sebastian's flight suit off him." Arms intermingled with arms, while the legs of his flight suit kept catching on switches and knobs, as everyone tried to rid themselves and Sebastian of their cumbersome flight suits all at once, and deposit them beneath their feet on the ceiling of the craft.

The air in the capsule was becoming very stagnant and unbearable with the smell of vomit as their oxygen supply was running out on them. The crew didn't have much time left in getting him or herself upstairs to the surface of the sea or Great Lakes out of the crippled capsule before everyone died from asphyxiation from the lack of fresh air and oxygen.

"When we do this," Chenco yelled out, "we have to stay together so we don't lose someone to the raging waters. We shall use the tow-line rope method leaving the vessel together. John, you go first. When you blast away the locked hatch, wait until the pressure from the water stops coming in on us. You will not be able to fight the flow of water against you as it is rushing in at you. We need to cover Sebastian's head so he won't drown."

"Is he still alive?" "I don't know, Gina, but I sure hope so!" Sebastian had made it this far, but would he make it the rest of the way home?

Would anyone of them make it any further in their desperate flight to freedom? It was hurricane season in the Atlantic, and since the big bang, the storms had grown in massive size and magnitude of strength. It all depended on their luck, if they had any left at all.

CHAPTER SIXTY

The Great Escape

The cloud cover they had observed from outer space a few days before coming off from the North African coastline heading westward toward the Leeward Islands and east of the United States was the first major hurricane of the season and the biggest the earth had ever experienced this early into the new hurricane season. Storms and weather around the globe were continually changing with the strengthening and weakening of the neutron force field that now surrounded the globe.

John slammed the mechanical triggering device to blow away the sealed hatch. The door flew out only a couple of inches then slammed instantly back against the capsule, leaving a gaping hole and opening of about six inches just above it. The waters from of the sea came gushing in at them, and when the outside pressure equalized itself with the inner pressure of the capsule, the loosened hatch door fell down and away from the capsule.

John at first was getting panic-stricken, as he was about to try and kick the hatch door away by himself before it fell. He knew what to expect, but his racing nerves were starting to get the best of him, and he knew if the door was stuck in place it would only be a matter of seconds, not minutes, they would all have left to live. What a relief it was when the hatch door slithered away down into the far off depths of the water out of sight.

John dove out of the hatch pulling a cable towline along with him in hand behind, frantically swimming toward the surface of the raging waters. Next, out went Gina, then went McGill, and then Gorbachaz holding on tight to Sebastian under his arms kicking with all his might toward the surface above, and then next out went Ludwitz. The rest followed with Chenco bringing up the rear, being the last one out of the capsule.

Ahead of going out the blown off hatch, John pushed out two inflatable rubber raft kits, and then pulled the cords to the Co-2 charges on them, to inflate the rafts. Everyone was hoping there would be at least one rubber raft and possibly the two of them bobbing up and down on the surface of the water to greet the crew when they all finally reached the surface.

They found way more than they had expected when they got to the surface of the sea. They were in one hellacious storm, and greeted with twenty and thirty-foot high waves bouncing and churning all around them.

One of the rubber rafts had blown away, and they were damn lucky the one John was holding onto did not fly away as well in the strong wind. Pushing Sebastian up and into the rubber raft first was a real chore for McGill and the others to handle with the immense swells of waves tossing them all around like loose bobbers in a raging river. Next into the raft were the three girls followed by the men. The waves broke over them as they would over a surfer who had just lost his surfer's riding board at the bottom of a great giant kahoona's surfing wave.

They were slapped by the wave of water coming down on top them like they had just made a huge belly flopping dive from off of the top of a ten or better foot high or higher diving board every time one of these huge pounding waves would break down over the top of them.

The two men along with Dominique all huddled together in a circle above and around Sebastian, Gina, and Krista. They tried their hardest to protect themselves and their unborn children from the ravage beating everyone was taking in stride of their horrendous situation.

The two girls' lives carrying the babies along with Sebastian still knocked out cold seemed the most important thing to them at the time. Sebastian lay limp and motionless between the two girls' laps, and was still breathing. Every time a wave was about to explode over the top of them, the two men and not the pregnant girls would take their battering positions again above the others to give them as much protection from the hammering wave as possible.

Chenco would yell out every time he saw a huge rolling breaking wave was coming getting ready to crest above them.

"Here comes King-Neptune again. He is going to flog the hell out of us again." The two men along with Dominique would stand tough with their six arms interlaced above the others, and take the punishment of the pounding water time after time to help protect the more weak and needy for protection.

All this being battered to death on earth by the anger of a raging sea and drowning a better way to die, than running out of oxygen and food aboard the space station and slowly suffocating, they all thought not.

Up and down they went with the rolling of the angered sea. Slap after bitter slap, the large waves continued pounding on them hour after hour and late into the evening until the darkness of the frightful night overtook them. They could not see the huge waves coming toward the raft after dark attacking them, but they sure could tell when one was going to crest over the top of them again.

The sounds made from the approaching thrashing wave was similar to that of the king of the jungle, a lion roaring in the distance protecting its freshly taken prey before the wave reached them and came slamming down on them like a huge wet fly swatter of water.

If it hadn't been for the rope encircling the out ring of the raft, and everyone tied together by it, one if not all would surely have been swept out, washed overboard of the raft by the hard pounding of water that came crashing down on them relentlessly time and time again.

This was the way of Old King Neptune telling those unlucky souls upon his back they were not welcomed on his surf. The ocean was

his home, and he did not want to be hospitable to the newcomers; especially the ones just returning back home from outer space.

The intense beatings lasted well into the late darkness of the night when finally the unstable waves of the ocean became friendlier to these newcomers riding upon the waters on her surface.

The two men and especially Dominique were exhausted from standing over Krista, Gina, and Sebastian every time they heard another approaching deadly wave come rolling toward them. There had been no more mammoth-sized waves come toward them for quite some time now, as the exhausted crew slipped off into a shallow restless soggy sleep, keeping one attentive eye and ear open for Chenco to call out for another wave to be coming. The waves were huge but rolling with smoothness as the rubber raft climbed up one side, and slid down the other side with ease.

As dawn over took the crew of the raft, the ocean became as quiet and smooth as a mirrored lake in the still quiet of a warm summer's day. There was not the least sign a raging storm anywhere in sight according to the quietness of the waters, but they knew better of it and could see the large circle of intense dark clouds around them, and could sense the rage within them.

The sun was brightly shining on the raft of cosmonauts, shining down through a huge hole in the circular canopy of clouds all around them. The clouds were swirling around them in a counter clockwise direction. The dark clouds looked like a huge doughnut spinning in the sky above them. Chenco knew they had just survived the worst part of a severe hurricane, knowing they could look forward to even more lashing from it when they entered the outer ring of the storm's madness once again. The only good thing about the other side of the storm if there was a good thing about it was that the returning winds would have had time to cool down and weaken before coming back at them from the north-northwesterly side of the storm if it went over cooler waters. It all depended upon their longitude and latitude position upon this angry sea.

The eye of the storm had to have been at least a hundred or two or more miles across from what they could guess from where they were in its eye. Gina had never seen or heard of such a huge eye in any storm in all the meteorological classes she had to go through and studied before becoming a cosmonautic astronaut. She had studied weather as her major in the Soviet college she had attended, and the size of this storm amazed her with the enormity of its huge eye in which she was now sitting in the middle of and in a stupid rubber raft.

The water was not as calm on the outskirts of the eye as they could see the waters churning in rage. For them it was clam as a mirror with only a little ripple to break its plain. They were all hungry, thirsty, and extremely exhausted from the torrential harsh beating they all endured during the prolonged night. There was not the least sign of a boat, a ship, or anything of any size anywhere out there to be seen, not even an outcropping of land, or a desolate volcano peak sticking up out the horizon above the sea anywhere.

They were definitely all alone out there, wherever there was.

CHAPTER SIXTY-ONE

The Capsule

Miraculously the only thing they could see sticking up out of the water was this steel round bottomed belled looking buoy with an orange rubber raft affixed to its outer circumference so to keep it from sinking to the bottom of the sea.

It was the bottom of their abandoned space capsule, and was truly a miracle it had made it through the night and had not sunk in the middle of the storm. They were glad it had not come crashing down on them during the worst of the storm as it would have killed them all. If they could get the capsule to float upright the way it was supposed to float, maybe they could use it for shelter from the blazing hot sun. It might also protect them as well from the other half of the raging storm they knew they would soon have to face again when it came their way.

They sat there in the storms middle watching the huge eye of the storm with its flotilla of clouds swirling around them as a militia naval convoy encircling them within its most inner circumference. Food, water, and a protective canopy for the raft was all locked away in a locker beneath the water inside the space capsule. In their hurried time to escape their sinking space capsule, they left behind these necessary items, not realizing the necessity of them until after reaching the surface. Going back down to retrieve them at that time in their desperate time of departure from the craft was ludicrous. It was a true miracle that any of the crew were still alive after spending such a frightful night and beating out on the open sea in a hurricane in an open rubber raft filling with water most the time. Never mind diving back down into a rough sea to enter a steel coffin bobbing ready to sink to the bottom of the sea at any given moment. It was time to see if any of the survival supplies had weathered the storm locked in their compartments in the upside down capsule.

Squid, both large and small, were floating everywhere the naked eye could see. There were so many of them that they looked like a huge blanket covering the surface of the sea all around them.

The crew welcomed the warmth of the water at the top of the ocean surface. If they had drifted much further toward the north northeast and had the storm hit them there, they could have died from hypothermia from the cold of the water that inundated them most all the night. They would have become too weak to fight for their lives.

Ludwitz volunteered to swim through the littered up water covered with the thick layer of slimy corpses of squid to the capsule's entry port, and then tie the tether line to one of the craft's two metal tie-down hoops so they might pull themselves over to it for some security. He had about five feet left to go when the length of the tether line attached to him ran out of length. "I need five more feet of rope," he yelled out to the others in the raft.

Chenco and Dominique both instantly slid down into the slimy water behind the raft, and they both began kicking with all their might to push the raft toward the capsule and Ludwitz. In the raft, Krista and Gina began using their hands as paddles, splashing at the water of the sea with all their might to move the raft forward toward the space module.

Ludwitz felt an object of some kind bump up against his legs. It felt like a floating oxygen bottle or one of the protective flight suit helmets they all wore during their flight or something hard like that beneath the water's surface. After mustering enough rope, he immediately crawled up out the water and onto the bottom of the floating space module without any time to spare. An enormous grayish black colored shark of some kind came careening up out from the far depths of the sea behind

him with its rows of ragged teeth showing bright and chomping at the air beside the module. Ludwitz heart went instantly up into his throat as he yelled out to the others still kicking hard. "Sharks!' Get the hell out of the water," yelled out Ludwitz in fear to the ones on the raft and ones still in the water. Dominique and Chenco both scurried out of the water as fast they both could move with some help from Krista and Gina. The two girls had taken their paddling hands out of the water as soon as they heard Ludwitz yell out.

The surface of the water around them almost instantly came alive with hundreds of hungry chomping sharks of all sizes swimming all about the surface everywhere their eyes could see. The splashing of the girls' hands in the raft and the hard kicking of everyone's feet in the water both behind the raft in the water and Ludwitz kicking his feet while swimming toward the capsule must have attracted the many sharks from the far off depths of the sea below. The hard noise of their hands and feet splashing must have sent a signal to the sharks below that there was food up above them for the taking. They were ready for the feast of flippers and bodies of seals, sea lions, walruses, or whatever it was that was causing all the ruckus on the surface of the water.

Ludwitz pulled as hard he could on the slimy tethered towline tied between him and the rubber raft, twisting it around his hands to grip it. The three girls in the raft screamed out in panic as the multitude of sharks were dragging their large dorsal fins up along the bottom of their rubber raft. The fins were pushing the soft rubber of the raft up against their bare feet and their undersides as they sat on the bottom of it. Shark fin after shark fin rapidly appeared out on the surface of the water. Multitudes of hungry sharks everywhere were devouring the dead squid floating loosely on the water's surface. An eating frenzy erupted all over the place surrounding the raft. All they could do now was to hope and pray none of the sharks' fins or teeth would puncture a whole in the bottom of their raft and all would become part of this crazy eating frenzy.

Ludwitz helped to keep a taught line on the tether line so it stayed up and out of the water most the time as he pulled the raft toward the module all by himself. He was exhausted when he finally got the raft pulled up alongside the overturned module. He helped everyone out of the raft and up onto the bottom of the space module.

They carefully pulled Sebastian up out of the raft and laid him down placing his head gently into Krista's lap again for her to watch over him. He was breathing normally but not responding to any one's voice or the water that had been splashing over him all night long. He must be in some kind of a coma they all thought or pretending to be fast asleep and not wanting to know what was going on around them, but they all knew better.

It seemed like the sharks eating frenzy went on for hours. How could there be so many sharks in one lousy place in the vast sea, everyone wondered. It looked more like a huge family reunion of sharks from around the entire world that someone had invited to join in this picnic feast of squid and fish, and they all had come. The thousands of dead floating squid seemed to be the sharks' appetizers, and their main choice of meal for all seemed partial to the dead or almost dead squid floating everywhere.

The crew worried while sitting on top the bottom of the module. They hoped these sharks were not going to be fancying one of them on their dessert menu. The scorching rays from the hot day's sun beat down on them relentlessly. They managed to pull their life raft up out of the water. They used it best they could for shade to shield and protect themselves from being burnt to death by the hot sun. Their bodies began to dehydrate from the lack of fresh water to drink, all hoping there was still precious water and food available down below in the module. At this time they were unable to get to it if there was any with the frenzy of sharks swimming all around them. No one dared to risk their life diving into a food bowl for the sharks to feast on by trying to retrieve anything from the module.

As the day slowly progressed, so did the approaching clouds of the storm. The center of the eye of the storm was moving away from them now, leaving them closer and closer to its most southern side. The quiet mirrored image upon the water's surface started to ripple more and more as the much larger waves could be seen churning off in the far distance coming closer and closer toward them.

The sharks had all but disappeared now and were full of dead squid, they thought, because the surface of the water was still quite messy with them, and a shark's fin hadn't been seen in quite some time. Maybe they were just waiting patiently for their dessert of one of the space crew to finish off their grand meal they had just finished devouring for themselves. Even though they looked as if they were all gone did not make anyone on the module feel any the safer for it.

The task of trying to maintain each other secure upon the bottom of the slippery module had become a real chore for the most part. The bottom of the module had become as smooth as glass upon reentry. The immensity of the heat applied to the tiled bottom of the craft had turned everything ice slippery smooth like glass, and to make things ever the more worse, the craft's bottom was more slippery with the slick coating of salty seawater along with the slippery slimy squid residue. They were all getting extremely tired of slipping and sliding, trying to stay alive on the curved round bottom of the space module that had brought them all back to this nightmare from hell they were all going through.

In just over an hour or maybe two, the awareness from the ravaged experience they endured the previous night, they were going to be plummeted back into it once again. Were they ready to be beat on by its mad force and cruelty one more time? This time being so tired and worn out from the heat of the hot sun and lack of sleep, something devastating was going to happen to one if not more of them during the next bout with the mad sea and its wicked forces.

Everyone looked at one another not saying a word about what their faces reflected, but each had the same thoughts about their dire situation. Everyone knew Sebastian would probably be the first to die and anybody's guess which of the other crew would go next. They just knew some one or more of them were going to die this next night as the night before was a miracle that none had died.

The water around them continued to become more aggressive with every passing moment. This really confirmed their worries. No one would survive trying to cling to the bottom of this slippery module seeing no one could hardly stay up on its glassy smoothness when the water was mostly calm. Would the beating they were about to experience a second time be as severe on the backside of the storm's eye as it had been on the forward side? They all hoped not, but knew it was going to be no picnic as it was not the last time.

The six mentally suspected not all would survive a second time around this time. The severe punishment they had all gone through the night before had exhausted them to the mere point of just giving up and letting whatever happens happen. If they were swept off the raft to die, then so be it, and goodbye to this miserable place called Earth.

Sebastian began to moan and groan and went instantly into convulsions. He began thrashing back and forth with his arms flailing out wildly in all directions. He began slapping out at anything and everyone one within arm's reach. He gasped for air to breath as his tongue slipped and curled back disappearing into the depths of his throat and trying to block his airway. Krista jumped in fear at first not knowing what was going on with him, and then tried to keep his head from falling off her lap and letting it hit the hard surface of the space module. Chenco put his fingers into Sebastian's mouth pulling his curled up tongue forward so he would not die from lack of air by suffocation. Chenco let out a blood-curtailing scream as Sebastian clamped his jaw down tight around Chenco's fingers, driving his teeth deep down into the flesh of his fingers.

Blood from Chenco's fingers oozed out of Sebastian's mouth, as the flesh of Chenco's fingers was severally punctured. He endured the pain so his friend would not die from suffocation, and left his throbbing fingers in Sebastian's mouth as a tongue depressor so his friend and comrade could breathe. After a couple grueling minutes, Sebastian quit his thrashing around and relaxed back down into the quietness of relaxation. He let go of Chenco's finger as he opened his eyes with them rolling around as if they were in a swirling saucepan and began to vomit. He had had an acute concussion with a large golf ball sized hematoma that had developed just above his left ear.

The increasing waves were becoming less than friendly as the first soft rolling waves of the storm and the darkness of night would soon be upon them again. They would all have to abandon their floating island of steel very soon. They needed to take refuge back inside the rubber raft knowing none could survive the night upon the capsule without a means of connecting themselves to it somehow. With the possibility it might sink this time around, it would take everyone down with it if they stayed. It was not worth the risk. They lowered the rubber raft back down onto the unstable rolling sea and carefully lowered Sebastian back down into it. He continued to moan and groan constantly, but would not or was not able wake up or come to from his unconsciousness.

Chenco was the last one to enter the raft as the wind blew harder and harder. The waves around began to swell and build significantly. Both the raft and the space module rose and fell in unison on the surface of the rolling sea. They would soon have to get far enough away from their floating island of steel so it would not cause them any harm during the night which was coming soon.

Chenco, being the highest-ranking officer in charge, was going to dive down to try and retrieve whatever supplies he could from within the overturned capsule. The fingers on his hand were a mess and still oozing blood from the gashes from Sebastian's sharp teeth, and a trickle of blood occasionally dripped off his fingertips every once in a while.

Gina begged him not to go, but he would not have it any other way. He was the highest-ranking officer onboard, and it was his duty to care for the ones under his control. "Think of the twins, Chenco, and you're bleeding fingers. Don't you have any common sense left at all?" Gina yelled out with fear in her voice for her husband.

"I am thinking of the twins and of you, Gina. You damn well need the food and the water for them as well as yourself to survive, and I am going to get it for you and the rest of us. We need the canopy from the module to cover the raft tonight and from the sun tomorrow. I don't know how we survived the storm out here last night; and without it, we will surely never see another sunrise ever again."

"Please, Chenco, the twins and I will be all right. Tomorrow we can get the supplies from the module." "I have made up my mind. Without any volunteers, it is my solemn duty to supply us with whatever supplies I can get today. Tomorrow will be too late."

"I will volunteer, Chenco," Ludwitz said. "I will retrieve whatever I can from the module if there is anything left in there to retrieve." Ludwitz put his head down over the side of the raft first, just barely beneath the surface of the water to look for lurking danger. With both eyes wide open and burning like hell from the salt water, he quickly looked both left then right. He looked forward and then behind them and then straight down toward the bottom of the sea. He was not able to see any sharks. He lifted his head back out of the water, and taking a deep breath of fresh air, took the cable towline behind him as he slid over the side of the raft on his belly into the water headfirst seeking out the opening to the capsule's hatch. He had to swim down and halfway around to the opposite side of the module before reaching the opening. He was running out of the breath of air he had taken to stay down much longer. Getting ready to swim in through the module's open hatch, Ludwitz pulled his head back with great fear for himself. His heart instantly began pumping adrenalin throughout his nervous veins as the inside the module floated a huge head of a fish gawking back at him with its eyes and mouth wide open. Ludwitz thought at first it was a huge hungry shark ready to attack him. It would have been too late to try to have escaped from it if it had been. He relaxed a little when it did not move. He recognized the lonely head of a very large Pope fish that had lost its body to the sharks during their eating frenzy. It must have taken place while the sharks were busy feasting on the many dead squid in the area.

His lungs were hurting and screaming for air. He pushed the bodyless head aside out of his way and entered the module in hopes that there was an air pocket still within it somewhere so he might catch a breath of air to keep on going, and there was. It was not much of an air pocket, but just enough to keep his lungs from bursting or collapsing so he might attempt to retrieve some very desperately needed provisions for their survival at sea. Ludwitz grabbed an almost empty oxygen bottle floating in the capsule, and turned the valve open. The bottle hissed some very much needed oxygen from itself, and he took another two great big breaths of air.

He busied himself by releasing the survival supplies from their storage bins beneath all the seats. A duffel bag full of sea rations was still intact and fell down to him when he released the latch to the first seat above him. He released another bin, and the other survival kit fell to him without the tarp in it to protect them from the torrent elements, but it did contain other important supplies for their survival at sea. He took a couple of the flight suits that had not washed out during the storm along with two flight helmets, and tied them to the tethered line. Two other compartments had come open during the storm, and their contents must have slipped out the open hatch during the turbulent seas. One of them must have contained the rubber raft protective tarp, needed to cover them up from the killer rays of the hot sun.

Ludwitz took another deep breath of air, bent down, and looked out of the capsule hatch to see a school of sharks swimming not far off to the right of the module. Chenco's bitten fingers must have dripped enough blood to attract the damn scavenger beasts to the area again, he thought. He pushed the Pope fish's head out the hatch, and the man eaters attacked it vigorously.

He didn't know what to do next. He couldn't stay hidden inside the module much longer for there was little air left for him to breathe. He couldn't go out of the hatch as he would surely be attacked by the sharks and be eaten alive or bitten and die anyway. What was he to do to escape the horrendous situation he was facing? He did not really have many choices, but to face the beasts and make a desperate swim for the top, and get into the raft as quickly as he could without them eating him alive.

He pushed the tethered supply satchels, helmets, and two flight suits out the door except for one flight suit left behind. He knotted the bottom leg openings of the flight suit and arms shut with knots, and then zipped up the front of the spacesuit. He then took the almost empty oxygen bottle sticking both out the hatch, placed the almost empty oxygen bottle into the flight suit's neck, and opened up the oxygen bottle's valve full force.

The flight suit instantly filled up with air making it a buoyant balloon. He let go of the oxygen bottle as he and the inflated flight suit shot to the surface of the water in a hurry. He swam quickly towards the raft ten feet away yelling "sharks" as he swam. Chenco and Dominique both reached out with their hands and arms to help Ludwitz back into the raft. As they both pulled at him from above, some thing or somethings were on the other end of him pulling him back down into the depths of the sea. His face turned from a dire look of concern to a horrid grimace of instant pain. Whatever it was that had tugged at him suddenly let him go, as both Dominique and Chenco pulled Ludwitz up into the raft, screaming with pain. He was bleeding profusely from several deep lacerations from a shark bite with razor sharp teeth had made on his leg.

He was lucky it had only been one of the many sharks in the water that attacked him, and not several of them all at the same time. Dominique and Chenco would not have been able to keep hold of him if they had, and he would have been lost to the scavengers of the deep for good.

Dominique pulled as hard she could on the tethered supply line to retrieve the survival supplies attached to it. Chenco pulled his shirt off and tore it up trying to slow down the bleeding with a tourniquet he made and applied to Ludwitz leg from it. Dominique felt several tugs on the tethered line as she tried to pull it in. The sharks bellow were busy biting at everything that moved as Ludwitz blood was drifting in the currents below them. Everything was mostly intact as the two duffle bags had only minor damage afflicted to them.

The flight suits did not look damaged, but one of the flight suit helmets looked almost crushed flat as if it had gone through a steel vise with large teeth, and a couple of teeth were still attached to it.

Chenco grabbed the first aid kit from the first survival bag that contained band aids for minor cuts and bruises. It also contained a tube of salve, eye drops, but nothing to patch up these kinds of wounds Ludwitz' leg had on it. He grabbed for another kit from the duffle bag. That bag contained a single poncho and other things that were for someone who did not need immediate medical attention. He grabbed

another one in a hurry, and this particular bag contained a single sewing kit.

"I have to sew these damn wounds up, Ludwitz! I know this is going to hurt like hell, guy, but I have got to stop this intense bleeding of yours or you are going to bleed to death."

"Go ahead", Ludwitz, said, "sew like hell and get it over with quickly. It cannot hurt one hell of a lot more than it does right now."

The salt water burned in his wounds like a blow torch. The sea was becoming angrier by the minute with every passing second it seemed, as Chenco hastily prepared for suturing. The ocean's waves were growing in size as everything around them was again turning into the nightmare they had just gone through the night before.

Dominique held Ludwitz' leg as still as she possibly could for Chenco to sew it up with regular clothing thread and needle as the rubber raft floated up one side of a wave, and slide down its backside. Chenco was doing the best he could with the unsteady movement of the raft. He was trying not to hurt Ludwitz any more than necessary with every stitch he took, as Ludwitz slightly moaned with every prick of the needle, but didn't yell out in pain like before because he knew he needed the needle work to be done on him or he would surely die from bleeding to death.

The sharks below must have known there was free-flowing blood in the raft above them because they continued to come up under it and drag their dorsal fins against the bottom of the raft and bump up into it with their strong pointed noses. Everyone in the raft expected at any given moment that a shark's head would come tearing up through the bottom of the rubber raft and take them one by one down below for lunch or dessert.

Chenco ran out of the sewing thread he was using in order to sew up the remainder of the open wounds on Ludwitz' leg. The long strenuous time of sewing up his leg had passed, and the time of day was quickly fading away into the darkness of night for Ludwitz. They had not finished sewing him up when they ran out of thread to stop the bleeding. Chenco quickly wrapped the rest of Ludwitz' torn leg with his own torn blood drenched shirt, and hoped that it would be enough

along with the salt water splashing in and around inside the raft to stop the remaining bleeding.

Not one brave soul sitting in the half-filled raft with water dared to bail any of the excess water out which had found its way into the raft. They were afraid that the residual blood in the water would attract the sharks. They would all be in danger of losing their lives to another eating frenzy should they contaminate the water around them with Chenco's blood should they decide to attack the raft.

Krista took the sharp shears from the sewing kit, and cut the top off one of the flight suits for Chenco to wear to protect himself the next day. She knew the next day's sun rays would cook him even crispier than his fair skin had already been cooked if they all be lucky enough to make it through another night from hell, like the night before that they had just gone through! They could hear the sounds of the huge horrid waves approaching again. The rain again began to come down on them in torrents by the bucket full, as it left them no choice but to bail out the excess water from the raft or sink down barely into the unfriendly waters just below the water's surface where the sharks would surely get to them.

Ludwitz's leg stopped bleeding at last. Poor Sebastian though was still in his coma state moaning and groaning constantly driving poor Krista and the rest of them insane. It upset her by not being able to help him more than to just hold his head up out of the deep waters in the raft, and try to comfort him as best she possibly could while holding his head up tight against her bosom.

CHAPTER SIXTY-TWO

The Gargantua 1ˢᵗ Wave

In the far off distance, the sound of huge waves began sounding closer like the mighty surf at high tide during a storm along a rocky coastline. The sounds of the waves grew more enraged with the passing of time as the inner outer circle of the storm approached the little rubber speck of a raft quivering upon its back in the open water.

Chenco could see the white of foam frothing from the first of the massive huge waves rolling in at them at a height greater than fifty feet in height, he thought. He yelled for everyone to prepare for the worst wave yet, as this was going to be the worst wave of all waves that would hit the raft. This was a rogue wave of massive height, he thought. The wave looked more like a huge tsunami tidal wave coming toward them in the dim light like the big wave shown in the movie "The Poseidon Adventure" with its peak licking at the sky above compared to the powerful big waves that frequently hit them during the storm the night before.

With it about to hit them, everyone took their same old trusty positions over the ones that needed protection the most. They braced for the worse, as this was definitely the worst wave that was going to hit them, and they all thought they were surely going to die from it. Everyone took his and her place in the center of the raft for the best of everyone's protection, if there was any.

Dominique being built so small in frame, thought for sure she was going to be about as useless as worn out tires on a race car in this task, but hunkered down just the same with Chenco preparing for the punishment coming right along with her fearless leader to protect the meek from the approaching menace. The first big wave to hit the raft was like the huge tidal wave Chenco had claimed it to be, as it came in over the top of them like a fly swatter. It was as he said it would be. It was nothing like any of the other waves from the same storm the night before.

The raft first went up the shank of the huge wave when suddenly to everyone's surprise, the raft shot down sideways and under the massive wave like a surfer trying to catch a ride at the bottom of a humongous wave and barrel roll through it as a cannonball roll. Instead of the raft riding the wave like a surfboard, the wave caught ahold of the rubber raft in midair grasping hold of the front portion of the raft. The wave instantly folded the front up tight over the rear half of the raft giving it a sandwiched effect, and almost threw those standing or kneeling in its middle out of the raft, but did not. It instantly sandwiched over the top of everyone in the raft as if in a big rubber bubbled sandwich. The wave instantly submerged the raft and its occupants beneath the torrent surface of the moving waters over it. It was turned over and over and over beneath the massive rushing waters. The force of the water's pressure compressed everyone inside together like sardines in a small can as it tumbled them like a top spinning the raft beneath its surface.

The massive pressure of the huge amount of water that surrounded them was almost unbearable for everyone trapped inside the sandwiched raft to withstand the compression being forced thirty or forty feet beneath the water's surface on them. Trapped motionless inside the rolling raft, no one was able to move or breathe for a couple of minutes.

While submerged for the short time, instant thoughts about sudden death quickly encompassed them all and passed around in everyone's distressing minds, except for Sebastian. Plummeted around beneath the water in the huge rolling wave tossing them and spinning them around speedily as if they were inside a flight simulator, but they were not able to breathe with no oxygen mask to benefit them. They all thought for sure that they were all about to die. They would become shark food and fish bait within the next several minutes or less.

The locked air caught within the baffles of the raft shot them to the surface atop the ocean like a sperm whale coming up out the water to empty its blowhole for a breath of fresh air. The raft shot skyward up out of the sea. It shot them high up into the stormy air, and then slammed them back down hard against the firm surface of the rolling sea. The raft flew open when it first came out of the water before settling back down onto the surface of the rough sea. The raft was still in great shape as if nothing at all had happened to it except for the six-trapped passengers held as prisoner inside.

The crew of the raft came down in a heap. Luckily no one flew out of the raft as none would have survived if caught under the huge wave all by themselves. They were lucky the raft opened up in midair the way it did because if it had opened up in any other way than it had, there would have had to have some been a serious rescue mission performed by someone to save the life of the one thrown out to the death-seeking sea. Not one in the raft was seriously hurt in this strange freak action of nature.

Everyone was just a little bruised from the involvement in the incident. Chenco instantly checked on Gina, Krista checked on Sebastian and Ludwitz. They all seemed all right or at least said they were, except for Sebastian. Chenco put his face down to Sebastian's mouth, finding that he was still breathing, and then Sebastian moaned out a loud groan into Chenco's ear. He was at least alive, but in great need of immediate medical attention as soon as possible along with Ludwitz and the two girls to be checked on for their unborn babies to make sure everything was still all right with everyone for what they had just gone through again.

The total dark of night was just about upon them now, and they knew like the night before, the sea was not going to be a nice place to be during this horrifying hurricane. If only they could hold out and survive one more trip through the torrent gates of hell, they might, just might, stand a slim chance to be saved by someone. It might be a slim chance at that, but at least it was a chance to hold onto and to fight for their lives.

Gina thought for sure the southerly side of the storm would be the weaker side of it. The other side of this storm if it were the southerly side, sure seemed to be the worst side yet, or was this the southerly side of the storm? The side of the storm they had already gone through, made this side of the storm seem worse to them, or were they just worn out from the first half?

Hour after long exhausting hour, wave after huge pounding wave, these six cosmonauts braced with one another against the elements of the ferocious tempest of pounding and pelting rain and furry placed upon them. They held onto each other with all their might for support, not wanting to lose anyone overboard, for whoever went missing out of the raft that night would surely stay lost forever. Everyone had all they could barely do to hang onto to their precious lives, as the torrents of waves continually attacked them, pounding them all down into frail little hunks of lost soaked souls of lifeless almost dead meat. The life raft should have ruptured long ago in the night from all the severe pounding it was taking from the people inside it twisting and turning their weary feet, just trying to brace themselves against the floor of it and its sidewalls of flexible rubber in order not be thrown out of the raft.

All six of the crew members should have all been broken down by now and dead, but somehow they all, including Sebastian, had managed to miraculously hold on to life and stay within the raft with arms and legs intertwined. It seemed to them that they would take a breath of air between raindrops and a lot of water in their mouths and nostrils, but somehow managed to get enough air to survive during each bout with the next huge wave.

To fight for life instills great strength in their mind and courage in their souls, enough to hang onto life in the most horrible of situations, even when Old King Neptune tries to beat the life out of you with his most ferocious of storms. No one in the raft including Sebastian not knowingly somehow wanted to give their lives up to this gargantuan storm from hell. Their want of life out weighted their fear of death, as everyone except the comatose one encouraged each other with each severe beating they took.

Krista held Sebastian's head to her breast with every crashing wave above them. She became his guardian angel, and would protect him throughout the night or until the sting of death took one or both of them away from each other. She kept thinking of her unborn child, holding tight the defenseless human being held tight in her arms along with the fragile life held precious in her womb. During the storm she had it in her heart to protect them both from this demon from hell.

She felt Gina, round as a beach ball pregnant with her twins, tirelessly trying to hold on and stay safe inside the raft. She fought hard against all odds not to become the first victim swept overboard out of the raft and sink into the depths of Davey-Jones's locker to her death. She looked exhausted, and just struggling to stay alive.

The raging storm threw everyone around and around in the raft all night long like swirling ice cubes in a bartender's mixing glass. No one could see one another after dark, but continued to talk and yell out to each other during the storm all night long, keeping tabs on each other during each attack of another wave, holding tight to whatever clothes, hands, feet, shoes, and sometimes even each other's hair, just to stay alive. Everyone was trying their very best to keep safe during the ravaging storm, no matter how bad it hurt them in the scary darkness.

Gina at times thought for sure she must have been a cave woman. There were times when someone in the raft would reach out in the dark grasping hold of her head by the hair to protect one another from being washed out the raft to their death. She could only imagine herself being dragged off to some unfriendly cave by a mad caveman holding a club in one hand and being dragged along by him in the other.

The heavy pelting rains and hard hail at times was strange for hurricanes. Finally the loud aggressive sounds of the huge large waves crashing down and coming at them, started to fade away slowly. The light of day began to break above them through the thick scattering clouds, as a spot or two of bright blue sky peeked its way down between the parting clouds of the mighty storm.

Why could the storm not have hit them during the light of day, they all wondered? In daylight, they could have prepared themselves much better for every huge wave that came rolling their way. Maybe they had been better off this way, so the dangers lurking in the night they could not see did not play upon their wondering minds. It may have played a real hard game against their psyche, if they had seen everything that was taking place around them, especially if it had been in the bright of daylight hours.

Not knowing what is taking place around one's self, whether in a horrific storm or in an apartment next door behind closed doors, sometimes is best unseen or not known about at all. If they had seen the giant lost empty oil barge drifting afloat all by itself during the storm that almost ran them over, they would have all jumped out of the security of their life raft, and tried to swim away from the beast and died in the huge surf of the angry sea. Sometimes things unseen during a storm are best out of one's sight and out of their minds in the dark of night. Strange noises that go thump in the middle of the night are noises best left alone and left up to the imagination to figure out their true cause.

Chenco thought for sure that he could hear the sound of water hammering hard up against the outer steel hull of an empty ship several times during the horrific stormy night, as did Dominique. Both strained their weary eyes until they hurt against the heavy pelting rains driven by the wind as they tried to search the area around them, looking as best they could into the storm for where the sound of the empty steel hull sound was coming from. In desperate search they looked for any light aboard a ship or a vessel that might be out there in the storm with them.

The slapping sound of water on a hollow steel hull seemed to be getting closer to them, as it sounded out several more times during the night, as they listened intently for another wave to come and hit them once again. The sound of the torrent waves coming at them, crashing hard up against this hollow sounding steel hull of the barge, was almost as good as sounding an alarm to the crew aboard the raft. It gave them fair warning that another wave was coming at them. They had no idea how lucky they really were because the barge took most of the fight out of the many harsh thrashing waves headed in their direction most of the night.

It was as if someone above had placed this huge barge, this fortress of steel, halfway through the night beside their raft to protect those trying to cling to a little ray of hope, in order to stay alive, as the barge bobbed up and down in front of them as a barrier.

The worst of the storm had passed by morning. The horizon over the earth's sea became very visible to them from the east with a brand new day dawning above them. Towards the north northeast, the horrendous stormy hurricane was leaving them in a huge massive circular cloudbank that stretched out for miles. To the west of them, the sky was clear, as was the sky to the south and south east was also clear as a bell. They had made it through yet another night of torture thrown at them by good Old Mother Nature herself. They were very glad the worst of it was over, or was it? Just because the sky was clear, didn't mean the sea would not become an aggressive field of menacing sharks again, putting their lives in danger one more time during an aggressive eating frenzy.

The dead squid were back along with hundreds of dead gutted fish lost from a fishing boat that were scattered all over the surface of the sea again like the day before. But there was no sign of a fishing vessel anywhere around to be seen. They didn't need another repeat from the day before as the bottom of their raft must be weaker now. They figured the seals of the raft would not withstand much more stress from a shark's dorsal fin, or was it that they couldn't stand the pressure of seeing more sharks.

Looking at one another with great big smiles, Gina started to laugh in hysterics and then began to cry out feverishly. She could not believe they had all rode out the night in the horrific storm and had come through the second half of the storm unscathed in just two days. Krista began to laugh wildly as well, and the raft echoed out in happy laughter for about ten long minutes as everyone aboard laughed in unison.

The storm left them hungry and thirsty from not eating or drinking any fresh water or food for the last two days. Chenco untied one of the tied up survival duffle bags from the tie down straps in the raft and passed a container full of fresh distilled water around to his wife Gina first, then to Krista who took a sip. They allowed Sebastian a try at sipping water, but he coughed it up instantly, so next the container went to Ludwitz. Chenco then gave the rest of the crew their turn at some of the refreshing liquid. Thank God, they had added extra nutrients to the containers at the space station. Someone special must have known this crew were going to end up in the brine of the sea or had guessed it and had added extra nutrients for a needy boost.

He next pulled out a container of sea rations from the strapped bag and proceeded to hand out to everyone a small snack from it to get their needed nutrients. In this position on Earth on top of the edge of the water, they could now see clearly how the world was round. They were like this tiny little germ sitting on top a basketball, looking out toward space. Never before on Earth had any of them ever experienced the significance of this sighting or feeling of how the earth's horizon was so round. This was a very different picture than flying in a jet or rocket above the globe. This was actually sitting on the smallest of positions on the surface where they could sense the massiveness of the globe and its true roundness. From outer space aboard the space station, they could see the roundness and beauty of the earth, but to sit here in the middle of its enormous ocean on this tiny rubber raft of no significance was to really see and feel the difference the location can make.

CHAPTER SIXTY-THREE

A New Day for Life

On the horizon in the far off distance, they saw a small black object like themselves bobbing up and down in the water. Could it be a ship coming their way, or was it just another raft like theirs floating up and down on the sea as they were? A short distance away to the rear of them was another object of orangey color, a piece of the rubber ring that once was the floatation device that had kept the capsule they came to Earth aboard afloat. Had they stayed with their capsule that night, they would have all surely died.

One of the horrendous noises they all had heard during the middle of the night was when the huge empty oil barge only yards away from them to their rear, rose up on one huge wave and came crashing down hard in the middle of the space module that suddenly drifted beneath it. It was a good thing that they had abandoned their space module when they did. If that first menacing wave of the storm had caught them on the bottom of the space module, they would not be sitting in the middle of anything at that moment. They would probably be beneath the sea if they managed to stay with it, and the oil barge would have surely done them all in.

Sebastian started to moan and groan again as the warmth of the sun beat down on them. He began to cough and gag for a split moment, and then opened his eyes wide as if he had just awoken from a good long night's sleep. "Where am I?" He questioned the others in the raft

394

around him. He did not remember a thing about the lottery contest, leaving the space station or anything else about the last several days' events. He could not image being back on Earth without remembering anything about how he had gotten there, and was now totally confused. All he did know was that he had this tremendous head ache along with a very stiff neck that hurt like hell when he tried to sit up and position himself away from Krista, especially with her husband looking at him as if he was taking advantage of her.

Chenco tried explaining to him what he and the others had gone through since leaving the safety of the space station a couple of days earlier. Sebastian could not believe what he was hearing that he was in a rubber raft out in the middle of an ocean, and thought for sure he was surely dreaming. He could not believe he was back on planet Earth, or fathom in his mind that he had gone through two different halves of a hurricane, and was now lost out at sea in a matter of less than forty-six hours. He thought for sure he was dreaming until he reached up and felt the large welt he had just above his left ear. It hurt like hell even more than if one pinched his or her arms to see if they were awake.

They showed Sebastian Ludwitz' leg and how Chenco had sewn up his shark attack tooth-torn leg with regular sewing threads, and then wrapped up what he could not sew with bandages made from his shirt. The sickening sight of the bandaged up leg wanted to make him vomit.

"How could all of this be happening to him", he thought out loud. Chenco handed him some water and told him to drink it very slowly for his own good. He still had a severe concussion and Chenco didn't know what consequences the sudden ingestion of water might do to his body and nervous system. Tipping the container of water up to drink from Chenco, his squinting eyes blocked out the bright sunlight became the size of large round silver dollars. He spotted a great number of sharks attacking the dead fish and squid scattered about the surface of the water. "Look at that", he yelled out. Turning their heads, Chenco, Dominique, and the rest of the crew watched as a large number of sharks started another feeding frenzy right there in front of them.

"Keep away from the outside rim of the raft," Chenco yelled out. We surely do not want to attract any unwelcome visitors aboard this raft, do we?

CHAPTER SIXTY-FOUR

The Long Wait

Several long nauseating days passed without them seeing the least sign of a ship, a small boat, an airplane, or an island of any kind sticking up out of the salty brine. Soon something would surely come along and rescue them they hoped as the life and death situation they were in aboard the raft was becoming more than just desperate. The food had all run out as had all the life supporting water they had. The tropical sun didn't care who was out of food or water on the open sea, as it continually beat down on them without mercy.

Everyone's skin was beginning to blister and crack from the intense heat of the tropical sun's hot ultraviolet rays. It was hard protecting everyone from the glare and strong rays as it reflected back up at them from off the water's surface and into their drying eyes. They were getting the rays from all directions from above and below.

Suddenly, Gina spotted the first living thing she had seen on Earth since landing in the ocean other than the million squid, sharks, and fish of the first and second days. It was hard seeing the seagull through the intense glare of the sun shining off the water. "Look! It is a seagull," she yelled out. She thought she could see a small seagull or other type of bird flying in the sky above the water off in the far off distance. Everyone looked in the direction to where she was staring, and pointing to see what she thought was a bird. Land and civilization could not be too far away she thought. Chenco didn't waste a minute of time and

quickly grabbed for the red flair distress signaling gun. He knew the object off in the far distance was not that of a bird, but the topmast or flag atop the bridge of a small boat or a ship. He pointed the flare gun in the direction of the tiny flag flapping in the air above the water and fired it off. The flag would pop up above the rolling waves of the sea and then disappear again back down beneath the horizon. Whatever it was, maybe a buoy above a hidden island from their position would rise up over the waves then fall back below them.

Excitedly, they all waited with great expectations in their hearts that there was other life out on the sea not too far away from them that might come and help save them from wasting away. They could see the top of the mast of a small boat sailing away from them as it hadn't seen their first distress call for help. The boat was sailing quickly past and away from them off in the far distance. They needed help immediately because one if not more would perish within the next forty-eight or less hours if not rescued soon.

Chenco figured it was now or never, and would give it one more futile try. He grabbed another signaling cartridge. He rammed it quickly down and into the throat of the chamber of the flair gun, and fired it off in the direction of the small flag atop the sailing vessel. He hollered out with all the might he had left in him in desperate anguish for someone on the tiny vessel to see their flair or at least hear his desperate call of plight.

"Damn it man! We are over here! What are you, damn it? Are you all blind?" Nothing happened as the mast of the small boat disappeared.

They again were being passed by, sitting in a very desperate time of need looking as if they were not going to make it back to land. They would die of thirst and starvation out on this mostly unoccupied ocean of an almost dead planet.

CHAPTER SIXTY-FIVE

A Tiny Sailboat

A white flair shot up from over the horizon from the direction the mast had disappeared. Chenco grabbed for another signaling flair from the emergency kit. He fired their last distress signaling flair they had up into the bright blue sky above them. The tip of the tiny mast reappeared above the horizon and grew in length as it sailed closer and closer toward them. Suddenly, the main sails of the craft appeared above the water and then so did the rest of the sailboat. Someone, thank God, had seen their distress signal for help and was now coming toward them to help, they prayed.

Gina screamed with excitement at seeing the boat coming toward them. She was becoming sick with fear as her body was becoming very sick from trying to keep her tiny twins alive in her womb without the help of much needed water and food. Krista was in the same situation, but not quite as desperate or in as much need of nourishment as was Gina.

Everyone on the raft had suddenly become overwhelmed with joy and excitement. It was a small sailboat, but it looked like the Queen Mary cruise-liner of hope to the very needy crew of the tiny space rescue raft. Sweet hope swelled in the hearts of everyone aboard the raft, especially Gina. She felt like she did years ago when her Papa came running after her to pick her up off the ground when she had fallen as a small child playing outside and learning how to ride her new bike. The mixed emotions brought forth by seeing the sailboat brought many different feelings into everyone's minds on the raft.

Pulling up alongside the life raft, they saw an attractive petite looking woman, guessing in her later fifties or early sixties, standing on the boat's deck. She was wearing a pair of dark sunglasses. She was a frosted blond haired person with gray mixing in, wearing a light blue bathing suit. She quickly threw the crew a tag line to secure the cosmonauts' life raft to their sailboat. On the aft of the sailboat stood an older looking gentleman, holding tight the large round helmed steering wheel for piloting their sailboat. He had mostly white hair of what they could see and was supporting a salt and pepper grayish mustache. On his chin, he sported a salt and pepper goatee, while wearing a red, white, and blue striped bathing suit. He had on very dark sunglasses and was wearing a duckbill captain's hat atop his head to protect him from the heat and rays of the sun.

He quickly released the sail tie down ringed ropes and let fall the main sails to the deck below so to allow their boat to drift on the rolling waters alongside them. He next scurried up the side rail of the sailboat's cabins landing short deck to help his wife with the crew of the raft.

"What in the hell are you doing down here" came the voice from the older looking man that had been at the helm steering the vessel. Boy, that voice sure did sound familiar to a couple of the ones in the raft. Taking off his hat and sunglasses, it was Commander Nelson Anderson from the Twitchel.

"Commander Anderson!" Chenco yelled out in pleasure, seeing him standing there on the deck.

"The one and only," he said, smiling back at them. "What in tar nation has happened up there? Why are you out here in the middle of this God- forsaken ocean, anyway? Has something drastic, something fatal happened to the space station?"

"Everything is fine aboard the space station, Commander, but we are starving and dying of thirst," said Gina out of concern for her new unborn babies. "We need food and water desperately, sir."

"Well come on aboard then young lady. Becky will fix you up with something to drink in no time. Becky went right to the galley and prepared to feed the hungry crew from the raft.

It was hard getting everyone out of the raft. Their legs and arms were extremely weak from going so long without any food or drink. Their experience of not walking or moving about in gravity made it all the harder for each of them to move gracefully around the swaying sailboat. It was a miracle at all that they had made it this far in the deprived condition they were all in, especially Sebastian. He was just barely holding onto life at all in his extremely weakened condition. He was still supporting a very large hematoma above his left ear. Ludwitz had lost so much blood, and didn't have enough food or water to help him reproduce more red blood cells to keep him alive. The others were hungry and thirsty, but not in as much danger of losing their lives as the others. Gina and Krista would make a quick turn around, but the two men were in for the long haul of getting better, if they could get better at all.

Commander Anderson, with great difficulty, managed to help move everyone from the raft to onboard his small vessel. He then helped bring Ludwitz down into the galley of his craft, and there made him as comfortable as possible on the narrow couch across from the dinette. His injured leg had become stiff as a board and needed medical attention as soon as possible or he might lose it.

Gina gulped at the water given her like she was going to drown herself in it. Becky told her to slow down and to take it easy drinking or she would waste it by throwing it all up. This would be a terrible waste of water as the sailboat only had a little water left onboard with every little drop now really counting. They would have to ration everything for a couple of days until they were able to sail on to Florida.

John began to tell the unbelievable story of their dreadful ordeal to Commander Anderson and his wife Becky. The two of them could not believe their ears or their eyes at first when they spotted the rubber raft adrift upon the water's surface. Commander Anderson knew right away where that special type of raft had come from. Now their ears were tentatively listening to a story of great survival about this very lucky crew.

What they had all gone through and endured since coming back to this mad earth! It was as if they were listening to a recorded fictional story from a bookstore someone had made up using their vivid imagination to write the book. Yet this story was a true story, and the words of truth were flowing out the mouths of the ones who had lived and experience the tale now, thanks to God, are still alive and able to tell their story to the world.

Commander Anderson explained to Chenco and the crew just how he and his wife Becky had ended up out in the Atlantic Ocean with them. They had been vacationed in Bermuda for a couple of weeks and were just getting ready to return to Florida when the storm hit.

It held them captive on their boat in a cove they were lucky enough to find on the north side of the island, to ride out the storm for a couple of long hard days themselves. If it had not been for the protective cove, they could have lost their boat and possibly their lives as well to this all-time record storm. As it turned out, the roughness of the storm tossed their craft up and down in the shallow cove. Sometimes the keel of their craft was hitting the bottom and causing a small separation in one of the internal keel ribs. They would have to be looked at when they returned to Florida. It did not cause their boat to be un-seaworthy, as long as another strong storm did not come along causing any greater damage to the hull before they returned to port in Florida to dry dock their vessel for repairs.

"I cannot believe the story you all are telling us!" Commander Anderson told the crew from the space station. "How could anyone endure what you six have gone through and made it out of that storm alive? Moreover, what the odds would be in us encountering one another in such a bizarre place as in the middle of the Atlantic Ocean? I just cannot believe it! I really cannot believe it could have ever happen." He was truly dumbfounded about the whole ordeal.

Colonel Anderson went on to tell the six survivors, the horrendous fate and ordeal that his crew and six passengers on the Twitchel had gone through on their return trip back to Earth, but in no way or comparison was it an ordeal such as theirs.

He was glad all had gone well for them, and when they go back to port, he would do whatever he possibly could do to help their space station family members in setting up a safe return home flight for them all. It might take an act of Congress, he said, but he was willing to do whatever he could possibly do to insure a safe return home for them, no matter if he had to pay for it himself.

They were now only a couple of days out from the coast of Florida, bearing in mind no more storms or difficult times with the commander's boat developed for their safe return back to the Florida coast line. He was in a hurry, and put a lot more stress on his weakened craft, trying to get them all closer to some very much needed medical attention for the malnourished, weather beaten, and one very weak shark-bitten crew member. Chenco, Dominique, and Krista, being pregnant, along with Colonel Anderson and his wife gave up their food and water for the less fortunate ones who needed it more than they did.

Gina was starting to experience minor labor pains, but she wasn't due to deliver the twins for at least another two or three months, according to her calculations. Krista in the meantime was not having trouble, but Sebastian's leg did not look the best in its swollen red-hot condition.

Medical attention was not close enough to suit him, and his leg throbbed severely with every beat of his heart.

CHAPTER SIXTY-SIX

The Watchful Eye in the Sky

Sitting at the main control station in the space laboratory, Commander Ivan had given orders for the remaining crewmembers to keep a continual twenty-four hour vigilant of monitoring the procedures of the space capsule and its journey back to Earth.

The reentry looked to be going well as the main parachutes opened up. They looked to be doing a fine job for the cosmonauts onboard. The crew aboard the space station all sighed a relief to see such a wonderful sight with all three huge parachutes holding the space module up below them.

Maybe their comrades would be able to convince the Americans to send them another mercy shuttle flight of food and supplies, and possibly take a few more lucky fellow astronauts back home with them on their return trip back to Earth. Time of rescue was of the essence for them, and Commander Ivan knew it. Whatever his fellow crewmembers aboard the capsule had to do, ask, beg or demand a mercy flight were now in the hands of his fellow cosmonauts. If they succeeded in this mission of mercy, God bless them, and if they did not, God bless them for trying.

As the space capsule fell toward the earth, it left a cloudy trail of hot burning steam behind it. When the capsule parachutes came out, the stream of hot gasses flashing off its hot bottom tiles immediately disappeared.

404

Commander Ivan knew by the way the capsule came to a sudden stop aloft drifting on the high jet stream of the earth's air currents, that the crew onboard the capsule were in some sort of trouble below. They were not going to land their craft on land at the Florida landing site that they first had picked out. They would definitely and eventually make it back to Earth, but where would they land was anybody's guess at the time. Would they land on the water of the sea or on the hardness of the land somewhere? It sure as hell looked to them like they were going to get pretty darn wet in the direction they were swiftly drifting.

If only Commander Khrushchev knew how wet they all were going to get, it would have given him nightmares for the next couple of nights. The capsule was speedily drifting along aloft stuck in the fast-moving wind currents of the earth's highest jet stream, heading north northeasterly out over the Atlantic Ocean.

The International Space Station zoomed out of sighting distance around the globe in its own speedy orbit before they could mark or plot a location where the capsule might have landed when they returned to where they last lost sight of the capsule.

It did not make any difference when they returned in their orbit from the dark side of the earth. They tried real hard to locate the module by looking down through their strong telescope. But to no avail, they just could not locate the capsule anywhere below. They must have drifted right into the outer-clouded ring of the large storm out over the Atlantic Ocean. If they had, he knew they were in serious trouble, but they could not have drifted that far, or could they have?

The next day, in the early morning hours, Commander Khrushchev was quickly called to the command post by his first lieutenant on post had spotted the capsule and crew. Some of them were on the life raft beside the orange ring of the overturned space module, as were some on the overturned unit itself.

The capsule was not supposed to overturn the way it did when landing. The floatation ring was supposed to maintain the module in an upright position when the craft landed in any water. What on Earth had gone wrong with their landing that had caused such a catastrophe

like that to happen? If only he had known the ordeal the crew had all gone through in their landing in the rough sea, and what a chore it was just to get out of the capsule, save their lives, and to get this far in their daring journey, he would have been truly flabbergasted.

The lucky or not so lucky lottery crew along with their overturned space capsule was sitting in the middle of a huge hurricane's eye below. It did not look very promising for them at this time. With the extended maximum strength of the powerful eye in the sky telescope, they could count every one of the cosmonauts to see just how many from the capsule had survived their first stormy night on Earth who were still safe in the raft or on the capsule.

It seemed from above that the cosmonauts were fine for the time being. Commander Khrushchev knew better. They were going to have to ride out one hell of a hellacious battle with good old Mother Nature's fury within the next few hours. It didn't look one bit good for them from where he could see their desperate situation. He couldn't believe they had all survived sitting on top of the overturned capsule with some in the raft all through the storm. It did not seem like a good choice for them to be making, and wondered why they had chosen to do such a foolish thing?

They saw them in the middle of the eye of the storm on its most inner circle of the storm's ring before the ring of menacing clouds began. Ivan could see the bottom of a ship afloat that looked as though it had unluckily overturned in the storm. Not far from the hull, he spotted a couple of empty life rafts adrift upon the churning waters, but there were no signs of any survivors in or around them.

Off to the lottery crews east southeast, he could see the huge hulk of a very large black looking oil barge freely drifting by itself, free of any towing vessel, and drifting all alone on the rolling waves of water not twenty miles or less from his fellow comrades. If only the crew of the space station knew what their friends had had to endure during the first night at sea, and to have been this fortunate enough to end up where they were now seemed impossible.

The crew aboard the space station would have all been in total shock at how anyone unless they were in the Special Forces and trained soldiers in very good healthy could have in anyway survived such an ordeal riding out a category six hurricane in a damn rubber raft without drowning. It was truly amazing that anyone down there was still alive, never mind all six of the crew!

Commander Khrushchev wished he now had postponed the damn request for the help mission and had put it off for at least another two or more days or even a week. Having seen the horrific storm off Africa's coastline several hundred miles east of the Florida coastline heading in a westerly north westerly direction.

He never thought the space module would never in a million years drift that far off course before touching down. The weather over the Florida landing zone at the time looked perfect when the capsule left the space station. It sure was pure hindsight, and too damn late to do anything about it now. There was absolutely nothing anyone onboard the space station could do now except pray for the unlucky comrades below who had really lost in winning the lucky lottery draw of life, instead of having won anything.

The following day, the raft and its survivors were located to the south west of the storm. All six crewmembers still aboard the flotation device somehow were going to make out all right after all. Just off to their north sat the bobbing barge, but no sign of the space module anywhere around them. It must have sunk during the harsh storm of the night, thinking it a damn good thing they had all abandoned it during the night, or they too could have come up missing.

In the next few days, several ships and sailboats had passed by the crew in their life raft just off to the north of it, while a couple passed off to the south of them. They seemed to be drifting along in an ocean current between the two shipping channels of the Atlantic Ocean.

If only there was any kind of radio communications still working down below on Earth, the lost raft could have been located and found by now with its radio transmitter beacon working in every space rescue raft had attached to it in order for the coastguard or any other naval military vessel to locate it. The radio communications man aboard the space station continued to broadcast the position of their friends raft below over and over all day long. They broadcasted their position all night long as well, hopefully wishing for someone down there would hear the desperate cries of help for their friends.

It didn't look very promising for the crew on the raft now, especially after the next couple of days out on the water cooking in the hot heat of the sun, unprotected from its rays. Everyone onboard the space station knew the crew below would be soon running out of all life support provisions of food and would desperately need water to survive.

Stone Deaf Ears

"International Space Station, calling NASA-ONE, over. International Space Station calling NASA-ONE, over, do you read me NASA-one, over? International Space Station calling NASA-ONE over, does anyone read me down there NASA?"

Silence fell over the radio messages like the closing of tomb doors behind coffins left in the silence of nothingness vaults for a future burial.

"NASA, international rescue team needed for life raft caught in middle of Atlantic Ocean, over. Six crewmembers in need of IMMEDIATE pick up, over! International rescue team needed A. S. A. P, for life raft victims, location heading north by northeasterly off Florida coastline, over, NASA!"

The many hundreds of radio messages they were sending were falling upon the thousands and thousands of dead silent radios around the earth. The electrical crystals needed the enhanced sound waves of the earth had been totally interrupted and silenced by the mammoth invasion of the neutrons spread worldwide.

There was no need for the space station's radio operators to try to send any type of messages, and they knew it. Everyone aboard the space station felt a need for it, a duty to try in any way possible they could to help their friends in this desperate need of help.

They, too, would soon need help, but their only thoughts about desperation were on their fellow friends and comrades below at that moment. For the next few days, the space station radio operators continued to broadcast the bearings and global positioning location of their friends drifting rafts whereabouts on the ocean's surface below to anyone who might hear their desperate plea for their needy friends.

The only ears hearing their calls were the many hundreds of communication satellites spinning around the earth in their own orbit right along with them, that also continually repeated the many pleading calls from them for help, over, and over again to the many silenced radio receptor towers below. The space station tried using Morse code in desperation to send pleading messages for their friends below. They repeatedly turned on and off the beacons around the space station as they passed overhead during the nighttime hours over all land, but no one responded back to any of their dire signals, not even from their Morse code.

CHAPTER SIXTY-EIGHT

The Seventh Day

On the seventh day of their observation, the assigned post officer in charge of the watch monitoring their comrades below observed a small sailboat crossing real close to the north of the life raft.

"Commander Ivan, there is a sailboat not far from the life raft, sir." Colonel Ivan took over the watch of the raft looking down through the eye in the sky, wanting to know what was happening to his friends below. Commander Ivan had all but given up hope for the poor souls adrift on the open sea. This was the miracle the crew needed to enable them to survive. The life raft and sailboat looked so damn close they had to have been within hollering distance from one another.

"Can't you see them? You sun's-of-bitches! Are you blind or what?" Commander Ivan was getting upset because the sailboat looked to be intentionally sailing by his fellow cosmonauts.

The Colonel was so damn mad at what he was seeing that he started jumping up and down floating in weightlessness while screaming out profanities at the sailboat, especially at its crew. "What the hell is the matter with all you down there? Are you all blind? Can you idiots not see them? The life raft is off to your port side for crying out loud. Come on damn it! They need you, you inconsiderate morons! Get your asses over there, now!

"YES, YES, YES." Shouted Commander Ivan as he spotted the sailboat coming about. "The sailboat has seen them," he shouted! The

whole crew in the control center screamed with joy, as the joyful sounds reverberated throughout the space station to everyone. The others in the space station came floatingly running to the control center quickly floating and grabbing hold of anything along the way they could to quickly get there. They wanted to see what all the happy hollering and joyful screaming was all about in there because they felt they knew and wanted to be a part of the rescue even if it was in their own minds in doing so. When the rafters were all safely onboard the sailboat, the crew on the space station screamed out in joyful jubilation. The once heavy burden of self-guilt they all felt had been lifted from everyone's shoulders.

The space station then passed out of visual contact again, as the space station zoomed away in its normal orbit around the earth for another orbit. The cosmonauts still kept a continual vigil upon their friends aboard the sailboat for the next couple of days, as they zoomed over Florida's east coast region of the Atlantic. They would bring up the power of the telescope just as they passed the halfway mark across the United States so they would be ready when they approached the eastern half of the country. They managed several minutes a day in their passes overhead during daylight time which enabled them to keep track of their friends below. Every second counted as far as they were concerned of what next was to happen to their friends.

They drifted in space having no idea if a rescue mission would ever be put together and come back to the space station for their rescue. They were glad and sad for themselves, but happy everyone below was safe and sound back home on Planet Earth once more, especially for Gina and Krista.

The space crew all felt quite sure that they would never see their homeland ever again. They took into account not seeing any activity at all taking shape on or around any of their own space-launching facilities back home in Russia. They really felt lost by not seeing the place around the Cape Canaveral launching site as well.

CHAPTER SIXTY-NINE

The Friendly Port of Call

Everyone's happy hearts were up in their throats aboard the small sailboat with a massive joy of relief in them as the sight of land came into view. This included Commander Anderson and his lovely wife, Becky. They were both happy for the six survivors they had just rescued from the deadly sting of the sea, especially Commander Anderson's happy attitude with his self-joy shared in with the six cosmonauts' lucky situation.

He still could not believe the odds of this particular situation ever happing to him or anyone else in the world. It was greater than one in a billion, a zillion, a bazillion, or whatever the highest number in odds was in the entire world that he would be the one to save his comrades from the sea. It could never ever happen again to anyone else on Earth, and he was very glad it had happened to him.

By just seeing the looks of happiness appear on everyone's faces when he and Becky pulled up alongside the raft was like looking at a child going to the zoo for the first time, and this thought alone made the commander's heart over-swell with joy. This feeling was even greater than when he and his crew first docked at the space station on their first rescue mission when everyone inside greeted his entire crew with wide open arms, smiles, and kisses, thinking someone cared enough about them who was willing to try to help save them.

The hoots, the hollers, the hugs of joy, even Ludwitz got up off the couch and hobbled along on his good leg to come topside above deck to witness and take into account the beauty of land, making everyone aboard feel relieved. They all screamed with joy so loud they sounded like foghorns of a ship lost in a fog bank, warning other ships they were in the immediate area. They were all so damn glad that they were in sight of good old terra firma Florida land at last. They all would now be able to get the much-needed medical services they so desperately needed, along with the special necessary food and water everyone needed, seeing they had run out of supplies again the day before. Who the hell cared anymore as they were all home safe now. This would be a new beginning for them all. They now could all return to all their old ways of life back home on Earth with all their families and friends back home in Russia, or could they? The way of living on Earth before had drastically changed, and they may never adjust to things the way they are now. It was still good to be back home on Earth again, or was it?

Were there any of their friends or their family still left alive on Earth to return back home to? Many of their loved ones along with many of their friends had long since perished from the surface of Earth that dreaded day or just shortly after the invasion of the Soviet neutron missiles that caused the frenzied reaction to all life on Earth.

Commander Anderson and Becky docked their sailboat just south of Cape Canaveral at the yacht club where he kept their sail boat, not far from where they now lived. Immediately, the rescued space crew were all rushed to the military hospital facilities at the base, and there were taken care of straight away. The salty seawater had helped preserved Ludwitz' leg from getting gangrenous, as physical therapy would be required to get him to be able to use it to walk once more.

The nylon sewing threads used by Chenco in his attempt to sew up the torn leg let the lacerations heal quite nicely, while some of Chenco's torn up shirt, the doctors had to remove surgically from the forming flesh intertwining with it where the leg's skin had started to use it in its healing process. He was lucky to be alive, and owed the most thanks to Chenco with his great sewing abilities, so the doctors said.

Gina had to be quickly rehydrated with a couple of intravenous units of fluids along with an antibiotic solution as an added precautionary measure, just to make sure everything would be all right with her and the twins she was carrying. Krista also had some intravenous units given to her along with antibodies to make sure she would do well in her fragile condition as well.

Sebastian underwent medical testing deep underground with electrical scanning units for the lump he had had on his head. Everything looked like it was getting back to normal for the present. He would have to return back to the hospital in a few days because of the clotting that had developed from the massive blow he took to his head and being knocked out for so long in a coma and having seizures when he first came around to being conscious again.

This concerned the doctors at the hospital, suggesting to Sebastian that he could still have some severe problems lurking in his head that needed more attention in the future, should they arise.

The remaining crew were all been given good bills of health, and were cleared to leave for home in Russia and Germany or stay within the United States to live, It would be their choice, whatever they wanted to do. The U.S. Government had given them all their choices, and would provide free transportation back to their native land of Russia if they so choose to return to it. It all depended upon them. In the meantime, they would all be put up in the military base-housing facilities, and await the good or bad news of loved ones from back home. Some would choose to stay if they had no one left to go back home to, while others would be more fortunate and would have at least one family member to return home to be with.

CHAPTER SEVENTY

The Last Shuttle of the Fleet

Commander Anderson went straightaway to the command center at the Kennedy Space Center deep beneath the surface of the cape's reconfigured space center. He contacted the Soviet Kremlin by way of a special underground wiring cabled system still capable in carrying a minimized amount of live current as long as it remained hidden beneath a certain depth in the earth or deep beneath the waters of the earth. The only insulators the wild neutrons around the planet's atmosphere would not or could not attack, as man found out the hard way with so many deaths in its many attempts.

The threat of war from electronically operated flying aircraft and accommodated rocketry was now a thing of the past. The world was probably a better place for it, for now the neutrons were in total control and governed almost everything in its atmosphere.

Commander Anderson held long conversations with the many Soviets now in charge who were desperately trying very hard to rebuild their devastated homeland. The big bang had hit them probably the hardest of all of the countries around the globe when the initial blast occurred.

The Russian's once superb space program was annihilated with their own big blast, losing every pilot capable of flying any type of space bound vehicle or aircraft for them.

They had no rockets readily built which could fly or the equipment to construct one. The only thing left of the Soviet Space Program were a couple of Soviet space modules still sitting in storage for future flights that would now surely never take place.

The fate of their remaining cosmonauts stranded in outer space they would leave up to another capable country in rescuing their cosmonauts because they were not capable of doing it themselves and would not try.

The new Soviet government wished they could help bring their fellow comrades home, but by no means were they capable of doing so now. When if possible they could put something together for a mission, it would definitely be too late for the crew above.

Commander Anderson in seeing they couldn't help in any other way than just wishing everyone good luck in rescuing their comrades, requested information pertaining to the crewmembers surviving families back in Russia for the six survivors who had just returned back home from the space station who were now resting comfortably at the cape's military hospital. Their kinfolk would like to know that their loved ones were back home safe and sound. The six cosmonauts back on Earth would like to know how their families were now doing back home in Russia. Seeing his last news he had brought with him to the space station was not very good for anyone several months ago, he hoped this new news would be more promising to the six now back on Earth.

The Kremlin would return his requested information as soon as they possible could, and thanked Commander Anderson for his attempt in trying to save their fellow astronauts from doom in his efforts to return them all back home safely.

Chenco stayed with Gina during her medical prenatal pregnancy physical examination, as did John with Krista. Gina's twins were doing exceptionally fine less the wear and tear on their mother, as they did not show any signs of trauma, so their birth should go well for her in the near future. Doctors recommended that Gina and Chenco stay in the United States until after the birth of their twins. This would afford the babies better chances in their survival and not risking them or her should any problems occur during the long journey of crossing the ocean. Not to mention the extended rough journey she would encounter getting back home in the back rough country of Russia where their relatives all lived, far from the city of Moscow.

Krista, on the other hand, passed her prenatal physical exam with excellence. Her healthy fetus of a strong-looking growing little boy was going to be a good football player, all the medics predicted. She and John were told they could venture back to their homeland at their earliest convenience or stay and live in the United States along with any of the crew who so chose to do so.

The requested information Commander Anderson received from the Kremlin was both good and severely bad. Sebastian's entire family of uncles, aunts, brothers, sisters, and grandparents, who mostly lived high up in the mountainous region in Russia in a small village, had all been laid to rest except for his father. He was the lucky one, or not so lucky one, having been away working when the blast occurred. His mother was one of the unlucky ones who was still alive back in the village who had been down in the root cellar getting food for the rest of the family, but who now had the mind of a three year old because of the high neutron count of the invasion in the region.

Chenco's family was also from a smaller village located within the same region as Sebastian's family. Drastically everyone in his entire family had vanished. There was absolutely no one left for him to go back home to. The only family he had left now was Gina and the twins to be.

Not one member in the entire space station's crew were without the pain of loss of a loved one; whether it be a mother, brother, sister, father, child, spouse, or relative of some sort.

The unprecedented missile invasion of neutrons on Earth's atmosphere left no family on the planet without heartache of a loved one or friend of some kind. Due to the greed of a small number of controlling want to be powerful greedy people of the world, living in a country full of wonderful caring beings. When Commander Anderson received the horrific information from Russia, he wanted to throw up from its most disturbing news. He had formed a strong family bond to Chenco, Sebastian, and the rest of the crew of the space station after having lived there among them for over a year, and felt a strong grieving feeling only a related family member could experience from such unbearable bad news.

He longed to help his fellow cosmonaut family in any way he possibly could, but not in being the bearer of sad news to them. He didn't want to be remembered this way, especially by the ones who helped save his life. He knew he had to tell his friends something, but he did not want to give them any of the bad news up front that he had just received from the Kremlin earlier that day. He didn't want to take away any hope that anyone might have in returning home to Russia to a life they had once so joyfully enjoyed in their youthful years. He would rather have his friends find out the bad news themselves when they returned back home to Russia and find out for themselves. He had a choice to make and knew whatever choice he made would be the wrong one now that he knew the real news of everyone's heartache.

His face showed great sympathy, apathy and apprehension when he spoke to his fellow cosmonaut friends later that day. Gina saw right through his deep feelings and emotions. She knew something of great significance was bearing heavily down on his kind mind, but that was all she could read in his troubled looking face. He was not his same old happy-go-lucky self today, and everyone around him could tell he was deeply troubled but unwilling to let go of the painful attacking alligator that was biting at his insides.

"What is it commander? What is wrong?" Gina said caringly searching. He had a way about him in turning his facial expressions of concern around and putting his outward appearance of concern toward a different friendly matter all of them together. He was good at covering up his emotions for the most part, and blamed this deep look of concern on the relief their fellow cosmonauts were not going to get from their own home country of Russia. Seems their country could not do a damn thing to help those lost in space or would not do a damn thing to help their friends aloft. He was not sure the United

States could or would send another dangerous shuttle mission skyward to help them out either. This was the look of despair he was wearing all over his face, and he was worried sick for his and their friends' welfare aloft, if nothing soon was to be done to help them!

He told them this little white lie to cover the looks of despair that covered his concerned looking face for them, but he had to tell them something about these damn concerns he was unable to hide that he had spread out all across his face. He knew right then and there as he was talking to them, that his government, the United States and their associates in NASA and from around the world, were coming together at that very moment in time to try to prepare another mission just for the purpose of saving the astronauts aloft. It would take another several days before the refitted shuttle could possibly be ready for launch if all went well.

He knew this would either be a mission to bring them all home, or some very unlucky souls would have to live out there until their elder years if they possibly lived that long within the space laboratory floating in an orbit of doom in space. Possibly burn up within it should the space station become entrapped in the earth's gravitational pull and be pulled back into the Earth's atmosphere, and burned up on reentry.

CHAPTER SEVENTY-ONE

Going Home

"We have a special military aircraft waiting and ready to take you all home tomorrow at 0800 hours at the adjoining airfield if you so choose to go. As you all know by now, and have witnessed things here on Earth around this globe of ours have changed significantly. We have made the best that we can out of a very difficult situation. Flying is very risky at times, as the "thing" in our atmosphere, all those wild neutrons, can snuff you out at the most unsuspecting moments in time.

We have lost a few aircraft since we started flying again, but we cannot tell if it is due to mechanical failure, pilot error, or that the life of the pilots flying these aircrafts had been snuffed out by this creature in our sky that dislikes anything invading its territory.

We are very limited in our hours of flight these days, as we can only fly during daylight hours, seeing we have no way of navigating in the darkness without electronics, lit up controls on our flight control panels, or lit up runways on the ground to land on. We especially do not fly during stormy weather if possible to do so, unless in a dire emergency condition.

Our flight engineers have designed and made up a hand-operated mechanical fuel injection system we use which allows the pilots to bring the multi-finned turbine jet engines up to full capacity in speed the same exact way the electrically operated flight systems we use to use did.

These new injectors are a little more mechanically cruel in nature, but they work quite well with our intended application for takeoff, flight, and in our landings.

The reverse thrusters on our aircraft, do not, and I repeat do not work as well as our pilots would like them to, so we need the entire length of our runways now to slow down and stop our aircraft.

I am certainly thankful that I had the opportunity to sail into your lives a second time in my lifetime. I'm glad I was able to offer my assistance a second time to you all for what you did for me and my crew of the Twitchel in our very desperate time of need in our lives. Listen up now! Sergeant Jones and Lieutenant August will be your own private limo drivers, your chauffeurs, for the remainder of your stay at the base. They will take you wherever you would like to go. Do not be afraid to use any of the services offered to you. Everything you want is on us, the people of the United States.

Do not be afraid to purchase whatever you desire in any one of the stores around to enhance your well-being, and remember to have a good time doing it."

The words flowing from Commander Anderson's mouth were like those of a well-prepared programmed computer talking while he was using his eyes to look into the eyes and souls of everyone who stood before him in the room. His own heart was bleeding in awful distressing pain for them as they were all his friends. He was intentionally withholding distressful life changing news form them and was having all that he could do in conveying the good news of the day while withholding the bad news, at least for now.

"I have to leave you all now and see if there is anything in this crazy world possible we can do for your fellow cosmonauts and Commander Khrushchev. Good day ladies and gentlemen." With saying that, Commander Anderson hastily turned with his eyes welling up with tears.

He felt self-betrayal of guilt in his heart that he had let his friends down by not telling them about their families, especially Chenco who had no one in the world left to go back home to. He felt like a little child about his actions, leaving the room weeping about his decision as he closed the door to the briefing room behind him leaving his friends and his other family from space.

Entering his outer office, Colonel Anderson informed his secretary, Linda, that he did not want to be disturbed for a little while. He went in and closed the door with a hurried push. She could tell by his awkward looks and hurried actions what he was going through, and would honor his request even if the president of the country, President Stallman, wanted to talk to him. Linda would put his life on hold for at least an hour or so because she had great respect for her boss, and would grant him his requested peace and tranquility to reorganize his self-esteem.

As he wiped away the tears from his eyes, he could not imagine where all these silly tears in his head were coming from. He had not felt this way in all his natural life. He had gone through losing several of his best friends in combat, even lost his grandparents to old age when he was small, and one to a heart attack, yet now he was crying. He was shedding tears for friends who were still alive. It didn't make any sense to him.

Was he crying for them, with them, or was he crying for himself? He did not really know why he was letting go now. After two long hours of emotional crying and feeling foolish from releasing all this built-up anger about the idiots who had caused this travesty to happen to the world in the first place, he felt much better about himself.

He again put on his old thinking cap, without his head filled with cobwebs and feeling guilty or shameful about his weak feeling toward himself or others. He had finally gone through the grieving process by letting go all the deaths in family and friends so he could go on being the same old reliable structure he had always been. Colonel Anderson felt greatly relieved by his final decision to not telling his dear friends about the slaughter of their families. The choice he made was right for the time being, anyway. The hurt and healing process would have to wait another day or two or maybe even longer for his friends. The ones who wanted to leave for home would do so the next morning, and he would see them off personally at the airstrip.

In the morning, Colonel Anderson met in the debriefing room, saying his goodbyes to the ones of the crew who chose to leave for home. He informed them about the new mission in progress being planned to save as many fellow crewmembers above still held prisoner aboard the space station as possible. With a little bit of luck and a lot of prayer, everyone aboard the ill-fated craft would return back to Earth on this last mission of mercy of his. If any chose to remain aboard the space station, they would be up there for the remainder of their lives.

This would be the last mission into space NASA was going to permit. The last of the shuttle fleet was now sitting in hanger number three, being outfitted for space travel as had been the Twitchel, and there were no more units left if something were to go wrong with this craft. The government was not all for this mission, but felt it was their duty to send this last mission because of what they had done for the crew of the Twitchel. This would definitely be the last mission sent into outer space.

Commander Anderson traveled on the bus with them down the base's airstrip where the jumbo Galaxy jet air-cargo aircraft was sitting ready for takeoff on the far end of the runway. It and its crew were ready to carry them back home to Russia. This particular aircraft was capable of carrying back the last two remaining soviet-made space modules with them to the United States in its huge cargo bay. The two modules would help in the rescue mission of the trapped cosmonauts stuck in the space station.

As soon as the modules from Russia were back and safely cradled aboard the shuttle in its cargo bay and the onboard hydrogen tanks and oxygen tanks filled, and the necessary electrolytes needed to charge the dry batteries aboard. The shuttle would be ready to shoot skyward for its final mission into space to rescue the remainder of the space station's personnel.

Colonel Anderson hugged everyone on the bus including the men before they boarded the air cargo aircraft as he bid them all a farewell. He watched as the huge jumbo jet revved up its four huge Continental engines, and taxied out onto the runway. The cargo jet shot off swiftly down the runway and into the early morning sky above. He had wished them all a safe flight home and a happy reunion with their families and friends when they all returned home to Moscow. He knew there would be some happy times and many sad times to be had by all.

He was glad they would be back home together with friends and family hopefully when the news of their losses was revealed to them, especially Sebastian with all of his losses. The only true family Sebastian had left in the world, even though they were not true blood relatives, was with him on that plane.

Colonel Anderson's only true wish for him was that Sebastian would soon find himself a wife, and that his family of cosmonauts would keep him well physically and mentally during his long transition of settling into this new way of life he was about to enter into. He would not recognize his simple-minded mother for whom she once was, and his father had passed away becoming yet another victim to the neutron masses when he had gone down the mountain to fetch some food and supplies for their home. His father was becoming fearful that he would lose his own mind trying to take care of his very sick wife, but he lost his life instead. Commander Anderson was sure of it. He had made the right choice this time by not telling any of the crew about the worst that had happened to family and friends. They would soon be in the country of their homeland and with people of their own kind who they could relate to better in this desperate time of need and a true soul searching experience.

He waved them off down the runway as the jumbo jet rose up into the clear morning sky above, and then it was gone. He returned on the bus with Gina and Chenco, the only two who chose not to return back home for the meantime to their temporary base housing unit. They were going to be staying there while Gina waited to deliver her little twins. It was going to be rough on Commander Nelson, but he was going to tell Chenco the bad news about his lost family when they returned to their temporary base housing apartment.

Commander Anderson felt it his true duty at this time, and Chenco would take it a whole hell of a lot better with Gina being there to console her husband. Sebastian at least had his mother to go back home to, even though the rest of his family was gone. But how would he take seeing the last of anyone he knew, who had raised him, acting like a child of a very young age?

Chenco had Gina and would have two little ones of his own running circles around him that would help keep him and his mind busy, hopefully helping in the healing process with his soon to be broken heart.

CHAPTER SEVENTY-TWO

The Last Flight to Space

Commander Anderson busily found himself rounding up the crew from his last mission aboard the Twitchel. This would be his last and final flight back into outer space, even though he had promised his wife, Becky, the last mission he commanded almost a year and few months ago would have been his last. Somehow Becky knew down deep in her heart, the second her husband recognized the six cosmonauts in the life raft as those being from the International Space Station, that there would definitely be yet another mission by her husband into space, God bless him, and he would be at the head of its controls.

Nelson was a good man, and would do anything to help another human being out, even if it meant losing his own life in trying to help whoever it might be in need of him. She knew it would not do her any good trying to reason with his kindness even if he had asked her permission in going to save his friends. She knew he would go against her denied permission and wishes anyway because of the caring man he was and for the many lives at stake. She could only wish him the best of luck in his quest, and for him to please come back home to her safe and sound. She loved him down to the last little strand of gray hair upon his aging balding head. Her hair was turning gray slowly. Not so much from old age that might have had a little to do with it, but mostly because of her husband's daring traits and his need to help others that were always in need of his help.

It was a bright early sunrise on another new Monday morning in time, when Commander Anderson knocked again on the front door of the quaint little farmhouse door in the Great Northeast Kingdom of Lunenburg, Vermont.

Ann was busy as usual preparing a healthy breakfast for her family, with her mother right alongside of her in the kitchen whilst her father answered the early morning knock at the door.

Her father could see the rays of sun beaming off the stern looking Commander's face, as the sun came rising up over the early morning horizon from the east. Her father, seeing Commander Anderson standing there, experienced an instant feeling of fear for his daughter develop in the pit of his stomach, that hit him like someone or something had just hit him hard in the groin with a baseball bat. If he did not have ulcers by now, he sure as hell felt like he had them when he opened up that damn door.

Commander Anderson said, "Good morning, Mr. Hamilton" to him, with a very firm sounding tone in his official sounding voice this time, not like before when he had asked for Ann.

"Good morning, Mr. Hamilton! Is your daughter Ann at home, sir?"

He knew damn well right she would be.

"Yes, sir, Colonel! She is in the kitchen with her mother, Dot, preparing our breakfast, thank you! Would you like to come in Colonel? The damn door is for you again, Ann! Commander Colonel Nelson Anderson is here to see you again, Ann!"

His voice was very jittery and loud when he called out to his daughter, and she could sense it in his trembling voice. Ann's usual morning happy-go-lucky smiling face of a very happy homemaker and mother suddenly turned sullenly stern like the granite rock of the "Old Man in the Mountain's" face. When she heard her father's voice echo out the name of Commander Anderson for you at the door again, it brought back the memory of the last time he had come to the farmhouse to visit, and that was not just to say hello then, and it sure as hell would not be just to say hello this time either.

She dropped the dishtowel she was using from her hand to the floor as she hurried out of the kitchen door to greet him at the front door. Memories from his last visit came rushing back into her mind as she stepped back in time for a reflected minute from the past. The sudden sick feeling she was experiencing that moment was as if she was a very small content peaceful little happy island out in the ocean in the direct path of this huge wake of an enormous tidal wave, a tsunami. There was nothing she could do to avoid being overtaken by its huge size and authority. It was a feeling like she was still in boot camp, and the instructor told the new trainees to jump off the so-called tower of death into the pool of water, and did it because of the authority the training instructors had over them. Colonel Anderson had that type of influence over her, and she was afraid she could never tell him no.

She had worked so rigorously on refitting herself into this new world and forgetting the past, and over the last year or so had had a very trying time to readjust herself back into the ways of this new way of life for her in this new world she had been so cruelly cast back into.

It was like being cast back in time, back into the dark ages of mankind and was just now starting to enjoy her every precious moments she shared with her children, her husband, Ben, and her mother and father as a family. She did not hate Colonel Anderson for who he was, but if she had never heard his name mentioned ever again in her lifetime, it would have been too soon. The mere mention of his name always brought back those lost moments without her precious children, and now it was too soon to hear his name mentioned again.

She was no longer dutifully bound to the United States Air force, or connected to NASA for that fact because her required contracted time of service to her country had long been expired. She was under no obligation to her country or anyone else except the obligation she had to help and protect her immediate family.

This person representing stringent authority standing at her door was an infringement upon her, and she did not like it one single bit. Tears rushed from her already swollen tear ducts after hearing his name mentioned. She wiped away the streaming flow of teardrops from her beautiful eyes with her apron. She picked up the spatula from the stove and whipped it into the sink halfway across the kitchen in total anger. She did not say or utter a damn word as she swiftly passed by her mother standing beside her, the children, and Ben sitting once happy at the kitchen table while they all were beginning to eat their early morning breakfast.

The look on Ann's face said it all, as did the changed looks on everyone else's stern-looking and frowning faces at the table, knowing damn well right what the early morning knock at the door meant to them all. It is funny how silence can say so much at times in one's life as this one did. Time stood still for a moment as she passed by her loving family members looking at each one of their very concerned eyes with theirs staring back at hers. With happy smiles on their faces, the children did not quite understand who this person was at the front door. They had felt quite content in having their mommy back home from outer space. They had their good old happy acting father back in the same old happy way he once was before the big bang occurred, and all was well living happily at their grandparents' farm. They had finally lost the fear they had once developed when at first their loving mother was so cruelly taken away from them for so long. The two were both cast into a life of turmoil into an unselected foster home not of their own making. Everything was as it was supposed to be now as a friendly family unit. They would not want it any other way, and if they had suspected by chance who was knocking at the door, their faces would have also been frowning with harsh looks of despair at their mother when she passed them in the room looking like she had just been stung by a whole bunch of angered bees.

It had been an extremely hard choice to make the last time, when she left her family the second time to return to space, and they were very cold to her again when she returned home from being gone only a few weeks. It had taken almost a whole year of the time from then till now to get their fullest confidence back that she would never leave them never again, and now came that damned dreaded knock at the front door she feared one day would come, wishing it would never happen.

Ann's mother had that caring motherly look spread wide all across her face with a slight bent smile looking very concerned what Ann would do to herself and them this time. Her mother still felt like Ann somehow felt she owed the remaining crewmembers aboard the ailing space station her life somehow, and would probably be gone for yet another spell of time on another mission of mercy. Ann was stubborn and would do whatever the hell she damn well pleased in suiting her own needs and those of others in need. Ben's look of instant fear, along with the anxiety in his loud vibrating very nervous voice, said it all. "What the hell does that man want from you now, Ann?" Ann didn't say a word. She just listened to the hot tempered words coming steam rolling from out his vibrating mouth, echoing out like an angry lion. He had a look of most deep concern imbedded in his deep old frowning wrinkled up face of total anguish. He had a similar look to the little boy's face who had adopted one of his dad's farm animals raised for meat for the family. A special little piglet for his own pet, and the day had come to have the now grown up pig to be slaughtered at the local butchers for meat for the freezer for the winter.

Ann closed her eyes and ears to her family as she quickly passed out the kitchen door and into the sitting room to meet her not so wanted guest at the front door this time. "Good morning, Commander. Would you like to have some breakfast with us?"

"That would be nice, Captain, thank you very much. At the farm this time Ann and her family were not as friendly toward him as they had once been on his last visit to Vermont.

Commander Anderson inquired how everything in life was going for her and her family living on the farm. He seemed very interested in what was taking place in the general public life outside military life on Earth for everyone these days. He was amazed at the progress Ben had made with all the old farm equipment that had been stored outback the barn, just left out there in the weather to rust when. The equipment was old, almost antique, but it did a fine job of running the farm again.

Ann had a very hard time explaining to Commander Anderson what the last several months back on the farm meant to her and how long it had taken her two little girls to readjust to her finally returning home to them. They both had been very skeptical about her presence most of the time this year. It was not until most recently that they had finally adjusted to her being there for them all of the time again, and how she had promised the two, including Ben, that she would never ever leave them ever again. She was sure that they would not ever get over a third time of their mother gone or Ben with her not being there for them. She felt in her heart that she would never return to them a third time. Just the very short few weeks away the last time caused such a drastic change in everyone toward her, she didn't think she could ever do that to the girls, Ben, or to her parents ever again, or to Ben, or to her parents.

"I sure hope, sir, this is just a social visit and not a demand that I return to active duty once again with you. I don't think I am quite ready for that kind of commitment just yet, and I know my family is not ready for it either. I can guarantee you that much, sir. So with all due respect, I do hope you are not here by the military or for the military to request my services again."

Ann had tears in her eyes as she spoke these words of truth to Colonel Anderson, almost begging him with her pleading eyes of mercy to reassure her that he was not there on a military request she could not possibly turn down or want to.

Colonel Anderson reassured Ann that he was there only on a personal note and not that of a military purpose. It was not a demand on her to return to the military or back to active duty or anything similar to that. This visit was just a friendly visit. "I am here as a friend, Ann, and that is all. I know you are no longer obligated to the armed forces in any way, and you have completed your tour of duty and your obligation to our country is well over. I am here to tell you about another mission I am about to undertake back to the International Space Station. This will be my last and final mission of my entire career. This will be my last grand pupa of all missions that I have had in order to help bring back all the cosmonauts aboard the space station. It is a mission of rescue and mercy to save all the lives still left up there in their lost orbit who are quickly running out of time to live, and will soon die. The Soviet Union, Ann, is not capable, they say, or are unable or very reluctant to help us out at this time. They are letting us use their only two Soviet-made space modules that they have stored away in mothballs to help us save their people. Rescue of the cosmonauts from the International Space Station is now been left up to the good people of our country to help you and me in saving our friends in space. We have the only capable rockets left to lift the last workable space shuttle to space and place it into orbit. We have the working knowledge and ability to reenergize its electrical power packs back to life which will enable us to have a very success mission this time. Without working electronics onboard, it would be truly impossible to send any other kind of recovery unit up there to the space station, other than through our existing space shuttle program. Yesterday morning, I left the airfield at Cape Canaveral after sending off several rescued crewmembers from the space module Commander Khrushchev sent back to Earth. He sent them back home to try and rescue his fellow Russians. There were nine of them on board all together." Ann wondered how nine cosmonauts could possibly fit into a module built for six.

"Six cosmonauts and three unborn space children, Ann," he said. What a story they will have to tell their children and children's children when they grow up."

He told the fairytale-sounding story about the rescue that he and his wife Becky made of the cosmonauts out at sea to Ann and her family. He was glad it was he and his wife who had found the Russians adrift on the sea and not some irate group of foreign sailors from another country who had lost loved ones to the big blast. They could have easily have taken out their wretchedness of grief and sorrow out on them, and blaming them for what had happened to the world around.

"There was almost as tragic an ending to their mission, as there was in their returning back home to Earth." He went on to explain to Ann and her family about the shark attack on Ludwitz leg, and how Chenco had to sew his torn apart leg back together using regular sewing thread, and some clothing. How Sebastian was knocked unconscious when they landed and unable to remember the hurricane or anything else about the horrid ordeal other than the last couple of days before their rescue. How if it wasn't for his wife Becky barely catching a glimpse of their distress flair for help, they would have probably all died out there all alone on the sea in a matter of a few more short days. He told how Commander Ivan gave up his lottery ticket so another life may be saved.

Ann could not believe all these parable fictitious sounding words coming out of Commander Anderson's mouth. The story sounded like a horrific tale right out of a science fiction writer's storybook portfolio of stories. Just like the neutron monster of the sky or the creature thing that wasn't fictitious at all roaming around up in the atmosphere of the earth's sky, controlling, absorbing, and draining every electrical impulse and power of the planet, and animal life alike. It was truly amazing; not every creature around the planet lost their minute electrical impulses in their insignificant little bodies, and not leaving all creatures of the universe destroyed.

The story about the cosmonauts sounded so unreal and made up that no one possibly could have survived such a horrific travesty as he had described, especially to have come through what they did and live to tell a tale about it.

"Several lucky winners of the lottery that Commander Ivan ran aboard the space station, flew home that very morning on a Galaxy 500 Paymaster cargo aircraft back to Russia. With a little luck if they had any at all, they should possibly make Moscow in the light of day, if they follow the light of the earth's rotation of daylight hours without having to fly into any darkness. If the dark of night was to have overtaken the aircraft, it would be lost to the fate of the darkness of night, unless there was a full moon out. Even then it would take a miracle to land any aircraft, especially one its size, without the use of runway landing lights. If the pilots were to feel they would be running out of proper daylight time before the end of their flight, they will have to put the aircraft down in Anchorage, Alaska at the Elmendorf Air Force Station's airfield, and wait out the night till the light of day was upon them once again. The news media around the world have not been told about the flight, and did not have the slightest in clues what United States was up to in its last rescue mission. The rescue news would have probably infuriated most the people of our country if they knew that our government was trying to help any Russian to live. The people of our country could care less what happens to those poor souls up there."

Commander Anderson told Ann that he would personally risk his own life one more time to save the ones in space who had so unselfishly set themselves aside in order to save the Twitchel's crew in their time of need. "Wouldn't you have, Ann?"

Ann did not say a word in reply to his suggestive quest of kindness. The world had become bittersweet, and Ann could not help but wonder about her stranded friends still held prisoner in orbit.

"This particular mission back into space is top secret," he explained to Ann and her family, and none at this table are at liberty to say a word to anyone about it."

He hoped his mention of it would not leave the mouths of anyone, especially Ann's dad who liked to brag about his daughter or Ben in his coming and going in town, or out around the countryside helping his neighbors at their farms. Commander Anderson explained to Ann and her family his visit to their farm was twofold. The first was as a friend, to inform her and her family of the progress her friends who were still living in orbit were holding out and doing. The situation with the cosmonauts aboard the space station was not very good at the time.

The folder he brought with him with information was to inform her of the last mission of his career. He hoped she would consider joining him in his last mission as his sole navigating officer, she having performed the job in a crisis of navigator so well in the past. The service performed on this mission would be strictly voluntary. There was no money or strings attached to it this time, and she was under no obligation to anyone to partake in it if she didn't choose to do so. He was not there ordering or making anyone on his last crew list make this last and final risky mission into orbit. There was always the possibility of something going wrong in any mission, and without her help as his navigator as in the past, this mission would be more likely to have something of a mishap happen than not, but he was going anyway. He owed his life to the ones still in orbit, and hoped she felt the same as he did.

The sounds of his words were more a plea than an order to Ann, but his words sounded the same as an order to her family. He shook their hands, and gave Ann a big long lasting hug as only a father would give

his own child, and then kissed her on her cheek. He thought the absolute world of Ann, more as a daughter than he did a fellow officer. If he had the slightest inclining that this mission would go wrong especially on this particular rescue mission, he would not have gone all this way up to Vermont to ask her to join him in it. He told her to think about the special mission. He gave her the secret code to use in notifying him if she so chose to join him on this last secret mission of rescue. "This is strictly up to you Ann, and your family. Please give it some very serious thought before you decide what you are going to do one way or the other. With this in mind, I will leave you now. Now please give it some very serious thought, Ann. Friday, 0800-hours, Ann is the latest if you are going to go with us. If we do not hear from you by then, Captain, we all will respect your decision. Thank you and to your family also for having both of us in for a lovely breakfast, Ann. 0800-hours Friday, Ann, and please give it some very serious consideration?"

He then informed Ann she was the first on his list of the Twitchel's last crew he was going to visit in trying to fill this crew of his for the upcoming rescue mission. Bill would be his next officer of the crew to visit and so on. By Friday, he had planned to visit all past crewmembers, every one of them personally, except for Lieutenant Charles. "That damn thing up in the sky took yet another good man away from us, Ann, as it has so many others. He was about to step into the cockpit of a converted fighter jet to test flight it. They modified the ignition system and the rocket-firing capabilities of it in order to protect the country from an invasion from any hostile country that might want to take over our land. It was unique in how they fire everything up now days. They use diesel power to do everything instead of electricity. Just as Ben has done so very well with everything around the farm here, they bring out a truck to the aircraft on the tarmac, and hook a piped up chute to the aircraft's turbine engine, and then begin forcing an enormous wind flow through it and then ignite the mixture of #2 fuels with a torch. If they happen to have a flame out during flight, they can re-ignite the turbine by the use of a flair gun mounted just outside the engine on its shroud. Ingenuity of the imagination has come a long way over the last few months, and years now, since the neutron creature has taken away all electrical power above the earth's crust.

Anyway Ann, back to what I was saying about the lieutenant. Lieutenant Charles and Captain Morris were about to go for their first flights in this new outfitted trainer jet since the poor landing of the Twitchel. Captain Morris had recovered fully from the injuries he had sustained in our dreaded landing. Lieutenant Charles was first up the ladder just about to climb into the cockpit of the trainer jet, when the neutron monster struck him dead. Captain Morris observed everything from about ten or better yards away, after having returned to the flight preparation room to retrieve the gloves he had left, and was retuning at a flat out run to catch up with Lieutenant Charles. Captain Morris literally watched Lieutenant Charles fry and die by being struck by that neutron thing. Lieutenant Charles went right into convulsions. His hands flouncing in the air, his body swaggering back and forth on the top rungs of the ladder to the aircraft, and then fell to the pavement and died. He was probably dead well before he even hit the ground, but nobody knows for sure. As I was saying, Captain Morris was about ten yards away from the lieutenant, when suddenly the thing from out the air struck him dead. Captain Morris heard this horrible buzzing crackling and moaning sound ahead of him. When he looked up to see what was making the gruesome sound, he saw that Lieutenant Charles was making the noise, more like the thing in the air was eating him when it took his life. Captain Morris saw an orange-greenish flourescent sheen of light that had engulfed the lieutenant, and then of course, he was dead. It happens the same way every time I hear of it happening. It does not matter if it is a bird in the air, an animal on the ground, or a human being. They smoke with a misty cloud of orange around them. The smoke smells similar to phosgene gas, similar the burning of hydrocarbon refrigerants or of ammonia. It is all so very strange. They say the smell of it is enough to gag a maggot, making anyone who smells it want to vomit. It burns your throat, your eyes, and nostrils. I am sorry, Ann, that I get pretty carried away with it all. Remember, Ann, 0800 hours Friday morning. I will see you then, good day."

Commander Anderson did not say another word. He did an immediate about face, and hurriedly walked from the front porch toward his awaiting ride. He left Ann standing there alone on the front piazza of the farmhouse, wondering what her next step in life would or had to be. Would she join her fellow crew of astronaut friends in this last and final mission to save her other stranded friends in space, or would she stay on the farm with her immediate family, her mother, her father, the girls, and Ben, and not give a damn about the success of this new last mission into space and its outcome.

By Friday morning, Commander Anderson's flight crew was almost complete with the exception of his lost friend Lieutenant Charles and navigator, Captain Ann Mitchell. Captain Morris told the commander he was not ready for space flight quite yet, but the Colonel knew he was, and he would certainly be there for him.

Commander Anderson had been very busy rounding up his new and old crew. On Friday morning at approximately 0600 hours, Commander Anderson found himself sipping a cup of coffee at his desk in his main office. He was awake half the night going over the new changes taking place on the next shuttle for its first flight into outer space. The same as he had when they had outfitted the Twitchel for another flight into the new unknown with all its new mechanical changes.

What could they possibly do different to make things a little more convenient for the crew of this new bird this time? What about the safety of the many cosmonauts that they would eventually have to bring back home with them to Earth in this very altered shuttle on this mission?

He knew Ann would just show up or send a message. He didn't quite know what to expect of her this time, but time was running out for her decision as 0800 hours was soon approaching. He knew it would be a very difficult decision for her to make between family and flight, as she was a dedicated astronaut right from the beginning and knew she would feel compelled to make the right choice in the end. This mission would not be as safe as the other missions had been without her being well groomed navigator she was in making all the right decisions that he knew she would. She was the best of the best when it came to navigating any type of space vehicle into orbit, or back out of its orbit, and back to Earth. It would surely make this mission one hell of a lot easier with her onboard than without her there with them.

Ann had waved goodbye to Commander Anderson, as his chauffeur drove him away down the road from the farm. She hurriedly returned to the kitchen almost at a dead run to clean up from the family's breakfast dishes that were still all spread out all over the kitchen table. She sent her very concerned looking mother packing into her sewing room to do her darning after she had already started to pick up after everyone went to do their chores.

Out of the kitchen doorway, her mother went being shooed away by her daughter. She went looking back at her daughter with surprise, the one who usually didn't like doing the job of cleaning up the kitchen all by her lonesome. She usually liked to talk about everything to her, but today she was on a mission of her own.

Her mother knew she wanted to be left in solitude to do her thinking in the quiet of her work. Ann wanted to be alone in the kitchen without anyone around, especially her mother. She knew her mother was especially sharp on how to read right through everything that was bothering her. Ann wanted to be alone to think and sort things out things while she cleaned up, and Ann needed time to think over what Commander Anderson had just said to her in his own sort of pleading way or just plain right out request of her to go along with him. He had not been direct in demanding her services, but he sure as hell pleaded in a hurtful sobering way that she had never seen him act before. He had treated her with kid gloves on trying his damnedest to try to guide her in her right decision making way at the time to get her to go with him. It suddenly began to work on her deeply troubled subconscious making her want to go with him in the worst possible way, but she had her reservations about the mission this time for what Scavonivich had done to her on the last one. Her wild emotions were bothersome and got the best of her. She then broke down and cried while holding the last dish in the dishcloth held tight in her shaking hands. Her mixed emotions felt like a runaway locomotive running wildly down a steep mountainside out of control. She had made a promise to her entire family, especially Amber and Sarah. her precious two little children she adored so much, that she would never ever in a million years leave them ever again for any reason. She wept like a lost little child who had just fallen off of her bicycle and had badly skinned both knees, and there was no one around to help her up off the ground or to take care of her extreme pain.

Ben came in from the living room and seeing her crying, put his loving arms snuggly around her midsection for comfort and self-assurance. He bent down stretching his neck around hers, and doing so gave her a big kiss on her cheek, and said, "I love you, honey."

"What do I do, Ben? Have I not done enough for those people up there already? Why does it feel like I have the whole damn weight of the universe, the entire whole world on my scrawny little shoulders, Ben? Especially the fate of those poor souls still left up there in orbit. I have a family of my own down here, and yet I feel like I am letting down my other family up there. My family needs me here, and their families need them home again, too. Some of them have not seen their loved ones in over two years and some over three years or better now. What the hell am I supposed to do?"

Ann turned in his arms with tears streaming down her cheeks and crying profusely. She looked like one hell of a mess of mixed up emotions to Ben, as he pulled her closer to him, and held her tight in his arms, as she whispered in his ear crying. "What am I supposed to do, Ben? What am I supposed to do?"

After a few moments in complete silence and hugging, he pushed her slightly away from him. He wanted to look deep down into the sole of her body through her eyes trying to give her as much comfort from his own eyes, when Amber and Sarah came rushing into the kitchen full of energy. They were full of great joy for the new day was bright and sunny outside, and Ann had promised them a picnic up in the apple orchard later on that day. "Ok girls, your mom needs time to be alone.

"We will go out back and see what Grandpa and Grandma are up to out there. I see they are about to go blueberry picking, and I think we can help them, what do you think?"

The kids just glanced over at their mom whilst Ben led them by the hand out the back door to be with their grandparents.

He left Ann to continue contemplating what to do next by herself, and hoped it would be the right choice, no matter what the decision was.

CHAPTER SEVENTY-THREE

The Choice of no Return

Ann returned to her wife and motherly duties after leaving the kitchen without a word about the rescue mission to anyone the remainder of the day. The only talk taking place was about the farm, the children, and the way things were going on around the town and out in the countryside.

"You know, Ben, old man Colby top the hill lost another one of his milking cows up in his back forty field yesterday. If the poor old boy loses any more head of cattle, he will be out of the farming business for good. He has already lost twenty head or so since that damn thing in the sky came to Earth. Poor old boy lost his only good tractor, too. The diesel engine seized up tighter than a bootjack on him. Happened the same day he lost his prize-milking cow too. You would have thought he would have known to have put some more engine oil into that diesel engine crankcase of his once in a while, wouldn't you, Ben? Those danged engine bearings will not last long without some sort of lubricant on them you know. He must be downright lost without any power from his tractor's PTO to run his milking compressors and cooling tanks. Can we spare the extra old pickup truck out back for a couple of days or so till he gets his tractor rig repaired or can get himself another one to replace the one that just seized up?"

"Sure thing, Pops, sure we can. We can do that for Fred. He has been a right good neighbor of yours for a good long many years, now hasn't he? After supper, we can bring old man Colby the old pickup truck up to him."

"Better to check the level of the oil sump first though; I would not want old Fred to seize up another engine, especially one of ours. We can jack it up, and put a v-belt on a rear rim to help him run his air compressor and refrigerant equipment."

"Much obliged, Ben! I sure do appreciate your loyalty, Mac, as a good friend, neighbor, and all that, you know. I do not know for sure just how I would have kept up with all my milking without the aid of the air-operated milking machines. That damn compressor sure does come in right handy when it comes time for milking all those cows and keeping their milk all good and cold. I should get my tractor back good as new by the weekend if I have any luck. Sam says he has all the right parts in stock from another job that he never started on in his workshop. He said the poor old gent from over Littleton, New Hampshire way was going to do the job for went by way of that damn beast in the sky. Frightening, is it not? One never knows when or where that damn beast thing in the air will attack you next and take your life out from under you or your animals. I kind of wish that beast had taken everything I got including myself and the wife, then I would not have to worry about anything anymore. I am just getting too darn old to keep up the way I should be doing things around here, especially without the help of a young lad like your son-in-law, Ben, there around here to help keep us going. The misses can hardly move anymore these days with all of her arthritis and her ailing bones and all the rest the pain stuff she is suffering from. Thanks again guys!"

"You would do the same for us, Fred, and you have. Good neighbors are good neighbors, so you can call us somewhat even. Consider this as a partial payback for all the help you and your misses have given us over the years, long before Ben here came along to help." "Thanks again!"

Ann sat with her mother and the two children in the living room while her father and Ben went up to the Colby farm to deliver and set up the spare diesel-powered pickup truck for him. Her mother was sitting on the couch with the girls reading the Bible to them, whilst Ann sat darning some holes in the kids' socks and repairing a pair of jeans for Ben. Clothing had become harder and harder to come by these days. Everything made from cloth was being mended once again and not discarded as old rags as they many times did in the past. Everyone was becoming more frugal with clothing, food, and other necessities of everyday living.

"The tattered sleeve on Ben's shirt there, sure was easier to mend using the old electric sewing machine, wasn't it, Ann?" Ann's mother asked her, as Ann put the threaded needle back through the separated cloth of the sleeve pulling it out again to mend the tear he had put in his work shirt while fixing and repairing a neighbor's hay rake.

Ann did not smile, nod her head, or even acknowledge that her mother had even spoken to her; she just continued to re-stitch the hole she was working on. In fact, she didn't even hear a word her loving mother was saying to her. She was lost in another world of confusion all by her lonesome. She was trying desperately to conclude on what to do about this supposedly last mission of mercy she was damn well betwixt and between about. The little stubborn yelling voice in her head was screaming at her. It was telling her it was her soul and duty to go along and try to help her needy fellow astronauts aloft. While another little soft voice in her subconscious mind was wrapping her up with guilt and shame if she was to leave her children and Ben behind again, especially after having promised each one of them she would never leave them or could never leave them, never again.

"Now take that no good for nothing electric stitching machine over yonder there in the corner. We got rid of the old treadle sewing machine. Traded it in for this here electric one, and now look at it. The useless thing just sits over there in the corner good for nothing and taking up space. Wish I had never traded that old treadle-sewing unit in for this one. We sure could use it now, couldn't you, dear?"

Ann just kept right on sewing, still not hearing a single word her mother was saying to her while trying very hard to make conversation. She turned back to the children and opened the Bible to another page and passage from the book of golden rules. She knew her daughter was in deep thought about another mission, and sure hoped she would use her head this time. She might lose Ben, and worse than that, they might lose her for good this time.

Subconsciously, Ann must have heard her mother talking. Her mind drifted, thinking about the inconveniences the massive amounts in neutrons caused the people around the globe. All the electrical conveniences of modern day living she had grown up with had vanished in a matter of seconds. Everything she had taken for granted was gone. They hadn't gone anywhere to speak of, but had all become useless pieces of junk in everyone's home no one could use unless they lived a couple of stories beneath the surface of the ground where the neutrons wouldn't or couldn't attack the power of the appliances.

Many of the earth's inhabitants were now becoming cave dwellers, just to have the conveniences the new old world ways of life they had grown up with and were so accustomed to having before the big blast, and the invasion of neutrons took away around world.

There was absolutely nothing, nothing at all for the trapped crew on the International Space Station to come back home to, that would better them for coming back, other than sustaining a life of cruelty for their being. Maybe it would have been better to have let them all fade away into oblivion from the lack of oxygen, than introduce them to this new way of life back here on Earth. The inhabitants of planet Earth had to adapt themselves to so many new ways of life and changes. Even Ann would have given it some very serious second thoughts about ending her own life and misery if it was not for her two little children. Everyone could have dealt well with the misery of her death if she had died in space, or could her children have coped well with it as she really didn't know.

Ann's timid mind was working at warp speed in overtime trying to come up with a good and levelheaded solution. She needed a quick answer to her overwhelming dilemma. Should she go with Colonel Anderson on his rescue mission to the space lab or not go with him and stay home with her family. She was becoming sick to her stomach again, the same way she had felt when she first became pregnant before her first child was born. It wasn't a very pleasant feeling then, and this nerve-racking sick feeling sure as hell wasn't a very pleasant feeling now,

and it wasn't going away by itself either. What in the hell was she to do? She felt her stomach coming up and ran as fast she could to the bathroom, and proceeded to vomit up what little evening meal she had forced down into the toilet bowl. She began shaking out of control with chills of mighty force all over her slender body. She developed an instant migraine headache, and felt like the size of Mount Washington. She was becoming dizzy with anxiety as she was so overly and desperately concerned in making the right decision for everyone involved except for herself. She wasn't giving a single damn thought about herself of what was good for her, but what was good for everyone else in her life and their feelings. She had come back from outer space to a husband she did not know or understand any longer at that particular time in her life. He had changed drastically from being a kind caring lovely man he once was before the big bang, to this very scared hard cored almost not caring individual. His mind had been slowly stimulated from the mental hardship and strain he had endured while she was gone. It was as if he had just returned home from the combat of war suffering from shell shock and living with constant depression. She was having a difficult time with that, and was trying desperately hard to adjust to the fact he may never change back into his good old happy self ever again. He was beginning to come around from it finally which was a good sign to her. Her two little girls had also become very distant from her being their mother, and they, too, had not accepted her for who she was when she first returned from space to them, especially on the second time back from the last mercy mission she had gone on. It had taken them all this while to re-accept her as their mother all over again. What in the hell would happen to her family if she were to go on a third mission? Just one more damn mercy mission and then what, what would happen to Colonel Anderson and his crew if she did not go? Ann was beginning to wonder what in the hell was life all about or would be for her in the future.

She stayed held up in the hallway bathroom at the toilet bowl with dry heaves until Ben got back with her father from the Colby farm. Ben then helped her to get up and into her bed. He thought she had eaten something that did not quite agree with her, and he was right about something. She had eaten something that did not quite agree with her in a different way, as she had ingested something into her mind that was making her sick and not by her mouth. She could not digest everything she had taken into her overly burdened mind, and it was not digesting anything there, and it made her sick as if she were suffering from a bad case of the flu or ptomaine poisoning of some sort.

CHAPTER SEVENTY-FOUR

The Decision

Thursday morning came to Ann in a way she had wished it would never have come to her. It was time for her to go. A time to go into a deep soul searching mode of heartfelt seeking and decision making. She had to make up her mind one last time, and seek out the decision of a lifetime for all. She was convinced that the choice she had to make would be the right choice. She was going to make a feast this day. A meal her family would not ever be able to forget. A meal made by her for her family to remember her for a long time to come as one's life by her. She kept herself busy all day long preparing this special dinner she had in mind for everyone to feast upon and enjoy. Her mind stayed busy all day long seeking, and then re-seeking the far depths of her soul-searching mind for the right answers. She thought for sure she had to come up with it, and would announce her decision at this very special meal of thanksgiving. She did not quite know how to go about giving the correct answer without sounding very selfish to all of them, but she would work on that during the day. That particular time of the day when she faced everyone, she would have just as well rather have skipped right over it, and gone on with her life like she had just woken up from a bad night of nightmares and dreams and not wanting to tell anyone anything about them.

Ann pranced around the house all day long cleaning everything in sight. She swept the floors twice. She then washed them twice to have something to keep her busy. She went around dusting everything, not once but twice, to make certain she had not miss a single speck of dust or dirt anywhere in the house that might have missed. She moved around quickly while putting back the smallest of trinkets and items not once but at least twice and sometimes three and four times, polishing every one of them as she dusted everything in sight a multitude of times.

Ann didn't really have to make this crucial decision until the very last second of the day. Her mind kept telling her it was time to go now, and no not to go around every second of every hour debating it with herself ever since Commander Anderson had left her standing all alone on the front piazza. She kept herself extremely active all day long like a little child who had just overdosed on Halloween candy trying to burn off its sugar content of high energy and had become overactive. She ran from room to room like a whirlwind cleaning windows, washing clothes, and cooking everyone's best holiday meal along with all their special dressings, along with an assortment of different desserts for them to enjoy after the meal.

Everyone knew something was brewing, and all thought the worst of it, even Ann in her decision. Everyone disappeared out of her sight for the day, leaving Ann to herself in the house alone to make the crucial decision of her fate. It would be her choice and her choice alone to make. Everyone had their own ideas about the outcome, and some were not too happy one way or the other about it, especially Ann.

At the close of the day, Ann's mother and father had brought the children home from a fun-filled day of trout fishing down at the mouth of Mink Brook where the tiny stream flowed quietly from the meadow under the bridge and out into the Connecticut River. They had a string each of fresh caught trout with them as they walked happily through the rear kitchen door and into the house. Ann looked up from checking on the fancy meal cooking in their gas stove oven. She having prepared a wonderful meal of the day for all, the meal of the century, wearing a great big pleasant smile painted wide on her very concerned face. She was well pleased that the girls, her dad and her mom had such a wonderful day out fishing together, and had caught so many wonderful good-sized fish to eat. The children both went on together happily jibber-jabbering about how their grumpy old grandpa had almost fallen into the Mink Brook trying gingerly to balance himself on a fallen branch in order to get a snagged fishing line and hook out from being caught up in a small tree's branch overhanging the water's edge.

Ann knew the two girls were in good hands when they were out with their grandparents as she always felt safe with them when she was a small child, and always had a good time with them no matter what they did or did not do.

Both her mother and father knew something was very much amiss the way their two beds in their bedroom looked rearranged and both been changed. Along with the rearrangement of their bedroom, there were two brand new handmade throws made by Ann over weeks past placed upon them. They found them when the two of them went upstairs to change out of their smelly fish clothes, and get dressed for supper. She had rearranged every piece of furniture in the living room three times during the day until she got it right the way she wanted it. Every room in the house including the attached woodshed was spotless and picked up. Not a sliver of sawdust or a wood chip could be seen anywhere, along with all the windows in the house having been washed and glittering clear.

Before them on the table lay waiting a fantastic meal Ann had arrange just so-so, very nicely spread out before them. Some of the hot foods were still on the wood burning stove to keep everything warm until the family could all sit down together at the table to eat and enjoy.

The dining room table looked to have been set for a Thanksgiving dinner they were about to partake in. Fancy linen napkins lay carefully folded underneath her mother's special silver wear. The dining room table was set with her mother's best silver tableware, along with her special green glasses she only took out for special occasions, mainly Christmas, Thanksgiving, and Easter. Ann was running around like the Tasmanian devil when her mother and father came back downstairs from changing, as if she was running a restaurant, and she was the only chief, cook, and bottle washer they had in the whole establishment.

"My lord child, what have you been doing all day," asked Ann's mother with a tone of deep concern in her voice as she spoke to her busy daughter running around.

"See if Ben is almost done with his chores out in the barn and is ready to eat supper yet will you Daddy?"

Her father quickly turned around, spun on his cane, and went out back to the barn to seek out Ben for dinner.

"Hey there, Ben, have you been in the house all day helping Ann with all those dang chores of hers, and not doing your own?"

"No I haven't, why?"

"Never mind. Supper is ready hot on the stove, and the table is all set up for us to eat. Ann wants to know how long you are going to be before you are ready to eat."

"What is the matter with you, Pa? What in the bloody hell is wrong? I can see something in your eyes that you are not telling me."

"Nothing, nothing is wrong with me, Ben! I think you already know what the matter is with me. I think Ann has gone and made up her damn stubborn mind again, and that is that. I think she has decided to goes off on that damn mission with that damn Commander Anderson fellow. The whole blasted house is aglow like a freaking Christmas tree at Christmas time, and the danged dining room table has been set up for the likes of a king and his queen to feast upon it. That is what is wrong with me Ben. I think she is a going to be joining Colonel Anderson on his foolish mission back to that stupid damned space station."

Ben slammed down the bucket of milk he was carrying very hard to the floor of the barn. The milk from the bucket went flying everywhere. "I can't believe it! Damn it! I just cannot believe it. Damn it, Pa! She promised! She promised me and the kids she wouldn't do this to us ever again." Ben began stomping his booted feet like a mad little child throwing a temper tantrum slamming his feet down running around the barn and screaming at the top of his lungs, all at the same time.

Ann's father stood there feeling the same pain as what Ben was going through. He felt like joining in with Ben screaming, and stomping his feet wildly, but could not, and did not. When Ben had finally calmed down, and stopped stomping his feet wildly and swearing uncontrollable obscenities aloud about his thoughts, he gently spoke to his father in-law.

"Tell Ann, Pa. Tell her I will be just a minute. Tell her I have to get the smell of the barnyard off myself, and then I will be right in, straightaway."

Ben took a cold shower out in the milk room of the barn to calm his raging nerves and to cool himself down before going into the house to eat with the children. The water stored in and from the big holding tank he had made in the barn was cold as ice, and he almost turned himself a purplish dark blue letting the open hose of very cold spring water flow over him for as long as he could stand it before he passed out from hypothermia. When Ben finally entered the house, he had cooled himself down enough so he would not lose his temper in front the children, her folks, and would talk to Ann in the private of their bedroom later on that night. If best, out on the front porch when the proper opportune time came about what was to happen, but for now. Now they would all enjoy the grand meal she had put together for them. Ann quickly placed the hot dishes from the woodstove onto the hot placemats on the table when everyone finally sat down to eat. "Mom, please sit yourself down at the table. I can handle getting everything on the table from the stove. What would anyone like to drink?"

"Water please, Ann!" Ann served everyone the drink of their choice, and then set herself down at the far end of the table to eat. She was still full of extremely nervous energy, not having used it all up in all she had done during her busy day.

Ann's father gave the usual grace before serving dinner, asking the good Lord above to please help rectify all that had to be done to help those left on earth and the needy ones held above in space. Ben just shook his head side to side when he heard his father-in-law ask for the Lord's help with the recovery of the cosmonauts from the space station. He almost got up from the dinner table to go out back again to the milking room in the barn to soak himself down again under the freezing cold water from the spring because he did not want to make a horrendous scene in front of his two wonderful girls. He did not give a damn if he blew up in front of Ann's parents or not for they felt the same way as he did. He did have enough self-control and thought of his children for their sake to spare them his faulty lousy feelings towards the damn Russian leaders, and not the Russia people that had caused this whole mess in the first place. He was totally pissed off at his father-in-law. The nerve of that old fart anyway, asking the good Lord for his help in saving the Russian cosmonauts in space. Help from the good Lord above, bullshit, he thought. If the good Lord above wanted any of them back down here on Earth, then he should send them a damn rocket to ride them back home in. Why in the hell did she have to go off and volunteer for this mission anyway? Why should she go and risk her own damn life all over again to save any of them? She already did it once, and almost got herself killed in doing it the last time. Ben was totally pissed off at the idea of it all and was having a real hard time trying to control his temper even though he didn't really feel that way about the poor souls still trapped up in outer space. He was angered and did not want to lose the love of his life. Scared to death neither he nor anyone else sitting at the table that day would ever see his lovely Ann again.

"Here comes your turkey, Ma." Ann's father passed the platter of turkey to his still very beautiful wife while everyone else picked up something different from the several serving bowls and started passing the food around the table. Ben's eyes looked red and bloodshot as if he had not slept a wink all night long for an entire week, as he sat quietly biting at his tongue at the table not wanting, or daring to say a word afraid he would lose his building up angered temper.

After Ann's father had returned to the farmhouse, he had let loose again with all the built up emotions he had stored up inside himself. He carried on like a lunatic, profusely crying in the shower, even getting some strong soap in his eyes while in the flow of the cold water, and did not give a damn that it burnt like hell because he was going through mental anguish anyway. No matter how hard he tried, he could not stop his hard crying while thinking about how lonely he and the children would be without her for those two or three long lonely weeks again. What if something was to go drastically wrong with this mission and none of them ever would to see her lovely being again. The thought of it drove him crazy, and the burning soap in his eyes did not mean a damn thing to him, except that Ann would say no to Commander Anderson, and now it was too late to change her stupid ego trip ways of doing whatever she wanted to do in the first place, and not give a hoot about anyone else.

Ben had had the hardest time trying not to cry at the dining room table, every time he looked over at his loving wife, Ann, or when glancing across the table at their two beautiful little girls. His heart just could not stand the pain any longer. He would want to die if she did, but knew he could not because of the girls. He felt like standing up right then right there. He wanted to grab the blasted table and flip the blasted thing upside down right in front of her. He was blind minded mad at her. He was turning his great concern for Ann into the most hostile anger he had ever felt before not knowing what or how to handle it any longer, except that he had to remain under control at least while the children were around, and then when they were alone together, he would let her have it with both barrels of his anger.

God he wished he knew what to do next and how to handle it better. He guessed it was time to turn to the Lord above for some help of his very own. The critical decision must lie in her hands, and her hands alone to make, for he knew what ever her decision was. He quietly said a prayer to himself asking for help from the Lord above for him and the girls. Would he support her choice, or would he not? If he left her and the children now, he would not have to worry for he would not know if anything went wrong, or put up with the hurt if something bad were to happen to her, or could he do that to his girls? Of course, he could not. He would always be there for those two little angels no matter what, and now he had to be there for her as well, even if he didn't like what she was about to say to them. Ben held his composure very well all the while at the dining room table trying to smile every once in a great while. He complimented Ann on a job well done with the spectacular meal she served to them.

He knew better than to ask the silly question about what the special occasion must be for such a grand meal in the middle of the week with no holidays anywhere in sight that he could possibly think of. The adults at the table were quiet while eating their meals just looking around at one another with silent questions all over their faces not asked. Except for the children who acted up as usual, when they sat down to eat by picking on one another. It looked like everyone was busy enjoying themselves with the great meal prepared before them. Having little to talk about, but that was not the case. No one wanted to open up the first complex issue, squirming loosely around in their timid concerned minds for everyone else sitting at the table, including Ann herself. She had never seen them so quiet, and no one seemed to care if the girls were loud or not. She knew they knew, and they did not want to be the first to talk, and neither did she.

"What has happened to your eyes Ben? They are as red as a fire truck?" Ann asked Ben, being very concerned for her husband's wellbeing.

"Nothing sweetheart, I just got a bunch of hay chaff, a little bit of wood chips and sawdust bedding into them, and soap from the quick shower I took out in the barn, that's all."

"They will be better off after a good night's sleep." Ben's father-in-law took a quick glance over and peeked up at Ben's eyes, and then quickly went back to his eating. He knew very well the real truth behind his swollen eyes, and it sure wasn't any hay chaff or sawdust specks in them.

After a most fantastic banquet several very lovely dessert dishes were served, one specially made for everyone at the table. Ann shooed everyone away from the dining room table including her mother out of the kitchen. She became an instant whirlwind again cleaning up the kitchen like the Tasmanian devil in action all over again. She flew from the table to the sink, the stove, then to the cabinets in the pantry. She washed the dishes, scrubbed the pots and pans, along with the silverware in record time trying to burn up the excess energy she had in trying to make the decision come to fruition with the right choice.

She was quite sure what she would do next, but after looking at her family sitting at the kitchen table next to her made the choice all that much harder to tell them. Every person in the world and in outer space deserved to be with the ones they all loved. Ann was with hers now, but for how long would she be gone, or ever return?

The children along with their grandparents got up from the table moaning and groaning a little bit with discomfort after eating way too much of the fine food prepared for them, and they found their way into the parlor. Ben thanked his lovely wife for such a great meal, and proceeded out the rear kitchen door to the back porch. He sat at the swinging lounge, swinging back and forth looking out into the outer space of nothingness and daydreaming. He sat staring out at the rolling beauty of fields and mountains of New Hampshire across the Connecticut River Valley.

In the far off distance, he could see Mount Washington standing majestically tall. No one uses the old cog railway anymore, ever since all those lives were lost on her peak that dreaded day when all of the neutron creatures appeared. Every time someone tried to climb or scale her majestic heights, they would all perish become an instant unintelligent zombie. With all that said, no one dared climb her majestic beauty any more. Even the bravest in mountain climbers would not climb any more mountains, for fear they shall all perish or become simple minded.

Ann watched Ben out through the kitchen window by the sink, as Ben stopped his swinging. He suddenly crossed his legs, putting his right elbow down on his left knee, and then wrested his chin in his right hand. He looked like the thinker statue at the science center in Providence, Rhode Island. He must be the most understanding caring man in the world, she thought to herself or at least he had been. He was definitely one of the most dedicated fathers around because so many had run away from their responsibilities after the big neutron invasion, while only a few remained faithful to their fatherly and husbandly duties.

Ann took one tall glass after another, drying the last few of them ever so slowly as she stood by the screen watching Ben out the window. She loved him dearly, even though he had changed drastically and who would not or had not. He had done the work of three men around her father's farm while still finding the time in his caring heart to help many of the needy neighbors who came to him for some help. No matter how tired he always seemed to be at the end of a long hard day of work, he always managed to muster up another hour or two in strength to help those in need around the countryside on the other farms in the area to help someone out of a bind.

She gently watched him with her own soft heart. He surely didn't know he was being watched, as he pulled his clean handkerchief from his rear pocket and began wiping away tear after tear she could see running down and dripping from off his chin uncontrollably. He suddenly slouched forward, placing his head face first down into both open hands, as his supported leg fell to the floor of the porch with a lurch.

She was trying to make the right choice for herself and other people's lives of the world, whether to help save her friends in space or not save them, and not really giving her own family the right to intervene in her own decision of making one of the utmost most important decisions she had ever had to make as she put the last glass away into the cabinet. She looked out the window just in time to see her mother put her caring hand down onto her loving son-in-law's shoulder as he put both arms out forward around her waist and wept like a child. Her two lovely children ran out onto the porch from around the front of the house followed by her father.

She put the dishtowel to her own weeping eyes, and knew then what she had to do. Ann had finally made up her questionable wandering mind. She was not going. She refused to put her family through another episode of grief like the last event she had caused, and even if she did come back safe and sound, she might never come back home to the same family she once knew. She ran for the closed kitchen door. She flung it wide open hard so everyone turned around startled from its almost cracking off its hinges and yelled out to them.

"I AM NOT GOING!"

They all smiled and sighed with the greatest of relief, especially Ben. He was so excited, he almost knocked his poor caring mother-in-law

over in his trying to get to his feet in order to get to the one he so loved the most in the whole entire world except for his two little girls.

CHAPTER SEVENTY-FIVE

The Last Mercy Mission

Four, Three, Two, One, Zero. We have ignition! The solid fueled rocket engines aboard the Omega one came instantly to life. The craft began to shimmer and shake as the hot flames shot out from beneath the tail section of the main launch booster rockets attached to the underbelly of the shuttlecraft. Commander Anderson sat at the flight controls along with Major Bill at his side. Both were getting ready if need be to help them in a straight smooth ride up into outer space and into an orbital path to linkup to the International Space Center.

The early morning weather over Cape Canaveral could not have been any better for the launch of any rocket, especially the shuttle. The sun had just crested up over the early morning horizon of the most eastern crest of the ocean shining bright, like a huge big red rubber ball all aglow up in the early bright blue morning sky. A few fair-weather clouds floated scarcely scattered about in the early blue as the temperature in air was between perfect and wonderful for the launch. The air was still without breeze with the ocean as calm as an ocean can be. If only they could swiftly make the out limits of the atmosphere before the negativity of the massive neutrons energy-absorbing field could attack them. The creature of the heavens had become very active lately for some very strange reason. It was as if it was trying to win a battle with another force over the planet, taking place by this other force field attacking it, that it was trying to win back its full control over the

universe. Might it be all the electrical power man was generating below the crust of the earth's surface, made it plausible that the earth was winning over the large neutron field by weakening it? Probably not, as it seemed to be infuriating the manmade creature into being more aggressive in movement and attack, or was it just growing in strength, and would soon one day suck all electrical currents no matter how small out of every living creature on the face of the planet and below its surface as well?

Some civilian and military aircraft now flew regular routes between cities and air bases around the country and the world. Most air travel was temporarily grounded because the threat of being attacked by the increased activity of the imperfection of neutrons. The neutron mass sought out the most minuscule energy field in living beings electrical impulses from within the brain who had sat inside the aircrafts at higher altitudes when it attacked absorbing the mainsail impulse from within them. It now was doing its best in attacking and absorbing the smallest of positively charged fields of any living being or creature living or flying above three thousand feet sea level. The littlest and largest of birds, butterflies, and insects were all falling from the sky in droves again like they had before when the immense neutron fields first invaded the atmosphere around the world. The rescue of any survivors from any of the downed aircraft if there were any was damn near impossible if there were any left alive. Without communication between the aircraft and someone on the ground, the chance for rescue was nil if not impossible. There had not been a single survivor recorded since recording of downed airplanes started just after flight had resumed. The last sighted crash of an airplane recorded was an attack by the neutron field at O'Hare International Airfield in Illinois, and luckily for some they were close enough to the ground when the big plane crashed for some of the passengers rescued from the horrific experience. The jumbo 350 jetliner was approaching from the north just returning from Anchorage, Alaska when suddenly it was engulfed by a yellowy orange and greenish sheen of death. The plane nosed up, turned over sideways, and then came crashing down on the runway on a wing tip, splitting the large aircraft in two, as passengers, luggage, and aircraft components scattered themselves all over the ground and along the runway. Of the list of 280 onboard, only twenty-two passengers were able to survive the crash. The lucky ones seated in the middle of the huge fuselage of the aircraft were the only passengers unscathed by the crash or by the massive neutron field attacking the plane. Many of the other passengers remained strapped into their seats. These passengers should have survived the crash. These passengers were lightly burnt and smoking, smelling of a strong phosgene gas odor from the massive neutron field attacking them. The ones seated in the aircraft's middle were protected from the massive attack by the field not reaching them yet when the aircraft crash landed. If the plane had stayed aloft just another second or maybe two to three seconds longer, the immense neutron field would have had time to finish its destructive job of snuffing out human life aboard the entire craft. When the inquiry into the accident occurred, there were only a few surviving passengers left for answering questioned about the accident. The ones left alive all repeated the same exact story about the mishap. The fuselage of the aircraft echoed with a loud buzzing crackling sound before it filled up with a strange smell in toxic gas, making everyone vomit from its strong offensive and very strange stench. The eyes of all passengers instantly watered, whilst their starving lungs all screamed for fresh oxygen because of the volatile strength of the putrid gas. The descent prior to landing became unstable, everyone's heads and arms being tossed from side to side as the aircraft twisted and turned just prior to its slamming down into the runway. It was a good thing the plane broke in two on impact for the survivors' wellbeing. Fresh air and oxygen came flowing into the plane's fuselage so the remaining passengers still alive could get a breath of much needed fresh air. They, too, would have surely all died from the strong putrid gas that had surrounding them that had taken their precious oxygen away from them. When the ones who could help, helped and saved everyone able to talk and move were off the plane, the very few strong men left, went back into the fuselage of the aircraft to help the others still strapped in their seats. Some of the passengers, and crew were still smoking and making sizzling cooking sounds just moments after the crash. There was no help for anyone who had this strange smelling smoke and gases ascending from their lifeless bodies and clothing. They all looked like dead seated mummies, still all strapped to their seats while the ones who had tried to save them were overcome with emotion seeing mothers with their small children still strapped to their seats seated beside them, and not a single solitary thing they could do to help save anyone of them, especially the little ones. Some of the survivors sat and lie along the runway in pain waiting for rescue when it began to rain.

Every fatality lately from the neutron monster was recently recorded during a rainstorm, just prior to or just after it stopped raining. The neutron sheens of rainbow colors in greens, yellows, and reddish browns danced among the rain clouds like lightning, but there was never the sound of thunder or the slightest sounds or rumbling associated with the sheen. Only once in a new blue moon would anyone hear the muffled sounds of thunder like noises mixed within the stormy clouds above.

Lately the muffled sounds of thunder were becoming more frequent and more pronounced with every new storm that appeared over the horizon around the planet.

CHAPTER SEVENTY-SIX

Safely in Orbit

Lieutenant Marsh pulled hard on the mechanical levers to activate the detonation of explosives attached to their ends to detach the main rockets from the shuttles undercarriage. Lieutenant Marsh had taken the place of Captain Ann Mitchell as the new navigator assigned to the Omega One's mission. The shuttle barely shook as the main thruster rockets used to get the Omega up into orbit separated from the cradle used to attach them to the spacecraft blew away. The rockets had spent their entire useful life, as the shuttle suddenly relaxed its g-force upon the crew inside the shuttle when the rockets exhausted their thrusting fuel. He then next pulled firm on another set of levers igniting the second stage rockets to finish placing the Omega One into its final rendezvousing orbit with the space station a few hundreds of miles ahead of them. The Omega shuttered slightly when the second stage rockets came to life, pushing its cargo and crew of astronauts back into their seats with more g-force, thrusting the Omega with its payload of space modules forward and upward into its needed orbit circling the globe on a well-predetermined and intended course.

Lieutenant Marsh was Colonel Anderson's second pick as navigator, and had him in training prior to him going to see Ann just in case she said no. He really thought she would be onboard the Omega One with him this last mission into space, and was glad he had had Jim start the training prior to his quest off to Vermont. Jim didn't have much training, but had shown great abilities in his previous performances in the space program.

As Colonel Anderson glanced back over his shoulder feeling the main thrusters depart the Omega One, he soon felt the second stage rockets come to life. This made the great weight of concern lift from off his wondering shoulders. The mission was going too good to be true, and they would be at the International Space Station on a well-predetermined time. Everything this time was going ahead like clockwork, and not like the last mission he had flown.

Breaking through the ionosphere was a spectacular sight for Jim. The star-lit canopy ahead of the Omega One out its windshield was the most spectacular, most brilliant of sights Lieutenant Marsh had ever witnessed in his entire lifetime so far, as this was his first time into outer space. He had never had the opportunity to see the heavenly display of stars upon its canopy of black this close up never before, and was totally awe struck with astonishment with its most magnificent beauty. Looking at it out the windshield of the spacecraft thinking he was dreaming for it was such a beautiful sight.

"Pressurize the cabin to sea level pressure, Lieutenant." Commander Anderson yelled back to Lieutenant Marsh, as Lieutenant Marsh followed through with his orders as the cabin in the Omega became less hostile to the crewmembers as the barometric pressure increase.

Everything prior to charging the batteries for power were done by hand, using pressure gauges and air tanks to do the job without the customary use of computers onboard to do the job, the way Lieutenant Marsh was taught when he first joined the space program before the deadly neutron attack. Lieutenant Marsh had been hard at work preparing for this big task of his every day for the past couple of weeks, working ten and twelve long hard strenuous hours every day since. He went over his every step of his assignment, lever, by lever, and valve by valve, and doing it in his sleep at night, continually practicing when awake or sleeping. He wanted to make his first time flight into outer space a happy experience, excited to be a part of the crew. Everything he touched whether it was a valve or some different levers for different jobs on the mission seemed to turn out to be golden for him and for the Omega One's crew. Who needed computers he thought with all these new fandangle mechanical devices affixed to the spacecraft. He turned out to be the next best navigator Commander Anderson had ever run into except for Captain Mitchell.

Not wanting to make another mistake like the one he had on the first mercy mission, Commander Anderson held onto the second stage rocket burn until they had exhausted themselves as the main rockets had done. He knew it would be easier to slow the Omega down on its final approach to the space station than waste the much preciously needed fuel in trying to catch up to the International Space Station this time with the Omega's manually operated positioning booster rockets. That had been the most crucial of blundered mistakes he had made on the last mission, and he did not want a repeat of it this time. They had been extremely fortunate in their last mission to space, having used up all the extra jaytoe bottles of fuel and still have a successful conclusion occur for everyone at the end. The outcome of the last mission could have been a devastating one, and a whole lot different if the main battery banks had failed them.

Once the Omega One was in its final orbit and closing fast toward the space station, the crew of the Omega One began filling the dry lead core batteries with its sulfuric acid life giving solution to bring the battery banks up to full power capabilities.

The Commander had the crew position the solar absorbing electrical shields toward the sun to absorb even the minutest amount of solar power they could possibly get from the sun, and began broadcasting radio signals to the space station immediately soon as the instrument control panel in front of them came to life and they had power.

CHAPTER SEVENTY-SEVEN

The Happy Eye in the Sky

Using the eye in the sky for the slightest ray of hope from below, the cosmonauts watched their American friends over the past week transport a new shuttle from one of its three huge hangers at the cape out to one of its launching pads. This meant one of two things, and Commander Ivan of the space station hoped it was his first guess of a rescue mission and not just that of a restocking mission for his crew. His crew was getting ready to die out there in orbit from the lack of proper food and nutrition along with a very critically low oxygen supply they had left in their tanked oxygen system, and the plants they had onboard were not thriving the way they should be in their producing usable oxygen. The best thing for everyone onboard this time would be rescuing, and not just restocking, but the latter would be better than the alternative of nothing happening at all.

Cape Canaveral had come alive again ever since the rescue of their fellow cosmonauts in their life raft and their safe return to Florida. The eye in the sky had been busy watching several times a day in their orbit every time they passed overhead of the cape. The lonely forgotten crew of the space station was in total bliss as the cosmonaut at the telescope gave a second by second account of this launch of a new shuttle from the Kennedy Space Center to them over the station's intercom and monitoring systems aboard the space station. The crews of the space station were lucky that they were in a position to watch the launch of the shuttle from its initial first burn right through its second burn, and then the eye in the sky telescope lost sight of the craft prior to the shuttle passing out through the earth's atmosphere and into space with them. The space station's speed in orbit took them out of sight out over the Atlantic Ocean and into their orbit around the earth to its dark side of blackness. Everyone onboard the space station felt a lot, if not just a little relief, knowing they hoped they were not the only ones in orbit now. They all had a ray of hope, a tiny sense of relief, knowing someone was coming for them or bringing them more supplies to sustain them from a failing life support system. With a little bit of luck, they all hoped, most the crew would be able to return back home to Earth if the Americans had retrofitted this new shuttle to carry more personnel back to Earth with them than the last mission did. It was only a dream for most, but one has to live on dreams sometimes just to stay alive. The thought of living longer, even if it was in space, rejuvenated the weary that had just about given up on life itself and were expecting the worst in life to happen to them in this void of heaven above their loved ones. They were beginning to think this was going to be their coffin just knowing they were all doomed to die, but not now.

Happy thoughts of going back home to Earth began to flow through the troubled minds of the ones who had just about given up and were ready to take their own lives rather than suffer the consequences of a slow death in space. They all became excited like little children at Christmas time, thinking of the coming of Santa Claus and all of his gifts. The shuttle, being the sleigh, and the gifts they were to receive would be more life supporting supplies or a free ticket back home to their families and loved ones with this crew.

If the Americans were capable of sending this spacecraft to re-supply them, then there should be no reason why in the world they couldn't send another, and another, and another until everyone onboard the doomed space station was back home safe and sound. At least there was a glimmer of hope now, and a little hope went a long, long way at a critical time in all their lives. The excitement aboard the space station turned to joyful bliss. Jubilation with it brought back many lost smiles to the many who had just about given up on their fellow Russians and men from below. The dreadful thought of dying by suffocation from the lack of oxygen was over for some of them for a while, or was it? Would the mere return home to Earth suffocate some of them in more mean ways than losing one's breathe in space? The loss of some loved ones and the loss of friends. The loss of entire families, and death to entire towns around the globe might be too much for some of them to manage now after being held captive in space for so long. Maybe suffocating from the lack of oxygen in space would be a more pleasant, a more humane way to let them all perish, than to bring them all back to Earth and let them face the music of reality the way it actually was on Earth now. Suffocating by realization might be more a slow agonizing death than seeing loved ones who have lost their soul mates, lost in such pain, half their once good minds gone by way of simplicity and foolishness, just barely surviving day to day in stupor, and in swaddling dirty waste and soiled clothing.

Unquestionably, a death in space would save them all from this most agonizing slow cruel mecca of madness waiting for them below on Earth.

A Friendly Voice in Space

"International Space Station calling the U.S. Twitchel. Come in please, Twitchel. Do you read us, over? International Space Station, calling the U.S. shuttle Twitchel. Do you read, over? International Space Station this is the U.S. Omega One space shuttle calling, do you read us, over. Space Station this is the U.S. Omega One space shuttle calling, do you read, over. International Space Station, this is the U.S. Omega One space shuttle calling, please come in space station, over."

The radio operator spun the frequency dial on his radio running the calling message out over all the different radio frequencies. Finally, the space station noticed the message broadcast from the Omega One, and returned its call.

"Omega One, this is the International Space Station, over. We hear you loud and clear, who is your Commanding officer Omega One, over?"

"Commander, Colonel Nelson Anderson is in charge, over."

"May I speak to your commander, please?"

"All channels open, lieutenant. How are you doing, Ivan? You can talk to all of us, commander, our channels have been all opened up for you commander, and how have you and your comrades been holding out up here?"

"Quite well, thank you Colonel Anderson, especially now that you are here with us, sir, or almost here with us commander. Food and oxygen supplies have been getting rather scarce in these cramped quarters of ours, Nelson. How are the crewmembers we sent back to Earth several months ago doing now commander, especially the two very pregnant ones?"

"Everything is going quite well with every one of your comrades commander, very well indeed!"

"How many supplies did you bring with you this time around, over?"

"We brought you and your comrades a couple of busses, Ivan."

"What do you mean a couple of busses, commander?"

"A couple of your own Soviet-built space capsules, Ivan, along with this very much modified shuttle with as many possible extra seats for your entire crew, sir. We are all going home together back to the earth this last trip, Ivan."

Tremendous jubilation exploded in the confines of the space station, as grown men cried happy tears of joy, while hugging and kissing each other like children in a daycare center learning they were going to the zoo. The female cosmonauts almost passed out by being so pleased and happy that they too would all be going home this time. Ivan had to take a seat at the control station from stand floating as he became so weak kneed and light headed from his own excitement.

This was it, their final ticket home, and now they had something to be overly jubilant about, maybe.

CHAPTER SEVENTY-NINE

The Docking

"Commander, we will rendezvous with the space station at approximately 1200 hours U. S. Eastern time, sir. We will plan to dock at portal one airlock platform at approximately 1300 hours, commander. It is 09:38 eastern time our time. Please set your timing instruments and devices to correspond with ours, Ivan. We will set the controls on both the shuttle and space lab computers to guide the Omega One through her porting positioning procedures to our Port A with both the crafts' computers synchronized to one another, sir."

"You have no idea how good it feels to have electrical power back again, Ivan. You all will not believe it whence you return back home to Earth. We now live as if we were back in the dark ages compared to what it was like before you and your crew left the planet to come up here."

Minds of the Soviets aboard the space station ran rampant, overjoyed with happy thoughts thinking how nice it was going to be to be back with their loved ones once again. The thoughts of just being back home on the family farm, back in the city of Moscow, or just plainly standing on the good old firm terra firma of the earth once again brought great joy to most everyone aloft. The only other thing that could possibly be more joyful than the moment at hand, would be to have already have landed back home on Earth, and already be with family and friends.

Some of the sad lonely crew sped off to their cramped living quarters. They took out the only picture or pictures they had of their loved ones back home from their closed lockers. Some had placed them away so not to constantly think about their loved ones back there. They began weeping over them with emotional joy, imagining the feeling their loved ones' arms would feel like wrapped tenderly yet firmly around them once again. Others imagined in tender thought about making love to their wives passionately, and showing just how much they had missed them over their time away from them. A couple the women cosmonauts thought how nice it would be to make love to their husbands in bed, and not making love to them using their imaginations alone in space. To touch one another was going to be bliss. Staring at the pictures of their children and family members brought happy smiles to their once so lonely, but now so joyful happy faces. Wondering how much taller, prettier, and more beautiful they would have become when they returned back home to be with them. Some thoughts of doubt about how their elderly parents and grandparents tolerated what had happened in their lives when they return. What would be the changes that had taken place in their communities during their absence?

If only the majority aboard the space station really knew what had drastically happened to most everyone down below, some would surely have rather chosen to stay on in the space station to live out their remaining days of life and pass away in their own silence. Some would want to take their own lives and most likely would rather than face the silence and emptiness they would find in their desolate homes back home on Earth. For some when and if they all returned back home, the pain of agony was going to kill them anyway.

Colonel Anderson, prior to liftoff had received word from the Kremlin on the status of all cosmonauts' families present and past history of those aboard the International Space Station, and for that very reason he had left the list of their families wellbeing, and not so well knowledge of being behind. He wanted all happy faces to greet him this time around when they opened the air locker doors between the two vessels, and did not want to disturb better than half the space station's crew before they were to return back home to Earth. He decided it was best left up to their own government to inform the lucky and not so lucky cosmonauts of the good, as well as the very sad very bad news about their immediate family's catastrophes whence they returned back home to their own country.

"The space station is coming into view, commander."

"Fire retro rockets, major." Bill reached over to the control panel to fire the retro rockets when Lieutenant Marsh interrupted him.

"Not necessary commander. The computer says we have one minute and counting before slowing mode takes over for us and slows us down for the docking procedures, sir."

"Never mind then, Bill. Let the onboard computers do their jobs. We do not have to do everything by hand anymore seeing we have electricity to do the job for us."

"It's very hard to accept that idea up here, sir, seeing we don't have to do all the work by hand anymore."

Just the way Lieutenant Marsh had said it would happen. The Omega One's retro rockets were ignited by the onboard computer calculating the exact time and distance between the two crafts, and the shuttle slowed down to intercept in the global course the space station was orbiting in, in order to prepare the two space vehicles for their docking. The timing between the two vehicles could not have been any more precise. The two onboard computers corresponded with each other precisely in preparation for them to link up with each other. If they had tried doing everything by sight and hand, they could have done the slowing down preparation manually, but it would have taken them twice as much longer in time to do the same job. The craft could have used up the much needed fuel they must use in their return flight back to Earth. The Omega One had already used up a lot of extra fuel in carrying the massive weight of the two space modules and its retrofitted cockpit to hold so many more passengers for their return trip back home.

"Space station, this is the Omega One, over."

"Go ahead Omega One."

"We are preparing to dock space station docking platform "A". Is everything cleared at main docking platform for docking, over?"

"Main link docking platform all cleared for docking Omega One. Airlock chamber platform "A" now ready to accept docking of craft Omega One over".

"We will let the computers finish doing their jobs, over."

"We will see you at 1300 hours, Ivan, over."

"Cannot wait to see and shake your hand, commander. It's been way too long since our last visit."

"Roger that, Ivan! Glad to be back for this special occasion. See you in about forty-two minutes, over."

"Forty-two minutes and counting, colonel. Forty-two and counting, see you then."

The friendly joyous sounds of metal to metal clatter of the docking clamps clamping tight to one another sounded like reindeer hooves on a roof and tones of sleigh bells ringing at Christmas time to the tired crew of the space station. What a beautiful joyful sound the two vehicles made as they engaged to one another, becoming one united vessel at the docking platform.

The joyful hearts aboard the space station finally beat with hope this time in them, instead of gloom, and doom they had all been beating with for so long a time, including Commander Ivan's saddened heart.

When the safety airlocks decompression chambers between the vehicles opened, happy beaming smiles began generating from everyone on both sides. The happy crew on the space station greeted their rescuers with hugs and kisses so dear like only family members would give them to one another. Lieutenant Marsh was overwhelmed with all the warm greetings he received, not knowing anyone on board the space station. It made him delighted he had so unselfishly volunteered for this risky mission, and receiving the overwhelming salutations he so deservingly received, he had not had the opportunity to live with these people for over a year's time in space in the past. He had not been on the first mission, but could only imagine the reception that crew received on their first mission. It was amazing the gratitude this crew offered for the gift of life they were about to receive.

If it was not for Colonel Anderson, and him almost having to get down on his hands and knees and begin begging NASA for this mission, all these happy people would have been but a mere thought in the backs of someone's blank mind back home on Earth, and thoughts of those few left alive that loved them.

CHAPTER EIGHTY

The Last Stage

After a healthy feast of thanksgiving with special foods and selected antibiotics that Colonel Anderson purposely brought with them, the work of the U.S. astronauts to return the Russian cosmonauts back to Earth began. For the next several days, both crews worked diligently with one another in the preparation for the shutdown of the space station, getting the two space modules ready with their retrofit, and the Omega One's retrofit for their reentry back through and into the earth's atmosphere.

Both Soviet space capsules were inspected back on Earth to see if they were space ready for a safe flight back home or not. All the makings for new battery life brought with the crew of the Omega to prepare their batteries in space for the onboard computers that both modules already had in them. The airtight seals aboard were inspected prior to occupation, or the cosmonauts onboard them could perish on reentry from the intense heat and sudden loss of oxygen.

Colonel Anderson had only hoped both capsules would be space ready when they were loaded into the cargo bay of the Omega One. It had been a crap shot in the dark, but one worthy of taking a chance on for the rescue of this well deserving crew. If all failed with the module, another rescue mission would have to be planned in the very near future, but not without an act of congress for its permission. NASA

476

was not in favor of this last one, and did not want this mission to take place, never mind possibly a third.

Extensive testing on the two modules took place several times over, to make absolute sure the safety of all onboard equipment they inspected. The oxygen system along with its reserve, the pressure seals, and power systems all checked out positive, giving everyone a good feeling. No one left behind this time to fend for themselves.

Practice landing procedures went on daily for the crew of the space station who were going to be using the space modules for their own return. Colonel Anderson informed them of the mistake the first capsule crew had experienced in releasing their main parachutes too early in their return flight, and it almost cost the crew their lives. Timing for the proper release of the main landing parachutes would prove to be the most critical of all procedures during their return flight back to Earth.

After several days, the three crafts had passed all their needed testing and retrofitting for their safe flights back home. Both Colonel Anderson and Commander Ivan were pleased with the outcome of the retrofit of the Omega and the extensive testing of both space modules. One of the modules had failed the life support system's testing. They took several needed parts from the space station's section B life support system in repairing the one space module. After removing the special equipment from section B, that section of the space station had to be shut down and sealed off. The crew jury-rigged the oxygen unit scavenged from section B into the module for its safe return flight. All went well with retrofitting it into the disabled module. At first, they thought it was a futile attempt, but with a little Yankee ingenuity by Lieutenant Marsh, and his good Irish luck, it fit without a hitch. It cramped the usable space inside the module for those using it, but would be worth it. Riding cramped up was better than the alternative of being left behind to die in space, or was it?

The time for their return back home to Earth was quickly approaching. The last assembly aboard the space station took place in the dining hall of the space lab. The schedule for the departure of the three space vehicles was finalized at the last meal with everyone onboard the space station.

The Omega One's crew would be the first to depart the space station. Commander Anderson would land his craft at Cape Canaveral first, and prepare the landing facilities to intercept the first space capsule, the second day after their initial arrival. The second space module would land the fourth day after Omega One, and then the entire space crew from the International Space Station would all be back on Earth and well, they hoped. If, by chance, the first space module did not make it safely back to Earth, the second module would still keep the same time schedule, landing on the fourth day, at the cape as planned.

The weather over the cape was discussed in great detail. None of the modules was to take any unnecessary chances this time. The weather was the biggest factor for them now, as the neutron field was very active during or around the formation or the disbanding of any storms lately. They wanted and needed perfect weather to be around the cape and even in the subtropics to guarantee a safe return home flight for all.

The space station ordered to alert the cape landing facility below by signaling it with its tracking light system the night before departure if everything looked favorable for the next day's landing. They would signal them below when they traveled overhead in the darkness by two and three flashes of their beacons. Two for thumbs up and three for thumbs down. Two to land the next day, and three to wait for better weather because the space station was not in immediate danger now of running out of food or oxygen. If it took a couple of weeks for everyone to return safely back to Earth, it would be well worth the wait.

The two crews parted for their quarters to get a good night's sleep before Omega One departed in the early morning hours, just prior to sun up over the cape and the landing facilities.

CHAPTER EIGHTY-ONE

The Return

"Space station, this is Omega One, over."

"Go ahead Omega One."

"It is a go space station, release docking clamps, over."

"Docking clamp release switch activated Omega One." With the squeal of the releasing clamp, the Omega One drifted slowly back away from the space station. This time there was no sad deathly feelings of desertion or fear in the ones left behind in orbit to die. The only fear was fear itself in the returning flight back to Earth some feared most.

The happy feelings among the last few cosmonauts left aboard the space station, including Commander Ivan, were ecstatic with self-pleasing pleasure with this timely event. No one left behind this time gave them all a most wonderful feeling, especially to Commander Ivan. He thought for sure right from the beginning that he would never see his loving family ever again.

It had been many days of hard mind numbing, and corporal work to ready both space capsules and the Omega One for their safe return trip back home to Earth. For most of them, except for the Omega One crew, it seemed like a dream to the many cosmonauts after having been lost in space for so many months. Soon they, too, would wake up from this horrid dream, and find themselves still in the dilemma of yet another more horrid morbid situation of being stuck back home in a dream they could not wake up from or escape.

This time going home had not been a dream, and when they awoke the work still continued until this day when the first spacecraft pulled itself away from their home from up in the heavens.

A couple of the crew from the space station leaving aboard the Omega One were half scared to death to leave the safety and solitude of the space station. They hadn't flown in so long and were experiencing the feeling of claustrophobia from all being so closely confined in the Omega's flight compartment, or was it just plain excitement for them in their returning back home again? They were all feeling like first time parachute jumpers, who had jumped for the first time and had committed themselves to the sky above the earth. Once out the aircraft doorway, it becomes too late for you for the wind of the earth's sky will take you away from the airplane's open fuselage door.

It becomes too late to change one's mind after jumping, wanting to return back to the safety inside the aircrafts fuselage where you had just mille seconds prior to jumping had been safe. Now the parachutists' lives are in the strength of the nylon straps as well in the nylon canopy of the chute above them in safely returning them back to the earth below. Control with these cosmonauts over their lives as parachutists given up and entrusted to the safety of the shuttle crew, strangers who were at the controls flying the space shuttle home. Not all these Americans were strangers, but none of these cosmonauts had ever entrusted their lives to anyone, especially not into the hands of enemies with a controlling power, only to the ones they had trained with prior to traveling into outer space. All they could possibly hope for now was that Commander Anderson, and his flight crews were as well qualified in their training as they felt they had been in theirs. It did not matter anymore now, for they were like that parachutist who had just went out the door above the earth, and had committed him or herself to the safety of the parachute and its nylon cords.

Home, sweet home, sweet home, sweet home, what was home now? The remembrance of going to the opera with one's family, or going fishing down side the canal by the power station. Going to hockey match games with friends and skating with children and friends on frozen ponds or at public skating rink, or flying to the French Riviera for a week or two of pleasure with one's spouse just to get away. What would life be like back on Earth with all these drastic changes being told to them by these strangers, who were not really strangers, but who were in control of their flight home to their new destiny in life.

What were these many changes to the earth going to do to them and this thing everyone has been calling the creature of the air? This neutron field that was deadly to all living creatures except the ones who lived beneath the sea or beneath the surface of the earth's crust. Whatever the changes, they would have to face them soon, and they did not really care what they were as long as they could be back home again with their loving families once again, or could they? No more electrical power to operate lights at one's desks to help them read or electrical power to fire engines in cars to travel. No more power above the surface of the earth to run all the conveniences in useful appliances they once grew so accustomed to having. Just the thought about all these new changes scared the hell out of most of them, but the worst would soon come to pass.

After landing, they would find out the truths about their devastated families and friends back home along with their new destiny. The thoughts of this creature the Americans kept referring to as the thing in the sky worried many of the cosmonauts. How could it be an invisible creature that took the life out of anyone if it was invisible? If it is not electrical, then how in the hell can it take one's life if it did not electrify them as everyone says it does? How can it make its victims smell as if all had burnt to death by acid when there is none in the air? The earth once known to them as home seemed invaded by aliens from outer space, and they were partially correct when they thought of this invasion from outer space this way. It was an invasion from space but not by aliens. It was caused by some of their over greedy leaders back on Earth who wanted to take over control of the planet by using power of dictatorship for themselves. They lost their own lives to this power they had created leaving the deadly creature in the sky to reap the power in their stupidity for years to come over the earth.

The cosmonauts returning to Earth were like new born baby fetuses ready to leave their mother's safe and secure womb up in the space station as and the flight back to Earth, their travels down the birth canal of their mother's birth canal releasing them out into a life they were not yet accustomed to. While they were in space, they were safe from hurt and many other outer cruelties that they would soon encounter by experiencing the massive hurt and confusion in their new environment. The safe haven of the space station was now over with, with the releasing of the docking clamps.

Releasing the Omega One from the space station's docking clamps was like the mothers first contraction before giving birth to her unborn child. The flight back to Earth, that special voyage down through the birth canal, and the landing the first cry of the newborn baby just prior to venturing out and growing up in their new existence.

"Fire thruster rockets, major." The landing crew at the cape had had their eyes pasted to the blue and partially cloudy skies for the last several days anticipating the return of their spacecraft, the Omega One.

The fire stations overhead garage doors were purposely being left wide open all day during the daylight hours in anticipation of the spacecraft returning soon, so someone on the ground could hear the sonic boom the shuttle would make on its reentry into the earth's atmosphere overhead. They were all ready to make a grand welcome home to the crew, and hoped their services would not be needed other than as a welcoming committee. The space shuttle Omega One was due back sometime this week. The ground crew did not know the approximate time or how long it would take the crews above to prepare everything on her and the space modules for their safe return flight back home to Earth for everyone. This landing would not be like the last ones. They were prepared this time for the shuttle's return. If there was to be one, it would take place between the hours of 0900 hours and 1200 hours, give or take an hour one way or the other. They would be able to see the Omega One soaring high through the sky like an eagle in flight high above the earth's crust leaving a vapor trail behind it like a tail as it evaporated any moisture around it into steam.

"Fire the retro rockets, lieutenant."

"No not yet, commander, the computer dictates two more minutes and counting, sir."

"Very well lieutenant. It sure seems nice to still have power doesn't it?"

"Yes Sir, commander, it sure does." Lieutenant Marsh counted down the last few seconds with the computer in its final countdown ready to fire the retrorockets. Three, Two, One, fire, the retro rockets fired simultaneously. This allowed the shuttle to slow down from seventeen thousand miles an hour downward to a slower reentry speed, and placed the craft into a 45-degree pitch angle for their rapid descent, allowing the Omega One to safely reenter the earth's atmosphere without burning itself up.

"What is the bottom temperature of this bird, lieutenant?"

"The clay-tiles are at 900 degrees Fahrenheit, and climbing, sir."

"OK Bill! Follow through with me now. Hold her steady at the 45-degree angle of descent firmly with me now. That damn neutron thing will take the computer away from us at any minute now, and we want to be ready for the floundering of this bird if there is any."

The Soviet passengers were able to listen in on everything going on in the cockpit which made them both excited and nervous about everything taking place all at the same time. Some were now beginning to get the sick feeling the force of gravity was having upon their week bodies for not having experienced gravity in over two or more years in space. It did not feel too pleasant to them now, and most did not think they would survive through the reentry and landing because it bothered them so. The flesh of their bodies began crushing down around their weak skeletal frames making them struggle to breath. The g-force grew stronger on them as they descended down into the extent of lightheadedness they thinking they would all surely all pass out from the extensive pressure. Colonel Anderson and his crew felt the discomfort of the g-force as well, but nothing like the discomfort their passengers were going through with theirs.

The yellowy brownish green orange sheen came as expected. The electrical power in the Omega One's instrument panel vanished into blackness when the massive neutron field snuck into the cockpit via the electrical wiring harness. It quickly vanished back out into the air of the atmosphere after not finding its way into any space suits trying to suck the life out if any of the astronauts had the slightest flaw in their suits. The batteries onboard were instantly drained of all their electrical power leaving the onboard computers a useless instrument for controlling the Omega One.

"Hold the controls back steady, Bill. We want to keep her nose up until we reach 10,000 feet." Bill acknowledged Colonel Anderson by looking his way and nodding his head in response. "According to everything prior to the loss of power we were right on schedule and due course. Lieutenant, pressurize the cabin so we can remove these helmets, please."

CHAPTER EIGHTY-TWO

The Sonic Boom

Suddenly the ground crew heard that all so familiar sound they had all been expecting to hear for the last few days of the returning space shuttle from outer space. It was that familiar sound of the Omega One breaking the sound barrier high up in the heavens. The firefighters fired up their diesel engines with their air jump starters. The sudden influx of air shooting through the starters whistled a loud defining shrilling sound as the engines of their vehicles came to life, and the blue smoke billowed out from their smokestacks. The ground crews pulled their rigs out to both sides of the runway to watch the magnificent scene of the Omega One touching down on what was supposed to be her last flight, or was it, they did not really know.

The ground of the earth below the Omega One shook from the sudden shock of the sound wave the Omega One caused by breaking the sound barrier above it. People on the ground looked up unrepentantly to see a rainstorm approaching with lightning flashing for the first time in as many months as they could remember. It would have been too good to think the power of the earth was winning its battle in taking back the extent of the strong neutron field of the atmosphere and retuning everything back to normalcy once again.

Scientist predicted a return one day to normality around the earth, if the massive neutron field in the atmosphere was somehow neutralized. With everything that was happening on Earth, the people of the planet thought it was a prediction similar to Newton's faulty, and the people of Earth were adjusting to their new ways of life without any hopes of normality ever returning.

The shuttle's crew scrambled down into the belly of the Omega and cranked down her landing gear, while Commander Anderson and Major Bill held her steady on course with her flight controls. Landing flaps needed cranking down into the landing position just like the landing gears. This was something the astronauts onboard the Twitchel had no control over on their first and second landings.

Lieutenant Marsh turned out to be as excellent a navigator as Ann had been on both her previous flights. Colonel Anderson was overly pleased with his selection of him and the job Lieutenant Marsh did for him and his crew was turning out to be an excellent one.

"Here we go, gents. Boy, does that black strip of tarmac look appealing to the eyes. Pull her back gently, major. A little more uplift, Bill. That's it, Bill, that's it."

The crew who had cranked down the landing gear of the Omega One had just sat back down in their seats and buckled themselves in just prior the tires of the Omega One smoking and coming to life rolling down the runway. Lieutenant Marsh let the braking chutes wide open behind the Omega One with a quick yank on some levers, and everything was going as planned for this rescue mission.

Commander Anderson could not remember a better landing even when everything was working onboard the old-fashioned way with electricity powered hydraulics for the flight controls and for the landing gears.

The anxious ground crew watched through their binoculars in amazement as this big bird like an eagle came zooming in out of the heavens above leaving a torrent trail of hot white mist in the sky behind her. She soared through the air like a jet under full throttle. This was the first space shuttle anyone had seen coming in on the runway in over three long years. It was a beautiful sight watching this particular craft come floating down out of the heavens and make such a wonderful landing. She touched down at the far end first part on the runway and came speeding down the runway the way she was intended to do with her beautiful red, white, and blue parachutes fully extended out behind her. It had to have been the best and smoothest shuttle landing ever recorded in the life of NASA.

The Soviet cosmonauts on board were astonished with the smoothness of the landing of the shuttle. They were expecting this hard usual bouncy sort of landing they were so use to having in the space capsules that hit like a rock on land, and preferred to land them in the softness of the water. They could find no fault even with the roughness of the runway. It was hard to tell in the landing when the lift of air holding them up in flight gave way to the support of the runway holding them up on the landing gear, except for the occasional soft bump of the asphalt beneath the wheels.

"I need some help with these brakes, major. Give me a steady pressure Bill. A little more Bill, a little more." Colonel Anderson and Major Bill both applied a steady strong pressure to the braking pedal system bringing the Omega One slowing her down to the runway.

"OK, Bill, release your brakes, I have her now." Bill took both his feet away from the hydraulic ruder braking system and let Colonel Anderson have full control of stopping his craft. Colonel Anderson lifted both feet from the two braking pedals so the Omega One could coast all the way down the runway to the awaiting line of fire trucks. Rescue personnel lined both sides of the runway in case a disaster might hit the Omega One on its landing, but nothing drastic happened. Commander Anderson let the spacecraft come right up to the line of fire trucks before he resumed applying breaking pressure to bring the Omega One to a complete stop. The firefighters brought the stairway ramp truck up alongside the Omega One's fuselage allowing the hatch to be opened allowing everyone onboard to offload to the awaiting vehicles.

By chance, the eye in the sky was in the proper location of its orbit to watch with excitement as the Omega One came to a halt at the end of the runway in front of so many vehicles. They knew some of their companions would be leaving for their homeland shortly, and could not wait to be back on Earth. Maybe with a little bit of luck, they all

could go back home to Russia together. It would only be a short, very long forty-eight hours before the next spacecraft would or could depart from its orbit in space and attempt a landing where the Omega One had just made its safe landing.

The next day, looking down from the eye in the sky, the crew aboard the space lab watched as the Omega One was on its way from its landing location to an empty hanger. The Space Station crew knew they were getting everything ready for another space vehicle to land there. The weather surrounding the cape and the Leeward Islands toward the eastern Atlantic looked very favorable for the next day's attempt at returning the first space capsule back to Earth.

That night when they passed overhead of the cape, the space station sent its Morse coded signal to the team of observers below, signaling them that they would be coming home soon, or at least attempting to.

0400 hours in the early morning of the following day, found the crew of the first Soviet space capsule sitting nervously in their seats ready to depart the space station. If all went well, which everyone hoped and prayed would, the other space module in another forty-eight hours to the minute, the last of the Soviet crew members aboard the space station would be on their way home as well.

"Commander, we are secure, and ready to depart, sir."

"Release holding clamps at will; see you all in a couple days, comrades. You all have a safe return flight back home, comrades. Say "hi" to every one below for us, and be safe."

"Will do, Commander Ivan, we will try to be, module one capsule, over and out." Commander Ivan took the pleasure of releasing the holding clamps securing the first module to the space station. He was thrilled to be able to set his people free from their bondage held captive in space. His only fear for their safety was in their releasing the landing parachutes too early in their descending phase, and feared they would drift out to sea as the first module crew had done before.

Off the African coast was another slight disturbance taking place in the atmosphere. He was sure this time it would prove deadly instead of lucky for the next module crew, if they ended up in the Atlantic Ocean this time around. Worse than being off course and landing in the water, his thoughts of fear were again in their timing. If they deplored their chutes too late, they would drill themselves deep into the hard crust of the earth's hard surface, like a falling meteor, and be lost without a trace.

Commander Ivan happily pushed the button control for releasing the module's securing clamps. The crew inside the space module heard the metallic ringing in their ears as the clamps of the space station released the module from its grasp, and let them float out into limbo drifting out away from the security of their dock. The release did not cause any sensation of movement to any of them, but hearing the sound of the clamps releasing gave them a feeling of insecurity knowing they were on their own now, and it was up to them from this point forward to perform on their own behalf or not perform it properly. Their lives were in each other's hands now, and all they could do was to pray and work together for their safe return back home to earth. Nervous sweat began to seep from the pores of the crewmembers in the space capsule.

The sky below was clear but pure reflections of the neutron's colorful sheen attacking the Omega One were stuck firmly in their minds. Everyone knew what they were about to enter, and hopefully pass through the realm of the beast safely before returning safely back home to the earth's surface without a mishap. Smiles, glancing from left to right to each other, giving happy signs of elation on their success of going home while their subconscious minds had thoughts of the dangers that lay ahead of them, and if this would be the last happy time they all would spend together before meeting their maker. Whatever happened, whether it be for the good or bad, at least they were all together in this hopeful voyage as one! It was their destiny now, to face the future whatever that future held in store for them. They fired the capsule's booster rockets, sending the module down toward the spinning globular ball below, putting them into a path of reentry while slowing the space capsule down so it could make its reentry into the earth's atmosphere without it burning up.

A couple of the older cosmonauts leaving the space station had never experienced a reentry flight back into the earth's atmosphere before. They were very nervous about doing it, and very glad someone experienced was at the controls of their module during this dangerous time in their lives.   When the capsule would lose its electrical power, hopefully their selected navigator would have the timing for reentry down flawlessly for discharging their parachutes well programmed in his mind for a safe execution of the critical landing device allowing them a safe and happy return to the earth below. It was an uplifting experience as they passed down through the outer ozone layer of the stratosphere. They felt the booster rockets ejected from the module when they threw the switches to rid them from the module. This would allow the retro rockets to burn up as they fell toward the earth below leaving the capsule with its heat shields to absorb the intense heat buildup the capsule was designed to absorb, withstanding the immense reentry heat before the parachutes were released for their safe landing. They shot into the atmosphere with their heat shields glowing orange hot with heat. The neutron field struck as was expected, absorbing away the power from within their craft's battery packs, as the critical time of reentry was now upon them. The next move for them would be to execute the landing parachutes in order to slow their decent back to the earth's surface down for a safe landing.

"One thousand one, one thousand two, one thousand three", the capsule's navigator was counting down the seconds quietly in his mind as they shot down toward the round sphere below. Having reached an altitude he thought was safe, and the heat contained in the base of the module, he blew away the safety shields surrounding the portal window in front of him. The sky ahead of him looked a crispy blue in color. The sun shone bright above them as the horizon of the earth was becoming enormously round in size as they descended downward toward it. He continually counted down, trying to open the parachutes at the precise time during their descent was nerve wracking to him, but very critical for a happy ending to their flight. They knew the eye in the sky was watching their every move as they made their reentry back to earth. Commander Ivan had planned for the reentry when the space station would be above them during its orbit.

Commander Ivan was at the monitor counting every second as well, from the time the onboard computer of the module told them to release the booster rocket package until the time they released the main parachutes. He felt and knew the timing for releasing the parachutes to be the most crucial of all the reentry, and wanted nothing to go wrong with the ones he was watching when it was their time to fly. If the crew of the first capsule released the parachutes too soon, he on the next mission would want to wait a little longer in his own timing before executing his judgment in releasing their chutes. If they released them too late, they were destined to crash. If that was to happen to them, he would then subtract a certain amount of seconds from the number of seconds counted to ensure a safe landing for his comrades if he and his fellow cosmonauts made it through the monster in the sky's habitat, that he looked forward to passing through without difficulty, he hoped. Boy was it hard judging the right time to release the main chutes without the computer working to help. The navigator watched as the earth's horizon became more and more pronounced, and extreme in size. He determined it was time to execute the hardest decision he had ever made in his lifetime, other than shooting down another human being during a dogfight with his fighter jet one day. He knew the outcome of that day was either he or the enemy who had been pursuing him, but this critical decision was for him and several of his very dear friends.

Commander Ivan and the space station were just about out of sight of the descending module when he saw the spiraling of a tiny chute flutter as it shot up above the capsule, pulling out the main parachutes attached to a long tethered line. He marked this time down on the chart in front of him, and would have to wait till their next orbit around to tell if the capsule made it safely back to Earth or not.

The crew of the capsule felt the huge parachutes fill quickly with air. It gave them a freaky sensation as if they had become attached to the end of a bungee cord attached to the space station, as it slowed the descent of the capsule down. They had all been quite comfortable in weightlessness during the first stage of reentry. Now the great g-force grabbed a hold of them when the three huge main parachutes brought

them to an almost sudden halt in their descent so it felt. The huge parachutes let the capsule and its crew fall toward the earth like the downy feather from a bird drifting softly on a warm summer's breeze. Things definitely seemed to be going way too smooth with this reentry. Something drastic was about to happen at any moment for they all thought the worst was still to come. Things were very quiet aboard the capsule as everyone was waiting for whatever it was to happen, and did not dare say a word to one another about it with fingers crossed. They did not dare look left or right at one another in fear they would see one of their fellow cosmonauts looking the strange yellowy green dead in their seat, after hearing the strange tails about what the strange monster in the atmosphere did to individuals.

CHAPTER EIGHTY-THREE

A Lonely Cloud

It was approaching late morning as Colonel Anderson and the ground crew looking skyward spotted a lone colorful cloud above them come floating out of nowhere. When suddenly beneath the bright colored cloud, there hung a dark cone shaped object. It was a remarkable sight for Commander Anderson to observe, as the first space capsule came floating down out of the heavens down toward them where they were standing on the earth. They were very close, very close indeed to landing right on target, Colonel Anderson thought. They might get a little wet, but that all depended upon the gentle breeze of the day as it was not blowing very strong this forenoon.

Whistles, horns, and bells rang out as the ground crew prepared for their next new arrivals from space. Every building surrounding the Florida facility came to life as everyone scurried to the windows or ran outside to catch a glimpse of the cosmonauts landing at the cape, or a sighting of them floating overhead as they descended downward. It was not that they had never seen a landing of a space module before on their monitors, but that they may never see one ever again, at least not in their lifetime.

The simple risk of space travel these days had multiplied itself a thousand folds more times over, since the loss of electrically operated electronics equipped space vehicles and the future risk of loss of life was not worth a single life to be lost. If Commander Anderson and his fellow crewmembers had not made it safely back to Earth on their first return mission from the space station, the lives aboard the space station would have all been lost because no one on Earth would have dared to chance the risk of an attempted rescue mission to save them. Even if they had attempted to send a rocket full of supplies to the space station, it would have failed without electricity to operate the computers on board to navigate the rocket to its destination.

Colonel Anderson instructed the driver of his rescue vehicle to drive to the far end of the peninsula, for he thought for certain his friends were about to get them themselves very wet, and he was right on the money. The capsule came floating down in shallow water fifty feet from shore, and bobbed up and down in the water on the shallow waves on its inflated orange ring. The space module floated like a cork in the water as the crew inside blew open the capsules door, and readied themselves for their immediate departure from it.

The rescue teams were at the module soon after it hit the water, and there was nothing but happy smiling faces staring out from within the capsule and in from without the bobbing module. Everyone in or outside the module were all elated, but not so much as Colonel Anderson was with himself. He was the happiest being on planet Earth alive at that very moment, as if he had just delivered his own newborn baby into life. Right now he felt he had just delivered sextuplets into the world from outer space. He only hoped he could be lucky enough one more time to deliver another sextuplets alive, and doing well in another forty-eight hours or so in the next capsule.

How happy were the crewmembers of the module? Happy, but how happy would they remain once they found out the truth about their families and friends back home on Earth? Colonel Anderson destroyed all the information he had pertaining to all their families that he had requested. He came to a final decision after many long restless hours of self-debating within his own mind whether to tell his friends before they returned back home to Russia or not. He found it best in his righteous mind not to let the cat out of the bag from him and destroy any good feelings they had had toward him as a caring human being. He did not want to make a single enemy of his dear friends from aloft before any of them returned back home to Russia. They would have their own downfalls when they all returned home, and he did not want any remembrance of him as the grim reaper of bad news to anyone ever again. He knew some would hate him for bringing them home, but he could live with that.

CHAPTER EIGHTY-FOUR

The Loss of a Mission

Commander Ivan Khrushchev was the last cosmonaut to pass out of the air lock hatch of the floating International Space Station in its orbit. It had been his home in the stars for more than a couple plus years. He slowly and lastly step floated out and into the second space module. He slowly turned around one last time to take a look before he left its sanctuary, and thanked the hulk of steel up in the heavens for taking good care of him and his fellow crewmembers for so long. He felt like he was deserting an old friend. He considered the Space Laboratory more like a family member now, a caring brother who had saved his life, and now he was turning his back on the one who had helped him and the others out so many times in staying alive in the hostile environment of space. Slight misty tears of emotion filled his caring eyes as a warm feeling of thankfulness filled his heart. Were he and the others lucky enough to make the flight back home safely? He would look back up toward the heavens as often as he could during the dark of night, and thank the lonely beacon shining bright in the heavens for his life in her. He wondered if ever there would be anyone lucky enough to venture back to the stars and use her cavity for their every experiment ever again as they had. He felt extremely sad by having to leave such an exquisite component of a learning facility vacant, to drift vacated in space, for there was no hope for her now in these hard times of Earth. There were many new learning processes to be reckoned with back home on Earth, and he hoped whatever this laboratory had taught him and the others in these last couple of plus years, he would be able to use its knowledge back home to make home a better place to live, and he was sure it would in some way or another. Filled with sadness for the craft, he turned off all of her interior lights. He had ordered all of her equipment to be shut down except for the reactivation controls so someone could if they did ever come back some day, bring her back to life before they were to board her, and have everything up to speed before entering her through her air locks. He left her sun-charging solar panels on and charging at controlled full power to keep her batteries fully charged. He left out her airlock hatch leaving her outer beacons brightly beaming in the dark of night forever. When the bulbs life of giving light to the darkness failed, she would become lost in the darkness of the heavens like so many other lost unused satellites had become over the years having all died from old worn out age as useless balls of nothingness as space junk floating freely in space, just waiting to fall into the earth's atmosphere and burn up on reentry. He set the internal timing device on the computer to release the capsule from its berth in twenty minutes, and then it would automatically shut itself down and remain on standby should someone in the future have to try and access the space station ever again. He saluted his old home in the heavens like an equal or better in rank. He then closed the airlock hatch behind him as he settled down into his piloting seat within the returning module.

Precisely twenty minutes after the commander set the computerized releasing mechanism's timer, the space module with the remaining crew aboard her drifted slowly away from its berth away from the International Space Station into the darkness of space. Hearing the metallic sounds of the releasing clamps from the space station sent cold chilling goose bumps running wildly up and down their spines. Two of the cosmonauts on board the space station had very mixed feelings about leaving their guarded posts in the heavens, as they did not have the opportunity to complete their original missions sent up into outer space to complete. Another two were sad to leave because they had formed such a beautiful family bond with everyone onboard her. The last two were with plain good old euphoric wonderful thoughts about going back home and seeing their loved ones again. Going back home to Earth was the best thing that could have ever happened to them, or so they thought. It was a capsule full of cosmonauts with very different categories of mixed up emotions in approaching their every need, as they slowly drifted out and away from the space laboratory.

Commander Khrushchev switched on the onboard computers reentry mode system. He quickly punched into the computer the deportment instruction code for reentry back into the earth's atmosphere. The craft departed the space station at precisely 0400 minus six second hours, as did the first module. Commander Ivan had to subtract the four minutes six seconds for the changing of time back on Earth for the reentry to follow the exact course of its fellow module craft of a mere forty-eight hours past, and hope the wind currents around the earth were precisely the same exact speed and bearings as they had been two days prior.

The disturbance in the weather pattern just off from northern Africa's most northerly coastline had become a swirling mixture of clouds and forming a huge storm's eye, as it was traveling westerly toward and nearing the outer rim of the Leeward Islands, but the weather over the Florida landing site still looked pretty peaceful at the time they departed, or was it?

Before closing the mechanical portable heat shields to cover their portal viewing port, the crew aboard the module watched as their orbit brought them around again from the dark side of the earth's nighttime to the dawning of a new day. The horizon above California was a dark royal blue with puffy high whispery high altitude weather clouds dotting its outline. Early morning was just breaking over the western part of the United States, as they were right on time and track to make their mid-morning reentry into the atmosphere above the Gulf of Mexico off the Florida panhandle coastline, which would land them right on target at Cape Canaveral, Commander Ivan so strongly hoped.

The computer fired the retrorockets, putting their craft into its final downward mode. Commander Ivan closed the windowed portal-viewing shields making the interior of the capsule black except for the lighted instrument panel, and prepared to start his final countdown for releasing the main parachutes when the retrorocket package was released from the space capsule by the onboard computers. He just hoped his timing would be right for he had all these lives at stake with him, including his own. He definitely cared about his own life, but was more worried about his fellow crewmembers than he was for his own welfare.

The g-force started to increase on them furnishing them all with that sick funny lightheaded feeling for not having experienced gravity for over the last couple of years. It made their stomachs churn as they wondered how stable their weak legs would be when they first attempted to walk again back on Earth with gravity pulling down on them.

The neutron mass engulfed the capsule as Ivan counted one thousand one hundred and ten. It was within two seconds time of the original time he had marked down on his chart from when the first module glowed orange from the orangey yellowy green sheen. Everything went black inside the module as expected, and all he could do now was to continue with his counting down of the numbers in his head until he reached the count of one thousand three hundred and eleven seconds before releasing the main landing parachutes. Neither he nor the crew could afford him having a brain freeze in his counting down now, or they would all surely die, or experience something they were not prepared to contend with when it did happened on landing. It seemed more like hours passing by to Ivan instead of only seconds as he counted down the time for this release of their parachutes. He recalled his training in flight school when they taught him to fly by the instruments of the aircraft no matter what the body or mind felt like and told him to do, as the instruments of the machine you were flying in were always right, and your mind and body were always wrong. Now all he had was his body and mind to rely on. His own subconscious was screaming at him to release the damn parachutes now as he continued with his count down, and ignored his own subconscious screaming at him to do the job right now. He knew better than to rely on his untrusting inner subconscious, and continued to count down to the end before he released the parachutes.

Ivan felt as if he had two personalities living within his own being, and they were verbally abusing one another first silently, then suddenly screaming at one another in the far off depths of his mind driving him crazy. This by far was the hardest mind over matter of mind control he had ever experienced in his lifetime, as he continued on silently counting down to himself. He never wanted to experience or ever having to experience a situation like this never again, if he was ever to live through this traumatic experience at hand. He was getting closer to the zero. Zero-hundred-hours when he could finally release the parachutes. His mind kept spinning with frantic emotion as he held firm his conviction on waiting till he hit the exact time to execute his hand, holding firm the lever to open the small tethered tied chute to his main chutes behind them. He wanted to vomit from the pain of his mind wanting to do everything but wait, along with fighting the feeling of the g-force exerted upon them, making him want to vomit as well as he counted. One thousand three-hundred and eight. One thousand three- hundred and nine. One thousand three-hundred and ten. One thousand three- hundred and eleven. It was now release time, zero hundred hours. Finally it came time for him to execute his own command. He yanked hard on the lever when his counting ended at the precise number count. He felt like passing out because it made him so sick anticipating the worst, but the faith in his training made him have to wait.

CHAPTER EIGHTY-FIVE

Manny Eyes Focused on the Heavens

Many attentive eyes were scanning the bright blue sky above the command center as a mist of fog started coming in off the changing temperature air flow over the Atlantic Ocean's surface. The different temperatures of the sea and land were fighting with one another, and the change was going to bring in an unsuspected cloudbank cover over the landing site at a most unfortunate time, if the space module did not hurry up and land very soon. The crew of the first space module to land were there with one couple standing as the others sat on the grass alongside the ground crew and Colonel Anderson. They all had very high hopes in greeting their fellow comrades back home from space. The ground crew had doubts about this landing being a good one, due to the many dark clouds swiftly coming in off the ocean and covering up the landing site were disheartening. If the Russian space module did not land soon, no one was going to see them above or have any idea where they might land. If by chance they were to end up out in the frothy waves of the sea, they had better be prepared to fight a hard battle with the hurricane coming in across the Atlantic toward them from the Virgin Islands, causing the surf along the shoreline to begin to rage a little. Everyone on the ground was getting rather panicky for the last of the crew from above to appear.

The cosmonauts aboard the space capsule were very happy folks, feeling the main parachutes attached to the capsule lift them up from

their rapid descent toward Earth to almost a stop, even though it gave them all a very funny sick feeling inside with the sudden yank of the chutes slowing them down. Things had gone way too smooth for this mission with the Omega One landing safely four days prior and then the first capsule, too. Something amiss had to go wrong with everything going way to well for them.

Either by the end of the day there would be a lot of rejoicing taking place on back on Earth, or a lot of grieving by the ones who had made it back to Earth safely. Whatever the outcome of the day would bring, it would be the end of an era of space travel until the restoration of electrical power to the world would come about, if ever possible. Everything about space travel had become a way of the past as of this day. It was too dangerous for anyone to attempt another try at conquering space travel the way things were on Earth now, and if it was not for pure luck alone or for the grace of God which it seemed to be. Whatever the reasoning, the good people from aboard the International Space Station would not be alive without the determined help of Commander Colonel Nelson Anderson.

Commander Ivan released the heat shield covering over the window portal. The brilliant sunlight almost blinded him as he looked directly up into the bright of the morning sun with it shining directly into his eyes. He closed his eyes for a mere second as the spacecraft turned on the gentle air currents aloft. When he reopened them, he could see the massive horizon of the earth getting bigger and broader and further away as they approached the surface of the earth. This was truly a day to rejoice.

One of Commander Ivan's crewmembers already on the ground spotted his comrade's space capsule first, as he shouted out in jubilant joy. "There! There! Up there!" He pointed toward the capsule floating down from above. Everyone's eyes had been looking toward the northwest sky, and the capsule was coming in at them from direct west. Two very large white chutes and a huge red chute with a large white Soviet emblem affixed to its side shown bright slowly drifting down toward them on the ground below.

If everyone onboard had come through the attack of the massive neutron field unscathed, it would be a day for rejoicing. If all or even one of their comrades had died from the neutron invasion on the capsule, it would not be so joyful. No one knew for sure what these masses of neutrons could really do to the unsuspecting public around the world as of yet.

They had all survived the neutron attack at reentry, but Commander Ivan didn't know if all had survived the reentry as of yet, and they were all so cramped up inside this reconfigured module. No one could really turn around or see how everyone had managed until they were able to get out from their cramped sitting stations.

No one on the ground would have to chase this capsule anywhere. The commander had subtracted the correct amount of seconds along with time change for the past two days, and then subtracted several more seconds to the countdown for the releasing of the main landing parachutes, because the first capsule had overshot its intended landing target by several seconds.

He would have rather been a couple of miles or more off course inland than a few miles off course out to sea with another massive storm approaching from the east. The space capsule came down right on the mark; the results of Commanders Ivan's careful calculations before deploring the chutes. The capsule was coming in real close to the ground crews waiting position. The ground crew had to move all their vehicles away from the descending space module.

It was an amazing landing. The space module landed directly across the runway in the soft grassy and sandy section of the compound. It bounced a couple of times. The first bounce looking to be rather hard that must have really jarred the occupants. The sudden stop was not their typical soft landing in the water where the water would have acted like a softening cushion during their touching down.

As soon as the capsule stopped, Ivan blew off the hatched door covering from the craft. Seeing the ground crew and their friends from the other module were rushing toward their space vehicle to see if everyone inside was either dead or alive. They all hoping for the latter of their two thoughts. It was as funny a reunion as anyone on Earth had ever seen before. Commander Ivan from the space station ignored Colonel Anderson's extended right hand in greeting him. He literally almost on purpose fell down to the ground to the good old terra firma beneath him. "Good old Mother Earth, he said," with a smile and kissed the grassy ground with a long slow emotional kiss, an embrace only a child would give his own mother. He tried jumping back up to his feet, but instead staggered from his kneeling position on the ground fighting against his own heavy weight against his feeble weak muscles. He fought the hard fight with Mother Earth's gravity, and then fell into Colonel Anderson's extended arms weeping with a great relief of emotion. He then staggered toward the space capsule that brought him and his comrades back home, as he tried to help the others out from within the craft without success. He was too frail and pathetically weak from spending too long a time in outer space without gravity to help keep him in shape enough to help his fellow comrades out of the space module. The ground crew from the compound helped everyone out of the passageway of the very cramped space module to their freedom and safety, while everyone, especially their fellow comrades, cheered for them as they exited out their space module.

CHAPTER EIGHTY-SIX

Home at Last

The reunion of the men and woman of soviet lineage from the space station was the best of the three return missions to Earth from space. All the astronauts finally rescued from aboard the International Space Station and its harsh environment of living in outer space that was not meant for man. The same went for the far off depths down in the seas of the world not meant for man to live or survive in without artificial help from some mechanical means of life support.

Home at last on good old solid terra firma to kneel down on and kiss for good luck. It was better than any hot-fudge sundae or a tall cold drink on the hottest muggiest summer's day during the month of August, July or any other hot day of the year for that matter. This would mark the end to a long time standing for man caught up in a saga of times in outer space that might not ever repeat itself. It probably would never happen again in the lifetimes' of those who were fortunate enough to have escaped the wrath of time in space. Who would remember this one, that had been saved from a fate of cruel happenings their own leaders of their beloved country had caused, and were going to leave them stranded aloft to fend for themselves and eventually die from lack of air and starvation.

The reward to Commander Ivan Khrushchev for saving the lives of the several Americans was life itself, extended back to him and his fellow Soviet crewmembers. Let's not forget the two Germans who

were definitely held prisoner in space by an awful obstructive want of selfishness by others. They, too, could have just as easily have played a role in sealing off the life-giving portal of the space station to the space shuttle Twitchel and its crew. It definitely did seem fair, a life for a life, but was bringing them all back to this new earth the right way of a fair reward for what they did for the Americans. Time back on Earth would prove to be cruel to most of the cosmonauts who returned after being saved. Were they really saved having returned to the mess the earth was in now due to some over egotistical greedy individuals?

CHAPTER EIGHTY-SEVEN

The Celebration

NASA gave a celebration of life party at the NASA space compound the week after the last space module landed. The party was to give honor and thanks to the Twitchel crew, the Omega One crew, their families, and the crewmembers aboard the International Space Station.

Chenco came along with his wife, Gina, who was due to give birth to another of their children at any minute from the first space capsule, the two crews aboard the last two capsules, and the two new brave officers who replaced Major Yeager who was lost to the neutron mass. They came to celebrate Lieutenant Charles' bravery and Captain Ann who decided not to participate in the last mission to navigate the Omega One into space for its final mission. Ann and her husband, Ben, arrived on Friday, six days after the landing of the last space capsule. The party included most the rest of the families from the shuttle's crew, including the wife of Major Yeager. This would be a way to allowing the families and crewmembers from the Twitchel and the Omega One and their families to give their own personal loving thanks to the men and women from the space laboratory for extending their hospitality to their loved ones at a dire time of need.

A couple of very lucky news media personnel from the highly respected newspapers in the Washington D. C. area were allowed to join in and attend this special party given by invitation only. Feeling privileged to interview the ones who told their stories about the horror

felt above, wondered what in the hell was going on in the world below. How could anyone around the earth hold these innocent caring people from the Soviet Union responsible for wreaking havoc caused by the few greedy tyrants who executed themselves during the first reentry of the deadly neutron missiles. If any were still alive, they would surely be in hiding, hiding mostly from their own people who would want them tried and punished by the tribunal justice system of the world. These few selfish people who caused world havoc in the countries around the globe, and by ignorantly destroying their own people.

It was a time for peace to prevail around the globe, and for everyone to turn to one another to make this sphere of ours a better place to live. Even without the aid of electrical power to fuel all the once conveniences of modern day technologies, lost forever, but maybe not forever if everyone would work together for a better world to live upon.

Colonel Anderson talked little about the creature in the sky at the party, and in the very few days leading up to the party. He let the medical team at the hospital help the space station crew regain their strength, and health. There would be plenty of time at the briefing the following week before most the crew of the space lab would be ready to venture back home to face the reality of destruction of human life, and turmoil left in the wake of the big invasion of neutrons in their country. Colonel Nelson Anderson remained kind during the briefing of the space station crew. He held back all the bad sad news he had obtained about their families, which he had destroyed after receiving the horrifying fax the day before he ventured back into space to help his fellow man out. He had lost many distant and close family members himself, and the ones he was debriefing had lost many more immediate close members of their own families than he had. If it was he who had lost what some of these space station crew had lost, he would have surely wanted to be forgotten and left behind inside the space station to die a sad sullen death like a hermit. Commander Anderson went on to explain the nature of the creature in the sky in great depth to all. He explained how it was changing its approach in its pattern of attacks on the many different species of animals, insects, and foul of the air around the earth.

In the beginning, it attacked anything in the atmosphere all of the time and now only attacked when there is moisture in the air during an approaching storm during or when the clouds are leaving the area. It has become truly unpredictable. With that all said in the norm, but there is no norm with this creature, and the norm as everyone had remembered it, is no more.

These few words spoken by Colonel Anderson confused the hell out of every one in the room retuning from space for the moment, but would fall into perception after the fact of how life use to be on Earth before this unforgiving creature came to the earth. It sits like a rattlesnake, he explained, all coiled up and ready to strike out, but without any warning. It does not have a tiny little rattler attached to it to forewarn any approaching victim. It sits in the air like a Great White Shark coming up from the far-off depths of the ocean's floor at forty-plus miles an hour, and attacks any unsuspecting creature floating leisurely on the surface of the sea. But in this case any creature around the world.

The space station crew tried to digest the quantity of dreadful news fed to them all at once about this new deadly creature thing living in the atmosphere. The main concept with the debriefing information was partially if not all unbelievable. The idea of it that it could not be me or my family stuck in many of the minds of the returning space crew. More than half the crew was in for some very bad news about their own families and friends when they returned home. They were the fortunate or less fortunate ones returning back home to Russia where devastation prevailed over most of the countryside and cities alike.

What use to be is no more, what should be is not, and that that is unthinkably true was true. Where their loved ones use to prevail are now an empty nest. The way of life they grew up to know from childhood had mostly disappeared, and a new way of life had started all over again as if everyone was living like the Neanderthal man from the past.

Upon their return, they would be born again into a life they did not know. Down through a birth canal from their spacecraft reentering the earth's atmosphere, and taking their first breathes of real air when they exited their spacecraft into a different world to begin life all over again.

Disbelief engulfed everyone's minds, thinking all should wake up soon from this horrific dream. Never the less, reality would soon set in on them when they all returned back to the bearing wastelands of reality where they all once called home where skeletal frames of buildings unscathed without any inhabitants with only remembrances from the past to cling to.

The new cities under construction beneath the earth's crust seemed like a story from some comic strip of yesteryear, but it was now the way of life for only the rich and famous. The earth was now lit up at night using gas, oil, or paraffin candles to strip away the bitter darkness. The stars and the full moon were the only natural light at night except on cloudy stormy nights. Then there was the casting out of the storm of green yellowy streaks of light with some faint sounds of thunder.

Insignificant traces of electrical lightning in stormy clouds was seldom seen, witnessed by chance alone dancing among the storm clouds if one was lucky enough to be looking in the right direction during the storm. Most the Soviet cosmonauts thought that the debriefing by Commander Anderson and his staff was nothing but a bunch of bullshit, and some built-up American scheme of propaganda. Commander Ivan Khrushchev knew Colonel Anderson would not say these things if they were not so. They mostly thought that nothing like this was possible to their families, to their planet, and certainly not to themselves. How could it possibly rain torrentially and have no lightning or thunder associated with it. Why had this creature attacked at all times when it first invaded the earth's atmosphere, and now lays dormant waiting, laying ready to strike out only at the beginning, during, or at the very end of a storm. How had it suddenly reactivated itself to strike again anytime it wanted to during a bright sunny day? It just didn't make any sense to them at all, especially to the ones who had studied science in college.

This neutron creature was very unpredictable. Man would search for a solution taking years to defeat the menace man had made for

himself against himself, and was now destroying the very planet they were trying to live on.

Why had this creature in the sky not taken the lives of those astronauts returning to the earth aboard the Twitchel the first time when the crew aboard the Twitchel reentered space a second time and returned once again? What about the three crews aboard the Soviet-made space capsules and the crew of the Omega One on its maiden mission into outer space? It must have had something to do with the close-knit seams of their flight suit uniforms that kept the neutron mass from entering their outer garments and sucking what little electrical field they had to operate their brains out from within them.

Whatever the reason behind all of it, the scientists from around the planet busied themselves by looking close at all the strange phenomena in it. They figured that any human wanting to protect him or herself out of doors, would have to wear one of these flight suits to guarantee their protection from the explosive neutron fields. With that said, the globe of the earth would become a planet with its intelligent creatures walking around outside dressed in protective clothing as if they were aliens from another planet visiting their own world. There were so many unanswered questions about the neutron creature lurking in the sky above it behooved everyone. What should one do to protect themselves from its lethal strike of death? When if ever was a big concern, would electricity ever be restored to planet Earth? Would man learn to be friends with this creature lurking in the sky or seek out ways to kill it before it killed them? Would man ever find ways in which to harness the strength of this neutron monster for man?

Through the want of greed, the modern day conveniences of the time were lost. Mankind might destroy himself searching for ways to neutralize this creature of neutrons, and in doing so who knows, the next big bang felt around the planet Earth might be its last.

EARTH LOST WITHOUT POWER

POWER

THE NEUTRON BOMB

L.S. WOOD

THE END

BOOK COVER

ILLUSTRATED BY

LARRY S WOOD

This book is a work of fiction. Everything within this book comes from the imagination of the author. Any reference to a person's name or names and places are fictitious in general. Any resemblance to persons living or dead and events are entirely coincidental.

OTHER WORKS BY L. S. WOOD

THE HEARTBROKEN LEPRECHAUN

Skip Into Trouble

A story about Skip, a young leprechaun with a broken heart who ventured out into the mortals' world to save his missing parents he loved, who at the time were presumably held captive by mortals as slaves in or about Dublin Town. With only a smidgen of his grown-up leprechaunic powers, he manages to get himself drunk and a stowaway aboard a ship bound to America causing grave trouble onboard and almost sinking the ship. Until he gains his full powers as a leprechaun, he has many upon many mishaps. With his Emerald Irish luck, he manages to accomplish the risky task he set out on in saving both parents held by an evil mortal and brings them both back home to Ireland from America. In this adventure, he makes two mortal enemies of leprechauns who befriended him, very rich and happy by going out of their way to help him when he had placed himself in great danger, and who helped to save his loved ones

CHIEF WHITE EAGLE

The Last Free Abnaki Indian

The first of a series of books about Chief White Eagle that begins with his birth into a free-roaming tribe of Abnaki Indians in the State of Vermont. The books harbor the many good and sorrowful adventures he faces throughout his lifetime as a lonely Indian trying to avoid capture by the white-man. The loss of his young bride and their infant son leads him to a life as a hermit, hidden away in a cave in the mountains of Vermont. By accident, he befriends a young white boy by saving the young boy's life during a hurricane. The boy who had just saved a baby eagle's life was about to step off a cliff to his death. A secret friendship evolved from his unselfish act that lasted a lifetime until the chief died. In the ending series, the white boy performs an Indian burial ritual, taught to him by the chief, to bury him beside his fallen bride and son. They had both died from the smallpox disease many years before when the chief was a young man, and living on a reservation governed by the white man. The story tells how when he was small, the tribe was made to move to a reservation, and how he became free to live as a hermit by himself in a cave on a mountains in Lunenburg, Vermont.

THE END

L. S. Wood lives in North Central Massachusetts in Winchendon with his lovely wife Rebecca of fifty years. They have two children together, a son Scott and a Daughter Jennifer. His son has four children, three girls and a boy. His daughter has one boy. His grandchildren keep him very busy when they are around which is most of the time. His son lives right next door to him. He would not want it any other way. His daughter lives a couple of towns away and visits a couple of time a week with her little boy who keeps his grandfather very busy when he is around.

He graduated from Mount Wachusett Community College, and attended Fitchburg State University. He worked for a bank before going to work in industry. He left working for others, started a real estate and construction company, and put up and sold many houses in the New England area. He started a home heating oil and delivery business after closing his real estate and construction business, giving the oil company to his wife, and has since retired.

He has written many children's books, science fiction, love stories, and more. Many of his books he has written sit on a shelf or in a file cabinet in his study collecting dust. He writes for the pleasure of putting stories down on paper. Due to family and friend pressure in sharing his works with the world, he is now just longing to publish his works, and hopes the people of the world will enjoy his books as much as he enjoyed writing them.

EARTH LOST WITHOUT POWER

BY L.S. WOOD

LARRY S WOOD at beclarwood@comcast.net

Larry S Wood

1335 Alger Street

Winchendon MA 01475

Tel 978-297-2326